Fiona and Minnie
The New Age

I0565543

Ken Coffman and Kristen Lolatte

Other books by Ken Coffman and Kristen Lolatte

The Reluctant Queen (Fiona Saga Book One)
The Moon Maiden (Fiona Saga Book Two)

Other books by Ken Coffman

Steel Waters
Alligator Alley (with Mark Bothum)
Twisted Shadow (with Mark Bothum)
Glen Wilson's Bad Medicine
Toxic Shock Syndrome
Immortality, LLC
Hartz String Theory
Endangered Species
Fairhaven
Mesh (with Adina Pelle)
The Sandcastles of Irakkistan
Fianchetto
Buffoon
Wales Detective Agency
Real World FPGA Design with Verilog

Fiona and Minnie: The New Age ©2025 Ken Coffman and Kristen Lolatte All Rights Reserved

ISBN Print 978-1-960405-60-9
ISBN eBook 978-1-960405-61-6

This book is sold subject to the condition that it shall not, by way of trade or otherwise, be lent, resold, hired out or otherwise circulated without the publisher's prior consent in any form of binding or cover other than that in which it is published and without a similar condition including this condition being imposed on the subsequent purchaser.

STAIRWAY⹄PRESS
APACHE JUNCTION

www.StairwayPress.com

Kristen's Dedication

For family lost and family found: I love you all
For friends old and new: I am forever grateful
For my favorite Scotsman: thank you for being my anchor
For mom: we miss you
For dad: malachite ice cream and endless Nantucket
memories. You'll always be my hero
For McNamara: love lives on forever
For my mancub: always and forever
For Ken: thank you for seeing this mayhem through to the end

Ken's Dedication

If you are reading this, you are a blessing to my life, and I
thank you. This book is for Judy and for the life we cobbled
together from odds, ends, baling wire and duct tape.

Credits

Cover Photograph by Wayne Fournier,
www.thruthesoberlens.com
Cover Design by Guy Corp, www.GrafixCorp.com
Some chapter icons by Olha Bondarenko
Cover Models: Madelyn Sweet and Kristen Lolatte

Author's Note—Kristen

I NEVER SET out to write; it wasn't even on my radar. Then, more than ten years ago, during a fateful Nor'easter, I found myself in a parking lot, picking up shattered glass. Later, I sat down and turned that experience into a short story. Why I sent it to Ken, I'll never know—but that's where our journey began.

In the decade since, relationships ended and began. Parents passed away and personal dynamics shifted. There have been struggles, triumphs and abrupt changes of direction. Yet through it all, Fiona was my constant, a presence—sometimes real, sometimes imagined—that carried me forward.

As Ken often reminded me, "this isn't your autobiography." But the truth is, I am Fiona—with a fair bit of Minnie mixed in. Our reluctant Queen remains with me, and she always will.

We poured ourselves into these pages, hoping readers will find joy in the world we've created.

Where do we go from here?

Only time will tell. But for now, Fiona's world lingers just beyond the horizon; that is where you'll find us.

Minnie: Under the Cover of Darkness

HOW LONG HAD the intrepid trio been driving?

Slowly, time slipped away from Minnie. In those early days, she and Gretchen would talk for hours, weaving stories and songs from thin air while Tor entertained them with his endless, meandering jokes. As time went on, silence reigned and Minnie lost her bearings. Day and night meshed. She was unsure about what day it was or where they were. Across Oregon, California, Nevada, and Arizona, they traveled on the blue highways—winding backroads carrying them through obscure towns.

Early in their trip, she occupied her mind with thoughts of Lacey and the Misfits—Mr. Danvers, and the school carnival. Her thoughts also drifted earlier in time to Fiona, Sean, and the Fachan. She pined for them and cried herself to sleep over losing them again.

Then there was the person she tried not to think of. The scamp. The troublemaker. The young man who made her insides tangle.

Philip d'GreenApple. The world's greatest kisser.

A month earlier, while standing on a rumbling truck's running board, she had looked into the eyes of a young man who used to be a scrawny runt. Now, he was a lanky, muscular young man with a crooked smile and wild tousle of auburn hair.

It took all her will, but she did not think of him.

Or hardly ever.

She often wondered about Fiona, who had pleaded with Tor and Gretchen—the wandering vagabonds—to spirit her adopted daughter away to safety. As they drove away from Cement City in the Pacific Northwest, Minnie heard the beating of troll drums in the forest and knew Fiona was going in to face them.

Alone and defenseless.

She could no longer reach Fiona with her mind. It was as if the string had been cut and only darkness lay between them. And here she was, curled up in the back of the VW campervan driving to who-knows-where with Tor and Gretchen.

She snuggled with Keela—who thankfully came along as well. At first, Tor had opposed the idea of carrying a little skunk across the country, but Gretchen and Fiona convinced him otherwise.

The last words she heard from Fiona echoed endlessly within her.

"Keela won't spray; she's Minnie's protector. Please keep them safe—the both of them."

Had it been hours or days? Was the sun rising or setting?

Minnie had no way of knowing. What she did know was they had stopped. How long they were parked, she had no idea but stopped and parked they were. Minnie stretched her arms, and Keela did the same—as only a skunklet could. On her back, Keela demanded belly scritches and scratches. Once the little beast was satisfied, Minnie decided it was time to get up and explore.

Tor and Gretchen must be outside. They are not here.

Minnie grabbed her coat and hat and wrapped a crocheted scarf around her skinny neck.

"Let's go, Keela. Let's see where we are."

As she slid the van door open, a waft of the freshest air came in—cool to the nose but flower-scented, dusty, and laden with pollen. As Minnie's eyes adjusted to the darkness, she realized it was the wee hours of the morning. She looked up and saw more stars than she could ever count, much less name. In the pitch black, she made out vague shadows of odd rock formations. In the distance, she spied a dying campfire and two shapes sleeping.

"Ahhh, we are camped here for the night, Keela. I don't know where we are, but I feel safe. Shall we ramble?"

On cue, Keela let out a trill and began waddling.

Minnie wrapped her scarf a bit tighter. A breeze picked up and she heard faint voices on the wind.

"She's here, she made it."

"She's safe and sound."

"Soon the others will come."

"Shhhh...she'll hear us."

Facing the darkness, Minnie stood with her arms crossed.

"I hear you fine—I'm not deaf. Show yourselves."

She heard the fluttering of wings.

Minnie decided it best to sit, so she did. Keela curled up in her lap and kept a watchful eye, ready to eat whatever tasty treat might fly by.

As she slowed her breathing and let her mind drift, something light landed upon her shoulder. Slowly, Minnie turned her head to look at a desert pixie perched upon her shoulder. Dressed in a wisp of dried rabbit hide and barrel cactus flower petals, this small one wielded a hornet husk shield and a Cholla-spine spear.

She felt it—this one was fearless and demanded respect. With caution, they eyed each other until Minnie spoke.

"Good evening, small one. I'm Minnie. And you are..."

"Small compared to you, Princess, but cross me and I'll put this spine through your eye. Do not toy with me."

"No disrespect intended. What shall I call you? Fierce and angry Eye-Stabber?"

"My name is Nyx."

"Pleasure to make your acquaintance, Nyx. Where are we?"

"You are in the midlands desert on the outskirts of Arabella. The wind tells me you will be here a while. Can we trust your human companions?"

"Absolutely, with no hesitation. Ever since we left Fiona behind, Gretchen and Tor have been my guardians."

Minnie's mind drifted through the ages. Tears filled her eyes. She wiped them away. On her opposite shoulder, something light landed and spoke with a melodious voice.

"Leave the Princess alone and stop filling her head with nonsense. She JUST arrived and needs to get her feet under her. Forgive the welcoming committee, Minnie. Nyx is a warrior and never lets down her guard. I am Breena and I am most pleased to make your acquaintance. We've been waiting for you. How was your trip?"

"Well enough, I suppose. Long."

"The desert is always thirsty, but there's no time for tears, young Minnie. You will be reunited with your kith and kin soon enough. For now, you are safe here. Spirits and mountain magic surround you. The desert elementals await your arrival. We are here for you and others will gather in force. Keep your eyes open and your senses keen. You must be tired. Go by the fire with Tor and Gretchen. Settle in and breathe the free air. Soon enough the sun will rise, and you will bear witness to the mountains waking in the morning light. Then you will see where you are."

Breena leaned over and kissed Minnie on the cheek—Minnie felt a tingle which made her giggle. It felt good to have magic around again.

Breena gestured to Nyx to fly away.

Nyx scowled, but with a sharp flick of her wings—stirring a puff of air—she complied.

Minnie and Keela walked to the fire and snuggled between Gretchen and Tor.

Tor opened an eye a fraction to study Minnie.

"Welcome, Sprout. Get comfortable and rest for now—we'll unpack soon enough. For a while, this will be home. But for now, just sleep."

"This strange place—I don't understand its feel. Where are we?"

Tor laughed. "Soon enough, you'll see."

Minnie frowned but accepted the answer. With Keela wrapped in her arms, she curled between the sleeping sacks and drifted away under the stars.

As she drifted, she hoped Nyx was right and that Fiona would be there soon.

Trevir: Troll Smoke

A BITTER-COLD WIND tugged at Trevir's collars and cuffs. Overhead, the cloud cover was a solid gray mass, and the midday sunlight was vague and diffuse. He wrinkled his nose at an acrid, disturbing odor emanating from the Earth.

"You are sure about this?" he asked Troll Srenzo.

"Surely you smell it," she said. "Surely you feel it. Shamble in the old-fashioned sense of the word. A place of carnage—a scene of great destruction."

Sensitive to any trace of mockery, he stared at her ugly face with its broken fang and coarse, tousled, boar-like hair. Red, hostile eyes were buried deep under her bony brow. Across naked breasts, she wore a semi-cured leather jerkin with patches of rank hair and flesh left over from a haphazard scraping. It reeked. Everything about her reeked, just the way he liked it. The urge to take her flowed through him—here in the wind in front of the wolves and her husband, Kelpht, the ohrkk. He pushed away the impulse and turned to take in the scene.

They were in a vast meadow—flat like a tabletop except in the dead center, where an earthen mound erupted like a ripe pimple. Hundreds of yards away, thick stands of Douglas firs and cedars crowded together like spectators at a crime scene. Nipping at themselves and the wind, the wolves roamed.

"What is your best explanation for what happened?" Trevir said.

Looking around, Troll Srenzo took a moment before replying.

"Your guess is as good as mine."

He couldn't prevent sarcasm from saturating his voice.

"My guess is the gutless trolls deserted and are hiding in an abandoned mine."

A wolf dropped something at his feet. Trevir knelt to look. It was a long fragment of bone wrapped in leather.

"Trolls are a lot of things," Troll Srenzo said, "but cowardly is not one of them."

"Hmmph," Trevir grunted. "You act as though this Fiona-creature is a great sorceress—capable of wielding true power."

"I didn't say anything like that. All I know is what I see. And smell. And feel."

He turned and walked toward the center of the killing field. The top of the pimple-mound was covered in emerald-green grass. At the center sat a nest woven of feathers, twigs, and straw; in the nest, something impossibly blue. He reached in to pluck it out.

A cat's-eye marble. Sapphire.

"I wouldn't touch that," Troll Srenzo said.

"You're right," Trevir said. "You wouldn't." He rotated and examined it. "Just glass. Open your pouch."

Troll Srenzo scowled. "I don't want it."

"But you'll take it just the same," Trevir said.

She loosened the drawstring of her heartsack and held it out. Trevir dropped in the marble, where it nestled among her other treasures: old copper coins, her father's rusty shaving razor, a desiccated baby finger, unpolished emeralds, and shreds of the bitterroot tobacco she chewed.

She pulled the drawstrings and stuffed the sack back under her leather vest.

He turned to Kelpht, the ohrkk.

"I think there are trolls in the woods, live ones. A dozen or two, give or take. Order the wolves to round some up. I will speak with them." He pointed at the mound. "And set up my chair here."

Trevir drained his wine and held out the jeweled goblet for a refill.

"Ever notice how much my Hungarian wine resembles rich, red blood? That's partly because of virgin female blood, isn't it? It is said the wine gains character when grape-stomping maids die screaming with terror."

As she poured, Troll Srenzo's face twisted and grew uglier, if such a thing was possible.

"So it is said, but who knows what they really use. Probably cow or sheep blood—what with fresh European virgins in such short supply."

Trevir sipped, then shrugged.

"Who cares? It's good."

The round meadow was flat, so from the top of the mound he could see all the way to the edges where dense trees hemmed them in. On the fitful wind, he smelled traces of smoke.

Troll smoke.

The gray sky oozed a greasy mist. It wasn't raining, but everything was wet.

"Do people really live in this dreary place?" he said.

With a dirty fingernail, Troll Srenzo picked at a shred of meat in her teeth.

"Some people like it. The air is clean, and it doesn't get bitter-cold like the Midwest."

The wolves herded a ragged figure toward them. Troll.

Trevir studied the squat figure, its full beard gray with flecks of green moss. Crooked nose. There was a scar across the left side of his face, and a half-ear peeped from under his floppy wool cap.

Trevir flicked his eyes at Troll Srenzo.

She cuffed the troll and bloodied his nose.

"Kneel when you approach your King."

The troll's voice was a low growl.

"Just kill me and make it quick. I've got nothing—not no more, I don't."

With a blow against the back of his neck, he collapsed to his knees.

"What is its name?" Trevir said.

"Arlyffe," he said. "Arlyffe the Bold."

"You don't look so bold to me," Trevir said.

Arlyffe shrugged. "In my day, I was bold enough." He struggled to his feet. "Bold enough to not want to die on my knees."

Carefully watching Trevir's face for clues, Troll Srenzo pulled her long blade from its sheath.

Ever so slightly, Trevir shook his head.

Not yet.

"I want to know what happened here. Every detail."

"I didn't see what happened. I was guarding, roaming the woods. In an hour, I was to be relieved so I could get me supper. Hungry, I was, and I could smell the squirrels and rabbits they were roasting. Truth be told, there wasn't much else I could think about—I wanted to sink me teeth into a juicy haunch of muskrat. Muskrat with leeks, lichens, and shrooms, that's my favorite. My road-wife was cooking me up a big, fat one. She wasn't much to look at, but she was magic with a roasting spit and stewpot. Couldn't think of much else, I'll tell you. A couple of acorns and a handful of rock tripe fungus, that's all I had since breakfast. You can't fill your belly on rock tripe, everyone knows, but that did not stop me, I did me job. There was nothing that came from my patch of brush, nary a fox or a bobcat could sneak by me. Not even a slug. Ever try to eat one? Good for a sore throat, me granny said, but I could never choke one down. Muskrat roasted over an open flame, that's what suits me."

"Okay, maybe not every detail," Trevir said. "I want to know what happened to my troll army."

"I done already told you. I was in the woods, so I don't know exactly what happened. I heard it, of course, every bit of it, but by the time I got to this meadow, it was what you see. Where there was soldiers and the camp with the women, children, cats, and ferrets, now nothing but brown Earth all torn up. It was like rocks came up and chewed everything to pieces, then sucked it all down its gullet, hungry like a giant land dragon. There ain't no dragons, not no more—everybody knows that—but that's what it seemed like to me." He gestured. "With a roar and the Earth quaking so much I could hardly stand, something with a mouth as big as this field opened up and ate us all down."

"You survived. How many others?"

"Maybe twenty. Hunters and other guards who were in the woods. And a few cowards who were quick-footed and ran. They didn't see nothing either—they was running for their lives."

In anguish, he dropped to his knees.

"Ten thousand or more, all gone in a minute. That's all I knows, so take me now with that evil sword and put an end to me misery."

Troll Srenzo shifted her weight and waited for the command. After a moment of thought, Trevir stood and gestured for Troll Srenzo to hand him her long blade.

"I'll do it," he said.

Arlyffe closed his eyes and stretched out his neck. Trevir examined the silvery edge of the blade. Gleaming and dangerous, it was thirsty. With a nimble flick, Trevir sliced off half of the troll's right ear, then sat back down.

A moment passed.

"Am I still alive?" the troll said.

"Stand," Trevir commanded.

Cupping his wounded ear, Arlyffe stood. Blood flowed through his stubby fingers.

"You hurts me," he said.

"Did any females survive?" Trevir said.

"Yes. A few foragerss. Servants. Maids. An old woman with more whiskers on her chin than teeth in her mouth. A young bride with a baby at her breast. And maybe a few more who are still hiding."

Trevir took a sip of wine.

"You are the new Troll King. Kill the cowards and breed the women quick, and we'll once again have more trolls than we know what to do with."

"King," Arlyffe muttered. "I got no use for being a king. What kind of game is it you're playing?"

A wave of anger washed over Trevir's face.

"I don't play. If you prefer your last image to be your head rolling across this dead Earth, then say so and I'll pick one of the other cowards."

"Why did you hurt me?"

"I don't want a Troll King called One-Ear. Arlyffe Half Ear is better. Choose. Be King or a head shorter."

Arlyffe considered.

"I supposes I could give being King a try."

Trevir laughed.

"I hope the decision wasn't a hard one. Now, go—get out of my sight. There is no time to waste. You have maidens to rape and cowards to murder."

Arlyffe raised his bloody hands. "Murder them with me bare?"

Trevir sighed. "Troll Srenzo will find you leathers and a blade that halfway fits your new station. Come see me if you get fresh information about what happened in this field. Useful information. Now, go before I change my mind."

Arlyffe bowed. "As you wish, sire," he said.

Trevir waved his hand around the field, then turned to face Troll Srenzo.

"If you had to guess, would you say it was the woman or the girl?"

"What did all this?" she said. "I'd say neither. Something came out of the ground and helped them."

"Nonsense. It was the woman. Fiona. She stood right where I'm standing and conjured something from deep Earth. She was to be my bride-mother and we would have had it all. Together, nothing could stand in our way."

From the top of the mound, he raised Troll Srenzo's blade into the sky. He tipped his head back and shouted.

"If you can defeat me, show yourself and let it be done."

From the dark bank of clouds to his right, lightning stabbed the Earth. Thunder cracked instantly—deafening, shaking the ground with its force. The land rumbled and quaked, but nothing else stirred.

"I didn't think so," Trevir said. He stabbed the sword into the mound. "Come up here and serve me, Troll," he said.

Troll Srenzo grumbled.

"Now? Here?"

"Yes," he said.

Grinding his teeth and trying not to hear Trevir grunting, Kelpht, the ohrkk, whistled for the wolves to follow, then turned toward the woods to help the new troll King find his wards.

Philip d' GreenApple

JUAN'S PROFILE WAS a roadmap of lumps and scars, a face that could make a mirror beg for mercy. Handsome? Not a chance; the man had brawled his way through life—with a flattened nose and ears puffed out like cauliflowers left too long in the sun.

I got his story over greasy truck stop chorizo burritos with jalapeños bleeding heat into the tortillas. A grizzled driver with a coffee-stained grin leaned over and whispered that Juan had once grappled under the Guadalajara lights as a masked wrestler known as Nacho Abuelito. Professional wrestling? It sounded like a fever dream cooked up by a guy with too much diesel in his veins, but hell, I'm just a Maine drifter; my expertise tops out at smelling out a moose at fifty paces.

I liked him from the jump, though I couldn't pin down why. The first time I laid eyes on him, he backed a semi-truck into a slot so tight you'd swear the rig was greased. One foot of clearance flanked each side—no clutch stutter, no second-guessing—just a smooth glide until the trailer kissed the dock with a metallic clank. He hopped out without glancing back and ambled toward the coffee shop as if he'd just parked a bicycle. It was impressive swagger from a stubby fireplug of a man.

Word was he wanted a road buddy, and after he stiffed me with the breakfast tab—those burritos weren't cheap—he jerked a thumb at the passenger-side door. No ceremony, no handshake—climb in or keep walking. I climbed in. We racked up miles, thousands piling up like desert dust on a dashboard. I tried counting once—10,000 and change—then quit. Numbers blur when the horizon's your boss.

He pried my life story out of me quickly enough, not that there was much of my story to tell: Dad, Mom, and a little sister who could nag the paint off a barn—all of us bouncing between traveler camps, carnivals, and Ren Faires, anywhere under-the-table cash could be earned. Earned was a keyword for our family. We worked and didn't expect anything for free.

Juan didn't think our story was odd. He'd been humping freight since he was ten, so my dropout tale didn't faze him. School? A racket—we'd take the open road over chalk dust any day. We'd been homeschooled, my sister and I, with GEDs in the bag by fourteen. Community college was an option, but sitting still is for suckers; I prefer engaging directly with the world and not wasting away staring at a whiteboard.

You'd think I'd chafe at being cooped up in a cab with a guy who spoke less than a mute monk, but I didn't. Why? I don't know.

Juan had a soft spot for the lot lizards: hard-luck women peddling more than smiles. He never sampled the wares, at least not that I saw, but a good sob story could pry a twenty- or fifty-dollar bill from his wallet. He'd insist it was lending, not giving, though I never saw a dime circle back. The rest of his spare cash flowed south, wired to shadows I'd never meet, leaving him with rice, black beans and a cold cerveza after a haul. But let's not forget the tin of Copenhagen chaw he'd burn through daily—sometimes two tins if the miles dragged on. It was my job to dispose of the two-liter spittoon bottles filled with disgusting brown fluid. Life on the road is not all rainbows and unicorns.

He lit up for anything I said about Minnie's magic and madness. I wasn't fully sold on her voodoo, but I'd seen enough weirdness to keep an open mind. Trolls devoured by spiders, an old coot knifing a hag and getting shredded for it—Juan lapped up these stories like a wide-eyed kid at a campfire. I'd never eyeballed that troll myself, but I'd once chucked green apples at his son—an oddball, so-called prince—and got him spitting mad. Minnie swore by hopping legs and other freak-show critters. There was never a dull moment with that girl and her step-mom Fiona.

Road rats spin stories which get increasingly lurid with retelling. Audit them at your own risk.

The kissing booth caper hooked him best. Here's the gist. The truck's clutch blew in Burlington in northwestern Washington State, so I hitched upriver while it got patched. I snuck into the line, stole a smooch that'd melt steel and ghosted. She knew it was me—she had to. I darned well knew it was her. Juan grinned through that one every time. Destiny's a funny thing—why is a magnet's north inevitably and invariably attracted to south? Don't ask me. Some things just are. Miles apart, her thoughts were a cipher, but her feelings? Every smirk, every sob—I felt them as if they were mine.

Juan wasn't just a wheelman; he was a cipher—a lumpy ex-brawler turned freight jockey with a past as cloudy as a diesel-stained puddle. Nacho Abuelito? Maybe he'd slammed bodies under neon, or maybe it was just 10-4 good-buddy trucker bullsnot. Either way, he hauled more than cargo: secrets and a taste for the absurd that kept us rolling. I hitched my fate to the highway, a Maine runaway with a GED piecing together the road's jagged truths mile by gritty mile.

One day, while the August sun baked the Franklin Mountains to the west—their rugged peaks looming like silent sentinels—we stopped in Anthony, TX. This town straddled the Texas-New Mexico border and buzzed with Tex-Mex taco trucks parked near the I-10 exit. They seemed to dance to a soundtrack of faint mariachi music from El Paso radio stations mixed with the occasional bark of a lonesome coyote dodging tumbleweeds.

It was the third time we'd run this play. Fresh over the NM border, we hit the Love's on I-10, and I'm stuck filling the saddle tanks—driver's side first, then swinging the rig around for the passenger's side, swiping Juan's beat-to-heck debit card. Long as I'm driving forward, he's cool with me taking the wheel in a parking lot, no sweat. Takes a good thirty minutes to babysit the nozzle, pumping close to three hundred gallons of diesel while the desert heat shimmered off the asphalt. Juan grabs clean jeans, his sharpest boots, and heads for the showers. Then I watch him stroll down Doniphan Drive toward the La Tuna prison with his straw cowboy hat jammed down on hair slicked back like he was auditioning for a border-town western.

Over time I had pieced it together. His kid, Mateo, was doing time. Usually, mules cross the river with no problems, but Mateo was unlucky—caught a two-year sentence and did the whole stretch due to trouble with the other inmates.

Juan let slip over greasy tacos at Carnitas Queretaro that Mateo was an *alacrán*. Scorpion. Looking at the photo from Juan's wallet, Mateo was like me—wiry and small. Juan wouldn't say much, leaving my mind going wild. My head spun with the Rio Grande's muddy pull, border patrol's halogen beams cutting the night, and the sour tang of La Tuna prison slop—watery grits and mystery meat. I didn't suffer a lack of imagination. With the slightest breeze, my mind could create a hurricane.

Back at the Love's lot, with dust swirling under I-10's sodium glow, I pictured Mateo dodging cops in the creosote scrub, quick as a zebra-tailed lizard, his boots kicking up sand where vinagrónes hid. Juan wouldn't spill, but the desert whispered plenty. Mateo was a spark in the dark. Dangerous like the arid Franklin Mountains looming over El Paso.

I nosed the rig into a corner of the dusty Love's lot, tires crunching gravel, the I-10 hum fading behind Anthony's creosote haze. Breakfast was Denny's—chorizo, greasy eggs, and coffee strong enough to strip paint, served by a waitress with a Juarez accent and a name tag reading Lupita.

Slowly, trailing Juan's lead, I could eat grilled jalapeños in my scrambled eggs—even learning to appreciate the charred snap biting my nose. I could handle 'em cooked, but Juan? His gut was forged steel. Jalapeños didn't faze him. Most of the joints he liked in the Southwest—the greasy spoons off I-10—stocked his kind of heat: Sorrentos and habaneros that would make an iguana cry.

A couple hours later, after I'd read the discarded El Paso Times newspapers—including the classified ads—a man dropped a business card on the table. The card didn't say much.

James Alvarez. Corporate Liaison. And a phone number with a Phoenix area code: 602.

I looked up at him. Despite the surname, he didn't look Hispanic. With thinning, short-cropped hair, he looked more like a husky, sun-burned, corn-fed white dude from Iowa. I could not restrain my brain—I could see him hosing off rubber boots after slopping pigs.

"That Wilbur was some pig, eh?" I said.

"What?"

"Never mind," I replied.

"I get it. Charlotte's Web. Clever. Can I sit?"

He didn't wait for my response. After settling his haunches on the bench and squirming to get comfortable, Lupita appeared.

"Just coffee, dear," he said.

After she hustled off, we stared at each other for a minute. I tried to guess what he wanted but came up short.

"I'm going to tell you things you'll be skeptical about. First off, I will give you a name. Seamus O'Toole. Call the local FBI field office. Ask for him. Then ask him about me. Jim Alvarez. He will confirm I am who I say I am. I won't give you the number—look it up yourself so you'll know it's for real."

With my fork, I moved congealed egg yolk around on my plate and analyzed my reaction to this man. He seemed okay, but there was lingering danger emanating from him. Not danger from competence—the image that came to mind was a blind man throwing rocks at windows. It was strange. He was more like a bureaucrat than a spy. Despite my wariness, I could not help it; I was intrigued. I didn't doubt he was a patriot—whatever that meant.

Was I a tool or a target?

Probably both.

I tasted the egg yolk. It needed salt.

"You gonna call?"

I couldn't decide, so I did my usual—let the universe choose. I fished a nickel out of my pocket and flipped it into the air, then slapped my palm over it as it landed on the Formica.

"Heads I call the Fed," I said. "Tails you amble off and leave me be."

Minnie: The Day Begins

THE MAJESTIC SUN slowly awakened the sleepy Faire grounds.

As night shadows retreated and daylight kissed the crowns of ghostly saguaros, otherworldly rock formations roused with the sun and shed their mystery. Minnie began to stir as the canyons hummed with life and desert animals took their first sips from moonlit pools left behind by a thunderstorm.

With a twitch of her nose, a gentle wave of a delicate finger, and a crack of her toe joints, magical elementals came to call.

She was half awake.

Were the elementals real or imagined?

The high-desert faeries were the first to arrive, waking the drowsy princess with kisses on the nose and tugs on her hair.

They were much different than the ones she loved at Sean and Fiona's home in the woods. These weren't brightly colored, nor did they flit about on the backs of dragonflies or fuzzy bumblebees.

These were drab in color and feistier. Adorned in the tones of the desert, their delicate skin was bronzed. Instead of gold and silver hair, theirs were sun-kissed browns and reds.

Minnie chalked it up to their environment; after all, one must be wary and camouflaged without overgrown greenery for hiding places and shelter. Mostly unnoticed by ordinary humans, these faeries took residence in desert saguaros or prickly pear cacti.

Often, they would ride atop hummingbirds or wasps—and many a desert faery came equipped with weapons of various sizes and shapes.

The unforgiving desert punished the unwary with quills, thorns, needles, stingers, claws and fangs. At a glance, it looked barren and lifeless, but nothing was further from the truth—every inch teemed with life, each creature fierce and beautiful in its own way.

The desert's magical folk weren't the quaint, pretty-in-pink faeries of the civilized East; these creatures would wage unholy war if necessary. In battle, these were the ones you wanted by your side. These were the ones that Ancamna would recruit and train.

As she sat up, Minnie let out a quiet sigh. Sick of hiding, she also knew all too well that Trevir would find them. She hoped for a while they would be safe in the desert, surrounded by the Faire folk. While they couldn't hide forever, she hoped their long journey would buy them time.

Due south of Sedona, the sleepy town of Arabella occupied a strange place, straddling both the low and high desert. The elevation sat on the border where saguaros thrived. In fact, in Arabella proper, there were more ghosts of saguaros than actual, physical ones.

Arabella was nowhere near as trendy and popular as Sedona—not as busy or expensive. It was just the way the locals liked it.

The town would soon awaken and witness the Renaissance Faire sprouting from the desert dunes. A caravan arrived under the cover of the new moon, beneath billions of stars—the only witnesses to their arrival. They drove in on I-17 just south of Flagstaff and wound their way through Oak Creek Canyon and Sedona.

Through a series of death-defying switchbacks and stomach-lurching twists and turns, trucks, cars, jeeps and buses brought their wares. There was no grand announcement—just a stealthy entrance through the moonless desert night. That's how the Faire gypsies worked; they preferred to move in and out under the cover of darkness. Enter in silence and leave without a trace, leaving the mind to wonder if they were ever really there at all.

Minnie, Tor, and Gretchen were set up in a tent on the outskirts of the grounds, but they were not completely alone. Trusted souls camped in tents nearby—people who didn't bat an eye at Minnie's comings and goings.

As Minnie wandered from tent to tent, the shopkeepers took notice but didn't stare.

Who was this youngling who had joined their troupe? Where had she and her makeshift family come from, and why were they here?

The Renaissance Faire people were a motley crew of Roma, artisans, actors, craft-folk and cooks. Often the outcasts of society, they were fringe dwellers and misfits who couldn't or wouldn't be put in a societal box—hardy souls who refused all labels.

They lived on their own terms and found community with others like them. Close, loving, and protective, yes—but slow to trust, they kept common folk at arm's length. Looking haggard and worn, these fresh strangers—Tor, Gretchen, and Minnie—had arrived in the dead of night. They spoke little of their travels, but it was well understood they needed protection.

Protection from what was unknown, but protection they would get.

Minnie moved from tent to tent, introducing herself and offering help wherever she could. It would take at least a month to transform this patch of desert into a proper Renaissance village—but transform it they would. As the day passed, Minnie mapped out the lay of the land, discovered who did what, learned about the wares to be sold and watched as entertainers rehearsed their acts.

There was scenery to build, costumes to mend and refit, scripts to run through, lines to rehearse. Menus were devised, jousts choreographed and practiced and old rivalries readied for the stage. As Minnie watched it all unfold, she couldn't help but wonder what Shakespeare himself would think of the spectacle. She laughed out loud, picturing him dropping into their midst and dashing off a sonnet or three about what he saw.

As Minnie was immersed in Shakespearean dreams, a minstrel

practiced his tune. Minnie twirled and danced around him as if he was the pied piper of Hamlin himself. She recognized it: *Renaissance Faire*.

Through the shroud of mystery
Turn a page of history
Feeling more than you can see
Down at the Renaissance Faire
Hear the minstrels play their tunes
They will play the whole night through
Special songs for me and for you
And anyone whose heart is true…

Gather lords and ladies fair
Come with me to the Renaissance Faire
Hurry now, we're almost there…
Fa, la, la, la, la, la, la, la, la, la…

"Well, my little one, I'm glad to see my music pleases you and calls you to dance. My name is Tobias. Whom do I have the pleasure of meeting on this fine day?"

"My name is Minnie and I'm not so young as I seem."

Minnie blushed as soon as the words came out of her mouth—she didn't mean to sound snotty.

"Forgive me, fair maiden—I meant no offense. Clearly, you possess wisdom beyond your years, as proven by your excellent taste in music."

Minnie burst into giggles, and just like that, all was forgiven. She quickly took to Tobias, delighted as he led her through secret corners of the sprawling grounds. As they walked, people waved and greeted them, glad to see Tobias back for another year—and full of questions about his new friend.

"This is Mistress Minnie, here for the season. She and her family are camped on the west side, beneath a cerulean tent—her comrades in the cyan and turquoise one just beside. It's perfectly clear she's exceptional, since she's already taken a liking to both myself and my music."

With that, Minnie giggled and offered a curtsy-bow to Tobias.

"Oh no, Mistress Minnie. It is I who should bow to you, for it is not every day one stumbles upon a wandering princess in the desert."

With that, the color left Minnie's face and she nearly collapsed on rubbery legs. No one here knew she was a princess or that Fiona was the queen—or at least she didn't think they knew. She quickly pulled herself together and chalked it up to thoughtless words Tobias said without knowing the truth behind them.

Minnie pointed to a large tent with teal and green striped sides.

"What's over there, Tobias?"

Inside was a mobile chalkboard fronted by a barn-door table. She noted long-plank benches on either side. The space could easily seat thirty, give or take. Minnie saw boxes labeled books and others labeled supplies.

"Oh, that, my dear one, is our school. As you will soon see, there are many younglings scattered hither and yon. While their parents work the Faire, the children attend school. What could be better than home-schooling and Faire-watching?"

School.

That one word sent Minnie's thoughts back to the Misfits and her school in Cement City. She missed Lacey and all her other friends. She missed the world they built there—the carnival, music, laughter, and stories. She even missed the homework and the drudgery of the daily schedule. She missed all of it. She sighed—a sigh that made Tobias stop talking and extend his arms to her.

"Memories are funny things, Minnie. Some bring sorrow, some bring joy; some bring confusion and some bring anger. Memories help make us who we are. Wallow only in memories that bring you comfort, Mistress Minnie. Perhaps a hug will help?"

Minnie looked at him with tear-filled eyes.

"Desert dust got in my eyes, that's all. But I will gladly accept a hug from my all-time favorite minstrel."

"Ah, that desert dust—always slipping into our eyes when we least expect it. Thank you for the compliment, but I daresay I'm the only minstrel you know, my dear. Come here, let me give you a hug. Soon, all will be right as rain."

With that, Minnie leapt into his arms and for a moment, she forgot about everything and simply enjoyed being Minnie.

Philip d'GreenApple: Three-Letter Agency

THE RECEPTIONIST PATCHED the call through quickly.

"ASAC O'Toole," a voice answered, clipped and dry.

"ASAC—what's that stand for?" I asked, with the tang of grilled jalapeños still on my tongue.

"Assistant Special Agent in Charge," he said, each word measured, like he was reading from a manual.

"In charge of what, exactly?"

He deflected smoothly.

"How can I help you, sir?"

I studied the man in front of me.

"I'm sitting with a guy dropping hints he works for a government TLA—three-letter agency."

Now interested, O'Toole's tone sharpened.

"I know what a TLA is. What's he look like?"

"Like a Midwest farm boy who ran from Iowa's cornfields as far as he could without going to California or Florida."

O'Toole let out a bark of a laugh.

"I know him. Jimmy Alvarez. He's the real deal—whatever that means these days."

I pressed.

"Which agency? NSA? CIA? DHS? NFL?"

"Hmmm." He drew it out like a bad poker bluff. "One that's not supposed to operate inside our borders."

I'd read enough Reacher novels to know that game.

"CIA."

O'Toole's voice turned hard.

"You said it, not me. Jim's solid and you can believe what he tells you. He's as real as it gets. Call me if you need anything else."

He hung up before I could push further. Sitting there, I stared at my plate of congealed yolks. My fork slipped from my hand, clattering against the chipped ceramic. Like a statue sand-blasted into nothing, Jim Alvarez's face was unreadable. We were walking distance from FCI La Tuna, where Juan's boy Mateo sat doing time for smuggling—maybe Jim was the one who put him away.

I shoved my plate aside.

"Let's hear it," I said.

Minnie: Wet Laundry

SMOKING, TOR LEANED against the side of his campervan. As Gretchen walked by carrying a basket of damp laundry, he hissed.

"Big G, come here. I need to talk to you."

"What is it?" Gretchen said.

"It's the kid. I'm worried about her."

"What do you mean?"

"I think she really believes in faeries and pixies and stuff. And she's always talking to herself."

Gretchen looked him over, left to right and up and down.

"Look at yourself, Tor. You're almost eighty, haven't had a real job since 1973 and you smoke more loose-leaf tobacco than a woodsman's chimney."

"What's your point?"

"Leave the kid alone. She's fine, that's my point."

"I—"

Gretchen interrupted.

"You gonna help me hang these wet clothes or what? We get them up now, they'll be dry by dusk." She pointed to her nose. "And, believe

23

you me, you could use a fresh shirt. Let's go."

Grumbling, Tor tapped out embers from his pipe, stuffed it in the chest pocket of his overalls, and followed her toward the community clotheslines.

Trevir: Mom's Pantry

HEAVY WITH LEAD shielding and bulletproof glass, the armored Escalade weighed almost three tons. Black, the way Trevir liked all his cars. The gloomy, waterlogged countryside passed by tinted windows like a silent movie. A creek had overflowed its banks—the SUV plowed through, spraying water and leaving a wake like a cargo ship. Trevir, Troll Srenzo, and the driver led the procession. Kelpht the ohrkk and the rest of the entourage followed in two trailing vehicles.

Ten silent minutes later, they passed a forlorn diner.

Mom's Pantry.

They were two miles past when Trevir decided.

"Turn back," he said. "We'll have lunch."

Troll Srenzo looked up from the hand-written runes of a leather-bound book.

"That dump didn't look open," she said. "There will be better places when we get to the freeway. Civilized places."

"A place like that will have yesterday's greasy meatloaf, green beans from a can and mashed potatoes from a box," Trevir said. "That's what I want."

"Wonderful," she replied.

Trying hard not to let her neutral expression change, she returned her attention to the book. Soon, after turning back, the motorcade crunched onto the gravel of Chet's parking lot.

"Everyone in?" she asked.

Trevir considered.

"No, just you and me. We'll send something out."

He waited until she came around and opened the back door. After clambering out, he reached his hands to the sky and stretched.

It wasn't raining, but the air was filled with mist like they were in a heavy cloud. Visibility was restricted to a hundred yards, and the trees in the forest behind the restaurant were gray. The air was gray. Everything was gray.

"I hate this weather," Trevir said.

Troll Srenzo shrugged.

"They say it doesn't get as cold as Boston."

"Boston weather sucks bad eggs too," he said. "Coffee-mate."

"What?"

"I'll bet they have fake-cream powder for the coffee."

She wrinkled her nose.

"That stuff is nasty."

"Soybean oil."

"What are you talking about?"

"One of the main ingredients of Coffee-mate. Soybean oil. This is going to be good. Let's go."

The front door creaked and tickled a bouquet of bells hanging from a hook. Inside, a crooked, hand-written sign: *Please wait to be seated.*

From the back came a gruff voice.

"Ignore the sign. Sit where you like."

They slid opposite each other in a booth covered with a stiff-starched tablecloth that faintly smelled of bleach. A tall, bearded man wearing an apron came out and dropped menus before them. His crooked nametag said Chet.

"I'm short-handed, so I will be your host, server, cashier, cook, busboy and dishwasher. Haven't seen my helper for a couple days— don't know where she and the sprout wandered off to. She appeared from nowhere and nowhere ate her back up. Coffee? I have Seattle's Best in the pot and a French press if you're fussy."

"Cremora?" Trevir said.

Chet laughed. "No. You'll have to make do with heavy cream from the dairy down the road a piece. You probably smelled it on your way up—can't have cream without the crap, that's life."

"We'll take coffee from the pot," Troll Srenzo said.

"Got it," Chet said. "The menu's good except for lamb. No lamb right now."

Trevir pushed his menu away and spoke with challenge in his voice. He'd already decided, if there was no meatloaf, Chet would lose a few fingers. Maybe all of them. The image amused him. It would be hard to chop onions when you can't hold a knife.

"I'll take the meatloaf."

Deep into it, Troll Srenzo studied the menu's fine print.

"I'll have…"

"She'll have meatloaf, too," Trevir said.

"Shit-fire," she muttered.

Chet left, then quickly returned with an insulated, stainless steel coffee jug and a tray with espresso spoons, sugar bowl, cream in a miniature pitcher and mismatched mugs. He didn't bother arranging things—he left the tray for them to sort out.

"On a day like this," Trevir said, "a little brandy would be good in my coffee."

Chet looked around the empty room.

"Don't have a liquor license, but if you keep it to yourself, I might find a snifter of Martell cognac in my private stash."

"Is your salad from a bag?"

Chet looked confused.

"No. From hot houses…we get most of our produce from this county, but a lot of our greens come from the hippies up in British Columbia. Do you prefer bag-salad?"

"He's messing with you," Troll Srenzo said.

"Ah," Chet said. "I see. I'll see to the hot rolls and creamery butter."

The salad was a serve-yourself situation, with lettuce, cherry tomatoes, sliced cucumbers and diced red onions in separate serving bowls. The dressing was mixed from cruets of balsamic vinegar and olive oil. This kept them busy until Chet appeared with their main course.

While Chet ladled pepper cream sauce on a generous slab of meatloaf, Trevir looked down at his plate.

"I expected ketchup, gristle and grease."

"Did you read the menu? I use morel mushrooms and top off my recipe with sliced truffles. The Yukon gold potatoes have pressed garlic. You don't like it, I will get you something else."

Trevir took a bite.

"Oh, my," he said. "This is good."

Troll Srenzo didn't like it.

Too rich for her belly, so Trevir ate half of hers too.

After the dishes were cleared away, Trevir rubbed his stomach.

"After all that, a piece of pie would be good."

Chet shook his head.

"Sorry, my pie-maker is missing. I have a nice blackberry cobbler and a bread pudding. I could probably spare a little more Martell's to spice things up."

Trevir studied Chet's face.

"I don't believe you. I think you have pie."

After a few seconds of stare-down, Chet gave up.

"Crap," he said. "There's a piece I'm saving. Might be the last I ever get. You can't have it."

Trevir grinned.

"Heat it up. Not in the microwave, in your oven. Then, slap on a scoop of ice cream and don't skimp."

Chet's shoulders slumped.

"Crap on a cracker," he said. "Okay."

It was ten minutes before Chet came back. There was a sticky dot on his mustache.

After staring down at the pie, Trevir looked up.

"You sampled."

Defiant, Chet responded: "I had to make sure it was good enough for you."

Trevir laughed.

"Fine." He took a big bite. "Summer peach is my favorite. All is forgiven. Give my compliments to your baker."

"If I see her again, I'll tell her."

Troll Srenzo had a contemplative look on her face.

"What was your baker's name?" she said.

Trevir scowled and interrupted before Chet could answer.

"Who cares?" he said. He examined the wreckage of their meal, then spoke again. "I'm satisfied. I think I'll actually pay the bill."

"A hundred dollars will do it," Chet said. "Morels are not cheap."

"You'll take five hundred and be happy," Trevir said. "Pay him."

Troll Srenzo reached into her leather bag for cash, then gestured to the entourage outside.

"What shall we order something for them?" she said.

"Screw them. They can find something at the airport."

Philip d'GreenApple: Bad Mojo

JIM SPREAD HIS fingers wide apart on the tabletop. It was a weird gesture, and I didn't know why he did it. His hands were uninteresting. Neatly trimmed nails. No wedding band or rings of any type—and no tan lines or imprints to indicate he'd removed his rings. His watch was a fake Rolex Air King—I could tell by its ratcheting second hand. It moved with noticeable one-second jerks, not silk-smooth like a real Rolex. His hands were soft and pink.

Desk jockey.

I looked at my own hands, burned brown by the sun—blackened with oil and grime that would only wash out if I didn't mind losing skin in the process. There was a lesson in the difference between our hands. He shuffled papers in an air-conditioned office. Whatever he wanted, I would take the risks and face the real-world consequences.

"There is a shipment we are interested in—specifically who takes possession of it. The pickup location is in Del Rio. The parking lot catty-cornered from the train station. The paperwork says it will be delivered to Lawrence, Kansas, but along the way, it will get reroute instructions.

To where? We don't know. That's why we need you. Easy. And better yet, as a government contractor, you'll get paid. Half up front and half after the handoff. All you gotta do is keep a tracker in your wallet and press your thumbs on a beacon when the exchange is made."

All you gotta do.

I was young, but I knew all-you-gotta-do is never really all you gotta do.

"You're not allowed to operate in the United States."

"You'll be paid in cash. No paperwork. And here's the good part. Any trouble along the way? Traffic ticket? Immigration checkpoint? State police? Call me and I'll take care of it." He tapped his business card. "Like the Monopoly game. Get out of jail free."

"Why me?"

Jim smiled. "What turns up if they do a background check on you?"

My dad wasn't a fan of government paperwork.

"As close to nothing as can be."

"In these days of ubiquitous databases, do you have any idea how unusual that is?"

I didn't, but I also didn't care.

At that instant, Juan appeared. Sweating, he fanned his face with his hat. His expression was blank as a poker player's, all stoic lines and hard edges, but I'd known him long enough to spot a telltale tic in his left eye. Trouble brewed.

He towered over Alvarez.

"You're in my spot," he said.

Alvarez looked up and grinned.

"I was just leaving."

As he stood up, he pushed a small leather bag—like a tobacco pouch—over to me.

"Detailed instructions inside," he said. "It's great to have you on board. I'll be in touch."

Juan and I watched him stroll away. Then Juan slid into the booth. With a sour look on his face, he pushed Alvarez's coffee cup aside and spoke to the tabletop.

"He tried to recruit me. I told him to *chinga* his *madre*. That man is all *frijoles* and no *sombrero*. *Mala vibra*."

I knew what that meant.

Bad mojo.

Juan didn't need to order. Lupita knew what he wanted.

She dropped a steaming, heaping plate of huevos a la Mexicana in front of him: scrambled eggs with diced tomatoes, onions, and jalapeños. Just like the Mexican flag, the plate was red, white, and green. Tortillas and frijoles were served on a separate plate.

"Mil gracias, Loopy," he said.

Reaching around, he patted her butt. She gently swatted his hand away.

I hadn't noticed on our previous visits, but they were comfortable together. I had to give Juan credit. Aging, she was in her forties, but plump Lupita was still pretty while Juan had a pot belly and a face like a bulldog. The man had something that worked with the ladies.

Regardless of the tab, he always paid with a hundred-dollar bill and didn't wait for change.

Was life as simple as that?

It was something to think about.

He stuffed his face like breakfast was a race.

I hefted the leather pouch.

"What do you think?" I said.

"I think you should keep a big gap between yourself and that man. He's a liar, and whatever he says he wants? That's not what he wants. He's not even a government employee—he's retired and came back as a contractor. Layers on layers. Nothing good will come from working for him. *Su esquina está llena de telarañas.*"

It took a minute to untangle that phrase.

His corner is filled with spiderwebs.

The image that appeared in my mind was vivid. Attic. Rays of light limning dust. Tangled webs. Eerie shadows. Danger.

There was no doubt Juan was right.

However, fear is a sure cure for boredom and I was curious.

"Do you forbid?"

Around a red and green mouthful, Juan grinned.

"*Nunca confíes en un vato con los dientes cafés.*"

He enjoyed my slow-witted, step-by-step mental translation.

Never trust a man with brown teeth.

What in the name of *la virgencita* did that mean? Juan had the brownest teeth of anyone I'd ever met. Jim Alvarez's teeth were typical norteamericano teeth—pearl white, straight and symmetrical, but not fluorescent. Juan was playing with me.

With a dirty fingernail, he dislodged something stuck in his amber teeth before continuing.

"On the road, we are free to make as many mistakes as we want." He tucked a hundred under his plate and took a final sip of coffee. "You get the bill and we'll get the rig rolling to San Antoine."

I stuffed the leather bag in my pocket.

San Antonio?

I didn't think so.

I didn't say it out loud, but my guess was that somewhere along the way, Juan's magic box would reroute us to Del Rio.

Trevir and the Parking Lot Gang

UNDER A GLOOMY sky, Cement City was a dismal, decaying town. Many of the businesses on Main Street were boarded up.

"These people have nothing to live for," Trevir commented.

Without moving her head, Troll Srenzo flicked her eyes at him.

"Congratulations. You just described most of the world's population."

"Customers. I just described our perfect customers. I'm almost ashamed at how rich we will be."

"Right," Troll Srenzo said. "Almost."

The SUV passed the high school. At the farthest corner, a group of young people were assembled.

Trevir pointed.

"Flip a U-turn. I saw losers I want to talk to."

Jimmy spat a wad on the parking lot's asphalt.

"If we can find another drummer, I think the Pisstols got a gig at the bowling alley down in Bug. Battle of the bands. If we win, it could be our break."

The garage-punk band Jimmy and the Pisstols owed everything to their musical heroes, The Ramones. Bug was a little town downriver— named for its ferocious mosquitoes.

At seventeen, Zeke was the oldest and the Parking Lot Gang's unofficial leader. He lit the stub of a stinkweed joint they smoked when there was nothing else and drew the smoke in deep. He spoke when he could breathe again.

"I thought the kegger by the river was going to be your big break. As I remember it, that didn't go so well."

After a fight with loggers camping nearby who didn't care for the thrashy noise, Jimmy's beloved Mosrite guitar ended up in the bonfire. Fished out quickly, it still played, but barely—not that it mattered for their music. This was a better outcome than his bass player's Mosrite, which was crosscut with a 48-inch chainsaw.

Jimmy's voice was filled with sad regret.

"They could have at least let us finish playing Blitzkrieg Bop. It's only two minutes."

Zeke had a rusty ratrod, a primer-brown 1961 Chevrolet C-10 pickup with a front bumper literally held on with baling wire. The Parking Lot Gang loitered around the truck: April, Albert, Jimmy, and Zeke. They were waiting for Calvin Long, who reportedly had pain pills stolen from his stepdad's medicine cabinet.

"I hope Cal has oxy," April said. "I hurt. Everything hurts."

"Shut your tongue-pit, Ape," Zeke said. "We're all tired of hearing about it."

Slowly, Trevir's black Escalade pulled up. He pressed the button and his tinted window slid down.

"What's up, kids?" Trevir said.

"Bugger off, pervert," Zeke replied. "There ain't nothing you want here."

Trevir scanned them slowly and laughed.

"You are so, so perfect. I love your truck. I love your spiky hair. Everything."

"You lost?" Zeke said. He pointed to the west. "Keep going. Wherever you're headed, you'll get there."

"And your attitude. Who said when you got nothing, you got

nothing to lose?"

"I think that was Joey Ramone," Jimmy said.

Trevir laughed harder.

"Deliciously wrong. Could hardly be more wrong. Love it."

He snapped his fingers. Troll Srenzo opened a leather valise and pulled out a baggie filled with shiny little black pills. Hesitantly, she handed the baggie to Trevir.

"You sure about this?" she said.

For an instant, Trevir clenched his teeth and hissed before turning and grinning out through the window. From the inside pocket of his jacket, he produced a card he held out to Zeke.

"Here's what I suggest. Sell this stuff and send me eighty percent of the money. When I get paid, you'll get more. There's a QR code on the card. Scan it with your phone and follow the instructions. Don't take any of it yourself. Sell it all. Got it?"

Zeke sauntered to the SUV, took the card, and studied it. There was nothing on it except the matrix barcode. He held out his hand, and Trevir dropped the plastic bag in his palm. He weighed it—it was surprisingly heavy, like the pills were made from lead.

"Give me one," April said.

Trevir shook his head.

"I don't recommend it," he said with a sad tone.

It was a deeply fake tone. Clearly, Trevir did not care one way or the other, not even a little. If these kids wanted to kill themselves, too bad, so sad. He wasn't worried about losing a customer—there were plenty.

Zeke pulled the ziplock bag open and held it out. Eagerly, April took a shiny black pill. It was small, smaller than a pea. Like the belly of a black widow spider, a crimson hourglass was imprinted on each pellet. She didn't hesitate—she popped it back and dry-swallowed.

While watching, for an instant Trevir's veil lifted and Jimmy could see the grinning, bloody skull under the man's lizard-skin.

Next to Trevir, he saw the leather-clad troll staring. With her broken fang, misshapen face, and hairy jowls, she was the most hideous thing he'd ever seen. In addition, he could see the future split before his eyes. Money and everything it could buy. Bling. Cars. Guns. Sex. All while he rotted from his core.

On the other path, his father said he'd pay for community college if he took useful classes like electronics or business. To make it work, he'd have to give up the band and get a job slinging burgers or washing dishes. He felt like he was being ripped in two. He looked at April—the color had returned to her cheeks and she radiated.

"Oh," she said. "I feel good."

Trevir shrugged.

"You will spend the rest of your short life trying to get back to what you're feeling right now."

"This isn't right," Jimmy said. "Don't do this, Zeke."

"Fuck off, Jimmy. When opportunity knocks, you gotta answer the damned door."

Jimmy shook his head. "I'm out," he said.

As Jimmy walked away, Calvin approached. He stood by Zeke and they watched the black SUV cruise slowly away.

"What's going on?" Calvin said. "I got Percs."

"I'm not buying anymore," Zeke said. "I'm selling."

Minnie: Walk

MINNIE STRETCHED HER arms wide as she stirred in the tent, careful to move as little as possible so she wouldn't disturb Gretchen and Tor—snuggled together in their sleeping bag behind a flimsy sheet, their makeshift attempt at privacy. The morning sun kissed the top of the tent and quickly moved downward while she decided what to do with her day.

Walk.

That's what she would do today: walk.

Where?

It didn't matter. She would walk.

Quickly and efficiently, she dressed: long-sleeved flannel shirt, floppy hat, sunglasses, rip-stop carpenter pants to protect her tender flesh—she had plenty of scratches and gouges and didn't need more.

Cushy cotton socks. Boots.

Tobias had found her a castoff pair of leather boots with a few hundred miles left in the soles.

In this area, there was no hiking without water and lots of it. Also from Tobias, she had borrowed a Camelback knapsack with a hydration pack. It held two liters, enough for a half-day hike. She made a mental note: she'd have to come back at noon or find a way to refill it. From a spigot, she filled the bladder, then hefted the backpack and adjusted the straps. Her hiking pole was a repurposed Kentucky tobacco stake with a leather string-strap. She raised the hickory to her nose and drew deep on the rich, chocolaty aroma.

So good.

She was ready.

Now, which way?

After closing her eyes, she turned in a circle until she was a little dizzy, then stopped.

North, cross-country, toward red cliffs glowing in the morning sun.

She took a deep breath of the cool morning air and set off.

After an hour, she changed direction and followed Oak Creek upstream until encountering a concrete bridge to cross. On the other side, tourists in Land Rovers and Subarus were parked everywhere they could. Minnie decided to follow in their footsteps to the Cathedral Rock scramble. After half an hour of climbing, the view from the trail end was spectacular and she noticed the END OF TRAIL sign placed exactly on top of a vortex—a small one that tugged weakly at her ankles. In greeting, she stooped and waved her hand through it and felt the tingle. This one was pale green—the color of a sun-baked prickly pear cactus—and smelled of old sage.

Looking down, she saw a little girl with huge brown eyes—maybe four years old. In braids, the girl's hair hung down on both sides of her round, flushed face.

"That was quite a climb for a little one like you," Minnie said.

The girl shrugged.

"My daddy lifted me on the hard parts."

"Did he tell you that you weigh a million tons?"

"No," the girl said. "He said I'm light as a dandelion seed."

Minnie laughed.

"What's your name?"

"Abby," the little one said. "What's yours?"

"Minnie." Slowly, Minnie reached for Abby's hand, then tugged it up to hold it over the rocks of the green vortex. "Do you feel that?"

The girl pulled her hand away and ran toward the shelf where her mother and father were making a cellphone video for their podcast.

"What is it?" her dad said.

"That girl is weird."

Her dad looked back.

"Do we have a problem?" he said.

Minnie smiled.

"In endless supply," she said.

After walking up to the ledge to join them, she looked out over the landscape. Eastward, there was a terrifying plane of rippling light. It wasn't a typical tornado vortex—it was more like sheet lightning zooming into the sky, old, powerful and scary. She couldn't bear to see it. She turned to the west. About three miles away, beyond the Cathedral hoodoos, rock outcroppings and valley scrub junipers, there was a vortex, a big, strong one—buttercup yellow.

She looked down at the little girl.

"It was nice talking to you," Minnie said.

The girl made a mean face and stuck out her tongue—it was stained purple, like the fruit of a prickly pear cactus.

Minnie couldn't help herself—she doubled over with laughter.

"You are a purple-tongued devil," she said.

As always, the climb down was harder than the climb up. At the bottom, she stopped, turned around and rubbed the backs of her burning thighs. High above, the couple still worked on their video. Standing at the edge, the girl looked down. Minnie waved. The girl did not wave back. It was too far away to tell, but Minnie imagined the vivid purple tongue flapping in her direction.

She turned to the west, where, at this angle, the yellow vortex appeared as a faint smudge on the horizon. Nearby, the Airport Mesa vortex shimmered with red and blue filaments, but years of tourists had left it threadbare and weary. The yellow vortex, by contrast, glowed strong and fresh—its power untouched. Minnie knew exactly what that meant: no tourists.

That also meant the Buttercup vortex must be a screaming bear to get to.

In between was a trail, Oak Creek, a dirt road, the highway, suburban streets, barbed wire fences, then open land—scrub brush: Pinyon Pines and Mesquite, Acacia, Manzanita, Desert Broom, Buckbrush, Mormon Tea, Graythorn, Wolfberry, Yucca, Ocotillo, spiny Cholla and the remnant ghosts of ancient saguaros. The terrain looked flat enough, but she knew there would be endless arroyos, outcroppings, washes, and lots of critters that would bite or sting if she didn't watch her step.

Given a choice, she would prefer not to be attacked by an eight-inch centipede. And there were colorful coral snakes. She recounted the warning in her mind:

Black nose touches yellow, kill a fellow.

What else?

Rattlesnakes, and tiny, powerful stingers on bark scorpions.

She decided it might be worth the effort.

In welcome, she stretched out her arms.

If the desert wants me, it can have me.

The trail would not hike itself. She took a sip from the Camelback's drinking tube and started walking. At the bottom, while dodging cars futilely trying to find places to park, she walked a few yards on Back O'Beyond Road. On a dusty-pink jeep, the printing on a magnetic sign caught her eye.

Norm, the Vortex Hunter.

Philip d'GreenApple: Old Soul

I WAS RIGHT.

Before the El Paso skyline—such as it was—was out of sight, Juan's box buzzed and the red light flashed. Instead of picking up pallets of Chevy transmissions in San Antonio, we were headed to Del Rio to exchange our leased Premier Trailer for a refrigerated unit.

"What does it say we're picking up?" I asked.

Juan looked over at me with a blank expression.

"Avocados," he said.

Right.

I opened the leather pouch. The first thing I pulled out was a condom in its foil package. I'd never touched one before, but it was flexible and felt strange with its rubbery ring. I showed it to Juan.

His face twisted in an expression I hadn't seen before. It was a mixture of resignation and sadness—as if one of his sons had grown up way too fast.

"*Forrito,*" he said. "Little cover."

I studied the package.

Sultán Prudence. Sabor Y Aroma. Mento.

Mint.

Do people eat these things?

I must have mumbled.

"What's that?" Juan said.

"Nothing," I said.

What would Minnie think if she saw me now?

I pushed the thought away and took the last item out of the pouch.

It was a credit card thing with thumb marks embossed on it. There were instructions printed on a removable label on the back.

Press on the front with both thumbs at the same time...help will come.

A voice in my head spoke up.

Don't count on it, kid.

I peeled off the card's label, wadded it up and stuffed it in the truck's ashtray.

"People forget I'm only fourteen."

Juan looked over at me.

This time, his emotion was clear.

Sadness.

"You got an old soul, Kiddo," he said.

It hit me—this was the third week of August. I ran the calendar in my head and realized my "circle-around-the-sun" day had slipped by unnoticed. I was officially fifteen now.

Time flies.

I wondered if that meant anything, if I felt any different.

I came up empty.

The Parking Lot Gang: Black Death

ZEKE KEPT TO the edges of the bustling hallways, slipping past open locker doors and clusters of students, always listening for April's voice. She was hunting him—everyone knew it. She was relentless, stopping teachers mid-conversation, quizzing staff as they swept the scuffed linoleum, even buttonholing classmates at their lockers. Between bells, her voice carried down the corridors—sharp, determined and impossible to miss. Zeke flinched at each echo, glancing over his shoulder while weaving through the noisy tide and doing his best to be invisible.

The night before, in his bedroom, he'd counted the black pills. There were 999. The bag had held 1,000. April got one. 999 left. This simple math obsessed him.

In school, the word was out. He had something. He was getting texts and voicemails—even a hand-written note handed to him as he scuttled between classes. In the hallways, kids caught his eye. Most were just curious.

What does you have? What's it like?

And, there was the big question.

How much does it cost?

Letting the World Lit teacher's words wash over him, he replayed the conversation with the weird dude in the Escalade. No resale price had been mentioned, he was sure of it.

What did this stuff go for? What did the thin creep expect?

Zeke finally decided: if the odd man cared about the price, he would have said.

His first thought was to charge a dollar.

That would be nine hundred ninety-nine dollars. Making the math easy, he'd send the weirdo two hundred, leaving eight hundred dollars in his pocket. Compared to the thirteen grimy dollars in his wallet and the twenty dollars he could get mowing a lawn over the upcoming weekend, that was a small fortune.

With the pills, how long would it take to make eight hundred bucks?

A week? Two?

The numbers made him dizzy. The year before, he'd had a thousand after selling the dirt bike his dad bought him for Christmas back when the old man was still living with them. He remembered what it was like to have money in his pocket. He was king of the world for nearly a week before it was gone. He bought decent weed from a Vietnamese cat at an isolated corner of the casino's parking lot. He bribed a homeless guy living under the bridge to buy cases of Miller High Life at the Liquor Shack, bought Cascade Burger baskets for his party of five and left a twenty-dollar tip, bought a hundred lottery tickets and won twenty-three dollars back. Thinking about that spending—and what he had to show for it—made his head hurt.

During that glorious week, he never had so many friends—they came from all over town and from the next town over. For a couple days, April's parents were away in Tacoma. That meant her house could host a party. He felt a twinge of guilt—after the two-day revelry, they left her house a mess and she had to clean it by herself. When it came time to sweep, mop, and take out the garbage, the party moved to the riverbank. She was on her own and didn't get any sleep that night.

Even after her cleaning, there were still a few Busch beer cans and a wine bottle under the guest room bed…along with a nasty condom filled with goo. Her stepdad welted her ass for that. She was an only child—there was no one else to take the blame.

Zeke was a solid C- student but he wasn't stupid. He disguised his intellect, but when he was younger, his 4th grade math teacher caught onto him. Something about how quickly he grasped carrying the ones when adding big numbers.

He kind of liked math but would not admit it to anyone. Only geeks, dweebs, and nerds liked schoolwork—especially math. More than anything, Zeke wanted to be cool.

Like lightning, there was a flash of light in his head.

What if the little black pills could be sold for ten dollars each?

Now he was really dizzy.

Ten thousand dollars, minus two thousand.

His knees weakened—he almost collapsed. In the milling hallway, he leaned his overheated head against the cool metal of a locker.

Is it possible to get ten dollars for one of the little black pills? Percocets went for twenty each. Oxy, even more.

Eight thousand dollars was not a small fortune—it was huge. A life-changing prosperity.

The numbers tumbled in his head. He realized he'd need to buy more pills when he ran out.

What if buying more cost a dollar each? What if they cost a hundred?

Suddenly, he could not tell if he was rich or poor.

Would selling pills for ten dollars each be like buying a hundred lottery tickets and getting twenty-three dollars back?

"Z, I've been looking for you."

Zeke shook off his trance.

April.

She pressed damp currency into his hand. He peeked—four wrinkled dollars. Pathetic, grimy dollars. Her palm was sweaty. The bills were damp. The feel of them made him queasy.

"I'll take four," she said.

He took a deep breath, then whispered.

"April, geez, I'm sorry. They're ten dollars each."

Her shoulders slumped.

"I heard they are a dollar."

His mind snapped to a decision. He pushed the currency back at her. She wouldn't take the bills. They drifted to the floor like autumn leaves.

"You heard wrong. Ten for friends. Twenty for strangers."

How would the man in the SUV know what he charged? He could report a dollar per sale and actually get ten.

Thinking back, there was something in the man's eyes.

No, his accounting had better be straight. No games.

"I have four dollars and I can get the rest later," she said. "You know I'm good for it. I don't need four pills, one is enough for now."

"Cash," Zeke said. He pushed her away. "Come back when you have it all."

"Meet me by the track. Under the bleachers. I'll do—"

Another flash of insight flooded his mind: he needed to distance himself from the customers and the transactions.

"Anyone who wants a pill needs to talk to Calvin. He has the baggie."

"Calvin? You have them, Zeke. I saw them."

His resolve stiffened. He pushed her backwards and entered the flow of bodies in the hallway. Everyone rushed—they had another minute to get to their seats.

"Go," he said over his shoulder. "Talk to Calvin. He'll take care of you."

He stood for a moment outside his Family Studies classroom before deciding to ditch.

I need to find Calvin before the word gets out.

Calvin Long was heavyset, beefy, and truth be told, not too bright. Zeke found him smoking a cigarette near the back door of the gym.

"Gimme a drag off that," Zeke said.

"Get your own," Calvin replied.

"Here's the deal…"

Zeke had to repeat himself more times than he liked, but Calvin eventually grasped the arrangement.

People would come to him for the little black pills.

"I will start you off with ten—we'll see how many days that takes you to sell them."

It finally occurred to Calvin to ask.

"What's in it for me?"

"I feel generous, so you give me all the money and I will rebate you back a dollar per pill."

"Rebate? What's that?"

"I will pay you—pay you back a dollar for each sale. You sell ten, you get ten bucks. Sell a hundred, you get a hundred. Don't take it from the haul, I get all the money and then I give you your piece of it. Got it?"

Calvin rubbed his stubbly double chin and picked at an inflamed boil.

"I get it. I'm not stupid, you know."

Right, Zeke thought.

Zeke fished the baggie out of his backpack.

"Got something to hold the pills?"

Calvin thought it over. "Pez candy. The plastic box? Chewbacca."

He made the Chewbacca growling noise.

"Waauggh."

Christ, what a moron.

After pulling off the top, Calvin upended the candy into his mouth, then handed over the Pez dispenser. Zeke carefully counted out ten pills, then rattled them in front of Calvin's face.

"Waauggh," Calvin said again, around the mouthful of candy pellets.

Jesus P. Christ.

"Ten dollars. Cash, no credit, no trades. And don't let April suck your willie in exchange for one."

Calvin narrowed his eyes like a brilliant idea had occurred to him.

Shit. He's going to let her. Damn it.

Zeke repeated the instructions.

"A hundred dollars for the ten pills. I give you ten dollars back and a fresh batch of pills to sell. Don't screw around, this is serious."

"Cash, no swapping, I got it. You can count on me."

Calvin could already feel the girl's mouth on his...what?

Pee-pee, Calvin thought.

Watching Calvin amble away, Zeke muttered to himself.

"I sure hope this works."

Philip d'GreenApple: Del Rio, TX

IT WAS AMAZING that Juan could eat after his big breakfast, but after sipping from a cold pint of yesterday's coffee, he pulled a concha from a paper bag and tore into the sweet bread like it owed him money.

"Del Rio by sundown," I said.

He grunted, eyes on the Chihuahuan Desert stretching endlessly—all creosote bushes, yucca spikes, and tumbleweeds.

On I-10 past Van Horn, 120 miles in, the Guadalupe Mountains loomed with limestone cliffs glowing gold against a washed-out blue sky. The road flattened into a sea of scrub and distant mesas; the kind of empty that makes you feel small. At Fort Stockton, 240 miles down, we passed the Paisano Pete statue—a 22-foot roadrunner, biggest in the world—its goofy grin a stark contrast to Juan's tight jaw.

"Mateo's getting out soon," he finally said, voice low, like he was tasting the words.

Sometimes I am clueless. I wondered what he was getting at.

After a few more miles unreeled, Juan spoke again.

"You're in his spot," he said.

Ah. Okay.

Regardless of Fed's play, this part of my life was ending.

After taking a quick look at whatever Alvarez was up to, it was time for me to head west anyway. My girl was calling.

No, not calling exactly, but ready, maybe.

In a month, maybe I'd be ready, too.

But ready for what?

I had the feeling that once we were together, nothing would pry us apart again.

We turned onto US-90 at Ozona and cruised the last hundred miles to Del Rio. The landscape turned greener with prickly pears and mesquite giving way to pecan groves along the San Felipe Springs, their waters feeding Del Rio's lifeblood. We rolled past the Val Verde Winery, its adobe walls baking in the late sun, and the Whitehead Memorial Museum, where a sign boasted Jersey Lilly, Judge Roy Bean's old saloon. Del Rio's border vibe hit hard—bilingual signs, mariachi drifting from a taqueria and the Rio Grande's muddy pull just south, where trucks and trailers like ours crisscrossed into Mexico and back.

After checking in and dropping the trailer at the TXS lot, we deadheaded back to a gravel patch near Amistad Dam with the sun dipping behind Lake Amistad's glassy sprawl, casting orange across the rig. Juan stepped out with boots crunching gravel and lit a cigarette, the ember glowing like a warning. I knew he'd hitch a ride to a cantina to drown the mala vibra of La Tuna's barbed wire.

Me?

I angled for a booth at Memo's Restaurant, the kind of joint where the menudo might—just might—calm the jagged edges of my nerves. Memo's sat a short stumble from the Palm Vista Motor Lodge, a 1950s relic that looked like it hadn't seen a fresh coat of paint since Eisenhower was in office. Juan, of course, knew a guy there—Juan always knew a guy. With a few palmed greenbacks, he'd secured us two rooms on the condition we kept our heads down and didn't show up until after 10 PM.

The Palm Vista wasn't the worst dive I'd ever crashed in, though that's a low bar. That dubious honor went to a Howard Johnson's outside Austin—a roach-infested hellhole I'd endured years back before they razed it—hopefully with a tactical nuke. At that HoJo, the bugs were so thick they held a convention in my room, skittering across the cracked linoleum like they owned the joint. Which they did. The scorpions, at least, gave me a wide berth, too busy with their roach buffet to bother me.

For all its faults—dingy walls, a carpet that crunched underfoot with God-knows-what—the Palm Vista had a bed, a real one, not the lumpy mattress in Juan's Peterbilt sleeper cab, where the blankets hadn't been washed since the Carter administration. A private shower, even one with a trickle of lukewarm water, was a luxury after days on the road, where hygiene often meant a quick splash from a truck stop sink. Juan wasn't big on laundry, and his cab smelled like a mix of diesel, sweat and regret.

With my knapsack weighing heavily, I shuffled to my room, the neon vacancy sign buzzing like a dying fly overhead. After fishing the key from under the doormat—a hiding spot so obvious it might as well have been taped to the door with a Welcome sign—I walked inside. The room was a mess, like the maid clocked out mid-shift and never looked back. The bed was a tangle of sheets, which I imagined as still warm from whoever had been there before me. Wet towels littered the bathroom floor, turning the cracked tiles into a swamp. For the twenty bucks Juan had slipped his contact, we'd been robbed.

Idly, I wondered if I'd ever see Juan again. At nine sharp in the morning, I was to meet Alvarez's quarry at the parking lot of the Del Rio Amtrak station. It wasn't too late to hop the Texas Eagle train to the west where I belonged. Despite Juan's lack of formal education, he knew a lot more about life on the road and human nature than I ever would. I was stupid if I didn't take his advice and steer clear of the Fed's game.

I sighed, hung the towels on the clothesline out back—where they'd dry in the desert air, or at least stop stinking up the place—and collapsed onto the bed. The mattress sagged like a hammock, but I was too tired to care. Sleep came fast, mercifully dreamless—a black void that swallowed the day and left me nothing but the promise of another tepid shower at dawn.

Minnie: The Vortex Hunter

THE OLD WILLYS JEEP was battered and sunburnt. Apparently, vortex hunting was not a path to endless riches. Amused, she stopped to have a look. Standing in front of the vehicle, she peered through the dirty windshield and caught the eye of the driver, who was halfway through devouring a foot-long Italian sub.

Slender, he was unbelievably handsome—in his early thirties, with a fashionable, carefully groomed three-day beard. Long, feathery brown hair framed his narrow face. He lifted his sunglasses and grinned. Bright-blue eyes and gleaming white teeth dazzled.

With a strand of lettuce hanging from his mouth, he said, "Didn't get lunch. Want a bite?"

There was a hungry churning in her belly. She hadn't had lunch either, but she wasn't going to eat a factory sandwich—not while there were organic pumpkin seeds and a couple of boiled goose eggs in her backpack.

"No, thank you," she said.

"Want to feel the relentless force of the Earth run through your teenie-tiny body?"

I thought that's what I was already doing.

"Sure, why not?" she said.

"It's two hundred for the first hour, a hundred an hour after."

She laughed.

"I don't have that kind of money. Not even close."

He flicked a lettuce shred off his face, then looked at the declining angle of the sun and the lethargic people streaming to and from their cars.

"How much you got?"

"Twenty dollars."

He scowled, then smiled after making a decision.

"No worries. I can take you to Airport Mesa for that."

She looked down at her boots. They were close to done with walking for the day. She fished around in her pocket for the wrinkled, lonely twenty.

"Let's hit it," she said.

From the passenger seat, she studied the side of his face.

"Your name isn't Norm," she said. "You're as far away from a Norm as a man could possibly be."

He laughed.

"No, I'm Al. Al Bailey. Bought the Jeep from Norm when he retired in ought-ten. Ain't got around to changing the name or the website. Someday, maybe." The wind whipped his hair. "Let me educate you about vortexes. They are energy-focus sites where spirit fields emit or are absorbed by Mother Earth. Downlifts are like swirling water going down the drain. Masculine uplifts like the Airport Mesa vortex are like an inverted tornado spinning up into a zero-point singularity in the sky."

"Do you believe any of this? Or are you just taking easy money from tourists?"

Al shrugged.

"I don't not-believe. There's something going on. How you care to describe it is up to you. I have most of a degree in physics from ASU. None of the instruments I studied measure anything at a vortex, but I can feel it. And in Sedona, I feel well and balanced. So, I will do anything necessary to stay here—including hauling around broke kids for a measly twenty bucks."

"Fair enough," Minnie said.

While stopped at a traffic light, Al studied her face.

"You're older than I first thought."

"I get that a lot," Minnie replied.

The Airport Mesa uplift vortex sat just off Highway 89A. Parking was scarce with only a handful of spaces and not a single one open.

"Scramble up and have a look. I will wait here so I can move if someone wants to back out."

Minnie shrugged.

"Okay."

It was an easy hike and Minnie's boots barely complained. At the top, on the flat rock promontory, the view of the valley and the red rock outcroppings were fantastic. She breathed deeply. Three photographers tended their tripods while four older women had spread yoga mats and worked on stretching and breathing. The vortex was barely visible. Like a parched well, it had been sucked dry. She walked to the vortex center, which was on the crumbling edge of the little mesa. She placed her hands on the rock to give back what she could. It wasn't much, but the red and blue hues brightened a little in appreciation.

This vortex needs more givers and fewer takers.

Aacross the valley to the east, the rainbow sheet vortex throbbed. That one scared her so she turned away.

Several miles to the west, the yellow vortex poured restless energy into the sky. It was vivid like a laser and nearly blinding.

Okay, she thought. That one looks more friendly.

Feeling lighter, she walked back to the Jeep.

Once there, she said, "This place is sad. Do you want to see a real vortex?"

He studied her face.

"This is all you get for twenty bucks."

"I doubt if you know this one."

"I know all them all. Bell Rock, Chapel of the Holy Cross, Red Rock Crossing, West Fork Trail."

"Nope," she said. "It's none of those."

"Schnebly Hill on the edge of the Mogollon Rim?"

"Is that the big, scary one to the east?"

"Yes."

"I don't want to hear about that one."

He mulled it over.

"You know one I don't? Bullsnot."

"Try me," she said.

"Okay."

She held out her palm and rubbed her index finger across it.

"If I lead you to a vortex you haven't seen before, I get my twenty back."

He laughed.

"No way. Rent's coming due and my gas tank is empty. I need this money."

She laughed.

"If I'm lying, I'll find another twenty and double your stash. Easy money. Okay?"

He scowled.

"I'll call that bluff."

They drove west a few miles on Highway 89A toward Jerome. Past the Lower Red Rock Loop, she told him to slow down. There was a dirt road by the Borrow Pit. She pointed.

"Turn left."

"There's a quarry out this way," Al said, "but the goat trail road is too rough for my Jeep."

Minnie was concentrating.

"Shut up," she said, "we're almost there."

On the rough rocks and potholes, they drove slowly for several hundred yards.

"Stop," she said.

After getting out of the Jeep, she looked up. The daisy-yellow energy field was like a huge, inverted pyramid. All the hairs on her arm stood straight out. She led the way across a dry wash and around boulders bigger than the Jeep. There was no trail; they walked a meandering hundred yards across the hostile desert. She could see where to go, but it was not easy to get there. Scrub trees, ravines and spiny cholla created a maze.

After some determined circling and a bit of backtracking, they finally arrived.

"Can you feel it?" she said.

"Maybe," he said.

"You're a fool." She tugged his arm and moved him closer to the center. "See how the junipers are twisted as they reach for the sky? You see this anywhere else? Not like this, you don't."

"I'm not sure."

"Some vortex hunter you are. Close your eyes."

She tugged him a foot to the right.

"Now, take a little step back. Five inches."

He hesitated.

"Go on, a half step, that's it."

He shuffled backwards until he stood directly over the funnel of invisible light. Slowly and unconsciously, he raised his arms and focused the energy.

And then, in an instant, he was gone.

She didn't have a watch, so she didn't know if ten or thirty minutes passed. Time is elastic. It was long enough for her to explore the immediate area...the prickly pears, the chunks of red rock, the birds and lizards and trees all baking in the sun's hot radiance.

Then, as quickly as he disappeared, he reappeared. Dazed, he looked lost and his eyes refused to focus. His knees were weak—he tottered back to his Jeep like a very old man.

"How was your trip?" she said with a smile.

He leaned back against the Jeep's fender and scanned the landscape.

"I don't want to talk about it," he said.

She held out her hand.

"Can I have my twenty dollars back?"

"No," he said.

She laughed and laughed as if that was the funniest thing she'd ever heard.

Minnie: The Vortex Hunter's Journey

FOR A FEW minutes, Al rested his head on the steering wheel until the temperature in the Jeep grew unbearable. Like he'd aged a hundred years, he slowly reached out to start the engine, turned up the air conditioner, and directed the vents to pour cold air over himself.

"No one lives here because they like the weather in the summer," he said. Waking up, he aimed one of the vents her way. "You okay?"

Minnie shrugged.

"To me, the heat is still a novelty. There's still a little moss growing on my bones."

"The nomads have it right. Go north in the summer. Come back in the winter. Tell me where you live—I'll drive you."

"Ren Faire," he said. "Ah, the rennies. I should have known. Where else? I know a back way; we can be there in twenty minutes."

The worst section was maneuvering across an unexpected flashflood washout, but the Jeep managed the task with its lift kit suspension and oversized tires. By the time they reached the Ren Faire's massive main parking lot, Minnie felt like a bobblehead.

"Think I'll take the highway back," Al said, laughing.

"You don't think I'm leaving before you tell me about your experience?"

He sighed.

"I suppose not."

"Spill it," she said.

He closed his eyes.

"It was not an illusion or hallucination. It was real. I was there."

Minnie let the silence reign for a long minute.

"Tell me."

"I stood at the edge of a dark forest on the edge of a meadow filled with wildflowers. Honeybees going crazy. On a knoll, there was a house, an old farmhouse. Veranda. Rocking chairs. A trickle of smoke from a brick chimney."

Despite the heat, cold fingers marched up her spine.

"Tilled Earth? Chicken wire to keep the rabbits out? Rows of peas, beans and corn?"

"You just described every family farm in the universe, but yes."

This irritated her, so she spoke more sharply than intended.

"One-legged hopper with a red bow."

He turned pale.

"I wasn't going to mention that."

"I know this place. Tell me everything. Now."

"On the porch, a woman in a swinging chair."

"That's Fiona."

"What's wrong with her?"

"She's dreaming and hasn't woken up yet, but she will."

"Let me start at the beginning. I walked through the tall grass and flowers, and..."

Impatient, Minnie said, "And what?"

"They invited me to join them for lunch."

"Lunch?"

"Yeah, rabbit stew with potatoes and carrots from the garden. Greens and blackberry wine. Simple, but it tasted like a million dollars."

"I don't care what you ate for lunch. Who all was there?"

"The guy cooked and served."

"Sean," she said. "He cooks."

"How do you know these people I dreamed up?"

"Never mind all that. Who else?"

"There was a young man—joking and laughing."

"This one I don't know. What did he look like? Fat? Thin? Tall? Short? Brown hair or blonde? Tats? Earring? Mustache?"

"Hold on a minute, let me think. Slender, not too tall. Handsome, like his face was etched from stone. Wearing a snazzy business suit. Long fingers, kind of delicate."

"I can't think of who that might be. They don't get many visitors— the farmhouse is not easy to find."

"I took an instant dislike. Fake smile, big teeth."

Oh, no.

"Real phony, like he'd be happy to cut out your heart and eat it. Everyone all friendly and polite, but there was a dark undercurrent. He was like a rabid weasel ready to pounce on a mouse. His aura was oily and black. Come to think on it, I've never seen an aura before, but a lot of people around here say they can see them. His was black as midnight and had warts. I halfway remember his name."

"Please don't say it…"

"Trevir, spelled with an 'i' not an 'o'. He said he was not really there, but would be, soonish. What does that mean? He certainly tore into the stew and soaked up a lot of the wine—bottle after bottle. A guy who eats like that should not be thin."

With her index finger, Minnie made an impatient motion.

Get on with it.

"What's an orc? Are they like from the Lord of the Rings or something? He said the orcs are coming, and they would burn the farm to the ground, like it was funny. Our host laughed it off, but I could tell he was worried—like he knew the walls would fall. What walls? There were no walls, just a forest."

"The forest is the wall. What else did they say?"

"That was it. Sean served apple pie with hand-churned ice cream and the ground cinnamon sauce smelled so good. But, before I could fork up a bite, I was back with you. Whoosh-zip-bang, back in the hot. I can still smell caramel and the spices of that pie, but here we are. Now, you tell me. Was I dreaming? Am I losing my mind?"

"No, you're just a messenger. It's a delicate balance. We have to enjoy the beauty of our day-to-day lives but be ready for war."

"I don't believe in war. I like harmony and nature."

"When the time comes, if you don't fight for good, darkness wins."

"That guy, Trevir. My mind made him up, right? He's not real? And, what is the Black Death?"

"No, he's real and Black Death is coming like a plague. It's already all around us."

"What are we supposed to do?"

She pondered before speaking.

"For now, we're going to live. Gather our strength and get ready. I don't think there is anything else we can do but savor peace and prepare for battle."

"If I see that guy, I will run and keep running until I'm far away."

"No, you can't run away. There's nowhere to go. On that day, you'll stand your ground and accept your fate like the rest of us. Die, probably. Live, maybe."

"I need a beer."

She took a deep breath and let it out slowly.

"Yes," Minnie said. "Enjoy a tall, cold one, that's what life is all about. Go about your day and be grateful for each peaceful second because everything will come to a reckoning and you'll be asked to pay the price—asked to put it on the line and sacrifice everything. Then you'll know what it really means to be human and to love—you'll know what everything really costs."

He fished the wrinkled twenty from the pocket of his jeans.

"I guess I owe you this back."

"No," she said, "buy yourself a good one—a microbrew ale, not factory swill—and remember each cold sip is a gift from God."

"You're a very, very strange young lady."

"You don't know the half of it," she said.

Philip d'GreenApple: Looking Back

I COULD PINPOINT the moment I stopped being a boy and became a man. One second, I was cloaked in youth's flimsy arrogance, shielded from the world's harder edges. Kids get that—most of them, anyway. I'd been luckier than most, dodging the worst of what people can do to each other. Men don't get that pass. They stand bare, braced for the world's jagged teeth.

For me, it happened in a gravel-strewn corner of a parking lot, just across from the Del Rio Regional Transportation Center. I'd hitched a ride from the hotel with a guy named Rafael, whose pickup rattled like it was coughing up its last mile. He dumped me in front of the station, a squat brick relic from the 1920s, spruced up with federal cash that didn't quite hide the cracks. I lingered, sizing up the arched windows and a vagrant howling about the government's sins. A Texas Highway Patrol cruiser rolled by, slow and suspicious. The lady cop behind the wheel gave me a once-over. I tipped my hat, playing the part. She smirked and kept moving.

Instructions from Alvarez included a map, scratched out in ballpoint like a drunkard's treasure hunt. I was off by a block. I had to backtrack to Main, head due north, cross the tracks, and wait by a scraggly stand of mesquites at the lot's far end. I shifted my rucksack, felt the straps bite my shoulders, and started walking.

In the stingy shade of a mesquite grove, two young men lounged with the practiced ease of those for whom waiting was both art and occupation. They crouched low, backs against the gnarled trunks, their silhouettes sharp against the Del Rio heat shimmering off the gravel lot. Short, wiry, with skin the color of burnt coffee, they didn't strike me as locals. Not Mexican, not with a guarded squint. Salvadoran, maybe, or Honduran—men who'd crossed borders less forgiving than the Rio Grande. Their eyes flicked toward me, quick and appraising, like they were tallying the worth of my boots and the trouble I might bring.

I gave them a nod. They returned it, barely, their faces blank as unpaid bills. The air smelled of dust and creosote, the mesquites' brittle leaves whispering lies about cooler days. I eased my rucksack off my shoulders, the canvas damp with sweat, and let it thud into the dirt. It'd make a fine pillow, better than the gravel, which crunched under my boots like a warning. I stretched out, trucker's hat tipped over my eyes, and settled into the Earth's unyielding embrace, feigning a nap.

The parking lot stretched empty toward the Transportation Center, its brick facade gleaming faintly under the noon sun, a monument to federal dollars and forgotten promises. Across the tracks, the town sprawled in a haze of heat and indifference—the kind of place where dreams came to dry out and die. The two men didn't speak, not to me or each other, but their silence was loud, heavy with the weight of shared secrets. One flicked a cigarette butt into the gravel, the ember winking out like a bad idea. The other toyed with a length of twine, knotting and unknotting it with fingers that knew restless work. They were waiting, same as me, but for what—or who—I couldn't guess. Not yet.

I kept my breathing slow, my body slack, but my ears strained for the crunch of footsteps or the low rumble of an engine. Alvarez's instructions had been clear: wait by the trees, keep my eyes open, and don't trust anyone who smiles too much. These two weren't smiling at all, which was either a good sign or a very bad one. In a town like Del Rio, where the Rio Grande whispered deals and the mesquites stood witness, you read the difference or you didn't last long.

A dusty Suburban growled across the gravel, snapping me awake from the half-sleep I'd been faking. The crunch of tires was loud as a debt collector's knock, and I blinked against the Del Rio sun, already brutal despite the early hour. The two men I'd been sharing the dirt with were already on their feet, brushing gravel from their jeans. They lined up like soldiers awaiting inspection, their faces blank but their eyes sharp, darting toward the idling SUV. I hauled myself up, rucksack slung over one shoulder, and fell in beside them—third in a row of nobody's heroes.

The Suburban sat there, engine rumbling, its black-tinted windows giving nothing away. It was the kind of vehicle that screamed trouble—too clean for honest work, too battered for show. A full minute ticked by, the air thick with dust and the tang of exhaust. Then the doors swung open and two men stepped out, moving with the easy menace of those who'd done this dance before. The first, lean and hawk-faced, peeled off toward the lot's entrance, his boots kicking up grit as he scanned the horizon for uninvited guests. The second stayed put—squat and broad, his eyes hidden behind mirrored shades that reflected the world back at itself.

The squat man—clearly the jefe—pointed a thick finger, and my companions shuffled forward, climbing into the Suburban's dark maw without a word. Then his gaze settled on me. I wasn't tall, not by Texas standards, but he had to tilt his chin up to meet my eyes. He studied my face like a man reading a poker table, searching for the lie I hadn't told yet.

He gestured at my rucksack. I set it down, and he rifled through it with the casual disdain of a cop who's seen it all—socks, a dented canteen, a paperback with curled pages. Satisfied, he motioned for my pockets. I turned them out: a few crumpled bills, a key, and the card. Plastic, edges worn, it looked like any credit card but wasn't. His eyes snagged on it, narrowing.

"*¿Qué chingados es esto?*" he said, holding it up like evidence in a trial I hadn't been invited to.

The hawk-faced man drifted back, his shadow falling across us. He glanced at the card, then at me, and shrugged, one shoulder barely moving.

"Computer money," he said, his voice dry. "Crypto bullsnot."

Jefe turned the card over, skeptical.

"Can we cash it in?"

Hawk-face grinned, a thin slash of teeth that didn't reach his eyes.

"Not without his thumbs."

The jefe considered this, his fingers rubbing the card's surface as if he could will it into cash. Then, with a flick of his wrist, he snapped it in half. He tossed the pieces into the gravel, where they glinted briefly before the dust claimed them.

That was the moment. Not a slow fade, not a gradual awakening, but a blade slicing clean through the boy I'd been. That card wasn't just plastic—it was my lifeline, my ticket out, the one thing Alvarez swore would keep me whole. Its ruin told me everything. Whatever came next—whether a ride in that Suburban or a knife in the guts—I'd face it alone. Something in me hardened, not like steel, but like bone, brittle but unyielding. The world's sharp edges were no longer a rumor.

"Hop in the buggy, *chavo*," El Jefe said, his voice low, almost lazy, like he was inviting me to a Sunday drive instead of whatever waited in that dust-caked Suburban.

I stood rooted in the gravel with the Del Rio sun baking my neck and flicked my eyes past the mesquite grove, across the empty lot to the train station's faded brick. There was still time to bolt—thirty feet to the tracks, maybe forty to cover behind a rusted boxcar. My legs twitched, muscles coiling, ready to eat the distance. In the woods back home, I'd run everywhere, and I figured ninety percent odds I'd make it before Hawk-face could draw, aim and fire. Better than the odds inside that SUV, where I imagined the air smelling like bad outcomes.

El Jefe caught my glance. His thin lips curled just shy of a grin.

As if skimming my thoughts, Hawk-face lifted the hem of his guayabera, slow and deliberate, revealing the six-shooter tucked against his hip. It wasn't pawnshop junk. Ivory handle, polished to a dull gleam. The kind of gun that kicked like a mule and hit like a freight train. He rested his hand on it, not gripping, just close enough to promise.

I recalculated. Ninety percent dropped to sixty, maybe fifty, with that look in his eyes—narrow, glinting, like he was praying I'd give him an excuse to pull and fire. He wanted me to run, to turn this into a story he could tell over warm beers in Ciudad Acuña, about the *vato* who thought he was faster than hot lead. My pulse hammered, but I forced my feet still, my face blank as the gravel underfoot. I wasn't about to let Hawk-face write my ending.

I gave a slow nod, the kind you offer when you're buying time, and walked to the Suburban. The rear door hung open, a black maw exhaling stale cigarette smoke and the faint tang of sweat. The two *morros* inside—the wiry, silent types from the grove—shifted on the cracked vinyl seat, making just enough room for me to wedge in my skinny ass.

One, the *pendejo* with the knotted twine, flicked his eyes at me, less curious than wary, like I was a stray dog that might bite. The other stared straight ahead, his jaw tight, as if he knew where this ride was headed and didn't like it.

The door slammed shut behind me with a thud that felt final, and the Suburban's engine growled to life. The tires kicked up dust that clung to everything, including hope.

Fiona's Endless Dream

IF SHE WAS QUIET, she could slip out of the house before everyone else was awake and avoid the dreaded morning hair-brushing. Her wild tangles, even chopped boy-short, hated brushes, combs and grooming of any kind.

"If this is a dream, I do not want to wake up," Fiona whispered to herself as she gently swayed in her chair. In her mind, she drifted back in time to Nantucket Island when she was young, eager, and wild-eyed with salt air blowing through her unkempt curls. Her skin was sun-kissed and freckled from the summer sun.

As she stepped off the ferry Naushon in 1974, she slipped off her shoes and felt warm cobblestones under her leathery feet. Nantucket in the summer was all about being barefoot and barefoot she would be. Seagulls swooped and asked for snacks. Fiona had saved a slice of Wonder Bread to feed to her beloved Sammy the Seagull. He appeared without fail, perched atop a wooden pylon, ever vigilant for Fiona to return for the summer. He saw her before she spied him and let out his signature screech. Fiona turned her head, spotted him, and went running.

He flew down from his perch and awaited his mistress.

"I've missed you, Sammy. Here, I saved you the best slice. Now don't go eat it in all in one gulp or you'll choke. There you go. So, tell me what I missed since last summer?"

In answer, Sammy squawked and cooed between bites of squishy bread. When he was done, he bowed his head and flew into the brilliant, cloudless sky. Fiona knew she would see him soon; he wasn't ever far from her when she was on the island—Sammy with the red dot on his beak; they would always find each other.

Fiona walked along Main Street, happy to be breathing in the sights and sounds of the island. She deeply inhaled the smell of the ocean and the shellfish-soaked wharf. On the breeze, there was the faint scent of drift whales and cranberries. Lost in a daze, she walked quietly along the sidewalk before being awakened from her trance.

"Hey, Fiona. You're here! I've been waiting for you."

Her eyes lost their glaze and Matt ran to her as if from a dream. This was her island mate, her sidekick, her truest friend. They embraced and began talking a mile a minute.

"Wait, WAIT! Let's go to the Sweet Shoppe and get ice cream. I want to hear all about your year on the mainland."

"Oooh! Yes! I'm in desperate need of a cone de la Malachite. Do you know? I still can't believe that no one off-island has ever even HEARD of that flavor? What is WRONG with humans? They don't know what they're missing."

Matt and Fiona bolted up the street, giggling and weaving between the ambling tourists streaming off the ferry. This is how her summer always began: Matt and green pistachio Malachite ice cream, barefoot and happy to her very soul.

Fiona swayed in her wheelchair, licking her lips and tasting memories of days gone by.

"No, not yet," she thought. "Don't wake me yet. Just a little more."

She fell back into her dream. She and Matt were at Surfside Beach—known for strong currents, huge waves, and soft, powdery sand.

"Miss me, miss me, now you gotta kiss me," they sang as they ran in circles, avoiding the wave wash. Eventually they got hot and ventured into the cold Atlantic surf. Fiona shuddered in her chair. The water never felt cold for long and soon enough, the body surfing began.

"Gaack," she called to Matt, "the entire ocean shore is in my bathing suit! Don't look, I need to empty this saggy sand diaper."

They giggled and swam, not even remotely noticing the cold water. The sun was hot and the towels were warm and dry on the beach. Somewhere, someone played music on a tape recorder. She knew the song—knew it well. Cat Stevens—Yusuf Islam.

Oh baby, baby, it's a Wild World. It's hard to get by on just a smile. Oh baby, baby, it's a Wild World. I'll always remember you like a child, girl...no wonder that song always made Fiona smile; it was their theme song on the island.

From Surfside, Fiona and Matt were whisked away to a lobster bake at Nobadeer Beach. It was a primitive, tough-to-reach patch of shoreline on the south side of the island. A hole was dug in the sand and driftwood logs were dropped in. Then came the layers of seaweed, freshly caught lobsters, clams and mussels from the ocean, followed by corn and potatoes and topped with more fresh seaweed. It was a feast for the senses as kids swam and skim-boarded in the heavy surf. As the sun went down, fireflies came out to play with sparks coming from the bonfire. Matt and Fiona ate to their hearts' content and then feasted on s'mores. Her memories were filled with woodsmoke and stories under the stars.

They walked along the back streets of town and stumbled into the Downy Flake bakery where they picked up lemon and raspberry bars, elephant ears and a loaf of Portuguese bread. The mainland had nothing on this little bakery. Fiona walked out with powder on her lips from the elephant ears. Matt couldn't take his eyes off her. Holding hands, they never stopped talking and telling stories.

They wandered into the Seven Seas gift shop and got rope bracelets which they swore to wear until they met again the next summer. By then, they would have shrunk to fit and would be soiled with dirt, sweat, laughter and tears from their year apart.

Fiona rubbed her wrist as she sat in her chair and wondered why her bracelet was missing.

They went to visit Madaket Millie Jewett, the local curmudgeon who long favored the presence of dogs to people. She who dutifully watched the seas and saved many a sailor from running aground. She once lifted a 283-pound driftwood log, killed a 300-pound shark with a pitchfork, and even drove away an abusive mail-order husband. She was crusty and crotchety, and Fiona loved her. Millie had a soft spot for Matt and Fiona and would always take a break from her sea watch to speak with them and train them on the ocean currents and clouds.

Just a little further on the West End, Fiona and Matt walked by Mr. Roger's Crooked House on Smith's Point. Sometimes he would be there and sometimes not; but if he was, he would wave and smile. Once, Mr. Fred Rogers invited them in for a bowl of hand-churned ice cream, and though it wasn't Malachite, it was the best-tasting vanilla they ever had.

Once he said, "I feel so strongly that deep and simple is far more essential than shallow and complex."

These words echoed through Fiona's dream.

They went into the Whaling Museum and marveled at the history of the island. They wondered what it would be like to be working on the massive whaling ships, gone for weeks and months at a time and maybe never returning. They sat outside and read the Obadiah Starbuck books and wondered what it would be like to be an island Quaker back in the day. They lapsed into laughter while talking about what it was like so long ago when the island was young.

"I can't imagine wearing a bonnet," she said.

"I can't imagine wearing clogs," he said.

Something tugged at Fiona. There was a gnaw, an itch, a need to open her eyes, but she was so happy living in her memories of Nantucket where everything was safe and pure. She drifted in and out, feeling an irresistible force pulling her to return to the real world.

Why, why, why couldn't she stay in Nantucket?

Why must she leave her endless dream?

What cruel magnetism grasped her soul…

Minnie: School

THE WEEK BEFORE opening day, the Renfaire folks worked hard, but weren't early risers. The sun had been up an hour, yet only a few scattered souls were up and about. Aimless, Minnie wandered. On the far western outskirts of the Faire grounds, the makeshift school and its weathered tables lay under a giant flapping tent. The rustic tables were built by various artisans and crafters; the long benches handmade and polished. Each piece was unique, funky, and perfect.

As Minnie looked on, it struck her—this was just like an old country schoolhouse.

It was a low-budget, multi-age school, made solely for the Faire workers' children. The teacher, Miss Epona, made it cozy by hanging blue and purple tapestries from the sides. This made it feel intimate and blocked out some distractions. Earlier in her life, Miss Epona taught in Boston-area public schools for twenty-three years. Now she was here.

There was an old chalkboard on wheels. And baskets—baskets upon baskets—of books. Old and new, well-worn and loved, each holding stories of bygone ages, new adventures, animals, science and history. Books that, when you felt them, you could hear whispers and feel their magic. Some of the kids were readers—not many, but a few—and when they needed a book, they sat by a basket and waited for a book to call to them, then they would be on their way.

The baskets lined the edges of the massive tent, showcasing Miss Epona's love of literature and storytelling. Scattered in between, one would find cushions made from the softest fabric; cushions and pillows that beckoned one to be seated, find a book, and be lost in the page-world for a while.

Literature was not the only thing Miss Epona taught.

She used decades of experience to craft and mold the young students who were alert and aware. In Boston, she had left behind the stifling rules and bureaucratic rigor of the education association. Here, she was free to do as she pleased and took on that responsibility with the utmost care and gratitude. If a young man (and, let's be honest, most troublemakers were restless boys) didn't like her style, he didn't have to attend. He could play video games all day if he preferred.

No longer limited to a standard curriculum, she helped mold young minds into true citizens of the world, for that is what they truly were. When it came to writing, each child was gifted a handmade journal, lovingly crafted by Miss Epona and other local artisans. Each was bound in some fashion of leather, carefully stitched and held shut with a leather tie. In these journals, they would write every day, for Miss Epona knew the power of words and thought, and how most didn't even know what they were thinking until they saw it displayed before their eyes.

With each journal came a handmade wooden stick pencil, which never seemed to run out of lead or need sharpening.

"Where were these pencils when I taught all those many years? My goodness, the amount of time my students spent at the pencil sharpener amounted to years."

She was grateful for these new pencils that never dulled or needed erasers and simply accepted their magic as was customary when they are bestowed upon you from a troupe of wandering gypsies. When one of her students felt the urge to publish and share their journal writings with the greater world, Miss Epona had an old typewriter set apart from the general tables. It was maintained by one of the Faire tinkerers, who relished the fact that he and the old typewriter could be put to good use.

As Minnie hovered, Miss Epona caught her eye and pointed.

"Take that group."

Minnie looked. With infinite stubbornness, three little girls diligently did nothing. They looked about five years old. Maybe the oldest was six. They were dirty—wearing torn clothes and old sneakers.

"And do what?" Minnie said.

"Think of something," Miss Epona said.

Crap.

Minnie looked around. They had old People magazines, construction paper, scissors and Elmer's glue.

"Let's do art," Minnie told them.

"We ain't," the oldest girl said.

"What's your name?"

The girl did not answer, but one of the others did.

"She's Steph. I'm Chloë." Pointing, she said, "And that's Penny. Penelope, but we call her Penny because she don't have one—she's flat broke. We don't have to do anything, so we don't."

"Good, you can watch me create fine art. Art that can't be beat—especially by lazy girls who don't have to do any old thing and no one can make them. I don't want your help and I'm happy you can't do anything."

"I didn't say we couldn't," Chloë said. "I said we don't."

"Splendid," Minnie said. "I know helpless girls who can't do anything when I see them."

She went through the magazines and carefully cut out pictures of people, cars, houses, and many other things.

"This must be done exactly right. I make beautiful people and beautiful things."

She pasted a dog's head on a bride dressed all in white.

"This is a dog-bride," she said. "She barks at the neighbor's cat all day long. Penny, please don't touch those scissors—they are for artists."

"I can art," Penny said.

Penny pasted a billy goat on top of a shiny BMW.

"Goat-car," she said.

An hour later, Miss Epona stopped by to see what the giggling girls were up to. There were slivers of colorful paper everywhere—glued on cardboard, on the ground like fallen leaves and tangled in the hair of all four of them. Steph held up her montage. It was a swimming pool filled with motorcycles.

"This is called The Garden of Useless Beautiful Things."

Miss Epona laughed.

"It will take a week for your mamma to get the glue out of your hair. I'm sorry, but you, Minnie, have made a big mess and cannot come here again. You are banned. Forbidden. Unwelcome forever."

Chloë stood up and faced Miss Epona with her hands on her hips.

"We like Minnie and she can art with us anytime she wants—and you can't stop us."

Miss Epona winked at Minnie.

"I see," she said. "I guess there's nothing I can do."

"I will take them to the bathroom and get a start on cleaning them up," Minnie said.

Grinning, Miss Epona replied.

"Excellent idea."

Philip d'GreenApple: Courier

THE SUBURBAN LURCHED forward, gravel crunching under its tires like bones in a sausage grinder. I pressed my back against the cracked vinyl seat, sandwiched beside the two silent morros who'd been waiting in the mesquite grove. The air inside was thick, a stew of sweat, cheap cologne, and the faint metallic tang of fear—mine, theirs, or maybe just the ghosts of past passengers.

El Jefe rode shotgun, his squat frame twisted to bark orders at Hawk-face behind the wheel. The engine growled as we swung out of the parking lot, past the Transportation Center's faded brick facade, and onto Main Street, where the noon sun bleached everything to a hazy white. I kept my mouth shut, eyes on the passing scenery: the arched windows of the old train station giving way to dusty storefronts, a taqueria with a neon sign flickering Abierto, and the distant glint of the Rio Grande snaking under the International Bridge.

Alvarez had promised easy money, a quick job hauling goods across the border, but snapping that crypto card had snapped something in me too. That card was my lifeline, my rescue plan. Now I was rolling toward

Ciudad Acuña with strangers who looked like they'd sell their mothers for a wooden peso.

And goods.

What did that mean?

Would it be something relatively benign like cases of counterfeit cigarettes? Bales of Acapulco Gold sativa? Or, huddled groups of *espalda mojada* undocumented immigrants who paid the steep coyote tax for a ride across the border.

Or something even worse, like trafficked children?

My mind did not want to go that way. Trying not to think, I looked out through the deeply tinted window at the world passing by.

We hit the bridge without fanfare. The U.S. side's border agents barely glanced at our papers—Hawk-face flashed a badge that looked like a challenge coin, muttered something in Spanish, and we were through. It was always easier to get out than get in.

The Rio Grande slid beneath us, brown and sluggish, flanked by concrete barriers and razor wire. The process was a little more involved on the Mexican side, but we were soon on our way. After passing ragged huts made of metal signs, Ciudad Acuña exploded in a riot of color and chaos: vendors hawking tacos al pastor from carts near Plaza Bella Acuña, their sizzling grills sending up plumes of smoke that smelled like cumin and charred meat. Neon lights from Happyland Casino blinked even in daylight, promising fortunes to the desperate. Maquiladoras hulked on the outskirts, factories spitting out cheap gadgets for gringo wallets, but our Suburban veered toward a rundown building with a chain-link fence drooping like a Fentanyl addict and paint peeling in the relentless heat.

The warehouse was a tomb of rust and echoes, crates stacked haphazardly under flickering fluorescents that buzzed like angry bees. Dust motes danced in the slanted light from high windows, and the air reeked of oil, stale sweat and something sharper—maybe fear, maybe desperation. El Jefe shoved me forward, the two morros trailing like shadows. A barrel-chested man waited inside, gold tooth glinting as he lit a cigarette. Vargas, they called him, the real jefe, his scar twisting his lip into a perpetual sneer. He sized me up, circling like a vulture.

"American? Fifteen? Runaway?"

I nodded, throat dry.

"Philip. Yeah, something like that."

Vargas exhaled smoke, eyes narrowing.

"You can drive a truck? Big one, semi?"

My father's lessons flashed—as soon as my feet could mostly reach dump truck pedals from the saggy seat, weekends making landfill runs from the Ren Faire, the clutch's bite, the roar of the engine. Dad was patient and apparently didn't mind the smell of a burning clutch. Eventually, I got smoother at it.

"Stick shift, even."

He grunted, appraising. I wasn't beefy, but I tried to project competence. Quick eyes, steady hands.

Talking to himself, he mumbled.

"Smart ass kid. Gringo. Capable. Give him to my brother to break in."

They led me out and across the weedy lot to a smaller building. Inside, I stood before a smaller version of Vargas. Smaller in stature, but also smaller in aura. More businessman than brute. His brother was scary and mean. This man was softer—there was no murder in his soul.

He looked me over.

"José Luis," he said. "That's me."

We went over the same details as his brother.

He decided and barked orders. They paired me with Raul, a wiry old-timer in his fifties, face etched like the canyons around Presa de la Amistad. Raul reeked of tequila and Marlboros, his laugh a rasp that could sand wood.

"Training? You watch, learn, don't talk."

We spent the afternoon in the yard, him showing me the rundown semi: a 1960s-era Freightliner with faded red paint and layers of patina from years of repaints, dents like war wounds, and a scorpion decal—stylized in black and gold.

Raul pointed at the decal.

"That's our passport."

I looked at the tarped crates being forklifted.

"The payload?"

Raul shrugged.

"Less you know, better for you, chico."

We carried on around the rig, beating on the tires with a rubber mallet and looking over the hydraulic connections for bad leaks.

Apparently, small leaks were okay.

Dusk fell as we rumbled out, the semi groaning like an arthritic giant. Acuña's streets blurred: Casino Villa de Acuña's garish lights, the *Museo Vida y Obra de Jesucristo* with its pious murals mocking us. The bridge again—the scorpion earned a wave from border agents, no hassle. Back in Del Rio, the creek walk's lights twinkled and San Felipe Creek trickled lazy under bridges, but we bypassed it, hitting U.S. 90 east through scrubland, mesquite and prickly pear clawing the roadside.

Once we passed the Air Force base, Raul pulled over at a wide spot and I took a turn at the wheel with him coaching.

"Easy on the clutch, like petting a cat."

My hands steady, mirrors checked for tails. Night swallowed us, stars pricking the Texas sky. Uvalde loomed ahead, a town of 16,000 with honey-sweet air and bitter memories—the school shooting scars, the Leona River's quiet banks. We veered off before city limits onto a dirt road near Cook's Slough Sanctuary, cottonwoods whispering, cattle grazing in moonlit fields, the spire of Sacred Heart Catholic Church a distant silhouette.

The handover was an abandoned barn, lit by flashlights held by a pair of pot-bellied Texans in cowboy hats. They inspected the crates, nodded and passed an envelope thick with bills. Raul pocketed the envelope.

"Good run, kid."

We switched to an old Chevy pickup, rusty but purring, and headed back west. The night air cooled through open windows, sage and rain scents drifting in. Crossing the bridge again, the scorpion a memory, I felt the hook set. José Luis waited at the warehouse, gold tooth flashing.

"You'll do," he said.

He pulled a wad from his front pocket and peeled off hundred-dollar bills—five for me and fifteen for Raul.

As I pocketed the cash, my mind raced—escape routes, the river's whisper, those unknown crates. In Del Rio's shadow, I'd crossed more than borders. Alvarez's failure was just the start; now I was in the game.

Minnie: A Million Butterflies

ROUSED FROM A deep sleep, Al fumbled for the alarm clock. It took him a few seconds to remember his alarm clock was broken. It was in the corner of the room, smashed. Al never did like alarm clocks and as a professional vortex hunter, did not have much need of them.

If it wasn't the clock, then what?

His cell phone, of course.

It was across the room lying on the dresser. He would have to get up.

Or, better—ignore it and it would stop.

That's what he did. It stopped.

But after a few seconds, it started up again.

Ugh, he groaned.

What time is it?

Bright light streamed through the edges and junctions of his blackout curtains. Standing and scratching his crotch under his loose jockey shorts, he picked up the phone.

"This is Al," he said.

The voice on the line was brisk and efficient. She was an enunciator.

Each word was crafted. Each syllable was sharply defined.

"I'm trying to reach Norm the Vortex Hunter."

"Oh," Al said. "Right. Speaking. This is Norm."

"The Vortex Hunter?"

He was beginning to wake up. This call was starting to smell like money.

"The one and only."

"I represent a certain party. I'm calling to make an appointment for a private tour."

"Ah, I do personalized tours for celebrities all the time," he lied. "Who?"

"If you sign a non-disclosure agreement, I can share the details. For now, I just want to nail down a price."

"Right," he said. "My schedule is tight, but I could work you in next—"

She interrupted.

"Today works really well for us. The G-5 will set down at 11:00 at your Sedona Airport. Tabletop Mesa. That gives you an hour and a half to prepare. The Mister does not like to quibble. We'll pay ten-thousand for three hours. Can you make that work?"

"Well…" he said.

"Okay, twenty-thousand, cash, and not a penny more. Yes or no?"

"I—"

"Let's be clear, Norm. The client expects something special. If you take them to a lame place from a cheesy tour book, you'll still get paid, but your Yelp will get bot-farmed into oblivion and your business will be dead in six months. Please say yes to acknowledge."

Al didn't have a Yelp and didn't know what a bot-farm was, but it didn't sound good.

"Well…"

"You are not good at following instructions and answering simple questions, are you, Norm? We'll see you in 87 minutes."

The connection ended with a click.

Al dropped the phone on his tousled bedding. He was frozen in place—he literally could not move.

Outside, the loud pipes of a Harley Davidson startled him. The spell was broken. He could move, but what was he going to do?

Jump in the Jeep and haul ass to the airport?

A minute stretched like a rubber band, then two.

Then he knew what to do.

He threw on yesterday's jeans, a moth-eaten Norm's Vortex polo shirt, and desert boots.

The Jeep started without complaint, and he drove like a maniac to the Ren Faire.

Minnie would help him.

Though it was technically still morning, the sun bit. Sweating under a jumper, Minnie hung up little sundresses. Colorful, they flapped in a light breeze. It wasn't a cool breeze; the air was heated by the desert.

By the time she finished a row, the first flapping frocks were already dry. She restarted at the beginning of the line, pulling off clothespins and layering the dresses in the basket. A hummingbird watched.

She put the basket on the ground and scolded the bird with her hands on her waist.

"You're about as useful as... a hummingbird on a clothesline," she decided. "And that's about as useless as anything can get. Shoo."

Most hummingbirds cannot laugh, but this one could. It giggled, then flitted away.

She took the laundry basket to the school tent. As she watched, a dust cloud was raised on the horizon.

"Someone is coming... and in a hurry," she mumbled.

Soon, she recognized the Jeep.

Al-Norm the Vortex Hunter. Or is it Norm-Al? Giggling, she decided that was not it. Al was definitely not normal. No way, no how.

It wasn't like him to be in a hurry.

I wonder what he wants.

She shrugged.

Surely it was nothing to do with her.

With a metal watering can, she doused a lemon tree growing in a terra cotta pot.

Lemons get real thirsty. Unbelievably thirsty.

After a minute of watering, she heard Al's voice.

"Minnie. Where are you? There's no time to waste."

This made no sense. She had all day and was looking forward to a siesta when the sun was directly overhead. In their tent, a rattletrap swamp cooler called her name. Do the morning chores, then rest an hour during the hottest part of the day. Lemonade. Ice cubes. Maybe a handful of almonds for lunch.

She watched him dart from tent to tent. Then, he found her.

"We have just enough time to get to the airstrip," he said, grabbing her hand. "No argument and no dawdling. I will explain in the Jeep."

She thought about resisting, but her curiosity was piqued.

"I'll need a bandana and a parasol. How are you fixed for water?"

"I have enough to drown a camel. Don't worry about water. No lallygagging."

She laughed.

What has Al in such a tizzy?

In minutes, they were on their way... driving fast on Al's secret cross-desert road.

"VIPs," Al said. "Big spending VIPs. We can make a fortune."

He thought about trying to lowball her but decided to be fair.

"Fifty-fifty, partner. We'll be rich... if..."

"If what?" she said.

"If you take our guests to your special buttercup vortex and give them a big thrill."

They pulled into the airport parking lot just as a Gulfstream biz-jet approached from the west. In a minute it was on the ground and the gangway was lowered. Watching, Al and Minnie wondered if the visitors would be anyone they recognized.

There were two figures, both tall. One was thin and the other was husky.

Minnie's jaw dropped.

Oh, yes. She recognized them all right.

It was the former President and First Lady.

Oh, my.

Her knees were weak, but she quickly recovered. Men with watchful eyes handled backpacks. Other men, even more watchful, watched.

"Secret Service," she thought.

The tallest strode quickly over and shook hands with them both.

"Robert," he said.

Al pointed at the dusty Jeep.

"That's our ride," Al said.

Minnie watched Robert's eyes. They gave away nothing.

Completely nonjudgmental, he said, "We'll follow you."

A woman in a blazer and short skirt walked up.

"Gwen," she said. "We spoke on the phone. I suppose you like to get paid up front."

She handed over a bulging manila envelope.

"Cash, as agreed," she said. "Shall we get on with it? The Mister and Missus have a fundraiser dinner in Scottsdale. Three hours, that's it. Chop-chop."

Holding the cash like it was on fire, Al leaned into his Jeep and stuffed it in the center console.

While watching the visitors load into their black Escalade, Minnie made a decision.

They weren't going to the yellow vortex.

To the west, there was a thin vortex like a laser poking into the sky. On the ragged edge of the Mogollon Rim, it was now aquamarine...the color of Navajo turquoise. From this distance, it was hard to see, but she knew it was there. Right now, it disappeared if you looked right at it, but if you turned your head away like you weren't interested, it blazed. It was a powerhouse but would be tricky. It wasn't continuous, it flashed like lightning. If it wasn't in the mood to play, they'd waste a trip in the desert.

But if things fell together in their favor...

Minnie pointed.

"That way," she said.

Al started to speak, then clapped his mouth shut with an audible snap.

He climbed in the Jeep and drove.

It took some back and forth, but they eventually got close.

Minnie waved her hand to stop him.

"We'll walk from here," she said.

Their guests wore dark glasses and stared at the world through them. The agents and escorts studied the terrain...looking for missile launchers or snipers or something.

In seconds, the thin man had beads of sweat on his forehead. He wiped at it with his palm and studied the moisture while the missus kicked at an anthill.

"You might not want to," Minnie said.

The missus shrugged and kept stirring the sandy hill with her toe.

Minnie settled her parasol at the proper angle to block the sun.

She thought about warning their guests about the desert's intense ultraviolet, but she didn't think black people worried about sunburn. However, the mister didn't look one-hundred percent black.

She poked Al in the ribs.

"Give him one of your logo hats."

"I usually get fifty bucks for them."

She didn't speak, just stared until Al's willpower broke.

"Okay," Al complained, "we'll give away the profits."

Grateful, the man took the hat.

"Thanks, my man," he said.

His voice was like cinnamon and honey in butter. Minnie felt something flutter in her belly. The missus seemed to be watching intently. He spoke like a poet with melody and rhythm. He could read from a phone book and make it sound like oration. It was hypnotic.

Don't antagonize the mama.

Gwen unrolled a floppy hat and arranged it on her head. The entourage had floppy camouflage hats.

They knew about the desert—they'd be fine.

A trilling tone was very out of place. A call for the mister.

Yapping on his cell phone, he looked around. He didn't seem impressed by the terrain. In fact, it was doubtful he even knew where they were. His mind was on his call.

"This way," Minnie said.

The vortex hid, but Minnie knew where it was.

There was great power in this region. Ancient spirits slumbered—

dangerous when riled. By its nature, all power held hazard. It wouldn't be useful if it was not.

Around the scrub brush and prickly pear cacti, they walked for ten minutes...stopped, then walked a minute more.

Minnie kicked at the ground. Dull rocks were scattered on the terrain, some of them lumpy and gnarly. She knew what they were.

Silver ore.

They stood on top of a huge vein.

There was a warning on the wind.

"I will say nothing," she mumbled. "But you must appear."

For a minute mister and missus looked bored. Gwen grew impatient.

"I didn't think this would amount to anything," she said. "Let's cut our losses and head back."

This was exactly the right thing to say.

The vortex decided to show off.

The blue light flicked on, and the world changed.

The mister dropped his cell phone. The missus swore and scratched her leg.

"Something bit me," she complained before everything disappeared.

They stood before a waterfall, but it wasn't water. It was something thick—flowing like maple syrup...the same golden color as syrup, too. The air was cool and smelled of citrus. Around the stream was deep green foliage with leaves shaped like nothing they'd seen before.

A word popped into Minnie's head.

Fractals. Everything was angular and fit together like a puzzle.

The scene wasn't the most striking part.

They were as one.

Everything was okay and all was well.

The missus laughed.

"I've never felt so good. I didn't know how wound up I was. All the tension is gone."

"It's like really good dope," the mister said, giggling and giddy. "Good thing I don't have to pass drug tests no more." He pondered. "Even better than choom. It's like sex with a virgin."

Minnie felt the flutter in her belly again, but stronger.

Careful.

"Jesus," Gwen said, "What is this place?"

The mister leaned over and dipped his index finger in the slow-moving creek, then popped it in his mouth.

"Tastes like orange marmalade," he said.

The sunlight was not white or yellow, it was a pale blue.

Something oozed from her skin and quickly turned dry and crystalline, like chalks of different colors. It felt strange... soon there was a crust that flaked off when she brushed at it. Underneath, her skin was warm and pink.

She knew what was happening—they were detoxing. Then it stopped.

The mister took off his hat and rubbed at his nappy hair. A dust cloud drifted away in a multi-colored powder, like they were in the glorious finale of a Bollywood movie. But it didn't last. In a minute the colorful dust was gone, and they stood around looking at each other.

The mister looked at his phone.

"No service," he said.

Minnie laughed.

Like iron filings in a magnetic field, she felt her cells aligning with the Earth. She didn't resist—she let the energy flow.

"I wonder if there's anything edible around here," the missus said.

"I could use a cigarette," the mister said.

Gwen walked over to Minnie.

"This is really cool, but we should get going."

Busy people. Too busy to relax and enjoy a moment. Too bad.

She walked to the edge of the stream. Gwen followed. Suddenly, they were surrounded by butterflies—at least a million.

Minnie laughed.

"I'm not sure the power will let us go."

Instantly, Gwen looked concerned.

"Say what?"

"I'm kidding," she said. "If you're sure, I will insist and we can go. We're not welcome here anyway. We disturb the force. We're polluters. Snap your fingers and we'll be back."

Gwen looked puzzled.

"Like this?"

She tried snapping, but it was weak and feeble.

"Do it like you mean it," Minnie said.

With an aggressive movement, she snapped as hard as she could. Nothing happened.

"This is good fun, but I don't want to be stuck here forever."

Minnie shook her head.

"A little patience, please."

After a few long seconds, Gwen opened her mouth to speak, but then they were back in the world—blinking in the bright sunlight.

"I have bars," the mister said.

His phone did not ring, but he put it against his ear anyway.

"Sorry, I have to take this," he said while wandering outward.

Al walked to the Jeep.

"I'll lead you out."

"We know the way," Robert said.

The mister whispered to Gwen as he climbed into the back of the SUV.

"Pay them double," he said.

"We already paid them double," Gwen said.

"Pay them double again," he responded as Robert closed the door on him.

With a sour look on her face, the missus shrugged.

"Big spender," she said. "What am I going to do with him?"

Gwen sighed and walked over to Al.

"I don't have cash... I'll messenger out another payment. Give me forty-eight hours."

The last of the doors slammed shut and in a cloud of sepia dust, they were gone.

Al looked at Minnie.

"We're rich," he said.

She giggled.

"Keep it," she said. "What would I do with it? Get in your chariot and get the A/C going so I don't fry my tender tushie."

"Yes, ma'am," Al said.

While the Jeep's cabin cooled, she studied the horizon to the east. The blue needle vortex flickered, but there was something beyond—something bigger and more primal. The Mogollon Rim was on the edge of the Colorado Plateau. It was ancient and held many secrets. She wasn't sure if she could see Mazatzal Peak or if she imagined it. Once you'd seen a map, it was hard to tell. At the Ren Faire camp, she had studied a geological survey of the wilderness and the names the settlers assigned filled her head. Spillway, Potato Lake, General Springs, Cypress Butte, Table, Hackberry and Lion Mountains, Strawberry Town, Verde Hot Springs, Cane Springs Mountain, Horseshoe Dam, Wet Bottom Mesa, North Peak and Chalk Mountain.

Those weren't the real names. The real names were complex and not assembled from a human alphabet.

She sounded out the rim's name.

Mug-ee-own.

Named after Juan Ignacio Flores Mogollon from the slice of history when this area was part of New Spain, then New Mexico. She could tell what it would be called in 500 years—something completely different. It scared her to know how everything would change, so she pulled her mind away.

Limestone. Sandstone. Silver. Copper. Endless forests of Ponderosa Pines. Sixty million years of history and things even older. Hulking, mysterious things. No, not things. Forces. The prehistoric soul of the Earth.

Closing her eyes, she smelled lavender.

The local version of the bigfoot legend hiding among the black bears, mountain lions and coyotes was called the Mogollon Monster.

That's not all that's there.

A shiver crawled up her spine.

There was something much bigger than Sasquatch living in the plateau. Unbelievably larger and if it was ever riled...

She looked over at the anthill. The Harvester Ants were still agitated and looking for a battle. Red garnets glittered in their rubble—blood-red Arizona rubies.

Why did the missus kick the anthill?

Minnie knew why. That's what some people did. She felt her mind spinning out of control.

What ants are to us, that's what we are to the old soul of the Rim.

She was used to feeling small but did not like the thought of being microscopic.

Al tooted the horn. It was cute—the clicking, chattering sound of a mockingbird. It pulled her out of a spiraling gloom.

Okay. Time to go.

She took a last look toward the east. It was not done with her. And vice versa. She had a vague sense of it. Somehow, the vast, unimaginable power could be useful if it didn't destroy her. She hauled herself up and onto the Jeep's seat. As Al turned, he spun the fat tires and scattered gravel onto the anthill.

She sighed.

It was okay. The ants would rebuild.

Al didn't care. His mind was consumed by the money.

It was enough to pay off all his credit cards. If Minnie really didn't want her share, he could ransom his old Martin guitar from the pawn shop and buy a new Jeep, then get it painted and wrapped with a new logo.

In silence, while he manipulated numbers in his mental spreadsheet, they made the trek back to the Ren Faire camp.

Minnie: The Wizard

THE FAIRE WOULD spring to life in a few days; the energy could be felt from miles away. The grounds were abuzz and ablaze with the energy of the upcoming opening day. Last minute preparations included mending costumes, arranging displays of wares, memorizing and refining lines and stage play scenes, tuning stringed instruments and rolling in kegs of honey mead and ale. The air was filled with the aroma of roasting turkey legs.

It was always the same: hurry up and wait then hurry some more— then panic because of some forgotten detail. Such was the way of life of the Renaissance Faire; such was the beloved way of life for all who chose this as their livelihood.

Most recently from a faire in Denver, Gwydion, the wandering wizard, arrived. He wholly looked the part with long gray hair and an even longer beard drooping from his chin like Spanish moss. Tall and gaunt, he was an irritating and pretentious man who sauntered around cadging free samples while waving his hands and fingers and speaking in the grandest of voices.

His robes, made of the Chinese silk, were long, elegant and artfully patched to give the impression of a long and weary journey. His pointy wool hat was steel grey, slouched and formed precisely to his head. With small, black eyes, he always appeared to be ignoring you—looking beyond to see if someone more important could be seen.

His real name was James Smith and though he claimed to be the human son of an ancient oak tree in Nottinghamshire, England, he actually hailed from a hog farm near Luther, Iowa. When he spoke, it was from a detached, third person perspective—as if he knew all and belonged among the gods, not grounded with his Earthly brothers.

He was never without his walking stick—the only authentic thing about him. Stolen from the estate sale of a collector, it was formerly owned by Old George Pickingill and had been hewn by a carver from the heart of a Colchester, England blackthorne tree. It held old magic within its crags and crevices. Tough as nails, it didn't splinter or split. Nestled into its top was a polished burl, smooth to the touch and hard enough to split a skull open if aimed just so. It was a weapon and a tool, and it was Jamie's sole claim to legitimacy in the world of wizardry.

Moody, sometimes, it scared him. At night, it talked but didn't make sense. It seemed to be composing a long, hostile letter to a bill collector. One night, Gwydion scribbled some of the words on a parchment...

> In contracts in which the performance depends on the continued existence of a given person or thing, a condition is implied that the impossibility of performance arising from the perishing of the person or thing shall excuse performance.

What did this mean?

Gwydion did not know, but the tone was threatening, and the stick's anger and menace grew night by night. In addition, it seemed to change shape—every morning it was slightly different. During the day, it was silent and frozen and compliantly followed him everywhere, but at night...at night it was alive.

He thought of burning it, but it was valuable. Through a factotum, he was offered over a hundred thousand dollars. Who the buyer was, the man would not say, but hinted it was a rich PayPal investor, or maybe someone from Facebook-Meta.

But it wanted to be stolen. If he sold, lost or burned it, he would die. Painfully. It never directly said this, but he knew.

He wished he'd never laid eyes on it, much less, on impulse, grabbed it. But the stars aligned. All the estate salepeople were busy selling pentagrams and magic carpets while an open door beckoned. Three seconds and he was out. Twenty seconds later, he was driving away in his van.

Now they were stuck with each other until it killed him. Which it would, one day. He knew it. He was sorry he ever pretended to be a wizard, but it was too late.

What else could he do?

Be an accountant? Work in a factory? Repair air conditioners or unclog toilets?

No.

During a show day, he could make two hundred dollars—or even three hundred on a very good day—by reading palms or casting toad bones and telling fortunes.

Minnie knew the fake wizard had arrived before she even slipped a toe out of her tent. As she walked along, she could taste the frenetic energy in the air. It was midday and the faire folke were all busy with their preparations for the upcoming opening day. Minnie stopped at this stall and that, helping where she could. By now she was as much of a fixture as any other worker. Animals, children and all manner of folke stopped to smile and wave at their princess.

As Gwydion approached, she stood aside and curtseyed as he did his customary wave while staring into the far beyond. She had no love of fakery, even if it was in the spirit of play-acting.

She sent out a mental greeting to the ugly stick.

Good morning, your holiness.

It did not interrupt its chatter.

As one looks at the common law as a whole, one must continually notice the insistent testimony which it bears to its feudal origin.

The stick was insane and dangerous, but Minnie was protected and safe. In no hurry, she watched Gwydion walk to a pub to beg for a breakfast pint of ale with a raw egg. Idly, she wondered why no one took notice of real wizard amongst them.

Seamus. The real wizard. Unobtrusive and quite unto himself.

His clothes were homespun—all earthen colors and hemp fibers, as befitting of an elemental Earth wizard. His shaved staff was a desiccated branch of an old ironwood tree and he did very little to tame it. Molded to his hand alone, once in his grip, there it would stay.

Seamus wandered the grounds, performing subtle miracles, unbeknownst to most and noticed only by those who could truly see. When Minnie was so lost in her thoughts that she felt barely connected to the ground, she would seek out Seamus and he would bring her back down. He need only hold her hand or put his finger on her third eye and she would become whole once again.

Once, Minnie said, "If only I were older, I would marry you," to which Seamus retorted, "Well, wouldn't THAT be quite the union: a wizard and a princess. But we know you're promised to another."

The vision of Philip appeared in her mind, and she felt his kiss on her lips.

With a wry smile, he responded, "No, not that lad. You know who I mean. Trevir, the black Prince. No, sorry, he's King now, isn't he? Regardless, he means to have you and he will."

Minnie shivered.

"You know that will never happen," she said.

"Never is one of those words that should not exist. Like always and forever, we don't know never and should not say it."

Minnie teased him.

"Never ever," Minnie repeated. "Won't never happen."

Seamus shrugged.

"For your sake, Your Hopeless, I think not, but we'll see."

Deep inside, Seamus knew her struggles without Minnie having to say a word about them; he knew of them through the ages. He knew of Trevir and his deeds; he knew of what was and what was likely and unlikely to become. Toward the heavens, he sent a silent prayer.

Help us, Master.

They would need all the help they could get.

Philip d'GreenApple: The Long Haul

I CLENCHED MY fists, noticing my knuckles were white like bleached bone under the dashboard glow. I'd been running loads for weeks now, but never alone—I was always the shadow of some driver with eyes like slits in a poker face, making sure I didn't veer off script.

The first few were cake—pallets and crates of who-the-hell-knows, dropped in dusty lots scattered around Bexar County. No questions, no chatter, just the hum of the diesel and the stink of exhaust chasing me back to base.

But this one?

This one felt like a gut punch from the jump. The yard boss, that fat prick with the toothpick eternally lodged in his gold tooth, had slapped the manifest on my chest like it was a love letter.

"Amarillo, kid. Long pull. Javier's your dance partner."

Javier was a bean pole, mid-thirties with tattoos crawling up his neck like vines on a prison wall—MS-13 ink, or some other cartel. He didn't smile, didn't shake hands. Just nodded once and climbed into the cab with a duffel that clinked like it was full of hardware.

Partner, my ass.

The man was a leash with teeth. He fired up the engine and the Cummins belched black smoke into the Texas night. The container hitched behind was a standard forty-footer, sealed tight, but something nagged at me.

Sloshing?

But as we rolled out of the lot with gravel crunching under the tires, I heard it again. It was important to be careful with liquid loads. Inertia.

Fluid in motion tends to stay in motion.

The manifest said Agricultural Supplies.

Javier lit a Camel, the smoke curling thick and acrid.

"Boss say you reliable," he said, accent thick as tar.

I grunted as he shifted gears as we climbed a grade.

Reliable. Yeah, that's what it's called when you're too scared to bolt.

Ever since the crap show in El Paso, where I'd stumbled into this nightmare, I'd been playing along. Hours ticked by with the rig eating miles. Javier didn't talk much, just fiddled with a rosary bead necklace, thumbing the cross like it owed him money. My mind wandered to the load. Kids in a container—Jesus, if that's what it was, we were hauling lost souls.

Human trafficking? Organ trade? The world was filled with harsh realities.

The thought made my stomach churn, bile rising hot. I glanced at Javier.

"What's in the box, man? Feels heavier than usual."

Javier's eyes narrowed.

"No questions, *pendejo*. We drive. We get paid. We don't ask."

Fair enough.

I pressed the preset buttons on the radio until a scratchy country twang about lost love and whiskey drowned out the silence. But the tension built like storm clouds, thick and electric. Around midnight, we hit a two-lane stretch north of Abilene—empty highway, no towns, just scrub brush and coyotes howling in the dark. That's when trouble hit.

Headlights flared in the rearview, two sets, closing fast.

Four motorcycles?

No, pickups—jacked-up Fords with roll bars, engines roaring like pissed-off bulls. He engaged the cruise control and the rig groaned as it tried to hold eighty.

"The hell's this?" Javier said. He answered his own question. "Ambush. Switch me."

I squirmed over him and took the wheel. It vibrated like it was alive. For this outfit, front-end alignments weren't a priority—they drove the beasts until they fell apart.

He unzipped the duffel and pulled out a long chain with haphazard nails welded to it. He grinned at me.

"Stop strip," he said. "Get in the other lane."

There was a name for these spike strips.

It would come to me.

Caltrop.

There was no oncoming traffic, so I eased over. The approaching trucks swooped over to pass on the right. Blinding lights filled the side mirror.

"Come and get it," he muttered.

Leaning out of the window, he threw out the chain and our pursuers fell back.

"Got them," he said.

But it wasn't over.

More lights—a third vehicle?

In front of us, lights snapped on. I saw flashes.

Gunfire. Our windshield erupted into stars.

I floored it and the truck lurched forward.

"Aim for the rear quarter," Javier shouted.

When we hit the pickup, it spun like a top while we rolled on. As the lights disappeared behind us, I turned to look at Javier. When it felt safe, I pulled over.

His pale face was sweaty. He took a round in the chest. My arm throbbed from shrapnel, but I ignored it, rifling through his pockets. Wallet, keys, a crumpled pack of smokes—and a folded paper. Instructions, scrawled in Spanish.

Toot'n Totum, Amarillo, backlot, 3 AM. Contact: El Toro. Password: Sangre Roja.

I flopped out of the cabin and vomited into the dirt.

Stinky yellow fluid dribbled out the back.

I walked along the side, then climbed up to look in on Javier.

Laboriously, he rolled down the window.

"What do we do now, man?" I said.

Javier turned his eyes to the road ahead. The headlights speared a hundred feet, but otherwise darkness was winning.

"Light me one, *Felipito*," he said.

At a time like this, the man wanted to smoke.

I leaned in, snagged his pack and fished him out a bent one. With a shaking hand, he pushed in the dashboard lighter and we waited for the click.

"I'm all tore up," he said.

You and me both.

I realized the thought was uncharitable. He took a bullet. I didn't.

Looking back, I could see flickers of fire like the upcoming dawn.

I could walk and leave all this behind. I'd probably get away clean.

That idea didn't feel right. Javier was unconscious.

I decided to drive.

As we pulled into Amarillo, Javier was still breathing. I was surprised. In a far corner of the truck stop, the overhead lights were out. I could see a few milling forms and pickup trucks.

I pulled up and killed the engine.

After looking over the cab with a flashlight, a man stepped up. I rolled down the window. This was a white guy tanned by the Texas sun. El Jefe. He wore a suede cowboy hat with a silk band.

"What's the password?" he said.

"Javier needs a doctor," I said.

His face twisted in a grimace.

"That's not it, *sabelotodo*."

I knew that one. Know-it-all smart ass.

I could have driven to a police station or a hospital.

Maybe I should have, but I didn't.

"You smell like leftover roadkill," he said.

After glancing at the dried blood on my arm, he jumped down and waved.

"Clean this kid up," he said.

While two burly men dragged Javier out of the cab and hauled him off, a woman in a nurse's uniform looked at my arm. With scissors, she chopped off the sleeve and studied my wound.

"An inch over and your arm would be waving around like *brazo de pollo muerto*."

Slowly, I worked out the translation.

Dead chicken arm.

With water poured from a plastic gallon jug, she rinsed away the dry blood and then smeared goop on the wound. I could move my fingers, so I guess there would be no permanent damage, but I'd always have a divot in my arm as a souvenir.

El Jefe wandered over and glanced at the wound.

"You'll live," he said.

She covered my wound with gauze and clasped an Ace on top with elastic bandage clips. Then she taped a plastic grocery bag over the top.

Cheap waterproofing.

She kissed two fingers, then tapped my arm.

"Lucky boy," she said. "Try to keep it dry."

"Take a shower and get a breakfast burrito," El Jefe said. "I'll find you a ride back."

Until that moment, I didn't know I was hungry.

My skin was covered in dried sweat and road dust, so a shower sounded good, too. Better than good. Heavenly.

Dazed, I didn't know what I was doing or why I was doing it.

There wasn't any way out, but there was a way through.

I didn't know how I knew, but it was true. 100%

After grabbing my knapsack, I jumped down to the gravel.

Looking back, I exchanged a look with Javier.

"Thanks, amigo," he said.

"Hang in there, *hermano*," I replied.

Already, two men were patching up the truck's bullet holes with Bondo.

One of them looked up.

"This thing running okay?"

I shrugged and pointed at something dripping underneath.

"Something got nicked. A little more baling wire and chewing gum and it will make another run or two."

The man nodded.

I turned toward the truck stop. After the shower, I dressed in clean clothes and felt nearly human.

Wearing a Sod Poodles baseball hat, a brown-skinned girl in a blue uniform was filling the display case with fresh burritos. She smiled at me as I reached around her. They smelled good, so I grabbed two.

She pointed at her nametag.

"Janet," she said.

I pointed at myself.

"Felipito," I said.

She thought that was funny.

I could see it all very clearly. I could settle here. We'd have five kids and be very happy. As taught by her grandmother, she was a wonderful cook and would pull off my boots after a long day driving a UPS truck in circles. She'd patch my jeans and make dresses for our girls. The vision was vivid and I almost forgot my heart belonged to another.

Yes. Minnie was her name.

"I love you, Juanita."

I don't know why I said it, but it was true. She was a good person and would make the right man very happy.

"I love you too, Philip," she said.

She winked at me and rang up my order—which I paid for with a ragged twenty-dollar-bill.

She didn't charge for my coffee.

Minnie: Palm Reading

AS MINNIE WANDERED about the Faire grounds, she felt the hustle and bustle of the upcoming opening day down to her toes. Artisans polished their wares and put them on display, trying to find the best way to capture the fleeting attention of wandering patrons. Blacksmiths hung swords from the tent tops and ensured that all weapons were peace-tied to prevent impromptu battles where a civilian might lose a finger or toe.

Face painters adorned themselves with the latest fae designs and braided their locks with local wildflowers. Costume shops were on full display with the hope that visitors would want to immerse themselves in the medieval experience and embrace their inner bard, prince, wench or monk.

Food vendors put the finishing touches on turkey leg recipes and the famous bratwurst boys sorted out the many varieties of meats, while the requisite fried dough and steamed potato huts geared up for long lines on hot days. Mead flowed and the friendly rivalry between ale vendors erupted in ribald insults. One of Minnie's favorites was the Sonoran dog cart. Made of meat, it wasn't the typical kind of thing she liked, but on a dare, tried a bite and a new addiction took hold.

All-beef vienesa with a solitary slice of crispy bacon. A locally baked torpedo-shaped Bolillo roll with pointed ends. These buns had a crispy crust and were soft on the inside. The dog was bedded on a tablespoon of warm pinto beans. On top, onions, diced tomatoes, yellow mustard, avocado, with a swirl of mayonnaise and a refreshing flourish of cilantro and a grilled jalapeño pepper on the side.

So good.

Eating while walking, Minnie took it all in, thoroughly enjoying the energy and frivolity. As she wandered and helped where she could, she noticed her left-hand tingling. At first, as she gobbled the last fragment of her hot dog, she thought it was an itch, then a bug bite, but it became too much to ignore. Within moments her entire hand was ablaze with prickling. Then her right hand started.

She let out a sigh.

"I'm busy, what do you want? And, must this be done NOW?"

She raised her hands toward the sun. The tingling got worse.

"Okay, fine. Let's find out what you want."

Minnie began wandering with purpose.

Hot. Cold. She let her hands be her guide. Between structures and under an awning, a nook. Palm Reading. There, Gwydion sat behind a card table reading a ragged paperback book.

He didn't know her. She didn't want to know him. But her palms had a different idea. They wanted his reading.

This is hogwash.

She marched up.

"Ohhhh, THERE you are!"

Gwydion nearly jumped out of his skin. With trembling hands, he dropped his book and reached for his staff.

"I'm sorry," Minnie said with a grin, "I didn't mean to startle you."

He placed the staff across his lap like it was a wall between them.

"Whatever are you talking about, Miss Minnie? I'm fine, totally fine. I'm just not used to rude people stalking me."

"I need to have my palms read. They're tingly and have something to say. So, I've come to you, the famous wandering wizard, because I want only the best."

"Oh, dear Minnie, thank you for those compliments. However, I'm not really in a palm-reading mood today. You see, for it to work I need everything to be aligned just so and well, to be honest, I'm not in that head space today. I'm sure you understand."

"I understand, but my hands don't. Not to worry, I can pay you— I'm no charity case."

"Oh, really? What do you have to pay me with? Rocks, crystals, pretty flowers?"

Minnie grew annoyed and her hands felt like they were on fire. She dug into her pocket and pulled out two gold coins that she'd found on her travels.

"Does gold work for you? I could give you one."

Greedy, Gwydion took one, weighed it in his palm and studied it carefully. ALFONSO XIII G S 1892. 20 Pesetas. He didn't know what it was worth, but it was a lot. He didn't want to touch Minnie's palms, but he wanted the gold. Greedy, he wanted both coins.

"I suppose I could do a reading if you gave me the pair."

She reached out to take back the coin.

His heart skipped a beat.

"Yes, one is well enough." After slipping the coin in the inside pocket of his robe, he leaned over his flimsy table. "Let's see those grimy mitts and get this over with."

"Finally," Minnie muttered.

Palms up, she spread her hands. She could hear Gwydion's staff complaining, though she couldn't make out the words. Gwydion had blisters on the palms of his hands. The staff was marking him. Who owned who was questionable.

James took Minnie's hands and studied her palms, side to side and bending her wrists up and down. He looked at the angle of her thumbs and pulled on her fingers. All the while he inserted plenty of "hmmm's" and "oh, that's interesting" and even an "oh, my."

Finally, he came to resolution.

"Your lifeline looks good and long with no breaks or interruptions. That's always a good thing. Your heart line looks healthy too; maybe you'll meet your true love soon. But then again, you're young so you should wait a bit before committing. Your head line cuts across your heart line—that's when your head and heart will finally work together as one. Lucky duck; most people only lead with one or the other. Your line of fate is rather short but that's okay, as we all know, fate works in mysterious ways. All in all, I'd say you have a wonderful life ahead of you; some mischief to be had, a few boyfriends here and there and overall good health. A fine hand you have there Minnie, a very fine hand indeed."

"Really, that's it? No Earth-shattering news? Just a plain old generic future?"

"Now, now, Minnie." He dropped her hands and patted her on the head. "Not everything in your life needs to be a grand adventure. Take it for all that it is. You're young, healthy and you have many true loves on the horizon. What more could you ask for?"

"I suppose. Thank you for your time, Gwydion. Have a wonderful day."

Minnie got up and walked off—with her head down looking at her palms.

Something isn't right. That's not why you were burning. There's got to be more to it than that.

Lost in thought, she wasn't looking where she was going and bumped into Seamus' back.

"OH! I'm sorry, Seamus. I wasn't looking where I was going."

Seamus turned around with a start.

"It's okay, Minnie. Here, come sit with me—I will share lavender lemonade sweetened with local brittlebush honey. We can talk. What's on your mind?"

Mimicking the turning of her hands and his verbal expressions, Minnie told him about the Gwydion palm reading.

Seamus laughed out loud.

"Well of COURSE you're confused. James-Gwydion is an actor, that's all, and can no more read a palm than a normal human can walk on water. Come, let me see your hands and let's see if we can't figure out why they are tingling and burning so much."

As soon as Seamus held Minnie's hands, he felt their heat and energy.

He looked Minnie dead in the eye and said, "There is a lot going on here. Bear with me."

He traced the various lines on Minnie's hand, the racettes along her wrist and the mounts along the base of her fingers. He visually measured the length between the bends in her fingers and looked at the angle of her thumb. He noted the placement of her fingernails, their width and depth. He shuddered when he ran his finger along her lifelines and shed a tear when he came upon her heart lines. When he traced her fate line, the color drained from his face. He noted where the planets were placed in her palm and how logic and willpower played into all of this. At the end of it all, he closed his eyes and held Minnie's hand between both of his and sat for a moment. He let out a huge breath and Minnie instinctively did the same.

As he opened his eyes, he looked into Minnie's and began to speak.

"Minnie, my goodness, you have a tough road ahead. Things are safe now, but evil is afoot. Tendrils of evil spread across the land and no one will be untouched. You will bear children…"

"What?!?! No. NO!! Children? I *am* a child."

"I'm not talking about today or even tomorrow. You're good for now."

"Tell me about these children."

"Hmmm, I can't tell if they will be conceived in love or hate. It's like that is unknown and could go either way."

"Tell me something helpful."

"Be wary of cuts you receive as darkness descends upon us. A drop of black blood mixing with a wound—that would not be good. You are loved, strong and healthy. Also, you are hated and vulnerable. Decisions must be made. Your road will be hard."

Silently, he gazed into her eyes.

Minnie's hands had stopped burning and tingling. Seamus had more to tell, but now wasn't the time. He'd seen things in her hand that no one should ever have to see—things he kept to himself for now.

She reached in her pocket and pulled out her remaining gold coin.

POR LA G DE DIOS. He translated the words.

"For the grace of God. I can't accept this."

Minnie shook her head.

"We're not negotiating. It's yours."

Seamus shrugged.

"Okay, so be it. I'll pay it forward. You have another one, so I think it will all be okay."

"You mean I *had* another one."

Seamus grinned. Three of his teeth were silver. They gleamed in the afternoon light.

"I'm not sure Gwydion earned his gold, did he?"

Suddenly, she felt the weight of the coin in her pocket.

It made her giggle. In peace, they sat in the shade and sipped the rest of the sticky lavender lemonade. So much to say, and so much to leave unsaid; but for now, there was sun, lemonade and a Faire opening soon.

Minnie: Finding Meg

FIONA WAS SLEEPING.

Who was Minnie kidding?

Fiona was always sleeping—she was forever stuck between worlds. Minnie wondered if Fiona would ever wake up. Minnie longed to hear Fiona's voice, to listen to her offkey singing, to hear her laugh and natter on about anything and everything. She missed Fiona. Sure, sure, the woman could be annoying, but Fiona was all she had. They had been through so much together; she just wanted to hear her voice again and to sit and cuddle.

These thoughts and feelings swam in Minnie's head as she made the journey between sleep and the waking world. Outside the tent-yurt, the sun was far from peeking over the horizon when the desert world would begin to wake. As Minnie slipped out of her dreams, she heard Fiona's voice in her head. Recently, Minnie had been getting up early—between 3 and 4 AM. She didn't know why, but the peace and solitude served something in her soul. This hour was halfway between the world of slumber and the waking world...a time when Fiona's voice was clearest.

"Go, Minnie. Go and find the Meg. She will teach you. Trust me, love, go find Meg."

As Minnie's eyes opened and the world came into focus, she still heard Fiona's voice echoing in her head.

Find the Meg.

Gretchen lifted her head.

"What is it, dear?" she said.

"I just heard Fiona. She told me to 'find the Meg.' Something about how Meg has something to teach me. Do you know a Meg?"

Gretchen thought for a moment as she tried to wake up. Reaching over, she stroked Minnie's hair. Minnie let out a quiet sigh.

"No, dear," Gretchen said. "I can't think of a Meg. Nor a Megan, Margaret, Nutmeg or Omega. Sorry. Maybe when I'm awake I will think of one."

"Sometimes I feel like I know everything. And sometimes I feel like I know nothing. And, there's no use in lying in bed while I'm wide awake."

"You roam, dear," she muttered.

Then, Gretchen was asleep again.

As Minnie wandered—wondering where she would be if her own name was Meg, she spied the bake shop. Behind the shop, a tall man loaded empty pastry racks into a panel van. Catching the lingering aroma on a drift of wind, her mouth said pretty please and many more.

Pretending she was exactly where she belonged, she walked in the back door and picked up a bundle of soiled trays and followed the man out to slide the trays onto racks mounted in the truck.

This was the last of the trays.

From behind, Minnie heard a boisterous voice.

"Hired yourself a helper, did ya, Benny?"

Minnie turned to see who was bellowing—it was a woman she'd seen around. Short and squat, her block-cut blouse framed her ample bosom—which was decorated with glitter and little foil stars. Minnie stared and wondered what it would be like to carry those plump melons around all day.

The woman addressing her was loud and gregarious for this hour early in the morning. Minnie had heard that booming voice before. The Faire wasn't open, but apparently the set-up workers and staff were customers. Or maybe the woman was warming up for the big show.

The voice echoed in her ears.

"Get yer Dorset Apple Cake! Costs nowt to gander. Get yer Kringles! Get yer Baboffee Pie! Don't be a wanker. Get your Spotted Dick! Authentic English recipes. They're ping and canny. Get yer Fairy Cakes! Bring your quid and nosh your fancy."

"Are you the Meg?" Minnie said sheepishly. "I am looking for someone named 'Meg'.

The woman threw back her head and laughed.

"No, I be a Susan. I sell Meg's bakes and make her lush quid, allright? Show her, Lemmy."

The driver slid the van's door closed to expose the colorful logo painted on the side.

Meg's Bakehouse. Authentic European Bakery.

"Look at her, Lemmy—a breeze would carry her off. Hang on."

She went inside and came back with two brown paper bags. Whatever was inside was rich—the bag's sides were darkened with oil stains.

"Apricot for you, dear. And Lemmy, I found a couple of Kringles that weren't on the dirty floor very long. They probably won't kill ya."

Lemmy laughed.

"Thanks, Sue. Back in a few."

He laughed again at his rhyme and turned to his truck and climbed up onto the driver's seat.

"Hurry up then," he said. "You want to meet the Meg? I'm off that way now."

While they munched on their pastries and arrived in town, the truck trundled on deserted streets. Grinning, Lemmie opened the cooler and pulled out a glass jug of milk. He peeled off the top and took a big drink.

"First swig gets the cream," he said. "Last swig gets the whey."

He handed her the quart, and she drank.

After the pastry, it was perfect.

In twenty minutes, they arrived at a self-serve car wash.

Lemmy parked the truck.

"Now comes the fun part," he said.

It took nearly an hour to hot-spray and scrub the trays. With a pile of towels from the van, Minnie dried and stacked them. Lemmy glanced at his watch.

"You saved me fifteen minutes, girl," he said. "I like it."

After the clean trays were back in the van, they traveled another ten minutes to a small industrial section of Sedona where there were a few buildings and warehouses. Diesel trucks rumbled.

"Here's where you will find what you're looking for," he said.

After latching the back door open, they carried the heavy trays in and slid them onto racks. On racks on the other side of the room were trays loaded with baked goods of all types. One rack of trays was labeled 'Faire.'

"C'mon, mewling, let's find us the Meg."

Inside, a female giant babysat a giant Hobart mixer. The hypnotic, enticing smell of yeast fermentation and baking caramelization filled the air. Minnie walked over and stared up at the giant.

The woman's face was framed by laugh-lines around her eyes and cheery dimples on her rosy cheeks. Looking up, Minnie was sure she was in the presence of a goddess. Tall and broad, her shoulders and arms were chiseled from years of kneading dough and working with bread. Her long hair was braided in a thick rope that ran down the length of her spine. With dewy brown eyes like those of a deer or cow, she had eyelashes to match and a smile that could melt the coldest of hearts. Her dimples could make Paul Bunyan blush. She had a commanding voice but delicately and deliberately annunciated every single word and syllable. Lowering her eyes, Minnie noticed her apron had a beautiful, fuzzy hand-stitched bunny on it.

Meg waited for the inevitable question to arise.

"I like your apron. The bunny is so cute. Does it have a name?"

"Why, yes, his name is Otis."

The next question came from nowhere. Until it left her lips, she had no idea it was coming.

"Do you cook and EAT bunnies?"

"Oh, heavens no, Minnie. I absolutely adore them, but not in the food sense. They are my friends. Otis is over there sleeping on his little bed. Do you see him? He is burrowed down under his blanket on top of that puppy bed. Some of the others are around here too, but he is the most social of the bunch, so he makes his presence known, even if just in slumber. You see, I carry a secret elixir right here in my pouch. If I learn that someone is fond of eating my fluffy friends, I offer them a taste of my 'special mead.' I put a few drops of this into their drink and they are henceforth disgusted at the very thought of ever consuming rabbit again. It is quite harmless really. Should they want to try eating rabbit anyway, then they will become violently ill and never try it again. It is the least I can do for our furry, fluffy little friends."

Minnie was completely entranced by Meg. Fiona definitely sent her to the right person.

"Now, for bagel making. First and foremost, you must always remember to be in a good mood when you bake. Sing, laugh, be full of whimsy and good thoughts. The bread is a living, breathing creature and notices your energy. If you are stormy inside, the dough will not rise. It will be limp and sour. Does that make sense?"

Minnie nodded.

Sure, why not?

"Well then, the rest is easy. You start with warm water, yeast, and bread flour. Spring water, Red Star yeast and Jovial Einkorn flour are my go-tos. This makes your starter. This is where you infuse your energy, your magic, your YOU into the process. After it sits and energizes for a spell, sprinkle in more yeast for good measure. Not a lot, just enough to liven it up a bit. Now here is my secret: dribble in a dram of honey. Use the honey dipper, two dips, no more, no less and, mind you, not the phony stuff that comes in plastic bears—real honey the bees cultivate from the alfalfa fields and are willing to share with you. Always ask them for permission and if granted, they will gift you the wildest and sweetest honey that they have. Now, add more bread flour and sea salt and once mixed, you will have the best dough. Now patience comes into play. You need to let the dough rest for an hour or so and then put it in the fridge overnight. So, as you can see, making dough takes planning. You are always making and rotating batches. Does this make sense so far, Minnie?"

Minnie nodded. She felt like this was not so hard at all.

It occurred to her that she had not mentioned her name.

How did the Meg know?
One way to find out.
"Excuse me. How do you know my name?"
Meg never wasted an opportunity to laugh.
"I hear things...things about a tiny, inquisitive girl with good diction and a wide vocabulary. I assumed and you didn't correct me, so I just know. Any other questions before I continue?"
Minnie shook her head.
"Now comes playtime. Some people weigh out their dough, so it is all uniform. Not for me. I eyeball it. So, you make lots of little chunks and roll them out into balls. It is like rolling playdough if you will. Roll them out like a snake, form them into a bread bracelet then put them on a rack to rise for a bit. While they are rising, you get the water, honey and baking soda boiling. Then you drop them in one at a time. Now is where you get to be creative. As I tell people, 'The longer the boil the chewier the bagel...it's all about the chew.' So, you get to decide that part. After the boil comes the toppings. Your only limit is your imagination so top them with whatever floats your boat. Savory sweet and salty-sweet, breakfast, dessert; dream it and then do it. There are no wrong answers in the land of bagels. Pop them in the oven and voila, you have bagels. Bake then boil. Are you ready to give it a go?"
"Absolutely."
Minnie spent the rest of the day making bagels with Meg. She made fresh dough to be used the next day and she used dough made the day before to make bagels for today. She experimented with the usual spices and even came up with new ideas. Fruited ones, spiced ones, savory and sweet ones. Baking came easy to Minnie, and she had fun singing along with Meg, doing their "bagel dance" and laughing away. It was a carefree day for Minnie and exactly what she needed.
"Well, Minnie, I believe it's time for you to venture back to your family and see about dinner. Take what you will and share your successes. I'll let you in on a secret. I made too many currant scones. They are coming out of all the bunnies' floppy ears. Do me a favor and take as many as you like. And you're welcome to come back anytime. It is not often that I have someone as skilled as you to join me. What an unexpectedly wonderful day we had here today."

Meg gave a deep, sweeping bow to Minnie who returned the gesture in a grand style, flour-stained curtsy. She patted Otis on the head, gave Meg one more squeeze then ran back to the back door.

It had in fact been a most wonderful day.

She got outside before realizing she had no idea how she would get back to the Faire. Across the parking lot, she noticed the *Norm the Vortex Hunter* jeep. Walking up, she saw Al Bailey sleeping behind the wheel. He started when she tapped on the window.

"Ah, finally," he said. "Ready to go back? Your chariot awaits."

"What are you doing here?"

"How else would you get back? Lemmy's sleeping. He gets up early, you know."

"What are you doing here?" Minnie repeated...allowing a little edge on her voice.

"Meg sent out the word. Business was dead today, so I told her I'd run you out." Pointing, he said, "What have we in the bag?"

"We," she said. "I recognize no *we* in our present context."

"Whatever," he said. "Fancy-pants girl and her big words."

Grabbing the heavy bag from her hand, he opened the top and stuck in his nose.

"Ain't Meg the best?" he said.

She grabbed the bag back, pulled out a flaky scone and waved it under his nose.

He snagged it.

"Like it or lump it," he said with his mouth full of pastry, "we're stopping at the drive-thru espresso hut."

He drove, talking around his scone.

"That money landed—we're sitting in high cotton."

She mulled over the phrase, half-smiling. That was not exactly the classic southern saying, but she took his meaning.

"You sure you don't want your cut?" he said. "It's a lot of cashola."

He said cashola, but in her head, she heard 'dough.' She reached for the bag...which held one last scone.

"Last one's all mine," she said.

"Hey, split it in half, pig."

She laughed and said, "No."

Philip d'GreenApple: Decoy Run

I WIPED THE sweat from my brow with the back of my hand, staring at the old Mack truck. It was a 1950's relic—patina in at least six layers. Idly, I wondered what color it was when it came from the Allentown factory—fresh and innocent and unaware of the rocky roads it would travel to get here and become this rusty artefact. In those years, it had been painted red in several shades, then yellow and black. I felt sympathy and realized that someday, I would be broken and old, too. The harsh reality hit me hard.

I shook it off. It didn't matter. I have things to worry about today.

The yard boss tossed me the keys with a grunt. He was acting weird—he tied a yellow ribbon onto the whip antenna, then handed me a wallet.

"Your name is Christopher Dodd. You're 23. College student. Princeton. Driving a truck as a summer job."

"I'm a teenager."

He looked me up and down.

"You look young for your age. Everyone says that. Rub oil and dirt on your face. You'll pass. Be happy—you're moving up. First solo, don't screw it up. Del Rio crossing to San Antoine, then jet back. Easy money."

I put my hand on a hot fender. For decades, this rig had been a loyal beast of burden, but it would soon be scrap. The retread tires had a barely legal eighth inch of tread and the engine coughed like a chain smoker. It was loaded with wooden crates marked *Machine Parts Hecho en México* tied down with yellow, oil-stained cargo straps. The whole thing felt weird. The truck didn't look like it would make it out of the parking lot, much less to San Antoine. I couldn't figure it out.

I climbed into the cab, the seat sagging under my weight. The dash was cracked and the air conditioner blew warm dust. After flipping the glow plug switch, I fired it up and the diesel rattled to life with a plume of gray smoke. Shifting into gear felt like grinding bones. As I pulled out of the lot, the truck groaned over the potholes.

Starting in Las Cuevas, I took the loop road starting west on Avenida Sur Poniente—which turned into Boulevard José Maria Ramón. The load felt light—like the crates were empty. My idle mind worked at that but didn't draw any conclusion. Through the dusty trees in the Parque, listless boys kicked a soccer ball. It was hot. I didn't know how they could stand it, but they weren't working too hard. No running—just booting the ball around and exchanging good-natured insults. The radio was tuned to a Tejano station—all thumping bass, wheezing accordions and blaring trumpets.

The International bridge was a concrete and steel span lurking over the muddy river connecting Ciudad Acuña on the Mexican side to Del Rio on the *Norte Americano* side. Trucks were lined up in the commercial lanes with engines idling. I pulled into the queue and unclipped the manifest from the visor.

Machine Parts for Export. Value $5,000.

The FAST lane for pre-approved shippers was moving quicker, but I wasn't certified for that. Nonetheless, the queue was short; I got to the checkpoint in only twenty minutes. The *inspectores aduanales* officer in an olive drab uniform waved me forward.

"Papers," he said, clipboard in hand. I handed over the manifest, bill of lading, and my CDL. He scanned them, then peered into the cab. "Origin? Destination?"

"Acuña to San Antonio," I said, keeping my voice steady. "Just parts."

"No," he said. "Where do the parts come from?"

"I don't know."

I did know. China, probably. That's where everything comes from.

There was a *supervía* from Mazatlán for Asian transport, but most of that highway traffic terminated further east in Laredo or Brownsville. He didn't really want to know; he was just making the interrogation look good for the security cameras.

He waved me through.

"Good luck," he said—which struck me as an odd thing to say.

Maybe he thought there was no way the truck could make it 150 miles to San Antonio. His eyes had lingered on the ribbon on my aerial. Maybe it meant something to him. Regardless, I was on my way to the other side—where things were different.

With his eyes lingering on the truck's rough shape, the CBP officer climbed up on the step.

"Pull over for secondary," he said

Secondary meant inspection. I eased the rig into the bay area, a concrete lot flanked by warehouses and X-ray machines. Officers in gloves swarmed—two with dogs, one with a mirror on a pole for undercarriage checks. The K-9s sniffed the tires and doors, tails wagging but no alerts.

"Out," an inspector said.

I stepped down, heart thumping. They popped the hood, checked the engine, then moved to the trailer. Seals were intact, but they broke them anyway as they pried one open: random gears and bolts, nothing fancy. But that wasn't enough.

"Full unload," the lead officer barked.

For the next hour, they opened the crates under the Texas sun, sweat soaking my shirt as I watched. They scanned everything with handheld detectors—no drugs, no contraband. Then came the X-ray van, a mobile unit that drove alongside the empty trailer, beaming through the farings. Screens flickered in their command post—clean.

But they weren't done.

"Disassemble," the officer said.

In border crossings like Del Rio, if suspicion lingers, they tear rigs apart. It's standard for high-risk loads: check fuel tanks for hidden compartments, pull panels for smuggled goods. Del Rio sees about 1,000 trucks a day, mostly farm produce northbound and used car engines and transmissions southbound.

They started with the cab. Seats out, dash panels unscrewed— wires and insulation exposed. I watched as they drained the fuel tank, probing for false bottoms. Nothing. The trailer floor came up next, planks pried loose. Empty. Even the tires were jacked up, deflated, and inspected. Zilch.

Hours dragged. I sat on a bench in the shade, nursing a vending machine Coke. Armed officers chatted about the heat wave, ignoring me, then a burly figure blocked the sun, then joined me on the bench. He was escorted by two men in uniforms. Not border patrol…maybe soldiers. His arms were loosely strapped behind his back with zip-ties. That was a tell. Comfortable, he could have easily slipped the cuffs. They were just for show. Without looking up, I knew who it was.

Alvarez.

I didn't know how I felt about this. Slowly, I did an inventory of my emotions but didn't reach a conclusion. Basically, I didn't care about him at all.

With his mustache, baseball hat pulled down with the brim low across his face and his aviator sunglasses, he looked like a cliché. Spook. Spy.

"How you holdin' up, kid?"

He probably knew more about how I was doing than I did. Silently, I watched the border agents destroy the truck.

After a quiet minute, he continued.

"We've been watching. Looking out for you."

I turned to him.

"In all of these loads, what are we carrying?"

"Chinese machinery—skipping on the tariffs and fees. Cigarettes without tax stamps. Avocados in the refer trucks."

I turned to him.

"I don't believe you care about avocados."

"True that," he said. "You're working for the wrong brother.

We're after the slippery one. Vargas."

This piqued my interest, but I wasn't going to let him know. I turned away and watched wiry little dogs sniff the truck's raggedy cabin.

"You're doing good. We opened a bank account. You're piling up cash. I told you we'd pay. We're paying."

"Bank account in my real name? Philip?"

"No. Christopher. You're going by that name for a while. Funny, right? Christopher Dodd, junior. Clever people will think you might be related to the Connecticut Senator, but I'm not sure how well that plays down here in Texas. I should get to the point. If Vargas offers you a job—take it, okay? He's crossing hot loads somehow and we haven't figured it out. The trucks we stop are clean."

"What's in a dirty truck?"

"Kids for trafficking. Fentanyl and worse."

I tilted my head and looked up at him.

"What's worse than Fentanyl?"

He sighed.

"They call it Black Death."

"What does it do?"

He spit on the concrete pad.

"It makes you feel better than you ever felt in your life."

"What's wrong with that?"

"You crash, then feel worse than ever. You'll do anything to get back up."

"There's a lot of money in that?"

His face twisted.

"Vargas has a submarine made out of gold."

I couldn't help it...I heard Ringo's voice in my head.

Sky of blue, sea of green, in our yellow submarine.

Donovan Leitch helped Paul with writing that line.

Why I knew that, I did not know. I might have been a little sun-sick.

My mind threated to unravel, but I shook it off and focused.

Pointing at the truck, I said, "I don't get this."

He pondered before answering.

"Sacrificial. Red ribbon means there's contraband. Yellow means the load is clean. They like to mix things up. If all the inspections were dirty, they'd do more. As it is, as long as they catch some loads and find some clean, the bureaucracy is happy. Everyone gets paid. The world turns."

"Why don't you bust the crooked agents."

"We don't care about little fish. We care about the whoppers. Like a giant tuna worth a million bucks at the Tsukiji Outer Market in Tokyo—a Pacific bluefin that fights for hours until you haul it in, throw it in on ice, sell it at the New Year's auction and make enough to pay off the boat and live like a king for a year."

My mind felt feverish, but now I was worried about Alvarez. My life was in his hands and clearly, he was crazy.

"If things get out of control, how do I get out?"

He pushed a card across the concrete bench.

"Make a deposit—exactly $17.76." He made a plucking motion with his fingers. "We're watching. We'll swoop in and get you. Vargas is in the bad stuff."

"What was in the truck when we had the trouble on the road to Amarillo?"

He grinned.

"Honey buckets. Portable toilets. Crap and piss. Sometimes they hide stuff in them, but that one was clean. As clean as sewage can get, I guess. Clean poop."

He thought that was funny. I was more convinced he was clinically insane.

While I watched the guards herd the dogs into a K-9 SUV, his minders appeared and helped him stand.

As they walked off, I called out.

"How much longer?"

He ignored me.

Eight hours in with the sun dipping low in the west, they finally wrapped. Like he was doing me a favor, the chief inspector gave me a manifest stamped: "Inspected."

"Clear," he said, tossing me a form. "Reassemble and go."

Reassemble? Alone?

The lot looked like a junkyard explosion with scattered seats, panels and crates. No help was offered. That's how it goes at the border—they tear down, you rebuild.

"What about my fuel?" I said.

"Hazardous waste. Don't worry, we won't charge you for disposal."

A thought flashed in my mind.

He and several of his pals drove diesel pickup trucks and liked filling up for free.

Someone was watching and within minutes a crew pulled up in a pickup with bedside toolboxes. The little brown guys were fast. By dusk, the rig was back together and they hand-pumped fuel from a rusty tank. As I fired it up, the engine sputtered before it caught. It was rattling worse but seemed drivable.

From behind, Acuña's lights flickered. I exhaled. My first solo was a sacrificial run. The road ahead blurred, and I wondered how deep this hole went.

I wasn't going to worry about it.

My job was to drive.

I drove.

When I approached San Antonio, my instructions had me skirt the city on the loop highway, then take 87 to the east. I passed the exit sign for China Grove and again, my overheated mind latched on a song. I didn't know the song or the band.

…they ain't lyin' when the sun goes fallin' down…

Truly, I was losing my mind. I'd never been high, but this must be what it felt like…like the world is an imaginary place where the rules we count on can bend and twist.

I didn't like the feeling and as I approached Latoya, things got stranger. The truck was changing into something alive—an old bull with smoke coming from its nostrils. Slowly, I realized I was smelling something burning—not steamy, something serious like brake or transmission fluid. Maybe the fumes were affecting my brain.

I was supposed to turn off on a stub of abandoned highway. In full darkness, I carefully watched for it. There was a dusty berm with lots of truck tracks on it. The mile marker matched, but something about this place felt off. The dirt barrier was high enough that I wasn't sure the truck could go over it. There was ghostly glow to the west. I decided go for it. In low gear, I revved up and hit the bump hard. I was glad to be wearing my seatbelt—otherwise, I would have bashed my head on the roof. Believe me, my head did not need that. We cleared the hump and after a turn and several dozen yards, the asphalt straightened and the ride got smoother.

As I approached the lot, the lights came into focus. They were still odd because they were flickering kerosine lanterns hanging from sagging power lines—tossed and turned by the wind. There was a motel, a big warehouse and diner—all abandoned with broken windows. Everything metal was rusty and the walls looked like they were dripping with old blood. I'd never seen a creepier place. There was a fire burning in the diner with flames rising from a barrel.

It was like an Avalanche party with the weird-looking crew cab Chevrolets parked at random around the diner. They were all dusty and battered to varying degrees. A short man with a flashlight gestured and waved me into a parking spot at the end of a line of old 18-wheeler tractors. These trucks were called bobtails. It was a bobtail graveyard. I felt an overwhelming sadness for this rugged old truck. It had served and this would be its final resting place. Its sad companions sat on deflated tires—some leaning and some with all the tires collapsed.

After I jumped down from the cabin, I turned. A few words seemed appropriate, but all I had in my head was *Yellow Submarine* playing at the same time as *China Grove*. There was a lot of change in my pocket, something like two or three dollars. I scattered it under the truck. It didn't make sense, but it was all I could think of.

Rest in peace, old bull.

In another fifty or sixty years, I'd be there too.

The lot attendant looked at me like I was loco, which was true.

He tossed me keys.

"White one," he said.

Under the dirt and flickering light, they all looked white to me.

No worries. With the fob, I would find the right one.

I nodded toward the diner.

"Any food in there?"

"*Cervesas, frijoles* and rice," he said.

"*Cafecito?*"

He nodded.

"The good stuff," he said. "Maxwell House."

"Perfect," I said.

I wasn't lying. Before that instant, I didn't know it, but that was exactly what I wanted. The coffee would be scorched and bitter and the fiery beans would swim in greasy pork fat. They would laugh at me for picking out chunks of habaneros chilis. That was okay, I knew enough insults to hold my own.

Out of habit, I stomped the worst of the dust off my boots before throwing open the door.

One of the men muttered.

"Vargas."

The name was like a magic spell. They would not trouble me. I wasn't sure how I knew, but it was a plain fact and as sure as anything.

A group was playing *Conquian.* They waved me over.

Back in Acuña City, I'd played with guys like them and they cleaned me out of all my cash in less than an hour. My body was safe from these hombres, but my money wasn't.

I waved them away and walked to the stew pot. Under chunks of port and grease, there were pinto beans, black beans, kidney beans and garbanzos—along with inevitable chunks of white onion, jalapenos and habaneros. If that wasn't enough heat, there was also a liter bottle of *El Yucateco* habanero sauce.

Fortunately, there was a cooler of fluorescent orange soft drinks, *Jarritos Mandarina.* I would need to quench the upcoming fire, so I took two, then looked for a good spot to eat.

There are a millions ways to live.

This is one of them.

After dinner, I wandered the parking lot, clicking my key fob until my pickup flashed. It was late and I was bone tired. I climbed in, reclined the driver's seat, and settled down. Even an hour after sundown, it was still ninety degrees—no blanket needed tonight.

I closed my eyes and was out right away. I knew nothing more until the morning sun blinded me and the cabin heated up.

Latrine. Breakfast. Then I was on my way.

Fiona: The Wisdom of Bees

SEAN LEANED FORWARD in his chair, staring at Fiona. A long, low, mournful sigh escaped from his lips as he tucked unruly hair behind her ears and studied her lax face.

"Oh, Fiona, what are we doing? What am I doing? I would walk to the ends of the earth and back for you—pass through endless lifetimes for you. This is slowly killing me, my love. Just watching you sleep. Tending to your needs but hearing nothing from you day after day—nothing but the rhythm of your breathing. Will you ever wake or is this how it all ends—with me being your keeper and sentinel until we pass into dust? How will it end, my love? How will this life play out?"

All was quiet in the house. There were no answers. Immersed in melancholy, he hung his head and buried his face in his hands.

"Air," he murmured, "I need air."

Outside, the fresh, cool breeze hit him soft and sweet; filling his lungs and infusing his soul. It always seemed like he stayed by Fiona's side for days on end and time stood still until he lost all sense of things. Breathing deeply reminded him that he needed to be outside more. Fiona would want that.

Tears welled in his eyes.

Fiona would want a lot of things.

He shook his head as if a fly had flown into his ear but kept walking to the corner of the grounds where a wildflower garden was planted. Despite the encroaching forest, it had grown and flourished. A woodsman assembled an elaborate beehive, and it was well known that the bees were friends and no one was to harm them. They provided, but they also kept for themselves. They were protected and respected.

Sean was drawn to them on this lonely day.

A fragment of melody drifted through his mind.

> *The joy is in the telling*
> *The sorrow in the soul*
> *Tears of happiness and sadness—let them flow...*
> *Telling the bees, telling the bees...*

He thought of Celtic folklore—which said honeybees were sensitive and should be respectfully informed about losses in the family—especially if something happened to the beekeeper. Bad news must be communicated gently and with sympathy.

Bees mourn, too.

If not? They might stop producing honey, desert the hive—or die.

> *Telling the bees, telling the bees...*

He half remembered reading an odd article in an old newspaper about a strange event in 1956 at the funeral of John Zepka, a beekeeper from the Berkshire Hills in Eastern Massachusetts. As the funeral procession reached the grave, the mourners discovered swarms of bees hanging placidly from the ceiling of the tent and clinging to floral sprays. They did not annoy the mourners—just remained immobile.

This curious case was taken as confirmation of the need to *tell the bees* and cemented the connection that exists between humans and hive.

His mind drifted. Like old John Zepka, the writer Edith Wharton was from the Berkshires.

One of her quotes drifted into focus.

There are two ways of spreading light: to be the candle or the mirror that reflects it.

And, wasn't there a poem? *Telling the Bees* by Deborah Digges.
Why do I remember the author's name and these weird details?
He had no idea.

> *Who makes the laws that live*
> *inside the brick and mortar of a name,*
> *selects the seeds, garden or wild,*
> *brings forth the foliage grown up around it*
> *through drought or blight or blossom,*
> *the honey darkening in the bitter years,*
> *the combs like funeral lace or wedding veils*
> *steeped in oak gall and rainwater,*
> *sequined of rent wings.*

Was there another poem? This one more famous? Who was the author?
It will come to me.

> *Trembling, I listened: the summer sun*
> *Had the chill of snow;*
> *For I knew she was telling the bees of one*
> *Gone on the journey we all must go!*

He remembered the author's name. John Greenleaf Wittier.
What a name. Sean made a solemn vow to change his name to Sean Greenleaf—a name for the ages.
Slowly, he approached the beehive and sat on a rickety wooden milk stool purposely placed in the garden to encourage sitting and communing with this farmland oasis. As he sat, he closed his eyes and breathed in the sweet smell of the wildflowers. Despite all odds, fragrant bee balm and lavender grew strong, tall sunflowers stood like knights moving with the sun and guarding the delicate bees while goldenrod, catmint and coneflowers were in abundance and poppies swayed with the passing breezes. Cosmos and calendula were sweetly nestled

amongst zinnias and anise hyssop. The blanketflowers glowed like sunsets come to Earth and allium reminded him of something from a Dr. Seuss book.

"Fiona loves this little garden," Sean murmured as tears slipped down his cheeks.

He took a deep breath and tried to meditate, but forced bliss would not come. All he got was an endless stream of questions.

"What am I doing here?"

"Why is all of this happening?

"Am I just wasting away?"

"Why, just why?"

The open road called to him. Hitchhiking and traveling to wherever the driver's car was headed. No pressure from time. No destination. Taking what came.

I could leave and never look back.

So many questions and yet no answers. Another sigh escaped his lips, but this time it was met with humming. Sean opened his eyes to see delicate honeybees hovering before his eyes.

"Well, hello there my friends. Am I intruding? Did my sour mood darken your day? I'm so terribly sorry if I'm disturbing you. Shall I leave?"

He held out his hand and the smallest bee landed on his outstretched finger.

"Please stay, Sean. You need to be here right now. Feel the sun on your shoulders, listen to the drone of our wings, glory at the beautiful flowers and taste of our sweetest nectar. We love you, Sean, and so does Fiona. She will wake when it's time and will be stronger and more beautiful than ever. Trust, Sean. Trust and be patient a little longer."

Sean smiled a small smile and closed his eyes.

"I've no choice but to believe you, my little winged friend. I have no reason to doubt. Perhaps I should bring some of your magical honey back for Fiona; perhaps it would lure her back to life. Maybe it would help me as well. May I be so bold as to ask? I'll not take much, just enough."

The bees flew about the flowers in unison while emitting an approving buzz.

"Of course, Sean. We are humbled and honored for you to take some of our gold back to the Queen. Take it from the left side of the hive—that is where the sweetest and most golden honey lives. Please though, sit a while longer. Let the sun kiss your forehead and ease your worries. Come to the hive when you're ready."

Sean once again bowed his head and gave thanks. He did as he was told: sat on the wooden stool and let the sun ease his worries and heart. Heady scents transported him away and the wind told him all would be well. With his toes planted in the warm, red sandy dirt he felt grounded and connected. He let out a deep sigh, and he felt himself return—return to himself and content once again to be in his skin.

Moving slowly, he stood and approached the hive from the left. He turned a sticky wooden spout and watched as sweet, golden nectar poured slowly into one of the Mason jars lined up on a fence rail. He took only what he needed and thanked the bees. The littlest one flew out and he once again stretched out his hand so she could land.

"Come back soon, Sean. You were gone too long last time. We are always here for you. We love you and Fiona and Minnie. We are with you always."

"I would tap you on the nose, but I fear I would squish you. Thank you so much for your wise counsel and healing honey. We love you too. Be safe and stay cool as high noon approaches."

"Yes, Sean, we have everything we need in this garden. We are well cared for and protected. Go now and enjoy our honey."

She flew up and gave Sean a kiss on the nose. It tingled. He smiled and laughed. As Sean left the garden he felt light again, light and filled with calm and purpose.

When he got back to the house, he placed the jar by the kitchen sink. In the sunlight, it glowed, and the bubbles twinkled as they bobbed up and down with the heat of the sun. Nature's lava lamp. He headed to the herb shelf and sat cross-legged on the floor. All the herbs were in alphabetical order and thankfully, Fiona had put descriptive labels on each jar. Ones for detoxing the body and ones to aide with hand tremors; ones to purify the blood and ones to induce dreams. Some would calm and some would excite, and others still served as aphrodisiacs.

Sean chuckled.

"Ah, yes, I remember what THIS one did," as he drifted down memory lane to a time that seemed so very long before. While not as intuitive as Fiona, he knew what he was looking for and as soon as his eyes landed upon them, he picked up the packets.

"Basil to refresh my mind and hyacinth to return mirth to my spirit. Lavender for a sense of peace and lemon to keep happiness growing between Fiona and me. A pinch of marjoram to banish the blues and rosemary to maintain our happy memories."

That should do the trick—or taste like boiled mud if I do it wrong.

Sean smiled and laid the herbs on a scrap of cheesecloth and tied it closed with twine.

"Enough for a whole pot," he mused as he turned on the copper kettle and waited for the water to reach near boiling.

He could hear Fiona's voice chiding him.

"Don't let the water boil, Sean, that will burn and ruin the herbs. Be patient and gentle and they will yield their magic and healing."

Sean rolled his eyes when she went on and on as if the herbs were her very children; but in essence they were, and he had grown to appreciate her loving and nurturing them. As he poured steaming spring water over the herbs, he delighted in the aromatic release and could almost hear them sigh with delight as if they were soaking in a warm bath. When he felt they were ready, he pulled out the cheesecloth, flicked out the debris and arranged the cloth on a plate to dry—to be used once again at another time. He drizzled in a spoonful of the glorious nectar from the bees and as he held up the warm cup, gave thanks for his day and his altered mindset. He was exactly where he was supposed to be and had made the most remarkable cup of tea.

Fiona would be proud.

"It may not be as good as your tea, Fiona, but this honey is truly magical. Maybe one day it will arouse you from your slumber. One day it will; and I will be by your side on that day. Until then I will patiently wait until I can gaze into your eyes once more. The bees heal," he whispered. "Always."

Another Edith Wharton quote came to mind.

Life's just a perpetual piecing together of broken bits.

126

That's me, Sean thought. Broken into bits and waiting for the cosmic repairman to glue me back together.

Sipping, he turned off his thoughts and emptied his mind...except for a persistent wisp of melody coming to him from beyond the singer's grave.

As old as these hills and old as the stones—I feel it down to my soul.

Fiona: Ghost Walk

A COOL BREEZE blew through the woods. It might seem quiet, but if you stop to listen, you'll hear a noisy chatter. The tall firs whispering. Owls hooting warnings at each other. Coyotes yipping at the fragment of moon floating on the horizon. The rustle of mice foraging in fallen leaves.

As always in life, the more you listen, the more you will hear.

Next to Fiona, Sean lay on their bed—soundly asleep; dead to the world. He held her hand to feel her pulse. Exhausted, he dreamed in random fragments of neither here nor there. He floated in the ether unaware of time and space. He simply was, and this brought him peace and deep sleep.

Fiona, motionless in catatonia, drifted back to her beloved Nantucket Island. Had Sean been awake, he might have felt her hips sway to the island breeze as the currents flowed through her blood. He may have heard her humming a tune from the island and see the corners of her lips curl up. With lips stained green and the taste of malt and pistachios on her tongue from Malachite ice cream, she was in her happy place, and it made her glow from the inside.

As she went back in time, she found herself walking along the cobblestone streets of Main Street. She walked past the Three Sisters brick houses, marveling at the architecture Joseph Starbuck designed for his sons in the 1800's. She wondered if he knew what Island icons their homes would become in their structured symmetry with porticos and granite stoops.

She wondered if he thought the whaling industry would continue until the end of time. While wandering and pondering, she eventually joined a group of tourists embarked on the Nantucket Ghost Walk. As a child with no money, Fiona had discreetly trailed the washashore tour many times—listening carefully to the stories. She enjoyed immersion into the lore of the whaling days and how the guides pulled the audience into their stories and how there was always something new to learn.

The dates, names and other details were always the same, but each guide had an individual style. The good ones embellished with colorful flights of fancy. A good story had little information—meaning the tour guide could add florid details without contradiction from inconvenient facts. On this blustery day, as Fiona flitted from doorway to doorway and listened to the tales, she felt the presence of someone, or something.

This was the dream world, but something felt real.

As they approached the Old North Burial Grounds, she glimpsed a suspicious shadow near one of the old trees. She remembered the first to be buried here were Abilgail Coffin Gardner and her husband Nathanial Gardner back in the early 1700's. Later, the rest of the Gardner family just began burying their dead on or next to the property, so there were all manner of stories and rumors about what and who were buried in the cemetery.

Fiona was in two places. Hiding in a doorway, she felt a cool breeze. Shivering in bed, she squeezed Sean's hand.

When they rounded the bend, a figure moved in next to her. It was an older woman dressed all in black with a shawl around her head. In her dream it was a cool island night, so nothing seemed out of the ordinary.

"Nice night for a walk about the Island. Are you enjoying the tour, Fiona?"

Fiona stopped in her tracks and turned to face the woman.

"You! What are you doing in my dream?"

It was the former Queen, the one who surrendered her life so Fiona and Minnie could live.

"Ah, you recognize me after all this time. Well, I should hope you would after all I went through. So, tell me Fiona, how are things? I imagine things are not all taken care of as I've had to visit you here in your dream on this most interesting island. Really, Fiona, this is what makes you happy? A cold island thirty miles out to sea? It's so...quaint."

"What exactly do you want?" barked Fiona. "Why do you invade my happiness?"

"Fiona, you are still asleep. It is high time you awoke from whatever you call this state of being—or nonbeing, I suppose. Trevir is on the move and he's not alone. He has a horde of trolls and all manner of foul beasts, and he's coming for you. He's coming for Minnie. He will dominate the world with his Black Death and mind poison. For his own amusement, he'll turn the world into a desolate wasteland. Only you and Minnie stand in his way. You know this, Fiona. Yet here you sleep and ignore what approaches your very doorstep."

"I'm tired. I went through a lot, and I need time to recover...trolls. I defeated the trolls. It took everything I had."

"Time is no longer a luxury you can afford. You have rested enough. Snap out of it, Fiona. This is your destiny. This is your lot. You drew this card and now you must play your hand until the bitter end. I did. You will."

"I did NOT choose this life. I never asked for it and I don't want it." An idea occurred to her. "What about you, my Queen?"

"Dead is dead, Fiona. Stop the drama and insolence—it won't work on me. You were trained. Many gave their lives to get you this far. If you won't willingly wake, then I will shove you back into your body by force. It's nearly time to decide. Live or die. Enough is enough."

"Wait! Don't I have a say?"

"No, not anymore, Fiona. We're done patiently waiting. However, I'll make you a deal. Go back into your body and wake up. You will regain your strength and plans will be made. Once this whole mess is sorted and should you, Sean and Minnie, survive what lies ahead, you can come back to this island rock and live out the rest of your days in isolated bliss. The outside world will trouble you no more. Deal?"

"Do I have a choice?"

"Yes, of course. You can choose death instead of the halfway house. It's coming, so be ready."

As the former Queen disappeared, Fiona drifted away from her Nantucket dream. Floating above the island, she heard seagulls singing their farewell, felt the salt air evaporate off her skin and slowly drifted back into herself. As her spirit melted back into her sleeping body, she let out a gasp as if she'd just swum to the surface of the cold ocean. She opened her eyes wide and squeezed Sean's hand. She turned to study his face and squeezed his hand again. In the dim light, his slack face seemed both older and younger than it should be. She was awake and she was back.

The temptation to wake him was overwhelming, but she pushed it away.

Just for what remains of the night, let him be.

Morning will come soon enough.

Philip d'GreenApple: Return to Ciudad Acuña

SAN ANTONIO'S SPARKLY skyline loomed in the rearview, a haze of lights fading as I pushed on back toward the border. When those lights disappeared, it would be 150 miles of nothing but armadillos, prickly pear cacti and literal tumbleweeds. Tumbleweeds everywhere—tangled in the barbed wire along the highway and floating across the road like a cartoon.

I was in a strange mood, feeling at one with whatever was happening. The image that came to mind was a leaf drifting down a placid stream with an ant clinging to its surface. I was the ant and there were rapids ahead. It was a stupid and clichéd image. I scolded my overwrought mind for creating it.

After the butt-pounding, spine-jangling ride in the old Mack truck, the Avalanche was the pinnacle of luxury and comfort. It was old, but someone cared for it. The leather was moisturized and plush. Everything in west Texas is dusty, but this truck's dashboard had been wiped down. The little pine tree air freshener hanging from the rearview was fresh enough to fill the air with its cloying scent. I was happy to ditch it when I stopped at the Castroville Walmart Supercenter to pee and get a bottle of cold water.

The CD player had a Banda disc. I let it play twice before I'd had enough of blaring that felt like a fist to the gut with trumpets wailing over a tuba's low rumble, the kind of music that made you think of fiestas and sweat-soaked regret. It was festive, but in that Mexican way—bright colors over dark hearts.

I ejected the disc and glanced at it.

Los Huracanes del Norte: Legado Norteño Corridos

My impulse was to sail it out of the window, but that would be stupid and wasteful. Though the roadside was covered in litter, I did not want to add to it. Besides, I didn't hate the music—it was part of the fabric of life in this area of the world. It would be like hating your arm. Pointless. Irrational.

I slipped it under the elastic band on the sun visor, then flipped the visor up so I would not have to look at it.

The yard boss's words echoed.

"Jet back."

But with the rig's guts spilled by the border boys, there was no *jetting* happening anywhere around here.

I goosed the pickup and passed a schoolteacher puttering along in a tiny Toyota Camry. What was her life like? What deep thinking went on under her unruly cloud of frizzy-white hair? In the back seat, I caught a glimpse of a three-year-old making an ugly face pressed against something smeared on the window. Strawberry jam? I put out my tongue and she laughed like it was the funniest thing ever. My imagination was out of control and that window would be a mother-bear to clean.

Clearly, my sanity needed to be carefully examined. My mind was freewheeling.

With the sun at my back and a lingering hint of cool in the morning air, I covered mile after mile along US-90. Through a crack of window, I enjoyed the scents of mesquite and memories of rain.

The Mexicans treated me like an adult, but deep inside, I felt like a child and I didn't want to give it up. But I'd seen things. I had experiences. The world was insisting that I grow up. And now, not later.

By dawn, the Rio Grande shimmered under the first light, and the International Bridge welcomed me like an old accomplice. The Mexican agents waved me through with barely a glance. Ciudad Acuña stirred awake as I rolled in: vendors firing up comals for breakfast tacos, stray dogs dodging early commuters and the faint strum of a guitar from a radio in a passing lowrider. Soon enough, the warehouse loomed ahead with its chain-link fence sagging under the weight of brutal sun.

I killed the engine and silence rushed in like a held breath released. José Luis waited, leaning against a rusted oil drum with a cigarette dangling from his lip. His eyes flicked over the dirty pickup—then to me, rumpled and road-weary.

"Felipito," he said, a grin cracking his face like sun-baked clay. "You look like hell, but you made it. Come on, *mijo*, let's get you fed."

Brusquely, he slapped a hand on my shoulder, steering me toward the smaller building where we'd first met. Inside, the air was thick with the aroma of chorizo sizzling on a hotplate with fresh tortillas warming on the side. A woman—his wife, maybe, or sister—piled a plate high: eggs scrambled with sausage, refried beans slick with lard and a stack of corn tortillas steaming under a cloth. She set it down with a nod, no words needed.

"Sit, eat," José Luis said, pulling up a chair across from me. "You did good. The run? Clean as a whistle. Kept the heat off the real loads."

I dug in, the hearty food hitting my empty stomach like a balm.

Around us, a few workers shuffled in, grabbing coffee and plates of their own. They murmured greetings and patted my back as they passed.

"*Buen trabajo, gringo.*"

No suspicion, no cold stares. Just quiet respect, the kind earned in the shadows.

Raul stumbled in and dropped into a seat, stealing a tortilla from my plate.

"Told you—easy money."

José Luis leaned in, voice low.

"Hermano Vargas is pleased. Says you're reliable. Got more work if you want it. Real runs this time. Pay's double. Not good. Stick with me, kid—you'll live longer."

I chewed slowly, the flavors grounding me. A warm welcome in a cold world—food, camaraderie, even a nod from the boss. But Alvarez's words lingered like smoke.

We're after Vargas.

"Double, huh?" I said, forcing a grin. "Count me in."

Outside, the sun climbed higher, casting long shadows over Acuña's streets. I was in deeper now, but for the first time, it felt like I had no choice.

Not even the illusion of one.

Minnie: Opening Day

AS SOON AS Minnie opened her eyes, she felt the energy. Instinctively, she knew it was around four in the morning. The Faire was awakening on opening day. The energy was palpable even at this early hour. Instead of trying to force herself back to sleep, Minnie got up to enjoy a few moments of relative peace before the inevitable chaos ensued.

As she strolled about the Faire grounds, the place came alive—she saw all manner of people stirring. Getting ready for the big day, blacksmiths stoked the fires in their forges, proprietors of food caravans and tents tended their ovens and laid out napkins and condiments, artisans polished and arranged their wares, actors and actresses did voice exercises and last-minute repairs of their costumes.

The mud pits were wetted down by bawdy mudders while roaming wenches primped, tucked and sprinkled glitter on their expansive bosoms. With children running and weaving through a sea of legs, musicians tuned their lutes, harps, fiddles and bouzoukis while minstrels and florid insulters studied tattered manuscripts with lips moving as they memorized the best lines.

While the sun peeked over the horizon, everyone was awake and abuzz. Minnie soaked it all in. A jester pushing a cart handed her an almond croissant dusted with powdered sugar—then he was lost in a crowd of jugglers before she could properly thank him.

The fluffy pastry was perfect.

As the morning progressed, Minnie helped where she could. She ran errands, delivered messages, helped to pull corsets ever so tight, braided feathers into hair, arranged baked goods and helped to set up shade tents. She was exhausted before the gates opened but there would be no sleeping until deep into the nightfall.

She wandered toward the main entrance. On the side, there were stairs to the overhang.

That would be a fun place to lurk.

"Ten minutes, folks. Ten minutes to gates."

She was surrounded by a swirl of color and noise.

"This will not do, sprite."

Minnie turned. She was surrounded by a troupe of singers dressed in long velvet dresses and tall, beehive wigs. Their makeup was so exaggerated and absurd, she could not help but giggle.

They spun her and there was a flurry of activity. In thirty seconds, they'd velcroed a dress over her jeans and t-shirt and tied the strings of a bonnet under her chin. There was a puff of red mist as a mushroom head powder puff was tapped on her cheeks.

There was a booming voice.

There was no way this tall, husky person was really a woman under the layers of skirts and shawls.

"Lipstick! Emergency! Who has?"

The massive woman studied a capsule that looked like a large-caliber rifle cartridge.

"Red ruby retro matte. Wonderful. Hold still, waif."

Minnie tried not to move while the lipstick was rubbed all over.

The woman stood back and examined Minnie carefully.

"Undeniable perfection," she declared.

Minnie didn't have a mirror, but she could imagine what she looked like. Ridiculous and one-hundred-percent silly.

She climbed rickety stairs and pushed onto the overhang—then gasped. In front of the gates were more than a thousand milling people clutching tickets. More cars jockeyed in the massive parking lot. There were young people, old people and everything in between. There were motorized wheelchairs, strollers, parasols, camera bags and knapsacks. Some were in costume representing varying degrees of effort—some with just floppy hats with feathers and some outfitted from head to toe. Two ten-year-olds took stances and fought with rubber swords.

On the overhang, the RenFaire queen on her throne shouted welcome at the crowd while her courtiers sang snippets of songs and greeted people picked out from the crowd.

"Red hat, you look wonderful."

"Man in the green coat, well played, m'lord."

It was bedlam.

As the wooden gates creaked open and patrons filed in, the minstrel began singing and welcoming the guests. He instigated and flirted, sang and yelled, introduced and played matchmaker between unsuspecting people. Minnie greatly enjoyed watching him at work; his ability to think and reply on the fly was a wonder and Minnie longed for that quickness.

She climbed down the stairs and lost herself in the mob and assisted all manner of people with finding their destinations, directing them to various port-o-potties and showing them where the medical and shade tents were. At one point she had to assist an older woman who fainted from the heat and excitement. She ran to find a medic who quickly came, rolled the older woman onto a stretcher and carried her away where she made a full recovery under their care.

As Minnie ran between here and there, she spied a small girl who was clearly lost.

"I want my mommmmyyyyyy!" the girl wailed helplessly.

Minnie knew that feeling all too well and immediately consoled her.

"There, there, little one. What's your name?"

"Sarah," she managed to say through her tears.

"Hi, Sarah, I'm Minnie. I'm going to help you find your mommy. Would that be, okay?"

"My mommy said never to talk to strangers."

"Well, your mommy is right, however, I can help you. Here, take my hand. Let's get you lavender lemonade and a pretzel. Then we'll have a sit under that tree over there. Once you're full, we'll walk around the Faire and see if you spot her. I'll also leave word with the medic and information tent that you're lost and looking for your mommy—that you're with me and to call me on the walkie talkie if she comes looking for you. How does that all sound?"

"I like lemonade. You seem nice. I like your name too. Okay, let's go, Minnie."

Sarah gave Minnie her little hand and they went off and did everything that Minnie had promised. In less than an hour, Sarah and her flustered mommy were reunited and all was right once again.

Morning turned to afternoon, then afternoon turned to evening and Minnie began to wonder if she would ever get a break. She'd been on the go all day and started to hit the wall. At long last, the final joust was announced and Minnie knew she was in the homestretch.

"Soon I can sleep," Minnie cooed to herself. "Just a bit longer…"

When the last patron was out and the wooden gate was closed and latched, there was an instantaneous "Huzzah" and a full cheer from everyone.

"Opening day. We did it! We made it!"

As everyone gathered to eat, drink, and tell stories from the day, Minnie found herself floating back to her tent. Her feet were tired from running around all day. She didn't know if they touched the ground as they took her home where she plopped onto her blow-up bed. It had been a long day, and she knew that deep sleep would come fast.

On the wind she heard a low, threatening voice.

"Sleep while you can, Princess, for soon there will be no more sleep for you or your friends…"

Fiona Takes Leave

AN HOUR BEFORE sunrise, Fiona sat on the front porch and soaked in the faint cacophony of the forest. There was wind in the trees and howling wolves in the distance. Out in the dark, life and death waged endless battles. Predator met prey. Some escaped, some didn't. There was a throaty roar, but Fiona didn't know what it was.

A cougar, bear or some unholy, mythical beast with horns, talons and claws?

On the breeze, she heard the murmuring of a baker talking to her rabbit and wondered what the Meg would think of their bunny stew. She respected Vegans and Vegetarians, but why did the Gods have to make rabbits and chickens so damned tasty?

"I'm sorry," she whispered to the world.

When the first ray of sunlight hit her, she'd be gone.

She had no idea how it worked, but she knew. After all his care and patience—it wasn't fair to Sean. She was sorry about that, too, but these things happen. Fairness was not her department. It was not her circus and not her monkeys. The decision was above her pay grade. The plot twist was not for the movie she is starring in. She tried to think of more clichés but came up empty.

She thought about where the wind would take her. The natural place was to join Minnie at her desert festival, and she would, but sensed there would be intermediate destinations. Ideas rolled around in her head, but she didn't focus on the question. It would be what it wanted to be. A realization hit her.

I'm not ready for battle.

She didn't want this to be true, but it was.

What does that mean?

I need to go somewhere where I can build my strength and slowly integrate into the wild world.

What kind of place would that be?

She thought about a tropical spa-resort or cruise ship. That would be perfect—somewhere they would take care of her. She could eat good food, get full body massages and take yoga classes. She could work on aligning her mind, body and soul. She could do free weight training and tone up her too-soft body.

As light gathered on the brightening horizon, the selfish idea made her smile. She could read books, make new friends and drink fine wine in the evenings.

Do I have a choice about what happens next?

She projected the idea to the universe.

All my friends could come. We could have a carefree party far away from dead trolls and the evil king.

Please.

It was certainly imagined, but she heard laughter coming from the trees.

As the sun peeped, the farm drifted into focus. Greeting the new day, an owl hooted, and their noisy rooster cleared its throat in preparation of announcing the new day.

A beam of morning light danced on her forehead...and she was gone.

Philip d'GreenApple: King of Dreams

WHILE WAITING FOR the trucks to get loaded and drivers assigned, we played the three- or four-player version of *Conquian*. They called it *Konkan* and it was similar to the Rummy my family played late at night around the woodstove. After playing the fool for a couple of rounds, I started winning my share…both the game and the respect of the other players. They played for a peso a point, which doesn't seem like much, but added up quickly at the fast pace they played. It was more fun to play with four than three, that's how it started for me. At first, my partner was reluctant, but after grasping the arcane strategies, I was in demand.

More than once, late at night it was just me and Raul. Of course, he cheated by peeking at my cards or bending the card corners. But I cheated too by dealing off the bottom of the deck or distracting him and being sneaky and sorting cards from the discard pile. Like everyone else, he smoked and drank endless bottles of Carta Blanca beer while I fortified myself with oildrum coffee and a strange addiction to a tamarind candy called del la Rosa mango *Pulparindo*. At first, I hated its bold, salty and spicy flavor—it was like a full-on attack on my taste buds, but late at night, it kept me going while my card-playing colleagues drank and smoked. It turned my teeth brown, but I didn't care.

The cards were fun, but they made me homesick—which was particularly sad because I didn't have a home. My people were transients. Traveling people. Home was wherever we were.

One night, it was down to me and Raul and we pushed stacks of pesos back and forth with wild abandon. At the far end of the warehouse, I spotted a familiar figure...one I hoped I would never see again.

It was that black Prince What's-His-Face. Like me, he'd grown up. He wore a black suit...shiny like satin. Probably silk. I didn't know anything about fabrics, but I could tell it was custom-tailored and expensive. He had an entourage. Notably, a man and a woman—along with three thugs—bodyguards with roving eyes and suspicious lumps under their jackets. The man and woman were interesting. She was tall and husky...her face was pale and she wore bright red lipstick. Black hair.

The black reminded me of something.

There is a coating material that is especially black. Blacker than black. Unbidden, the name popped into my head. Vantablack. It was patented, trademarked and not to be confused with Black 2.0 or Black 3.0. I even knew what VANTA stood for: Vertically Aligned NanoTube Arrays Black. I didn't know how I knew, I just did.

It wasn't the color of her hair or the suit that brought this to mind. It was their auras. Blacker-than-black.

I shrank within myself and disappeared as much as I could. This was not physical, it came from something deep inside. I was an unobtrusive pinpoint. Barely there—or anywhere. It worked. They barely glanced my way and did not see me.

Of all places, what were they doing here?

His name popped into my head. Trevir. I didn't want it, but it came anyway. The black faerie Prince...now King. I try very hard not to hate anyone, but I hated this psychopath with a blinding fury. Bizarrely, if I had a green apple, I would chuck it at him. I had to push my heasted emotions deep inside or they would see me. Like a spotlight in a cave, they would see me.

Trevir gestured and the large woman produced a plastic bag filled with shiny little black dots.

I knew what the dots were.

Black Death.

At up to a hundred times stronger than morphine, fentanyl was dangerous. 40 times stronger than fentanyl, nitazenes were unimaginably dangerous. What came after that? Super addictive and hazardous even in tiny quantities? Black Death.

It was 2:30 in the morning. Most of the warehouse workers and drivers were asleep.

Raul laid down his cards and raked in the pesos.

"Gone out, amigo," he said. "*Estás bien güey.*"

He was right, of course. I am a fool.

What was I doing here?

It was one thing to work for José Luis. There were no direct victims of his crimes. Smuggling. Skating around tariffs and duties. As life goes, this was not super troublesome. But it was clear. I was going to work for Vargas and didn't want to. I really—deep in my soul—did not want to. I needed to get out.

But how?

I didn't like Alvarez…and I didn't trust him. He wasn't a solution to my problem.

I did a rough count of the pesos. Raul had cleaned me our of about four dollars. He could not have been happier.

For this day, I'd had enough. I needed to sleep—and to think.

"I will get it all back tomorrow," I said.

Raul drained his beer and laughed.

"We'll see, *cabrito*," he said.

Cabrito.

My mind stumbled on the translation.

Baby goat.

Kid.

I got it.

To avoid attracting attention, I moved slowly and slipped out of the warehouse, then eased the door shut behind me. My truck was parked in a dark corner of the yard. As the lights faded behind me, the stars woke up. We were in a semirural area and the city lights were dim. I got in the Avalanche and pressed the button to recline the seat.

I didn't want to dream, but I knew I would.

The King.

The cards.

My dilemma.

I surrendered to sleep.

Misfits

PARKING LOT.

With her eyes closed, she turned on her heels and breathed the air. It wasn't winter, but the fresh, clean air held a coolness that warned about the upcoming cold. From the damp weight of the atmosphere, she knew where she was. The Pacific Northwest. Cement City. After opening her eyes, she recognized the High School—the school Minnie had attended. She stood on the gravel and asphalt parking lot where the fund-raising carnival was held.

It seemed like a million years ago.

Why here? What was the point? What do I do?

Feeling disoriented and weak, she thought about the immediate future. How long was she gone? Were her clothes and furniture still in Chet's rental house behind the restaurant?

Was she supposed to settle back in her old life?

Whatever spell she'd been in—it lingered. It would take time before she would be grounded and fully engaged in this life. Her life.

She knew Minnie was far away in a different state with a different family and a different climate.

This is weird. Why here?

What am I supposed to do?

Though the summer break was imminent, school was in session. She could see cars in the parking lot...including the teacher and staff section.

She did an inventory.

How did this work?

She was dressed.

Thank the gods for that.

She had everything she'd left with. Shoes. Red, high-top Chucks. Blue jeans. A t-shirt under a heavy sweater. Her purse. She could tell it was stuffed with all her random junk.

Keys. Chapstick. Kleenex.

I'm transported through time and space with all of my clothes and belongings. What weird logic did the universe use?

There was trail mix in her bag. She wouldn't starve.

Her wallet was in her purse, and it surely had money. Thinking hard, she remembered almost $200 from a week's collection of tips—grimy dollar bills and loose change. The burger place was across the busy highway, but she wasn't hungry. Behind the burger shack, the creek burbled.

It was all so absurd, she had to laugh.

She tried speaking.

"My name is Fiona and I don't know W-T-F I am doing."

About half the words came out. Her throat was dry and her voice rusty.

How long had it been since I last spoke? What were my last words before dying?

Straining, she thought back.

I am nothing.

No, that was her last thought, but those were not her last spoken words. She could not remember her last words. She remembered the scene—the trolls and ugly carnage.

I don't know anything.

There was a phone at the burger shack. She could call for a ride. But a ride to where? Upriver to Chet's restaurant? Downriver toward the Emerald City? Fighting tears, she felt an overwhelming desire to wrap Minnie in her arms and squeeze her tight.

She turned toward the school. That felt like the right direction.

She imagined walking in and trying to explain everything that had happened. The thought made her laugh.

They'd lock her in the funny farm and throw away the key.

A strange idea filled her head.

What would happen if I embrace a vow of silence and don't say a single solitary word?

After walking to the school, she opened the door and walked down the hallway to the admin office.

Sitting behind the reception counter, the first person she encountered was Harriet.

Harriet was a very large woman wearing a mid-calf dress like a tent. Her thinning hair was pressed into pin curls...dyed blue. Fiona had seen the woman around but didn't remember ever speaking to her.

Harriot cocked her head like a dog.

"Can I help you, dear?" Harriet said.

Fully passive, Fiona stood and stared.

From behind Harriet, another woman approached.

Patty. Fiona studied her.

She was tiny, maybe five-foot-two and eighty pounds. A breeze could blow her into the next county. Bobbed black hair framed her round face. Vietnamese, Laotian or Cambodian, but part faerie, too.

"I know this woman," Patty said. "It's Fiona. Minnie's, uh, caregiver. Mother. Stepmom. Something like that."

To Fiona, she said, "We haven't seen Minnie for what? Six weeks? What happened to her? Is she okay?" Looking into Fiona's eyes, she said, "Are *you* okay?"

"This is weird," Harriet said.

"You think everything that can't be put in a spreadsheet is weird," Patty muttered. "She just needs to catch her breath."

Patty's forehead crinkled with concentration.

"We don't have a replacement for Miss Thomas yet. Fiona can use her room."

All the way down the hallway, Patty chattered.

"School nurse. Miss Thomas. Lovely lady, nervous type. Not suited for the role, you know. Didn't make it. Her boyfriend landed a program manager job at Microsoft. What's a program manager do? I have no idea. Poof, she was gone. Dual role. Two jobs, one paycheck. That's how we roll. Nurse and social worker. Cleaning scratches and applying bandages. Giving pads and Midol to the girls who need it, if you know what I mean. Greif counselor when the bus driver had a heart attack. Remember? Alvarez Rojas. Sweet man, used to be in the Army. MP. Military Police, did you know that? No one knew, but in the office, we see all the paperwork. Wounded when a car tried to crash through the front gate in Kabul in Afgooberstook. Stray bullet and flying glass. You never know about people, you know? What they did and what they went through. You been in the soup, I can tell. But don't worry. Take all the time you need. Even sleep here if you like—I'll warn Enrique so you don't scare the daylight out of him when he's buffing the hallway floors."

In the room, Fiona looked around. The room smelled like incense and sweet oils—the lingering odor of a diffuser. The scent was warm and welcoming, like sweet grass and cedar with a hint of white sage. The oils protected the space; sending evil back from whence it came and encouraging positivity. Under it all: tobacco.

Patty wrinkled her nose.

"Miss Thomas said something crazy. 'If you want to know what the kids are thinking, sneak a smoke with them under the bleachers.' Principal Gorton knew, but he didn't make a thing about it. Danvers liked Miss Thomas and that was all our Principal needed to know, I guess."

Fiona didn't know Miss Thomas—as far as she knew, had never laid eyes on her—but she liked her too.

One wall had a Grateful Dead poster with red roses and a skeleton playing a guitar, the other featured Taylor Swift and a blue-eyed cat. Around the room were second-hand couches and cushions. In hanging pots: spider plants with droopy leaves. Someone had been tending them; they were plush and green. Scarves were thrown over the table lamps to create soft, ambient lighting. Silk curtains shielded the room from outside light. In a corner, a seashell windchime hung from the ceiling.

"I gotta go back to work; make yourself comfortable. Toilet's down the way a bit. Shower in the gym. Get hungry, you can order a pizza, I guess. Send an email if you want something. Clean panties, toothpaste, deodorant or an accordion. You know. Anything."

While standing at the door, Patty took a long, lingering look at Fiona.

"Whatever time you need," she said.

After a quiet hour of thinking about what use she might have for an accordion, there was a knock on the door—a soft tap followed by the door slowly opening.

A young girl, maybe 15, appeared. Her hair was tousled like she'd just awoke from a long nap. She wore black and white striped tights, combat boots, a short black skirt and a black t-shirt with a cartoon faery on it that said MISFIT in block-letters. She had a silver hoop through her nose and jet-black eyeliner. Her eyes were sad and far away. A kindred spirit. Fiona smiled.

"Miss Patty said I could come here. I won't stay long. I just want to sit and be quiet and see who you are. Is that okay?"

Fiona nodded.

"Okay. My name is Tara. Thank you."

Tara stared wistfully out the window. Fiona could feel sadness rolling off her but remained quiet. Tara would speak when she was ready. Or maybe she simply needed someone to hold the space for her so she could simply exist. Either way, Fiona was there and they were safe.

"My grandmother was the only one who understood me," Tara said. "And now, she's gone."

Fiona nodded.

The girl sobbed. Fiona handed her a Kleenex.

There was more.

Everyone was talking about a new drug…a little black pill.

"Unless someone stops me," Tara said, "I'm taking one. I'll do anything to find peace."

Fiona stood, walked around the desk and wrapped her arms around the trembling girl.

"No one cares."

Fiona held the girl at arm's length and pointed at herself.

"You care?" Tara said. "Why?"
Fiona shrugged.
She didn't know.

As the days and weeks went by, Tara and many more students came to Fiona's room. They talked about deaths in their families, how they'd lost friends to drugs and how their pets died of old age. They spoke of loss and love and annoying teachers. Fiona never passed judgement and never offered true advice; she just led them down the garden path so they could reach their own conclusions. They always seemed to leave more at peace than when they came. For that, Fiona was grateful. Day by day her strength grew, her cognition returned, and her voice became stronger.

Being here gave her purpose and will to continue.

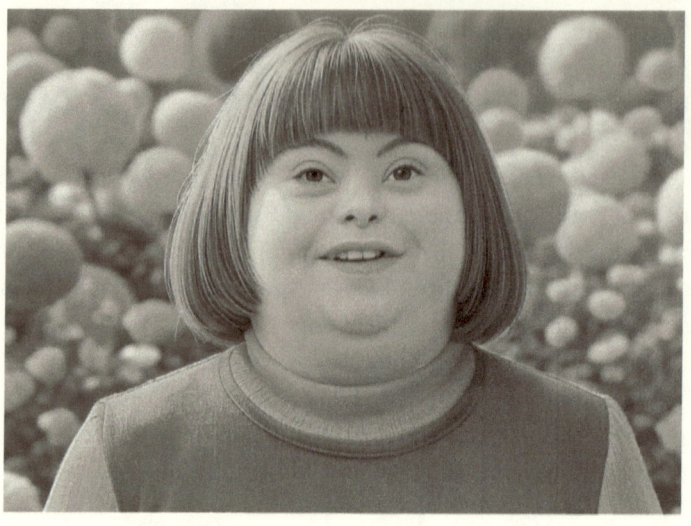

Daphne

DAPHNE HAD A round face framed by an oval pageboy haircut. Everything about her was round: hands, feet and body. Her laugh was round and so was her attitude toward life. Downie. Down's Syndrome. She understood little about life, but that did not stop her from being relentlessly cheerful.

As a small school, Cement City High only had six special-needs kids. Daphne was one of the six, a senior. She had a job…bagging groceries at the supermarket. On some long weekends, she took home fifty dollars in tips…carefully stuffed into a pot-bellied piggy bank. Her dad routinely cleaned out the pig and deposited the money in a credit union account. Her balance was over $6,000.

Almost everyone loved Daphne, but there were always those few…

Before school, unless Fiona had another visitor, Daphne would stop in to discuss the previous day and her upcoming plan for the day…the only things she knew anything about. Today was a big day. She had a date in the woods with Stan.

Stan had been grooming Daphne for months and this was finally the payoff. He spent time with her and gave her little gifts—all in secret.

Today, she had a pink ribbon in her hair and wore her best jumper, white socks and saddle shoes.

"I'm getting flowers," Daphne said. "At lunch. Flowers." She giggled. "Stan will wait behind the little shed."

At the far corner of the school property, the little shed wasn't used anymore. It held rusty, abandoned rakes, shovels and rotting, forgotten hoses. A normal girl would know meeting a boy there was a bad idea.

A very bad idea.

Fiona wondered what she should do.

Daphne deserved a good life. She had a supportive family with means—in no way was she a burden on society. Fiona knew the plan. Stan and his pals planned to run a train on Daphne. Fiona didn't know what that was until she googled it and then wished she hadn't. Fiona's mind ran amuck. She considered many options—including calling the police or gathering a sympathetic group of football players to beat the train *engineers* into bloody pulps. She even considered finding a pistol somewhere and shooting those nasty boys. Surely they deserved it for even thinking of violating an innocent girl. And, there was no one more innocent than Daphne. She was and always would be a child—even if her body was mature.

However, there was no way Fiona would get a gun. She'd never touched one and never would. But the problem remained.

What should she do?

While the girl babbled, Fiona studied Daphne and knew something. Daphne was innocent, but was not helpless. She had power. Perhaps she could use a little nudge.

With her mind and spirit, Fiona reached out.

At noon, Daphne couldn't wait. With her hair flying and heels kicking up dust, she ran from the playroom. As inconspicuous as she could be, Fiona followed. The boys were waiting—Stan and his three friends. Behind the shed, the grass was trampled and considerately, they'd spread a blanket.

As certain as anything, Fiona knew the boys were about to learn a valuable lesson. She didn't know how she knew, but there was no doubt. The wind in the trees settled. Except for a faint hissing from trucks on the highway, there was total silence. From a hundred feet away, Fiona could hear everything.

"Hello, Stan," Daphne said. "Where are my flowers?"

"We'll get to the flowers later. Come and lay down on this nice blanket."

"Why are your friends here?"

"We're going to play a game. It's fun. Let me lift up your dress."

"I like games—very much I do. Almost as much as I like flowers. And you, Stan. I like you a lot."

"I'm going to pull down your panties, but it's okay because I love you."

"I'm not supposed to let you touch me there. Not until we're married." She raised her hand and wiggled her wedding finger. "You gotta put a ring on it."

"It's okay," Stan said.

"Stuff a sock in her fat mouth."

"No, that's my favorite part," Stan said.

Fiona heard the sound of zippers—then panic.

"Where is my..."

"What happened to my..."

Fiona couldn't see, but she imagined them looking like Ken-dolls—smooth and featureless in their midsections.

One of the boys screamed.

"What is happening to us?"

Like the devil was on their heels, they ran past Fiona.

The spell would wear off in an hour and they'd be fine.

Daphne was in no hurry. As she strolled past Fiona, she spoke with a loud, happy voice,

"I like flowers," she said.

Fiona Gets Stronger

THE DAYS MELTED into each other in an endless stream of solitary hours punctuated by the noisy bustle of the hallways and the kids who visited and shared their problems.

Slowly, something occurred to her.

Day by day, she was getting stronger—both in body and mind.

After midnight, she spent time in the school gym dribbling and shooting baskets on the hardwood court, lifting free weights and stretching on a borrowed yoga mat. She walked the hallways and up and down stairs all around the building and helped Enrique mop lonely corners where the buffer would not reach. Like her, he did not speak, but he did not need to.

They communicated just fine without words.

In her wandering, she heard voices but often couldn't make sense of them. From the magic land, she heard faint voices and wished her friends would stop by to visit. Then, one day as she sat up from the nurse's office trundle bed, they were real. Sebastian and Brutus bowed deeply, and Sebastian hopped on her lap.

"Fiona, do you remember me?"

Fiona smiled and nodded.

"My beloved Sebastian from lifetimes ago and yesterday all at the same time. And Brutus, I remember you too. Tell me, what am I doing here?"

Sebastian and Brutus looked at each other as if wondering how much to say.

"Think of this as a halfway house—a gentle stage of life between the magic and hard worlds."

"I know that, silly. What am I supposed to do here?"

"Whatever you're doing, of course. That's what you're supposed to do. Just like the rest of us. We do what we do."

Fiona blew out an exasperated breath.

"Okay, let's try this. How does all this work?" She waved her arms all around. "Most people around here can't see you. You're from a strange land where the rules are different. In fact, you're from a place where there are no rules. Animals talk. Faeries fly. Rocks think. Spirits are real. It's very confusing."

"That's easy," Sebastian said. "Rules are what you think they are. If you free your mind, anything is possible because nothing really exists. Everything is a construct of the fat and saltwater of your brain. From your senses, your mind constantly creates reality. And what are your senses? Nothing, that's what. Electrical signals connecting to nothing. See, hear, feel? Ha! Just waveforms…nothing physical. The physical does not exist, you just think it does."

Brutus sputtered.

"Nonsense, poppycock and equine manure." He glanced at Fiona. "I apologize for the crude imagery, m'lady. This is no time to think of steaming horse biscuits, Of course the objective world exists. Our senses and brains are imperfect and thus our understanding of the universe is flawed—we don't completely understand the cosmos and its laws, so some things seem mysterious and will until we have better models, equations, formulas and algorithms. But, one day, our math will be good enough and we will figure it all out."

"You always say that," Sebastian complained, "but you don't really exist, so it doesn't matter what you say."

"I *do* exist and if you keep saying I don't, I will punch you in the head and we'll see what's what. Maybe a fractured skull will convince you."

Fiona pushed Sebastian off her lap.

It was obvious these two had been having this argument for a long time.

They were not helping.

There was time for a quick shower before the teachers arrived.

Philip d'GreenApple: Ponderosa

WHEN I WOKE, the cab was uncomfortably warm and the humidity was high. Thunderstorm weather. Tornado weather.

My parking place was remote. My bladder was hot and swollen. After taking a quick look around to assure privacy, I let loose a rusty stream into the thirsty gravel. I was dirty and smelled bad. My mouth felt like it was coated with fungus. I wet my toothbrush with bottled water, then coated it with salt from a baggie. Why my fellow truckers brushed their teeth this way, I have no idea, but I felt better after rinsing my mouth and spitting out the salt water.

Leaning against the truck's fender, I looked around and wondered what I was doing here. I had no distinct memories of what I had dreamed about, but there were flashes before my eyes like tired clichés. The Black King surrounded by ugly, mythical creatures. In particular, the woman dressed in reeking raw leather with tusks like a boar. One tusk a stub, broken off. The illusions a mind could conjure were embarrassing.

The stink didn't hit me all at once; it crept in slow, like regret. My nose started complaining. I should've peed farther away. But that was just the surface. What I really needed was a long, hot shower—and a new life.

My belly growled. I wanted breakfast, but not here. It was after 9:00, so Tierra Bendita would be open. I had wads of pesos, so I could afford to get a breakfast burrito. I hauled myself into the truck's cab and drove. Breakfast was good enough. The service was friendly, but the burrito was nothing special. After eating with the drivers for a couple of weeks, everything tasted bland unless it sopped with hot sauce and chilis. The restaurant was close to the international bridge, and I thought about just driving across and carrying on as fast and as far as the V8 would take me. Maybe Vargas wouldn't miss me, but sure as anything he would track down his truck. Besides, the idea did not seem right. I was not done here yet. That said, I was in no hurry to get back.

The Mexicans are crazy about baseball, but the Bravos de Acuña were not playing so I didn't bother with driving to the Estadio Emilio Sosa ball field. I didn't even know if it was baseball season. Too bad, the colorful spectacle would make for a pleasant afternoon.

Aimless, I wandered the dirty streets. I was filthy enough that no one bothered me except I was claimed by a skinny kid named Pablo. He was determined to help me with whatever I might buy. He tried everything. Onyx chess sets. Enameled toads playing fiddles. Scorpions in Lucite. Mescal and Tequila. Loco weed. Cubanos cigars. Antibiotics. Pain killers. Ritalin. Viagra. Coca powder. He seemed particularly baffled that I did not want to meet his virgin sister. Apparently, she was very friendly. I bought three boxes of Chiclets gum from a six-year-old girl and gave them to him.

His English was good but seemed weird. Then I realized he was speaking a mix of Spanish and English garbled together. I was taken aback when I realized how much I understood and how I hadn't noticed his mix of languages. I didn't know what it meant about me. Nothing good.

After nearly an hour of cajoling, he decided I was a lost cause and wandered off.

I didn't know where the day went, so, as monstrous thunderheads gathered and the afternoon waned, I walked back to the pickup. It was time to head back.

By the time I arrived back at the warehouse, the sun cast long shadows toward the east. In the distance, lightning stabbed the Earth and distant rumbles of thunder washed all around us. I walked up to a table of animated Konkan players and watched them for a few minutes. Raul looked up at me.

"Vargas has been looking for you," he said. "Better hustle to HQ."

HQ was a two-story compound. I had not been inside, but I heard it was nice. Really nice. In no hurry, I strolled across the yard. By the time I reached the front door, I was pelted with giant raindrops. There were two guards.

When did face tattoos become a thing?

These guys did not need them. They would be plenty scary without facial ink. The one on the left popped open the door and waved me in.

The scene inside was a surprise. Outside, it was rusty metal and looked decrepit. Inside, it was a ranch house lit with hurricane lamps with buck horns on the walls, a hanging chandelier made from a wagon wheel and a huge stone fireplace with a set of Texas longhorns mounted above. The stuffed furniture was maroon and to the right of the fireplace was a huge glass case filled with old rifles. To the left was a fancy dining room. The inside walls were peeler logs with gaps filled with mortar.

Vargas sat at a desk drinking something brown from a China coffee cup. He gestured for me to sit.

"Recognize the place?" he said. "Ponderosa Ranch."

I must have looked baffled. That would make sense, since I was.

"From the TV show," he continued. "Bonanza?"

I shrugged.

He looked despondent.

"Young people don't know anything. Hoss? Adam? Ben Cartwright from one of the most iconic and popular TV series of all time? We duplicated the ranch house to the last detail."

"Cool," I said.

He gave up and leaned back in his chair.

"I hear very good things about you."

I didn't know what to say.

"Cool," I ventured again.

Weak. I know.

"It's dangerous for me to cross over, but you and me…we're taking a run—right after we make a man of you."

I didn't care for the sound of that. I was a kid and wanted to stay that way—at least for a while.

What did it even mean?

"Want a belt, before? To settle your nerves?"

Before what?

"I don't drink. I don't even take aspirin."

He nodded.

"I heard that about you. I respect that. Go up the stairs. Second door on the right."

I'm naïve. I admit it. I still didn't know what he was talking about.

His face hardened.

"You'll go now," he said.

"I'm fifteen," I said. "Just turned."

He exploded.

"I don't care. Get your ass up there and don't come back down until you know more about what life is all about." With a fingernail, he fished something out of his cup—which he flicked away. "*Mosca chingona*," he said. "Damned houseflies think they own the place."

I was in no hurry. I took the stairs one-by-one while studying the details of the elaborately carved walnut staircase. Eventually, I stood with my hand on the doorknob of the second door on the right. I let the moment stretch as long as I could before turning the knob and walking inside.

Ken Coffman and Kristen Lolatte

Philip d'GreenApple: Girl

YOU'RE PROBABLY WAY ahead of me.
Inside the room, there was a girl.

Fiona: Black Death 2

UNTIL IT APPEARED before her, there was something Fiona did not want to think about…what the kids called Black Death. That day, it was early. Calvin sat before her and mumbled.

"I can't do this anymore," Calvin said.

That's easy, Fiona thought. Whatever it is, just stop.

"We're hurting kids. I don't know what to do."

This was true. Two kids had died and one was in the hospital.

To get out of a hole, the first thing to do is stop digging.

It was a stupid cliché, but Fiona couldn't prevent herself from thinking it.

Calvin's voice had a whiny tone.

"You're supposed to help. Tara said you helped."

I don't work here and I don't know that I'm supposed to do anything. I don't have a contract or a job description. I'm just here.

She sat, looked at Calvin and said nothing.

He pulled a wad of money from his overalls. It wasn't all ones, there were twenties and hundreds in the mix.

From counting tips, she had a knack.

It was at least a thousand dollars.

"I don't want this money. It's dirty."

I don't want it either.

After a minute, she made no move to take the money, so he stuffed it back in his pockets.

"I didn't take it directly. This was clear. Zeke gets all the money, then he hands back my commission. So, I will give him the cash back and I'm done. All I ever did was what he told me. I'll undo my part of it. What else can I do? Thanks, that's helpful."

After his decision, relief was genuine, but she couldn't tell if his last comment was sarcastic.

Trevir: Sales Meeting

THE COST OF THE private jet landing at the Skagit regional airport was far more than any profit Trevir would earn from sales at Cement City High School, but he didn't care. Something was wrong and he would not rest easy until they figured it out and solved the problem. To him, the strategic was always more important than the tactical.

As always when visiting the Pacific Northwest, Troll Srenzo enjoyed the green landscape and clean air. On rare days when the weather was good, there was nowhere more beautiful. However, as they traveled upward into the foothills, her unease increased. For her taste, this was too close to the troll's final battleground. Surely it was imagined, but she thought she saw troll smoke on the horizon.

It took a little more than an hour before the driver pulled the leased Escalade into the high school parking lot. She pointed to the corner and the driver eased the car around.

With one exception, the cars were the rusted-out beaters she remembered. The exception was a shiny, cherry-red Camaro with wide tires and a crumpled fender. The windshield in the passenger area was starred with cracks fanning out from an impact area. For whatever accident they had, the driver had been wearing a seatbelt. The unfortunate passenger had not.

Troll Senzo smiled with approval.

She pressed the control button and the tinted window servoed down. The lanky kid with pockmarked face approached. Proud of herself, she remembered his name.

Zeke.

He immediately launched into his speech.

"I'm up to date. Online banking transactions, just like you told me. You never told me how much to charge, so if it ain't enough, that's on you."

"Sales are soft, "Troll Srenzo said. "The boss does not like the trend."

Zeke pulled a quart-sized freezer bag from his jacket pocket. It was stuffed full of gleaming black pills.

"I have the inventory. No one is stealing from you. Take it back if you want."

She glanced at the bag.

"We want money, not product. Why are your sales going down? They should be increasing."

Zeke's voice had a shrill tone.

"F-F-S. Some of our customers died. Is that my fault?" His desperate brain landed on an idea. "There's a woman. A waitress from upriver. In the old nurse's office, she talks to people and they stop buying. Well, not exactly talk. I don't know what she does. She doesn't talk, but you know what I mean. Go see her. Tell her to stop and sales will go up, I promise."

Troll Srenzo's lips twitched.

A promise from this creep was not something she could take to the bank. However, her curiosity was piqued. She would find this woman and sort things out. She reached over and tapped the driver on the shoulder.

"Leave the engine running," she said. "I'll be right back."

After marching up the steps and pushing through the main entrance, she stopped at the reception desk.

Harriet looked up.

"Sign in, please."

"I will not be signing in," Troll Srenzo said with a mental push. "Which way to the nurse's office?"

Harriet pointed.

As the troll continued down the hallway, unconscious students cleared the way. When she got to the nurse's office, Patty stood by the door.

"She's with someone," Patty said. "I wasn't listening in."

Troll Srenzo grunted and pushed by the tiny woman. Inside, Fiona was with a strung-out girl. The name filled Troll Srenzo's mind.

April.

She remembered April but was surprised she was still alive.

Barely.

She was emaciated and dirty. Her lank hair was greasy. Startled as she sipped from a steaming cup of tea, she spilled half of it. Shaky hands. Nervous tremors. A front tooth was missing. Her skin was covered with lesions. This girl was nearly done. Zeke would need a new customer soon.

Troll Srenzo searched her conscience. She should care but didn't. This girl was a bug and had no one to blame but herself.

That wasn't wholly true, the sad girl had a tough ride.

Her problems started from one of her mother's boyfriends. "Uncle" Wesley. Then, chronic pain from a broken leg that didn't heal right. Recently, the only good thing in her life was the black pills, but they didn't work as well as they once did and coming off them wracked her body and soul with pain. However, her pain would end.

Soon.

Troll Srenzo pulled up a chair and sat beside April, then slowly raised her eyes to gaze at the woman across the desk.

"This one is mine," the troll said.

Her eyes finally found Fiona's face.

"Oh," the troll said. "I know you. I even remember your name. Fiona. What did you do to my trolls? And don't say you did nothing, because that would be a damned lie. A filthy, lame-ass, fake excuse for mass murder. You think you're pure and high and mighty, but you're a disgusting, evil monster."

Inside, Fiona was scared to death. The tall woman she faced wore a mask. The mask was attractive. Wide, blue eyes. Lustrous black hair. A silk blouse, unbuttoned to show off mounds of plump breasts. But, with her head tilted at just the right angle, Fiona could see her, really *see* her. Broken fang, tufts of bristle on her chin, everything. Evil in the flesh.

But, also, this creature had no choice. She was Trevir's slave. It was slavery she embraced and nurtured, but still, she had no free will. Deep inside, she wanted to live in peace with her husband, Kelpht, the ohrkk, but had no power to make it happen.

This beast would kill Fiona without a second thought. She could see blood dripping down the monster's chin as it ate her heart. A part of her wanted to lay down and let it be—get this hard life done. Like April, let her troubles be over and enjoy blissful peace.

The black emptiness of peace. She yearned for it.

But...

No.

From her spine, she felt power. The power of good from the Earth. The power of love. The power of the grateful joy of being alive. It flickered inside her, fitful and weak, but growing.

With a claw, Troll Srenzo reached out to flick April's carotid artery. It would be a mercy—an end to needless suffering. It was so inevitable, the spray of pulsing blood already flowed.

But...

No.

For an instant, a bleak despair washed over Fiona.

April's fate was not up to Fiona.

April had to choose for herself, and the weight of the cruel world had crushed her. She was already gone, destroyed by pain, destroyed by suffering, destroyed by the hard people who made her a victim of sad circumstance.

Fiona looked around for a weapon but found nothing. A knife. A hammer. Anything. Her eyes rested on a brochure. Evergreen Pines treatment center. The booklet was colorful—a cartoon hiding the harsh reality of painful recovery. The subtitle was chilling.

Boot camp for lost souls.

At a boot camp, they broke you down. They terrorized and traumatized you into nothing—an empty vessel that could be refilled with a new personality.

It was expensive, but helped some people, including a few famous ones. At the same time, this is where the actor Penelope Phelps committed suicide. And, the rock star, Mel Anderson. They didn't make it, but April might if someone believed in her and could finance her journey.

With the razor-claw hovering a fraction of an inch from her death, April looked at the brochure Fiona pushed across the desk and decided.

She pushed the troll's hand away and reached for the booklet.

It was worth a try.

Inside, Fiona shuddered with relief.

That was close. Too close.

Troll Srenzo growled with frustration, turned and raised both claws. Enough of this nonsense, she thought.

Fiona summoned and for an instant thought there was no hope.

Then, from the walls and the Earth, came energy that flowed around April and protected her. Troll Srenzo recoiled like she'd been electrocuted. She turned to face Fiona.

"This is not over," she said.

Fiona raised her hands, palms up.

Let me show you something.

Fiona let herself go. Her atoms and molecules aligned with the fabric of the universe and she disappeared. Everything was waves and fragments of waves. Formless. Structureless. Dissolved like sugar in tea.

Concentrating, she pulled herself back together, then reached for her paper pad and pen. She scribbled a note to the troll.

You can disappear.

Troll Srenzo shuddered.

"How did you do that?"

Fiona shrugged.

It didn't matter how it was done. Once you knew it was possible, you could figure it out.

Fiona gestured.

"You can't have my treasure," Troll Srenzo said.

Impatient, Fiona gestured again.

Troll Srenzo rolled her eyes. *Pussywillow*, she mumbled, then pulled a leather bag from the pocket of her jerkin. She weighed it in her palm before dropping it on the desktop. Then she left.

As soon as the door closed, Fiona felt like her bones had liquefied. She melted into her chair like a jellyfish. April was stunned and senseless—clutching the colorful brochure to her chest like a rescue rope.

Patty poked her head in.

"Is everything all right in here?" she said.

Fiona pointed at the brochure clutched in April's desperate fingers.

"It's expensive," Patty said.

Fiona summoned enough energy to shrug, then pointed at the leather sack on the desk. Gold coins.

They had enough.

Outside, after walking across the parking lot, Troll Srenzo opened the SUV door. Inside, laying on the passenger seat was the plastic bag of pills. She looked around. The cars were gone.

Trevir was not going to be happy.

Trevir: We Need a New Drug

ON THE SEVENTEENTH floor with a stunning view of the Seattle skyline, the executive team was gathered around the conference room table.

"I need answers," Trevir shouted.

After a few uncomfortable moments, one of the nerds mumbled.

Trevir stomped over.

"I didn't catch that," he said.

"It would help if our product didn't kill our customers."

Trevir wanted to twist off the man's head but stifled the impulse.

"Unhelpful," he said.

"Sir, if I might…"

This speaker was young. Too young. He looked like he was twelve.

"And you are?"

"Albert Woo. Chief Financial Officer."

"What happened to the last CFO?" Trevir said. "Oh, right—flayed and dissolved in acid. Fun day. Speak your mind."

"You have fourteen-billion in cash and cash equivalents. You could spend a million dollars a day and not touch the principal. Why not declare victory and cruise around the world with Miami yacht girls? You could replace them every five minutes when you got bored."

Trevir crouched so he was at eye-level with the lad. His tone was dangerously mild. The young man didn't have enough sense to be scared.

"Let me guess…that's what you would do."

"Sure, why not? The finest wine. The prettiest girls. An endless search for eternal sunshine."

Trevir stood and walked to the windows to look out over the city, then turned to address the room.

"That's why you're you and I'll be President of the world. Worship me—or die screaming. We need a new drug. Let's have your ideas. Now."

The nerd raised his hand.

"Ozempic, Adderall, fentanyl, mescaline. Thinner, smarter, painless. Calibrate the doses and customers won't die right away."

Trevir grinned.

"That's what I'm talking about. Fresh ideas. What else do you have?"

Albert raised his hand. Trevir crouched before him.

"Speak. What?"

The young man's voice broke.

"By my calculations, you need a thousand psychopaths to work in sales."

Trevir stood and resumed his pacing.

"Great. How are we going to find them? Not next year. Now. There's no time to recruit and train them."

Albert took a sip of water.

"You have money, sir. Go to where they already are and buy them. Start with state governments and go up from there. Washington, DC."

Trevir stopped, turned and stared.

"I'm beginning to like you, kid," he said.

Fiona Hits the Road

SOMEHOW, FIONA HAD acquired a suitcase—it was filled with donations. Toothpaste. Clean socks and panties. With a jacket folded over her arm and an umbrella—one didn't dare going anywhere in the PNW without an umbrella—she stood inside the nurse's office door and looked around, trying to figure out what was forgotten. She hadn't come with much; she was leaving with a little more. She'd miss the smell of the place. And the kids. She'd miss them a lot. But she was done, and it was time to move on.

Fiona didn't want any fanfare. She'd arrived quietly and wanted to leave the same way.

There was a side door. Emergency Exit. A sign said an alarm would sound, but that was a lie. Everyone knew the alarm was disconnected.

She didn't hesitate—she pushed through and walked around the building to the parking lot. The whole school was assembled at a pep rally—cheering and stomping their feet. She was urged to attend but refused. Through hallway chatter, she learned they planned to give her an award, but Fiona was not there for awards, gifts, plaques or trophies.

She still didn't know why she was there, but it wasn't for honors.

It was a mystery.

She turned to look back at the school. It wasn't perfect and never would be, but there was a subtle glow around it. It was headed in the right direction. Good kids would pass through its doors and wander its hallways. Productive lives would be launched and lifelong relationships would be forged.

She looked toward the corner where the Parking Lot Gang usually gathered. It was lonely and abandoned—just oil-spotted asphalt and empty, wind-blown fast-food containers. She fought an impulse to find a garbage bag and clean up the place. If she started cleaning, she'd never be done and would never leave.

It was an unwholesome thought, but in this case it was one hundred percent true.

Cleanup was someone else's job.

On the highway, she stuck out her thumb.

In a very few minutes, she had a ride and was gone.

After three rides, she stood by the I-5 offramp in Mount Vernon. Across the highway, the cheery yellow and blue sign of a Denny's restaurant called her. Sitting at the breakfast bar, without thinking, she violated her sacred vow of silence and ordered a thousand calories of pecan and banana pancakes.

She thought about her journey—the personalities, the vehicles and scenery. All her deep thoughts. All her emotions. The weather, the lonely periods where no one would stop, the inevitable smell of beer, vapes, yesterday's lunch, cigarettes and flatulence. It was like a grand Ken Kesey adventure. Sometimes Another Great Notion with modern day cops, cowboys, traveling saleswomen and ranchers.

She overheard an older man telling the cashier he was going to Everett. All dressed in white with a golf polo, slacks, shoes and belt, he didn't look like a serial killer. She gathered her courage.

"Excuse me, sir. I could use a ride to the bus station. Everett Station."

He looked her up and down.

"I don't generally pick up lady hitchers." He pointed at his wedding ring. "False allegations, get it? Imagine it, the missus gets in my car and it smells like Bum Bum Cream. But, you look like a schoolteacher. I'll move my golf bag to the backseat and give you a lift if you promise not to stab me in the liver with a pig-sticker."

She crossed her heart.

"I promise," she said.

Philip d'GreenApple: Rope Swing

I STOOD IN the doorway looking at her. Pretty, she was dressed like an Old West housemaid with petticoats and a bonnet. We were about the same age. We stared at each other for a few seconds before she got up and pushed the door closed behind me. She recoiled at my scent.

"Lordy," she said. "You stink like a dead cat." She gestured at a door. "Take a shower. Scrub up good. In the washroom, there is a plastic garbage bag. Put your clothes in and we'll burn them later. For jobs like this, they should at least give me a clothespin. Seeing confusion written on my face, she continued. "To plug my nose. Get it? With a clothespin on account that you stink so much." She pointed. "Go. Now. Go."

I eased around her and headed to the bathroom.

She stopped me.

"When you come out, you want me dressed or not?"

I couldn't help myself. I looked her up and down. She was small and delicate, maybe five-foot-two.

"Dressed, I think," I said.

She nodded.

"Most men want to undress a girl themselves. Part of their fun. I get it. You wash good. Everywhere. Do you understand? I want you clean from head to toe and everywhere in between. Use the toiletries. Deodorant. There's no hurry—we have all night."

"Got it," I said.

I walked in the bathroom and turned the privacy lock. The door could be opened in two seconds with a paperclip, but it was better than nothing.

She was right. I needed a shower—maybe as much as any boy ever did. Fresh clothes were laid out. They thought of everything. I cleaned out my pockets and was surprised at how much I was carrying. Money. Folding knife. Keys. *Pulparindo* candies. Fingernail clippers.

Then, as she demanded, my old clothes went in the garbage bag—carefully tied to trap the stench.

In the shower, I scrubbed until the water ran clear. It took a while. After, I wiped steam from the mirror and looked at myself. Apparently, under all the dirt, there was a boy. A boy I barely recognized. There was a little fuzz on my chin. I decided to leave it. I rubbed Old Spice under my armpits and dressed in the clean clothes. Someone knew my sizes well enough. The jeans, belt and Amistad Reservoir t-shirt fit fine…loose enough to be comfortable. I tied the laces on the Adidas running shoes. I could not stall any longer. I was clean and dressed.

"You still alive in there?" she called out.

The bathroom had a window. I was afraid to look out because it was my only chance to escape. If there was no way out and no way to clamber to the ground—I'm not sure what I would do. I confess, I considered just going along with the plan. She was pretty, with a personality that seemed too pleasant for the job. Who knows? Maybe she'd be in big trouble if she did not complete her assignment.

Her assignment being me, of course.

I wasn't afraid. My overwhelming emotion was curiosity. The universe would do what it wanted with me. Maybe this was the way it was supposed to go. But I didn't think so. A path that started with her and me getting intimate led to many other things. Pleasurable things, maybe. A man without vices isn't a man, I know that. But we had to control them—not the opposite.

I opened the window and peeked. It was a long way to the packed

Earth. I'd break my neck if I jumped. There was a giant oak tree—too far away to reach the nearest branches. Then I noticed a truck tire hanging on a rope from a tall branch. If someone untied the tire and threw me the rope...

A hundred feet away, a boy sat under another tree playing with a flashlight.

He waved.

I gestured for him to approach.

After a few seconds of confusion...

Yes, you, boy.

He ran up and I whispered what I wanted.

He nodded and got to work untying the rope from the tire.

It took a few throws, but, leaning out, I finally grabbed the end of the rope. Assuming the branch held, I would put my foot in the loop, soar out into the air and safely reach the ground after some gut-wrenching swaying.

I took a deep breath, then stepped out into the void.

Fiona: Greyhound Flixbus

IT WASN'T RAINING, but a steady, characteristic Pacific Northwest mist dampened her hair as Fiona stood beneath the glow of a lonely streetlight at the bus stop. There were other lights on poles, but they were all smashed and broken. Across the bustling street where cars and trucks sloshed on the glistening roadway, Everett Station stood with its vibrant, historic mural shimmering faintly through the haze. One-way ticket. No return. The journey to Medford, Oregon would take 18 hours and 25 minutes, give or take. Why south? Why Medford? She didn't know. She just knew that's where her path led. Was she ready? No. Would she ever be ready? Probably not.

Is any great Queen ever ready to take up her rightful throne?

Deep down, she knew it. No way. She laughed to herself.

Queen my ass. I'm no queen. I'm nobody and lost like everyone else. But I guess I'll be lost down south.

And east.

The Greyhound pulled up and idled for a few moments. The drivers switched, and then Fiona boarded. She showed her ticket.

"Ah, another one headed for Arizona, I see," the driver said as he settled in his seat. "Well, make yourself comfortable, miss. This carriage will be your home for a good while."

Arizona? Who said anything about Arizona?

Other than the vague feeling that her route would go east from Medford, she didn't know where she was headed.

Fiona smiled and looked around. Most travelers were sleeping or half-asleep. No one seemed dangerous—or at least, not as far as Fiona could sense. The bus was less than half full, so there were many seats to choose from. She met eyes with a dreadlocked young woman. They smiled at each other.

"Ah, that is where I shall go," Fiona mused.

Quiet like a cat, Fiona walked up the aisle.

"Is it okay if I join you?" she asked.

The girl nodded. She seemed relieved to have protection. Strength in numbers. Fiona thought she looked like a baby bird flung from the nest all too early.

"Fiona, be gentle with this one," she told herself.

Within a short span of time, the bus began to move. The engine found its rhythm and began its long southward drive. As soon as they left the city, for a few minutes before the lights of Seattle conquered, the sky was black as ink. Stars showed themselves like lights through a Lite-Brite. Fiona smiled; she had always loved her Lite-Brite and refused to follow the patterns, instead creating her own worlds—worlds no one else could understand. Adults called her works *chaos*, *unmanageable*, or worse, *nothing*.

The girl spoke quietly.

"Imagine we're trapped in a paper cup covered with ink-black paper and pierced with a scatter of air holes. What if those twinkling stars are not distant suns but beams of light piercing through, cast on us by a single, mysterious source? Picture a cosmic lantern with a glow fractured into a constellation of holes, shining down on our fragile world with an ethereal dance of shadows and light."

Fiona looked at her and said, "Maybe we're a grand experiment by neurotic aliens. If so, I hope they're learning a lot."

The young girl smiled.

"I knew I liked you. My name is Nova. Nice to meet you."

"My name is Fiona. Tell me your story, Nova. I can tell you have one, and I'd love to hear it if you're willing to share."

Nova let out a sigh.

"Who sent you, Fiona?"

Fiona took the question seriously, but the idea that she was important enough to get sent anywhere was silly.

"Life is a pinball game and I just go where the cosmic flippers send me."

Fiona studied the girl. She had long dreads—not tidy, neat ones done in a salon. These were real, with beads and feathers scattered here and there among the braids. Nova was a light brunette with streaks of blond and red highlights. She had big, beautiful blue eyes that seemed to change color.

Was it a trick of the light?

They would shift to green or gray, blue or blue-gray, and sometimes a brilliant blue. It was all very subtle, but for those who watched, it was magical. Nova had full, pouty lips and a piercing through her septum, through which a delicate hoop was displayed. A spattering of freckles crossed her nose and cheeks, giving her a childlike quality. She was bundled in leggings and Birkenstocks, a bulky sweatshirt, and a quilted crossbody bag. She had a big backpack in the overhead storage, which Fiona surmised contained all her worldly possessions.

Nova took a deep breath and looked out the window at the bright lights of the city blurred by rain.

"My mom said she'd help me, support me, stand by me, but it's their job to say that, I suppose. She supported me, alright—supported me right down to the bus station and told me to go far, far away. She didn't really want any part of helping to raise a baby. You see, Fiona, I'm pregnant. Seventeen and pregnant. I had a lapse in a movie theater bathroom. He said he had a condom and I just wanted to feel something. Anything. It was stupid and I didn't think anything of it. I missed my period but still didn't think anything of it until my boobs started hurting. I picked up three pregnancy tests; figured one test could be wrong, but not all three. Lo and behold, all three showed I had a little bun in the oven. I went to Planned Parenthood, and they confirmed it. I told my mom; she said it was my decision. I told my therapist. I asked her what about all the meds I'm on—would I have to come off them? Would the baby be born addicted? I have ADHD and schizophrenia; my therapist said the baby would be fine."

Turning away, she scrawled something in the fog on the window. Something random. A rune or something she'd seen spray painted on an alley wall. It meant something, but Fiona didn't want to overthink.

"My mom said she hoped nature would take care of this, but nature has a different idea of what is and should be. So, she sent me on my way. So here I am, headed south. Alone. Seventeen and pregnant. That's my story. Glamorous, huh?"

Fiona sat quietly. Such an odd little bird—strong yet scared, independent yet yearning for a mother's touch and advice.

So close, yet so far away.

"For what it's worth, Nova, I believe you and your little one have an incredible future ahead of you."

"Are you just saying that, Fiona, or do you really believe it?"

"You don't know me, Nova, but I have a sense of people. I can read energy. And you, my dear, are very strong. You're scared, and rightfully so. This is all new for you. It wasn't planned, but you're not one to shy away from a challenge. You know what I see? Family and a home. A new one. A different kind. Family isn't always your own flesh and blood; family comes in all shapes, sizes and colors. And a home like a bird's nest. Get it?"

Nova looked skeptical.

"What do you want? I don't have any money. I don't even have food—not since breakfast. Yesterday. Is this religious—some kind of holy roller thing? Will you give me pamphlet? A tiny Bible?"

This made Fiona smile. An hour earlier, she wasn't hungry but—on impulse—had bought a ham sandwich and a Snapple at the AM/PM convenience store. They were stuffed in her jacket pocket.

"I don't know anything about religion, but I don't have a problem with it if it helps you sleep at night. We all need to find our own way." Fiona shifted in her seat, raised her hands and wiggled her fingers. "I know a magic trick. Want to see it?"

Nova shook her head.

"I don't got nothing better to do at the moment."

That wasn't good logic, but Fiona let it slide.

She reached in her jacket pocket.

"Presto! I conjure a sandwich."

Nakedly hungry, Nova stared at it. Fiona dropped it on the girl's lap.

"I couldn't possibly…" Nova said.

"Shush and eat. Guess what? That's not all."

She pulled out the peach tea Snapple.

While tearing the sandwich' plastic wrap with her teeth, Nova said, "That's my favorite."

Fiona laughed.

"Of course it is, dear," she said.

It took nearly the last of her cash, but at Medford's Front Street Amtrak station, Fiona bought Nova a train ticket to LA. Nova's dad's sister lived in Glendale and would probably take her in. Nova protested but eventually took Fiona's remaining cash. It wasn't much. Maybe a hundred bucks. While watching the old train trundle off, Fiona wondered.

What now?

She would go south eventually, but not quite yet.

It's no good standing around.

She walked eastward down Central Avenue. Half a block away, a scent teased her nose. She walked faster and caught sight of the awning.

Butterbloom Bakery.

In the window was displayed a slice of cake—orange with honey buttercream. It looked so good, Fiona's knees grew weak. Dragging her eyes away, she saw in the corner of the window a handwritten sign with near-professional calligraphy.

Help Wanted

And in smaller print…

Overnight shift—Pie Maker

Working in a bakery is hard work. Brutal. And working all day and sleeping all day really stinks. She hadn't even started yet and her back and knees ached.

She walked in. The owner looked up as the doorbells tinkled. Pale, she had flushed cheeks dusted with flour and streaky blonde tangled hair pulled up in a scrunchy. Her nametag said Kimber.

"Does the pie-maker job include lunch—payable up front?" Fiona said.

Kimber laughed.

"Only if you like spicy bison chili and cornbread."

Fiona had never heard of anything that sounded so good.

Kimber pointed at the outdoor camp tables.

"Plunk yourself. I'll assemble a bowl, and we'll talk."

Fiona: Buttercream Clouds

KIMBER, LIKE FIONA, had an innate sense of people. As she fixed up a heaping bowl of Bison chili and cornbread, she studied Fiona through the kitchen window. Kimber felt the woman radiating as she decompressed and her soul relaxed.

Giving in to an urge, Kimber closed her eyes and thought about what Fiona might like. Chopped green onion was a no-brainer.

Now what?

Radish sprouts.

She arranged a tuft.

There's no sense in going crazy.

The stew already had ancho chilis, black peppercorns and brandy.

The tray looked complete enough after adding a crock of locally churned butter blended with alfalfa honey from a farm upriver. On impulse, she put an absurdly large spoon on the tray—an antique silver serving spoon.

Smart people have a sense of humor.

She only wanted to work with smart people.

After adding a pot of hot water and a collection of teabags to the tray, she walked outside and placed the tray on the picnic table.

Fiona laughed when she saw the spoon.

"You must think I have a mouth like an alligator."

Kimber busied herself with selecting a teabag and did not respond.

"Okay," Fiona muttered.

The spoon was large in her hand…like it belonged to a giant.

It was like a shovel, so Fiona started shoveling and soon scraped the bottom. She polished off the last of the sauce with a fragment of cornbread.

"This is the best meal I've eaten since—" Fiona said. She took a breath. "I'm not normally a meat eater. But this, this could turn anyone around. Sorry, buffalo, but you tasted real good and your sacrifice is appreciated."

"It's my secret recipe. There's magic in every bite."

"Ever think about going vegan?"

Kimber sighed.

"Only every day. For the folks inclined, we offer no-meat dishes. But look around. We have a veneer of modernity, but underneath, this lovely valley is stuck in the 1950s. Today I'd go broke if I led the way, but tomorrow? Who knows? Hope springs eternal."

The silence stretched, broken only by the clink of the giant spoon. Fiona raised her eyebrow and only then noticed Kimber was staring at her.

"How long have you been on the run?" Kimber said.

"Oh, I'm not running. Or maybe I am. I'm not so much running *away* anymore. I'm running *towards*. Trying to build up my strength and resolve for my future, or lack thereof."

"The crows foretold of your coming. Or rather they told me a great pie baker would come and lo and behold, here you are. I'm Kimber. Not Kimberly. Kimber like the handguns my papa liked. So, tell me, Miss…?"

"Did I not say already? Fiona, my name is Fiona. The crows often lie, but this time they told it true. If a hundred customers can be trusted, I make excellent pies. I could bake you freebies to see if they meet with your approval."

With eyes narrowed, Kimber tapped the spoon against her mug as if waiting for a trick to reveal itself.

What could go wrong?

With vigor, the crows complained.

It was like they were saying, "Don't be stupid."

"Hmmm, okay. I like your confidence and your energy. Let's give it a try. When you're done with your tea, peruse what I have in the pantry and walk-in. Surprise me."

Fiona smiled. She liked this Kimber-gun woman.

A good soul, she thought. Young, hardworking and trusting. Out of the box thinker and not afraid to take risks.

"Fruited or sweet?"

Kimber calculated.

"You choose."

"Okay," Fiona said.

Both, she thought.

She could have taken an easy route with her crowd-pleasing Snickers pie, but that felt like cowardice.

"Buttermilk pie it is," she mumbled.

As she toiled away to make the crust from scratch, she found her hands moving in the old familiar way. Muscle memory is a glorious thing.

She began singing along to the upbeat song playing on the Southern Oregon University radio station.

> *I preach what's on my mind, in my heart, and my dream time*
> *But don't be fooled, not pretending I know*
> *Life keeps rolling by and all we can do is try*
> *And send out love, even when it hits a stone...*

Kimber wandered back.

"Ah yes, Xavier Rudd is a favorite of mine too. He is so completely in connection with the Earth and all that is...."

She swayed wistfully to the tune. For a moment she and Fiona shared one spirit.

Yes, Fiona would fit in well here at the Buttercloud Bakery.

Fiona pushed a strand of hair behind her ear, leaving a flour comet across her temple. Like a magician, she gestured at her secret Buttermilk Pie as well as her signature Nectarine-Blackberry Slab pie. Both were unconventional but the taste and textures were irresistible.

"You did all this," Kimber said softly, not a question.

"They did all this," she said, nodding at the pies. "I just listened." She found a towel and wiped her hands. "Seeing is one thing. Tasting is another."

"Don't forget the aroma. They smell heavenly."

"Let's sample them in flights."

"Flights of pie." Kimber grinned. "Buttercloud Airlines."

She stepped inside the kitchen and pointed with a finger hovering over the custard.

"What's this one?"

"Buttermilk. From your fridge. It needed to be used before it went bad."

Kimber laughed.

"How does buttermilk go bad?" she said.

Fiona shrugged.

"Good point," she said.

"We start with this one?"

Fiona nodded.

"It's honest. If it tastes right, the rest will follow."

Kimber made two plates, careful with the knives. She ate like someone meeting a person in private. First bite was assessment, second was a negotiation, third was the handshake. She closed her eyes on the third, the way you do when you want to hold something in your mouth longer than physics allows. When she opened them, Fiona had already guessed.

"You're dangerous," Kimber said. "If people taste this, you'll ruin them for store pies for the rest of their lives."

"They'll forgive me," Fiona said. "Or they won't, and I'll be down the road before they can get mad and burn me at a stake."

Kimber laughed, but it wasn't quite light.

Down the road.

She turned to the slab pie, its fruit glistening with the discipline of a good glaze. She was brave and took a big bite. The black pepper showed up on schedule.

"There it is," she said. "I love that you trust the customer to let the bite be strange before it's perfect."

"I can't bake afraid," Fiona said. "I tried. The pies sulk."

Kimber savored the work and love that went into the baking. She tasted the care in the crust, the daring in the spices.

Fiona watched as the telltale smile appeared on Kimber's face.

"Fiona, you are absolutely exquisite in every sense of the word. I don't know your past or your future, but it would be my honor to have you here, working by my side as long as you'd like. If you need a place, I live above the bakery. It's a little boho studio—plants, books, sunlight. There's a futon you can crash on, full kitchen and bath. I can pay you five hundred a week. What do you say?"

In a week I'll have enough cash to keep moving, Fiona thought, but aloud she said, "That sounds like a dream. You're a gem, Kimber. I'll take it. When do you want me to start?"

"Let me show you upstairs and you can get settled. Sleep now and you can start tonight if you'd like. How does two dark o'clock sound to start? We can monkey with the schedule as we sort things out. But I feel like that will be a good jumping off point."

"Fantastic. It will take me a bit to get used to working nights again, but it shouldn't take long. Lead the way, Kimber."

Kimber put up a sign that read "back in a few" and showed Fiona around upstairs.

Outside the crows watched and squawked their approval. They would carry this news through the wind and it would be known that Fiona's destiny would have to hold off for a detour. Long detour? Short detour? The universe would decide.

Ken Coffman and Kristen Lolatte

Trevir: The Psychopath Pipeline

TREVIR CLAPPED ONCE—sharp, surgical.

"Get me a map and convert this suite into a war room."

Within minutes, the conference room transformed. Screens blinked awake. A digital map of the United States glowed on the wall, pulsing with red dots.

Albert leaned in.

"Each dot marks a confirmed sociopath in public office. Verified by voting records, donor trails and leaked texts."

Trevir's eyes gleamed.

"You built this already?"

"We had a feeling you'd ask."

Trevir turned to the room.

"This is why I don't kill all children. Occasionally, they're useful."

A woman in a lab coat raised her hand.

"Sir, we've been testing a compound—tentatively called Soma. It induces euphoria, suppresses empathy and boosts verbal aggression. Ideal sales vehicle."

Trevir frowned.

"Soma? That's lazy. Has Huxley's copyright expired? Never mind. I have lawyers, too. Side effects?"

"Hallucinations. Nosebleeds. Spontaneous freeverse poetry."

Trevir grinned.

"We'll market that as a feature. Everyone's a creator now."

Albert tapped his tablet.

"Deployment in three phases. First, microdose state legislators. Second, flood the lobbyist ecosystem. Third, weaponize the influencers."

Trevir paced.

"I want results. Not next quarter. Not next week. Tomorrow."

The nerd spoke up again.

"We need a slogan."

Trevir stopped.

"Yes. Something punchy."

Albert cleared his throat.

"Soma—Because Empathy Is for Losers."

Trevir laughed.

"Print it. Tattoo it on influencers. Pay MrBeast whatever he wants. Skywrite it over Portland."

The woman hesitated.

"Which Portland, sir? The weird one in Oregon?"

"All of them. Do I have to do all the thinking around here?"

"One more thing. The drug works best with a visual trigger. Something primal. Something that bypasses reason."

Trevir's eyes narrowed.

"Like what?"

She tapped her screen. A grotesque, smiling face appeared—part clown, part predator. It pulsed with hypnotic rhythm.

Trevir stared. "That's me."

Albert nodded.

"We'll call it the Trevir Protocol. Subliminals everywhere. Drug them. Brand them. Take their money. Make them beg for more."

Trevir turned to the window, the skyline now a chessboard in his mind.

"Tomorrow," he whispered. "We start the harvest."

Philip d'GreenApple: Three Kids Under A Tree

ONCE I WAS on the ground, my terror subsided. With my feet solidly planted, I gripped the rope like a lifeline for a few moments to catch my breath as my heart rate and stomach settled. I watched the boy saunter back to his tree where he crouched—folding into himself like he'd never left. I walked over and studied his face. He had pale, gringo features— which was surprising. Everyone else around here had brown skin of various shades. He was young, maybe 9, and his clothes were ragged and filthy. His shoes were held together with duct tape. There was a flicker of something in his blank, masklike face. Jealousy, disgust, disdain. Whatever it was, it was gone in a flash.

Patiently, he guided me through an elaborate handshake followed by a fist-bump.

"Gracias, amigo," I said.

His English was accented, but perfectly understandable.

"You don't think I did that for free…"

Of course.

"How much?" I said.

He looked me up and down as if trying to figure out how much I could pay.

"Hundred pesos," he said while extending a dirty palm.

Just over five dollars.

As I pulled my wad of currency from my front pocket, I tried to decide if that felt like a fair market price for my rescue. We looked up as a voice called out to us.

"*Hola, charros de cartón,* I want to come down, too."

Cardboard cowboys. The insult amused me.

We're all cardboard cowboys.

I peeled off another bill from my wad of currency.

"I'll pay for her, too."

The practiced way the rope was tossed and caught—and the smooth way she was so quickly on the ground filled me with a brief fit of anger. I thought this was *my* smart idea. Clearly they'd done this before—perhaps many times. My pique passed quickly, washed away by the absurdity of it all.

She handed him a Snickers candy bar.

"I already paid him," I said.

They ignored me and walked back to the tree. The boy flapped a blanket and then spread it out to protect her fancy dress. Listening to them chat, I followed, then stood and looked down on them.

"She's my cousin," the boy said as he unwrapped his candy bar.

She shrugged.

"Everyone in Mexico is his cousin."

"What's his problem?" the boy said with his mouth full of chocolate.

She looked me over.

"*Joto,* maybe?"

This flustered me, but before I could protest that I am certainly not gay, the boy spoke.

"Could be. He smells nice."

"Old Spice. Sea Spray. Cool, breezy, subtle. You should have smelled him before. He went heavy on the Old Spice—Dead Possum."

The boy deepened his voice like he was reading advertising copy.

"Bold enough to wear roadkill. Subtle enough to get away with it."

These two really thought they were funny.

I didn't know what to make of this. Any thought that I was more sophisticated or smarter than them flew away quickly. Interestingly, I didn't know I carried around a superior attitude until it was gone.

"All right, you two." I gestured. "Shove over. I don't want my clean pants to get dirty."

Giggling, they couldn't be more pleased with themselves, but they scooted to make room for me. I fished a *Pulparindo* out of my pocket. She held out her palm.

"You get one when you tell me your name," I said. "Two if you tell me what is going on here."

"Two then," she said. "Marisol."

I fished out another, then discovered they were my last two.

"Drat," I mumbled.

Seeing this, she pushed the second one back at me, then unwrapped hers and popped it in her mouth.

"Keep it. We don't know what's up."

"Tell me what you do know."

She sighed.

"At the *quinceañera*, I let a boy get too familiar. *Mi viejo tío* is punishing me or trying to teach me a lesson or something. This is a test or something. Uncle Vargas is weird."

I mulled this over and still didn't understand.

"When you say *familiar*, what do you mean?"

She scoffed.

"Handsy, but not even under the blouse."

The boy's face twisted.

"Gross," he said while chewing the last of his Snickers.

By now, it was full dark. We watched as the guards—with cigarette tips glowing red—circled the building every few minutes. Winking fireflies flickered. The situation was so odd that my mind gave up trying to make sense of it. I would just let everything be what it was and stop trying to figure it out.

"What happens next?" I said.

She shrugged.

"We hang out here for an hour or so, then go in for dinner."

"How do we get back up there?"

The boy leaned over to look me in the eye.

"I have a ladder."

"Or we use the stairway on the side. Or we walk around and go in the front door. No one cares."

"What did your uncle think would happen with us?"

She twisted around to look me in the eye.

"If he knew what was going to happen, he wouldn't have done this. Why would he bother?"

That made no sense. Why was I with these two knuckleheads? What was I doing under this tree? What was I doing in this foreign country? What was I doing on this planet? My mind was a jumble.

"Why did you offer to get undressed?"

She elbowed me hard. It was going to bruise.

"I did no such thing."

I thought back and tried to picture what happened as accurately as possible.

"You said, 'When you come out, you want me dressed or not?'"

"Yes, I said that, but that wasn't an offer. I was just curious about what you'd say."

"I assumed..."

She interjected.

"I know what you assumed. It was written all over your red face and shifty eyes. I am wearing my pretty *quinceañera* dress. I am not a *puta*. I will never be one. I'm educated. I wear a uniform and go to the *Ecclesia Catholica Colegio América* school. I am going to marry a lawyer and have 12 kids. Not you. Uncle is weird. That's all. Get over it. Get over yourself."

She gave me a lot to think about.

The boy got up.

"I'm going to jet. I'll see you losers later."

We watched him wander off. After he disappeared, she spoke.

"Tio Vargas loves me and for some reason, likes you, too. He's messing with us. He would never harm a hair on my head. But you? I think you should be careful. He will use you as a tool. What's the word? *Desechable*. Expendible."

That I knew. She didn't need to tell me.

"What now?" I said.

"Can you smell it? Dinner is ready."

Daintily, she held out her hand.

I stood and offered my hand to help her up. Once she was up, she brushed off the back of her dress. She turned her back to me.

"Am I okay?"

I couldn't help it. I laughed.

"Yes, Marisol. You're okay. Very okay."

She took my hand and we wandered around the building to the front door. We walked in and made our way toward the dining room. It was crowded and no one paid any attention to us. As appetizers, there were soups, salads and tortilla chips with guacamole and salsa. The main course was a platter with several roasted chickens. It was good.

Fiona: Life in the Buttercream Clouds

OVER THE NEXT week, the kitchen became a thunderstorm with oven-heat raising sweat, cool drafts slipping under the back door and dark clouds rolling in thick and low. With sleeves rolled, hair pinned back and an apron streaked with flour, butter and canned cherries, Fiona floated in the storm the way hawks ride thermals.

Muscle memory guided the sequence: weigh, whisk, chill, roll. Rest. Roll again. Crimp. The dough flourished under her palms. She pinched a fluted edge so clean it looked stamped, then ruined it on purpose with a thumbprint—an imperfection to make the pie honest.

As she worked, something called to her. At first, it was a whisper but soon came into focus. Her pies would be better with fresh fruit. She knew nothing about the Rogue Valley. She'd never been there, she'd never heard of it, it had never crossed her mind a place like this existed.

She should have known. There is magic everywhere.

She started with thinking she might only bake for a week—long enough to make enough money to buy a bus pass and trail mix for the road—then be on her way. But, the week, as they do, turned into two, then four as she settled into a routine. Baking was like a fever when the oven heat takes hold. Egg-browned crusts welcomed custard, pale gold. Apple pies called for cinnamon bark shaved so thin it curled like ribbon. Pecan pies begged to swim in molasses dark as midnight.

She made pies without thinking, using whatever she discovered in the cooler, the walk-in or the pantry. She didn't decide; the ingredients decided for her. Nectarines and blackberries presented themselves like a dare; the slab pan waited, almost smug. Fiona obliged, macerating fruit with brown sugar, salt, lemon, a whisper of brandy from Kimber's desk drawer stash—and a grind of black pepper that wouldn't announce itself until the third bite, when someone would pause and look around, thinking, what was that...?

By the end of the week, the tinkling doorbells were chiming more often. There was no denying it, the pies drew in customers.

When the shop opened, Kimber would peek in the kitchen but would not interfere. Fiona's kitchen did not invite conversation; it was a whirlwind chapel. She caught the crows' silhouettes through the transom window—three on the pole, one on the sign, two on the power line—fidgeting and watchful in a way that wasn't strictly ornithological. It made her smile.

In the back, Fiona worked until the ovens glowed hot enough to cast small shadows of the pie tins on the wall. She rotated trays like planets, shuffled pans as if dealing cards. Every timer was a bell in a monastery. She was tired, but fatigue didn't matter. Her hands were awake, everything else could rest later. The radio offered a run of unexpected songs: Xavier Rudd, yes, but then k d Lang yearning. Then an old Gillian Welch tune that sharpened the room to a single point, and finally a strummed demo tape from a local college band, earnest and a little out of tune, which was perfect. She harmonized without thinking. At some point she laughed to herself. The mix of voices sounded like her mother singing with her sister, which felt like a good omen and a warning.

By early afternoon the cooling racks were crowded, the stainless counters a landscape of pies and flour drifts, a battlefield won by butter. Fiona leaned against the walk-in door, breath coming steady, sweat at her hairline. Emptied and full at once—there's no other way to put it. The kitchen air had changed: less push, more glow. The storm had passed.

Kimber came in, standing at the threshold taking in the scene with eyes moving as if reading text. Her mouth made a shape that wasn't quite a smile and wasn't quite anything else.

After work, Fiona was exhausted and empty. At Kimber's suggestion, she began a new routine.

The Route 10 bus hissed at the curb, its doors folding open like a sigh. Fiona climbed aboard, dropped coins for her fare and slid into a seat by the window. The vinyl was warm from the last passenger. The driver nodded once, as if he already knew her destination.

Downtown Medford fell away in a blur of pawn shops, taquerias and faded billboards. The bus gathered speed, humming south along the valley floor. Out the window, orchards stretched in neat rows, pears hanging heavy, their leaves flashing silver in the wind. Beyond them, the hills rose dark and close, stitched with pine and oak. The sky was a pale bowl, clouds drifting like slow ships.

At each stop—Phoenix, Talent—new riders climbed aboard: a woman with grocery bags, a student with headphones and a man who smelled of sawdust. They nodded to one another without speaking, as if all were part of the same quiet pilgrimage. Fiona felt herself included, though she carried nothing but her handbag and the scent of flour still clinging to her sleeves.

The crows followed. She saw them through the glass, black commas on the power lines, lifting and resettling as the bus rolled on. Once, a dust devil spun across a field, scattering dry leaves against the windows. The woman with the groceries crossed herself. Fiona only watched, thinking and not thinking of ovens and thunderstorms.

As the bus climbed toward Ashland, the air sharpened. Vineyards appeared with their trellises taut with grapes. Roadside stands flashed peaches and melons under shade cloth. Fiona pressed her forehead to the glass, and for a moment the reflection staring back at her wasn't entirely her own. The eyes were hers, but older, as if the valley itself was trying her face on for size.

Then the bus curved past the university, and Lithia Park opened green and dappled with creek water flashing like quicksilver. The driver pulled to the curb and the bus doors folded open wide. Fiona stood, her knees stiff from the ride, and stepped down into the shade. The crows scattered into the trees, their calls echoing like a benediction.

Lithia Park breathed around her. The air was cooler here, touched with creek-spray and pine resin. Ashland Creek ran quick and clear over its stones, flashing like a ribbon of glass. Children raced past with paper cups of Kool-Ade, the liquid sloshing bright red against the waxed rims. A few drops spattered the path, staining the dust like watercolor. Their tongues were already dyed crimson, laughter sharp with sugar. The air carried that unmistakable scent—cheap powder and hose water—sweet, thin, and oddly comforting. Fiona breathed it in and felt a tug of memory, as if the valley itself were reminding her that magic didn't always arrive dressed in silk, Sometimes it came in paper cups and sticky fingers.

Couples strolled beneath the sycamores, pausing to watch ducks swim in the shallows. The whole place seemed staged, but not false—more like a play that had been running for a hundred years and never lost its freshness.

Fiona sat on a stone wall and let her body unclench. Flour and butter still clung to her sleeves, but here it felt like tithes. The crows had settled again, black punctuation marks in the branches, watching without judgment.

A woman approached from the shaded path, carrying a wicker basket lined with leaves. She looked like she belonged to the orchards with sun-creased skin, hair streaked copper and silver. Stopping in front of Fiona, she glanced at the dusting of flour in her frizzy hair and reached out as if to brush it away.

"You've been baking," the woman said.

Fiona opened her eyes and looked up.

"Hello."

The woman smiled and held out the basket. Inside lay a handful of plump strawberries.

"Hand-picked this morning. Try one."

Fiona chose not the biggest, but the reddest. She bit and sweetness spread across her tongue like a satin secret.

She swallowed, then asked, "Who you be?"

"Marigold Rosen. Call me Mari. I work at Harry & David. The corporation owns the name, but the land still speaks."

Fiona studied her. Mari carried herself like management, though dressed down in a sundress, canvas hat, and Birkenstocks. Not wolf in sheep's clothing—something more wholesome, more innocent. Competent, though. Very competent and confident.

"And you recognized me by a little flour?"

Mari's smile deepened.

"Flour in your hair, yes. But also the way you carry yourself—like someone who listens to ingredients instead of ordering them around. That's rarer than you think."

"What's a Harry and David?" Fiona asked.

Mari laughed.

"We make fruit baskets."

Right, Fiona thought. And Tiffany's makes diamond rings.

They sat together, sharing strawberries while the creek burbled. For a moment Fiona felt seen—not as a traveler, not as a fugitive, but as a baker whose hands carried truth.

"Let me tell you about our valley," Mari said. "Our harvest seasons start with strawberries, then cherries. Apricots, then blackberries, plums and peaches. All are good, the best in the world, or I'll—" She glanced up at the crows. "Or I'll eat a crow. But if you want something truly special, it's our pears. World class. Hand-picked. Perfect."

"I don't think a crow would taste very good. Stringy and gamey. Like eating your sandals."

The crows did not like this. Overhead in a sprawling sycamore, they squawked and rustled.

Fiona thought about what she would do with a perfect pear. She wouldn't get fancy. She'd heat simple syrup in an iron skillet until it was on the edge of scorching, then caramelize the pears. That would make a good pie.

Mari leaned closer.

"We'll deliver in the evening. There won't be an invoice. I just want one pie. Every day. The first one out of the oven. Deal?"

"How do you even know about me?" Fiona said.

Mari grinned.

"Small town. People talk. You want more? Fine. When I send the car to pick up my pie, the driver will bring you here. No more bus. Done."

She stood, brushing her skirt.

"Keep the basket, dear. We have plenty."

On impulse, Fiona stood and hugged her quickly, awkwardly, then sat back down. The crows broke their silence, wings scattering against the sky. When she glanced back, Mari was already halfway to a black Mercedes sedan waiting at the curb.

An owl in a crow's costume, Fiona thought.

There was one strawberry left. She admired it, then ate it.

Fiona: Life in the Buttercream Clouds—Part 2

FIONA ACQUIRED AN apprentice. It was 3:00 in the morning and the world was asleep. In a flurry, pies moved from prep deck to oven to cooling racks. She imagined herself an octopus, arms waving. Pies-pies-pies.

A pounding rattled the back door.

Another of the homeless?

Graffiti in the alley marked the bakery as an easy handout. Feeding one meant feeding a hundred, but she couldn't say no. Anyone who asked politely got a sliver of day-old pie or a broken cookie. Tonight there was a tray of over-browned oatmeal-raisin cookies from the day shift. Still edible, but imperfect.

She picked one up and opened the door.

The girl standing there was not homeless. She was all circles—round face, soft body and hands like dinner rolls. An uncharitable thought flickered.

The last thing this girl needs is a cookie.

The girl brushed past.

"I'm going to help you," she said.

There's no room in the kitchen for the both of us.

As Fiona followed, the girl turned her head.

"I'll wash," she said.

The girl did not wait for permission. She tied her hair back with a scrunchy band from her wrist, rolled up her sleeves and found the sink. Within minutes she had a rhythm: rinse, soap, rinse, stack. She moved with surprising economy, never in Fiona's way, never clattering pans or demanding attention. She seemed to know instinctively when to step aside as Fiona spun from counter to oven to rack. The kitchen was still a storm, but now it had a center of calm.

By dawn, the counters gleamed. Sheet pans leaned in neat rows; bowls nested like Russian dolls. Fiona realized she hadn't had to stop once to wash. The girl had anticipated every need. It was unnerving and wonderful.

When Kimber came in later that morning, she stopped short at the sight of the stranger at the sink. Her eyes narrowed, then flicked to Fiona.

"This is...?" Kimber asked. "Someone else I can't afford to pay?"

The girl dried her hands on a towel and turned.

"Marta," she said simply. "I'm helping. For free. I want to learn to bake. Fiona is teaching me."

Kimber raised an eyebrow but said nothing more, because just then the deliveryman shouldered through the back door with four flats of strawberries. He set them down with a grunt, wiped his forehead, and left without a word.

Kimber stared at the berries.

"I didn't order these. And I can't afford them."

Fiona stepped forward, lifted one berry, and held it up to the light. It was perfect, sun-red and fragrant.

"It'll be okay," she said. "Trust me. These will pay for themselves."

Kimber muttered something about invoices and margins, but she didn't argue further. Marta, still at the sink, smiled faintly as if she already knew Fiona was right.

By midday, the kitchen quieted. Fiona wiped her hands, untied her apron, and stepped outside where the black Mercedes sedan waited at the curb. The driver held the door open. Fiona turned back to Marta.

"I don't want to assume..." Fiona began.

"I'll be back tomorrow," Marta said, matter-of-fact. "If you'll have me." After a beat, she continued. "And share the secret of browning a crust."

The words filled Fiona with a joy she hadn't expected. An assistant was never part of her plan, but here she was, a gift dropped at her door like a blessing. She slid into the car. The door closed with a soft thump. Fiona pressed the button and the passenger window slid down.

Kimber, leaning against the bakery's doorway, spoke to Marta intentionally loud enough for Fiona to hear.

"There goes Her Majesty, off to court in Lithia Park. Can't you see her prancing at the Shakespeare stage?"

Marta didn't miss a beat.

"Every Queen needs a kitchen," she said. "And someone to keep it clean." The word *Queen* filled Fiona with tangled, unruly emotions. She was no Queen. She baked pies. Shaking off the storm, she spoke through the lowered window.

"Luxury offered is no sin," she said. "It would be stupid to say no."

Marta and Kimber looked at each other.

"Did I say something wrong?" Marta said.

"I never noticed, but she does have kind of a royal Queenliness about her. If there is such a thing. Which there isn't."

The sedan pulled away, crows lifting from the power lines to follow with their wings scattering like black confetti in the bright noon air.

"Have you eaten?" Kimber said.

"I've been nibbling," Marta replied.

"I'll make you a sandwich."

Fiona: Life in the Buttercream Clouds—Part 3

LITHIA PARK SMELLED of pine needles and damp wood benches. A ragged circle of amateur actors in thrift-store costumes milled around the park's outdoor stage, their voices rising and falling in half-remembered lines. Someone's Juliet wore sneakers under her gown; Romeo had a bandanna for a sash.

The director, a wiry man with a clipboard and no patience, barked, "We need a royal Queen. Just for the last lines. You—"

His finger landed on Fiona, who, practicing invisibility, sat far up the knoll enjoying the ragged spectacle.

Queen. There was that title again. A clichéd shiver ran up her spine. She shook her head.

"I'm no—" she called out.

"You can read. That's all it takes. Come on."

Two extras ran up the hill and grabbed her arms. On the way down, the last page of the script was shoved into her hands.

The troupe parted, grinning at her reluctance. A few clapped as if she'd already agreed. Fiona stepped onto the stage boards, which creaked under her weight as if they remembered every amateur who had ever stood there. Gingerly, she held the page as if it might bite.

Above, the crows shifted on black tree branches. They followed her here, of course. They always did. One gave a dry cough of a caw, then another answered until the whole tree muttered disapproval. Apparently, this was too trivial for their seriousness.

Fiona cleared her throat. The words on the page blurred, then steadied. She read them flat, without flourish, but the lines carried their own gravity.

For never was a story of more woe
Than this of Juliet and her Romeo.

The stage went still. Even the director stopped scribbling. The sneakers-Juliet pressed her palms together as if in prayer. The silence that followed was not reverent so much as unsettled, like ionized air before a storm.

The crows broke it. They cawed in unison, ragged applause or revulsion, who could tell? Their wings beat once, twice, then settled again as if they had delivered a cue.

Fiona lowered the script. She wanted to laugh, to hand it back and step down, but something in her chest shifted. The words weren't hers, but they had landed in her mouth like a dare. She looked out past the stage lights, past the benches and into the trees where the crows watched. Their eyes were small, black coins, and they did not blink.

The director clapped once, sharp.

"Perfect. That's the ending we needed."

He pressed a plastic cup into her hands.

She looked down.

Beer.

She tried to hand it back.

"I don't drink—"

"Nonsense," the director said. "Tonight you swill ale with the rest of us peasants."

Fiona stepped down from the stage with a cold beer in one hand

and the script still warm in her other hand. She thought of Kimber, of pies cooling in ranks, of the luxury sedan car waiting somewhere on the busy street. The crows cawed again, softer this time, as if to say the play is over, but your part has just begun.

The next day, the driver kept making eye contact in the rearview mirror. He had something to say, but she teased him by watching the valley stream by and pretending not to notice. Eventually, she decided on mercy.

"What's on your mind?" she said.

"Lithia Park is a perfect place, but I'm yours all afternoon if you want to do something different."

Clearly, he had a plan, but she wasn't done gently torturing him.

"I suppose we could stop at Zoey's for an ice cream. That would be a wild and crazy way to shake things up."

He looked so disappointed she could barely stifle laughter. She decided to give him a break.

"You've got an idea up your sleeve. We won't debate or agonize, we'll just do it."

He pulled the car onto the freeway on-ramp and accelerated.

"Here in the Valley, the Rogue River is placid and mellow. But elsewhere, it earns its name. I'll show you."

In the mirror, she looked into his eyes.

"I suppose I should know your name…"

He stared back.

"Elm," he said.

Puzzled, she frowned.

"Elm, like short for Elmer or Elm like the tree?"

He shrugged. "Elm. My parents are hippies."

She laughed.

"I like it. If I ever have a son, that's what we'll name him in your honor."

He couldn't tell if she was mocking him. But he was eager to give her a geography lesson, so he carried on talking as he drove, pointing out ridgelines and naming creeks as if they were old friends. The freeway gave way to two-lane blacktop, then to a road that narrowed and twisted, climbing into pine country. The air cooled, resinous, and the light thinned into green.

"The Rogue is a trickster," Elm said. "It shows you one face here, another there. Up ahead, it vanishes. A whole river goes underground."

She raised an eyebrow.

"Nonsense. Rivers don't vanish. They meander. They sulk. They roar and rampage. They don't do magic tricks."

"You'll see."

They parked at a turnout where the thunder of water filled the air. A short trail led through basalt outcrops and moss-slick stones until the river appeared, frothing white, then—impossibly—slid into a black hole in the lava rock. One moment it was a torrent, the next it was gone, swallowed whole.

Fiona stood at the railing, leaning forward. Mist cooled her face. The sound was enormous.

"It's like the Earth is drinking," she said.

Elm nodded.

"They call it the Natural Bridge. The river runs under the lava tube for two hundred feet before it rushes back up. Some people say it's haunted. The native Americans say it's holy."

Above them, crows wheeled, their cries sharp against the thunder of water. They perched on the black rock, watching, as if they had seen the disappearing trick a thousand times and were unimpressed.

Fiona shivered.

"It feels alive. Like if you leaned too far, it would reach out and pluck you."

Elm smiled.

"That's the Rogue. Beautiful, dangerous, never halfway."

She glanced at him, hearing her words echo—*I don't know how to mean it halfway*—reflected at her by the river. The crows cawed again, ragged and insistent, as if to mark the moment.

She stepped back from the railing, clutching the script page she had never quite let go of, still folded in her pocket. The words of Shakespeare and the roar of the river tangled in her head.

For never was a story of more woe...

Elm touched her elbow.

"Ready to see where it comes back up?"

She nodded, though she wasn't sure if he meant the river or herself.

They followed the trail upriver, where the Rogue re-emerged from its stone throat, foaming and furious, as if insulted by its brief confinement. Fiona leaned on the railing, hair damp with spray, and laughed.

"It's been reborn angrier."

Elm grinned.

"That's the Rogue. Never the same river twice."

They lingered, walking the loop, watching the water vanish and return, vanish and return. Fiona pulled her jacket tighter, but the mountain air was already cutting through. The sun had dropped behind the pines and the shadows carried a chill.

She rubbed her arms.

"Okay, Professor Elm. Geography lesson complete. I'm freezing."

He looked at her, half-apologetic, half-pleased.

"Back to Medford, then?"

"Back to Medford," she said, and the crows overhead gave a single, ragged caw, as if to mark the decision.

The drive down was quieter. Fiona leaned her head against the window, watching the trees blur into twilight. Her body was tired in a good way, the kind of tired that comes from walking and laughing and being surprised. She thought of the stage at Lithia, the beer she hadn't wanted and the words she spoke that weren't hers but felt like they could be. She thought of the river swallowing itself and roaring back, unchanged and yet not.

Elm tapped the steering wheel in rhythm with the radio, some old rock song fuzzing through static.

"You know," he said, "most people's idea of a crazy adventure is to stop at Zoey's for ice cream."

She smiled without opening her eyes.

"Insult ice cream—especially locally churned—and we will no longer be friends."

By the time they rolled back into Medford, the valley lights were scattered like dropped coins. Fiona stretched, yawned, and laughed at herself.

"Thank you for a day."

Elm glanced at her in the mirror.

"You're welcome," he said.

The crows followed them down, black flecks against the last of the day. They settled on the power lines as the car pulled into town, muttering their approval or disapproval—it was hard to tell.

She was too tired to care, and it felt like freedom.

The next day, she spoke as soon as she slid into the car.

"I love Lithia Park. Truly, love-love-love it. But today, let's do something different again."

It was as if she'd said magic words. Elm's face lit up.

"I was hoping you'd say that."

Overeager, he pressed too hard on the accelerator and the car hopped with tires squealing. He caught her gaze in the mirror.

"Sorry. I hope you're wearing comfortable shoes."

Fiona shrugged.

"I'm a baker and on my feet all day. Is there any other kind?"

The freeway unspooled north, then narrowed into a road climbing past orchards and basalt cliffs. Fiona rolled down her window, breathing in dust and pears. Ahead, a mesa rose flat-topped and improbable, as if a giant had set down a table in the middle of the valley.

"Table Rock," Elm said, introducing her to an old friend. "It's a hike, but at the top you'll feel like you're standing on the roof of the world."

They parked at the trailhead. Fiona eyed the slope.

"That's not a hike. That's a dare."

Elm grinned.

"You'll hate me on the way up and thank me at the top."

The trail was steep and rocky, switch-backing through scrub oak and manzanita. Fiona's breath came fast, but she refused to let Elm see her falter. She filled the climb with chatter—about Kimber's pies, about the crows that seemed to stalk her and about how she hated the word *moist*. Elm listened, laughing, pointing out lizards darting across the path.

Halfway up, the crows appeared, black flecks against the blue. They circled lazily, then settled on the rim above, waiting.

"Your entourage," Elm said.

"They're critics," Fiona replied. "And they never clap in the right places."

At the top, the trail leveled onto a broad basalt plateau. The valley spread in every direction—Medford's grid of streets, orchards stitched like a green quilt, the Rogue glinting like a blade. Fiona walked to the edge, wind tugging her hair and felt her stomach drop.

"It's like standing on the edge of the world."

Elm joined her, quiet for once. Crows lined the rim a few yards away, muttering among themselves.

Fiona sat on the warm rock, knees pulled to her chest. She was tired, but it was the good kind—the kind that made her feel real. She glanced at Elm, who watched the horizon as if it might reveal a secret.

"Okay," she said. "You were right. Totally worth it."

He smiled, still looking outward.

"Told ya."

The sun-bleached plateau stretched wide. Wandering, Fiona drifted toward a shallow depression in the basalt. The air there felt different—charged, as if the ground itself hummed. She crouched, pressing her palm to the stone.

A current curved through her, not upward but sideways, as though the Earth bent like a magnetic field. For a moment she wasn't on the mesa at all but under a tent in a hot, far-off place. Minnie. Sleeping. Waiting.

When she first arrived in this valley, she hadn't guessed its charm. The history and geography tugged at her. It would be easy to settle here, to make a home. But that vision wasn't hers to keep. Minnie waited. Somehow, Fiona needed to reach her. Not today, but soon. The thought filled her with both happiness and regret. Through the vortex, she stroked Minnie's hair. The girl stirred, as if sensing her touch. Fiona pulled her hand back.

"Sweet dreams, my angel," she whispered.

Elm approached, curiosity etched on his face.

"Did you see a rattlesnake?"

Fiona waved him off, but he stepped into the depression anyway, stopping with a puzzled look.

"What's happening? Is it warmer here?"

"Never mind," Fiona said. "Let's go back and look over the edge."

They stood together, gazing out.

"It's a long way down," Fiona said.

"That's called restating the obvious," Elm replied.

He worried that he'd gone too far, but she held her mock-irritated look only a beat before breaking into laughter. Relieved, he joined her.

They stayed until shadows stretched long across the valley. On the way down, Fiona slipped once, catching herself on Elm's arm. He steadied her and for a moment neither spoke. The crows cawed above them, ragged and amused, as if they'd been waiting for that stumble.

By the time they reached the car, Fiona's legs ached and her shoes were dust-stained, but she was grinning.

"Comfortable shoes," she said. "God's gift to women."

Elm laughed, starting the engine. Below, the valley lights flickered on, scattered like embers. Fiona leaned back in her seat, exhausted, reflective and completely happy.

The next day, as Fiona settled into the plush leather seat, she caught Elm's eager eyes. She knew what he wanted to hear.

"No park today," she said. "Surprise me."

He'd been holding his breath. He exhaled loudly.

"I have an idea," he said.

She grinned.

"Somehow I knew that."

The highway bent west, tracing the Rogue as it narrowed and quickened. The orchards gave way to pine and fir, the air sharpening with altitude. Fiona leaned her head against the glass, watching the river flash silver between the trees.

"You're taking me into the wilderness," she said.

Elm smiled.

"No, I'm taking you into history."

They turned onto a gravel road that rattled the car's frame. The Rogue pressed close now, steady and insistent, its surface flashing against black rock. Finally, Elm pulled into a clearing where a weathered cabin crouched above the riverbank. Its cedar shingles were dark with age, its porch sagged, but it carried a stubborn dignity.

"Doesn't look like much," Fiona said.

"Bite your tongue, cretin." Elm said, reverent. "Western writer Zane Grey's place. He came here to fish and write. Said the Rogue was the only river wild enough to keep him honest."

Fiona stepped out, the scent of river moss and woodsmoke ghosts filling her lungs. She touched the porch rail, rough beneath her fingers, and imagined the writer hunched inside, scratching words by lamplight while the river moved outside with its patient strength.

"Feels haunted," she said.

Elm nodded.

"By him, maybe. By the river, definitely."

The crows arrived, black commas against the sky, settling in the firs above the cabin. Their calls were sharp, like editorial marks in the margins of the scene.

Fiona walked to the edge of the bank, looking down at the Rogue. It slid past, green and muscular, indifferent to cabins or novels or visitors. She thought of her own words, the ones she'd spoken on the Lithia stage, the ones she'd felt echo through the basalt at Table Rock. Words that weren't hers but had claimed her anyway.

Elm joined her, hands in his pockets.

"Can you hear him?"

She smiled faintly.

"Maybe it's just the river, telling its same story over and over."

The crows cawed in agreement—or dissent. It was hard to tell.

Back at the cabin, the door groaned on its hinges and the air inside was cooler, redolent with cedar and dust. Fiona stepped across the threshold and stopped.

This time, it hit her like a wave. Not the smell, not the dim light, but the mass of words. Zane Grey's words. They pressed in from the walls, from the shelves, from the very grain of the wood. She felt pummeled, as if every novel, every frontier sermon, every fish tale and gunfight was pressed onto her shoulders at once.

The cabin was small, but it felt enormous—swollen with sentences, paragraphs and chapters. She could hear them, a low murmur beneath the steady voice of the river. Here, the Rogue didn't roar; it slid past, green and heavy, its current patient and muscular, whispering against stones as if it had all the time in the world.

She gripped the doorframe, steadying herself. Elm joined her, looking around with boyish awe.

"Can you believe it?" he said. "He wrote here. Right here."

Fiona nodded, though her throat was tight. To her, it wasn't awe but assault. The sheer productivity, the relentless voice of a man who had poured himself into the page until the page became a monument. She thought of her own words—few, fragile, scattered like crumbs— and felt them fragment smaller still, as if the river itself was sweeping them away.

Above the rafters, the crows shifted, their claws scratching the old wood. They muttered as if amused by her discomfort, as if they too had seen this trick before: a mortal crushed beneath the weight of another's story.

Fiona stepped further in, forcing herself to breathe. The river's calm voice outside steadied her, reminding her that even Grey's words were only echoes.

She wandered from the porch, following a faint path through alder and willow until the river opened before her. Here the Rogue was not loud but deliberate, sliding past in a green plane. Its voice was low and steady, like someone speaking just out of earshot.

She crouched at the edge, letting her fingers sift through damp sand where the current had curled back on itself. A small, heavy shape pressed against her fingertips. She lifted it, rinsing away grit.

A nugget. Not dazzling, not theatrical—just a dull, dense lump that caught the light in a way that made her pause. It was the kind of gold you could almost mistake for stone until it warmed in your hand, until its weight told you it was something else entirely.

For a moment she held it, listening to the river's calm voice. The nugget seemed less a prize than a message, as if the Earth had quietly pushed it forward for her alone. She thought of Grey, chasing stories of fortune and wilderness. She thought of Minnie, waiting far away, her future as uncertain as the river's next bend.

Above her, the crows shifted in the branches, muttering their ragged commentary. One gave a dry cough of a caw, as though to say:

Careful. Gold is never free.

Fiona slipped the nugget into her pocket beside the folded script page. The two objects knocked together—words and weight, story and substance. She stood, brushing sand from her knees and looked back toward the cabin.

Elm called from the porch.

"Find something?"

She closed her fist around the secret in her pocket.

"Just the river," she said.

The Rogue slid on, patient and unhurried.

When they finally got back in the car, for the first time, she got in the front seat. Elm glanced at her but did not speak. No longer driver and passenger, they were now simply friends. As they pulled away from the cabin, Fiona kept her face turned toward the river until the trees swallowed it. The Rogue's undertone faded, but its pull clung to her.

Zane Grey's words, the gold in her pocket, the crows' restless muttering—it all pressed together, too much to carry and too precious to drop. Elm hummed along with the radio, content, but Fiona's chest ached with a different rhythm. She knew these days—these strange, charmed excursions—were numbered. They glittered like coins tossed in sunlight, already falling out of reach.

Something gathered, a convergence she could hear beneath the crows' ragged calls. She closed her eyes and saw the bakery: the glass cases, the smell of sugar and yeast, Marta's steady hands. And someone else—someone not yet there but already moving toward it. A figure at the threshold, a woman's shadow stretching across the tiled floor.

Fiona shivered, though the car was warm. She pressed her palm against the nugget in her pocket as if it might anchor her. But her melancholy only deepened.

While Elm was distracted, stopped and watching for a gap between log trucks, she slipped the nugget into his jacket pocket as a secret tithe to days already gone.

Magic days end. And when they do, something else always begins.

Philip d'GreenApple: Chibson

AFTER A NIGHT of trying to sleep while wind and hail battered the pickup, I woke to tapping on the window. I reached out, pressed the button and lowered the glass. I didn't recognize the man.

"Everyone up," he said.

The parking lot was milling with drivers. Near the main building, a semi-trailer was being unloaded. From this distance, I couldn't tell what the cargo was. After relieving myself in the weeds behind a rusted dumpster, I followed the crowd and took my place in line. The sun, already hovering low on the eastern horizon, was hot against my back.

Vargas supervised. He caught my eye and grinned like he was genuinely pleased to see me.

Had I passed some kind of test?

My brain was foggy from lack of sleep. I didn't want his attention—nothing good would come of it. I forced a grin in return, but it probably looked more like a grimace. The man was crazy.

A crew was unloading acoustic guitar cases—dozens of them. One per driver. They were heavy, at least forty pounds each. After hauling mine to the truck, I studied it. The Gibson logo was a sloppy silkscreen job. Unconvincing. I knew what it was: a knockoff. Chinese fakes of expensive Gibson guitars were called Chibsons. I didn't know how I knew that. My brain refused to behave.

The latch was sealed with a large yellow zip tie. We were also handed slips of paper—handwritten, barely legible. I glanced at my neighbor's. We were all headed to different destinations. Mine was Uvalde. Not far up the highway toward San Antonio. A day trip. Out and back.

The parking lot was teeming. I did a quick count—at least fifty trucks, a mélange of color and condition. Mostly battered old Nissans, which, for some reason, were popular down here.

I couldn't process it. A flotilla of pickups crossing the river, each headed to a different town. Most would make it. Some wouldn't—that was the cost of doing business. The drivers were paid well. The ones who got caught? Expendable.

I decided I wasn't going to follow instructions. It was over a hundred miles out of my way, but I'd take MX 29 down to Eagle Pass and cross on the old bridge.

The long drive gave me time to think—about what I was doing, and why. No good answers came to mind.

I crossed the border from Piedras Negras smoothly with no hassle. Then I drove until I found an IBC Bank. They opened at 9:00. I was early, so I waited in the truck, then went in and deposited the signal amount: $17.76. Alvarez would take at least two hours to get here. He'd complain, but I didn't care. The man was going to get me killed.

I was tired of Mexican food. The bank teller gave me directions to the local Starbucks. That's what I wanted: charred coffee and overpriced Egg McMuffins. I spent an hour watching plump girls walk out with frozen drinks topped with whipped cream and caramel drizzle and cowboys leave with Venti cups of black drip. I took my triple espresso and the remains of my sandwich back to the truck and drove back to the bank to wait. When the heat climbed, I ran the engine for the air conditioning and dozed.

Just after 11:00, I woke to a rap on the passenger window. Alvarez. I unlocked the door. He opened the back crew cab door and studied the guitar case.

"What did you make me come all the way out here for?" he said.

"I risk my life and you complain about a commute. Bite me."

The way he looked at me—I knew in a flash. This scene had played out before. I wasn't his first undercover kid. There were others. Maybe several.

"What happened to the ones who came before me?"

I saw it on his face. That question hit home.

I was here because I was curious and open to letting the universe guide me. Follow a path and see where it leads. But this was serious. My life was at risk.

And for what?

He studied my slip of paper.

"Uvalde," he said. "We know this place."

He pulled a knife from a leather holster on his belt.

Just as I said, "Don't...," he sliced the zip tie and slipped it into his pocket.

"Don't worry about it," he said. "We carry all the colors. I got yellow."

Inside, packed tight, were more than a dozen one-kilo plastic bags filled with what looked like shiny black lentils. They weren't lentils. I knew what they were. This was pure evil. I didn't want anything to do with it.

It was as if Alvarez could read my mind.

"The only way to defeat evil is to confront it," he said.

How do you fight monsters without becoming one?

And besides—how was this my problem? How was this my battle to fight?

I saw a path in my head. I'd go to a convenience store, buy lighter fluid and wooden matches. Then I'd drive to a remote area, soak this death and light it on fire. It felt right. I even thought about the wind. I wouldn't want to breathe the smoke. The hot wind was steady from the south.

These details felt real. This was a version of reality that could exist—and should.

"No, that's not the way," Alvarez said.

He seemed to know what I was thinking.

He continued, "Just get him to cross the border. We'll grab him, and you'll be free."

What is he talking about? I'm free now.

"Serious," he said, gesturing. "Do you know how many people this sh—uh, this stuff—can kill? This is important. Get him into our hands and you're done."

"How exactly do you expect me to do that? Shall I say, 'Hey, *tío* Vargas, let's grab brunch at the 830 Kitchen in Del Rio'?"

"You're a clever lad. Figure something out. The U.S. government will be in your debt. You'll be rewarded with life-changing cash. We'll give you an award—a walnut plaque—and a medal. Photo op. The President will shake your hand. Lives will be saved. Children's lives. What else do you want—a parade?"

He was throwing things out, hoping one would stick. Hoping to find something I cared about.

Lost and confused, I walked around the truck. There was a soda can on the sidewalk and thirty steps away, a garbage bin. I picked up the can and dropped it in. In the trash, a newspaper headline caught my eye: *Child Dies from Overdose.*

Okay. Message received.

I walked back to the pickup.

"I'll try," I said. "One last time. Then that's it."

Alvarez nodded. "I won't ask for anything more."

"Take that stuff," I said. "I don't want anything to do with it."

Alvarez shrugged and handed me a yellow zip tie.

"Sorry. You have to deliver it."

I didn't like it, but I did it anyway.

The drive to Uvalde was uneventful, but the silence felt loaded. I kept the windows cracked just enough to let the wind carry the heat out and the dust in. The guitar case sat in the back seat like a coffin. I didn't look at it.

Uvalde crept up slowly—low buildings, faded signage, a few gas stations and a Whataburger that looked like it hadn't been cleaned since the last flood. I passed a school, then a feed store, then turned onto a side street lined with cracked pavement and chain-link fences. The drop site was behind a shuttered laundromat, next to a dumpster that smelled like bleach and rot. Empty little plastic bottles of Fireball whiskey were scattered everywhere.

There were no instructions on my paper—just a place. I parked, killed the engine and waited. Someone was watching.

Ten minutes passed. Then twenty.

Covered in dust, a silver Tacoma pickup pulled in, windows tinted darker than legal. The driver got out and nodded. I took the case from the back seat and walked it over. He plopped down the tailgate. I set it down gently, like it might explode. He didn't say a word. Just pushed in the guitar case, closed the tailgate and drove off.

No handshake. No confirmation. No code word.

I stood there for a moment, watching the truck disappear down the street. A dog barked in the distance. Somewhere behind me, a screen door slammed. The wind picked up, carrying the smell of mesquite and diesel.

I walked back to my truck and sat behind the wheel. My hands were shaking. I didn't know why. Maybe it was adrenaline. Maybe it was guilt. Maybe it was the weight of knowing I'd just handed off something that could kill thousands.

I started the engine and pulled out slowly, merging back onto Highway 90. The sun was high now, and the heat climbed. I didn't turn on the radio. I didn't want noise. I wanted silence. I wanted distance.

I passed a roadside memorial—plastic flowers, a wooden cross with a child's name carved into it. This could not have been true, but it looked like my name. I didn't slow down. I didn't look away. As I passed the Air Force Base, I was thinking about the river. We called it the Rio Grande. The Mexicans called Rio Bravo. Unruly River. Wild River. I liked their name better.

By the time I reached the outskirts of Del Rio, the case was gone, but its weight wasn't. It clung like sweat. Like smoke.

On the bridge, traffic was light. The cameras took my pictures and the border agents asked their usual questions and then waved me through. When I pulled into the lot, I was one of the last ones back. The lot was full. I found a lonely parking spot in a far corner. The lot boss looked at me for a long minute before checking me off on his clipboard. I probably had one of the shorter runs and was the last one back. If not a red flag, then yellow. I thought about inventing an excuse but dismissed the idea. These guys were all professional liars—they'd smell my deception a mile away.

"Go see the accountant," he said. "There might be a few pesos left."

Calling the money-man an accountant was a joke. On payday, he set up a card table and handed out wads of U.S hundred-dollar bills in racks and stacks. With a pencil stub, he crossed names off hand-written entries on a yellow tablet. How it worked was a mystery, but it seemed accurate. Or, maybe it was dangerous to protest. Maybe the complaint department was a hole in the desert.

He'd already packed up, but when he saw me coming, plopped the suitcase back on the table and opened it. I couldn't read his expression. It was something, but I didn't know what. He handed over two racks. Twenty-thousand dollars. That was a lot—a substantial brick of currency.

"The boss wants to see you," he said. "He's been waiting."

"José Luis?" I said hopefully.

He shook his head.

"Vargas."

Great.

It was an irony, but my money was safe in the truck—I didn't even have to lock the door. No one dared to steal—you'd lose a finger for petty larceny and a hand if you irritated the big guy.

Vargas wanted to see me, but I was in no hurry to see him.

I walked around the blocky building to the back. Beneath the sprawling tree was a figure. I assumed it would be the kid but as I approached, I could see it was the girl, Marisol, dressed in ragged stone-washed jeans, the kind that somehow cost two hundred bucks. To complete her outfit, she wore a tank-top decorated with the green Wicked witch. The dialog bubble said, 'I'm off to see the wizard.' It must have been her idea of a joke, but on her dirty feet, she wore Cruzado huarache sandals with truck-tire soles and soft leather straps. They were decorated with a silver coin. Sol. The Sun.

It all meant something, but I didn't know what.

"*Te late si me estaciono aquí?*" I said. This meant something like 'Cool if I park here?' or close enough.

Her shrug was barely noticeable, but I took it as permission and settled beside her. We watched a hairy tarantula idle by in front of us. Unlike us, it had someplace to go.

"This is quite a change from your *quinceañera* dress," I said.

She glanced at me.

"Q-party dress. My *quinceañera* is next year."

We sat in silence watching the guards pass again, their boots grinding gravel in unison, with smoke trailing behind them like banners. The air was thick with the tang of tobacco, and every exhale seemed to hang low, refusing to rise against the heat. I could hear the rattle of their gear, the metallic clink of keys and buckles and it struck me that they all moved with the same weary rhythm as if the job had hollowed them into copies of one another.

Marisol watched them without expression, her eyes half-lidded, as though she had seen this parade a thousand times and it no longer registered. For me, the silence between us grew heavier with each step of their boots. I wanted to say something clever, something that would cut through the weight pressing down on us, but every thought dissolved before it reached my tongue. The tree above us creaked in the breeze, and an acorn plonked between us like a punctuation mark. I stared at it, absurdly grateful for the distraction before forcing myself to speak.

"To me, the difference between a dream and hallucination is subtle. Either way, I don't like them."

The way she looked up at me, I couldn't interpret her expression. She didn't get up and wander away, so she must be interested.

"Either way, I am not in control of my thoughts," I continued. "I prefer being grounded in reality."

After a beat, she spoke.

"Norteamericanos are weird."

"So what?" I said. "Mexicans are weird, too. Everyone is weird."

"I'll tell you what I don't like. My body is changing and things are getting complicated. Life was simpler when I was a kid. In an hour, I could give a boy what he wants and it could change the course of my life forever."

I didn't know what to say, so I didn't say anything.

She continued.

"Do you believe in magic?"

I thought it over before responding.

"I know people who do."

She changed the subject.

"Do you have a girlfriend?"

Another hard question…

"I have something much deeper than a girlfriend."

She twitched like I shocked her with a cattle prod, then scooted back to look me in the eyes.

"You're too young to have a wife."

"Right," I said. "But I'm not too young to have something more than that…a soul mate. Crap, that's a weak cliché. She's the translator of my unspoken, the resonance chamber of my half-sung notes, the one who makes them music."

Marisol scoffed.

"Who talks like that? Besides, she'll break your sentimental heart."

I couldn't help it; I emitted a bark of laughter.

"There are a million surprising things Minnie could do—but breaking my heart isn't one of them."

"How can you be so sure? When it comes to other people, you can't count on nothing."

Her statement made no literal sense and briefly, my mind stumbled on it, but I knew what she meant.

How did I know?

"How do you know your *jefecita* loves you?"

After thinking about it, she said, "There's not one way. There are a thousand ways."

I felt an unreasonable sense of extreme relief for the easy answer she gave me.

"Exactly," I said. "That's exactly it. Besides, I'm so lovable and charming, how could she not?"

She elbowed me in the ribs.

"Easy," she said. "You're annoying. And if she really loved you, she'd be here."

"No, she'd be where she is and I'd be where I am."

She paid no attention to me.

"She would not like seeing us sitting together under this tree. She'd be *encabronado*. How do you say it? P-O'd. Pissed off."

"No, she'd be fine with us like this."

"She wouldn't like to see us kissing. *Besuquearse*. All slobbery tongues. *Fajar*. Making out. She'd shoot you in the belly with a *una fusquita rosa* she carries in her belt.

In a flash, she was all over me—holding my hand against her chest while covering my face with sloppy kisses.

Like everyone else, she wanted what she could not have.

I won't lie and say I didn't like it. I did. She was innocent and cute. But I knew. The instant I grabbed her and forced myself on her, she'd be done and things would go very bad for me. So, I left my hand where she put it and let her cover my face with saliva until she got bored. It didn't take long. She pulled back and rested against the tree. Her cheeks were flushed and she was out of breath.

"First firefly," she said. "Dinnertime."

She got up, brushed dust off the seat of her jeans and then walked toward the big house.

As I watched her leave, I felt Minnie watching from afar.

Laughing at me.

She was solid before my eyes.

"Resonance chamber of my half-sung notes," she said. "What is that?"

"I don't know," I said. "It just came out."

Her expression turned serious.

"It's nearly time for you to come home."

"I know," I mumbled. "Soon."

Leaving behind the faint scent of sage perfume, she was gone.

No, I don't believe in magic.

But I knew people who did.

The silence Minnie left behind felt heavier than her presence. I stayed under the tree, staring at the place where she had stood, or seemed to stand, her perfume clinging to the air like a ghost that refused death. I rubbed my palms together, half expecting to feel the warmth of her hand, but there was nothing—only the grit of dust and the faint tremor of my own nerves.

It unsettled me how easily she could appear in my mind's eye, solid as stone, and then vanish. Was it a dream, memory, hallucination or some trick of mental exhaustion? I told myself I didn't believe in magic, but the line between memory and apparition was flimsier than I liked to admit. If she could watch me from afar, laugh at me, scold me then summon me home—what part of me was still my own?

In a breeze, the old tree creaked, and I realized I was holding my breath. I let it out slowly, forcing myself to move, to follow Marisol's path. Better to chase the smell of roasted pork and the promise of a cold Coke than to linger in the company of ghosts.

I wanted that Coke so badly I could already taste the syrup, feel the carbon dioxide biting my tongue.

As I walked, I waved annoying fireflies out of my path.

Fiona: A Farewell to Buttercream Clouds

A WOMAN STOOD at the counter, travel-worn. Canvas bag, sun-hollowed cheeks, hair braided for practicality, a tan line that didn't care about fashion. She ordered coffee, black, and didn't blink when Kimber mentioned the day's pies. The woman took a sip, then nodded at the coffee pot as if it had done her a big favor.

"Strong and black, like my heart," she said. "Good. I'm dead tired of Circle-K swill."

"Headed where?" Kimber asked, not nosy, just mapping the world in the way of small-town gossip-meisters.

"Nevada," the woman said. "Past Reno. Long drive. I hate I-5, so I'm taking the back road. Tonight, if I can make it."

Kimber's eyebrows moved a fraction.

"That's a long road for sure. The long long way? K-Falls, a slice of California by Goose Lake, then Nevada through the reservations. No one goes that way."

The woman's mouth made a shrug.

"I prefer to go around the Siskiyous, not over them. Even if it means skipping Weed. You gotta love a town called Weed."

"Past Reno? What's past Reno?"

"I'm meeting a guy in Hawthorne. Business opportunity."

In the back up to her elbows in a mixing bowl, Fiona heard *Hawthorne* and felt an interior color change—some rooms lit, others dimmed. Hawthorne. She knew the town from a dirty finger on a paper map, a line of highway, a block of lake and rumors about ammunition bunkers and a ghostly quiet that wasn't just absence but something that watched. If you were allergic to the I-5 freeway in California's central valley, you might know this place. A place people endured, not embraced. This woman spoke the name without dread. That was its own kind of warning.

Hawthorne was a nasty place, but it was on the way.

On the way to where?

She pressed that thought away.

Fiona set her pie plate down, walked to the doorway and leaned on it, the frame marking a border her body wasn't eager to cross. If you were at point A and wanted to get to point C, sometimes you have to pass through point B—even if it was not a place to linger.

Kimber glanced back at Fiona, then back at the customer.

"On your own? Ill-advised," Kimber said with just enough humor to make it sugar, just enough steel to keep it salt. "I've made that trip. There be dragons. Miles and miles of no gas stations. No cellphone service. As a single woman, I wouldn't."

She glanced at the woman's hands.

At least thirty dollars of fingernail work.

"Get a flat tire and you'll break nails. Guaranteed."

Fiona wiped her hands on her apron.

"I'll come with."

The sentence surprised the room. It was the kind of declaration that lands like a coin on a table—a small sound, but everyone knows what it means. Kimber's eyes went to Fiona's, then down to the flour on her hands, then out to the crows on the sign, as if to check the world's opinion. The crows did what crows do when humans need a theatrical cue: cawed once, together, which is either confirmation or coincidence, depending on your appetite for myth.

The traveler—she hadn't given a name yet—studied Fiona with a neutrality that felt more like courtesy than caution.

"You pack fast?" she asked.

"…and travel light," Fiona said. She looked at Kimber with regret. "It's time. Marta can take over. I can leave you a list of labeled portions. The custard won't keep; serve it today or eat it yourself. The slab wants morning customers. The apple will forgive the afternoon."

Kimber came around the counter and put both hands on Fiona's shoulders.

"Are you sure? I hoped you'd stay forever. And then a day. Maybe take a week to think about it? Or three? Or a year?"

"No, I'm not sure," Fiona said, which was truth, "but yes, I will go." She smiled crookedly and calculated what she'd saved up. It was more than she needed. "Stay too long in one place and you can get stuck."

Kimber exhaled, then made a sour face.

"I could sell a thousand of your pies if we had them. This place will be here for you if your road turns. I mean it."

"I know," Fiona said. "Get Marta some help. Don't make her work alone."

They stood in a silence that was awkward and holy. To pop the moment like a bubble, an older man lugging plastic grocery bags asked for a slice of something sweet to take home to his wife; Kimber took care of him with automated choreography.

The traveler finished her coffee, tapped the rim once like a bell, and set it down.

"We're burning daylight," she said mildly. "Hawthorne isn't closer when you talk about it."

Fiona untied her apron. The knot resisted for show, then yielded. She folded the cloth, set it on the counter the way you'd leave a goodbye letter. She washed her hands with more attention than necessary, dried them on a towel she'd used all afternoon and hung the towel up on a rack to dry. She thought about the pies cooling in serried ranks with crusts that fractured just right when a knife broke them open. She thought about sleeping on the futon upstairs under Kimber's plants and waking to bake and then bake some more in the dead of night.

Briefly, she thought, about staying. Then, as if summoned, Marta appeared, crestfallen.

"No one makes a peach pie like you."

"You can do it," Fiona said.

Marta looked surprised as it occurred to her. She could. Actually, she really could.

Fiona took Marta's hands and pulled her close.

"Here's a secret," she whispered. "For the crust, sprinkle the salt in the form of a cross. *Para bendecir la masa*. To bless the dough."

With tears streaming, round Marta whispered back.

"Thank you for everything, Fiona."

Kimber interrupted the moment.

"Wait," she said, then disappeared into the back office. She returned with a small box, bakery white with a loop of red twine. "Emergency provisions. Bison chili and cornbread ends."

She placed the box in Fiona's hands.

Fiona laughed. She felt something behind her eyes, then not, then again, then gone.

"You're trouble," she said, meaning it as praise.

The crows announced a clock change and lifted to a higher wire. Shadows lengthened. Fiona looked at Kimber and Marta.

"I'll message if I find a signal. Or I won't. If I don't, assume I'm fine."

"That's not how assuming works," Kimber said. "But I'll pretend. Go do your unstoppable thing."

Fiona and the traveler stepped outside. The air carried sugar, heat and the smell of the creek, Bear Creek burbling and mumbling—a silver idea under the valley's afternoon sun. The light had that near-evening thickness that makes decisions feel heavier and more buoyant at once. The traveler's vehicle was not a statement so much as a tool—dust-brown, two doors and a windshield with sun-cracked spider veins, the kind of car that will never forgive you for what you did to it.

"What do I call you?" Fiona asked.

"Call me Jan," the traveler said. "Short for Jannelle."

"Call me Fiona, short for nothing," Fiona said.

At first glance, Jan's Hyundai was unimpressive.

It smelled like French fries and Burger King Whoppers. The passenger seat held a constellation of old coffee cups. After clearing a spot, Fiona placed the bakery box on her lap, tucked her rucksack bag at her feet and found the seatbelt, which worked after a firm negotiation. Jan started the engine; it answered with a second's delay, then a commitment. The crows argued among themselves. Some were happy that Fiona's journey would continue. Some said Fiona should stay, but they were mainly thinking about the pie crust remnants tossed in the alley.

Kimber stood in the doorway, one hand shading her eyes, the other tucked into her apron's pocket as if it held a talisman. She didn't wave. Waving felt like asking for something. Instead, she held still and watched, the way bakers watch ovens—alert and practical.

Jan put the car in gear.

"You ever been out this way?"

"Not this way," Fiona said. "But it's the same sky."

"You say that now," Jan said. "Give it four hours."

They rolled into the road. The valley's veneer of modernity softened as they cleared the town's last traffic light. Fiona felt her throat loosen. The bakery receded behind them, butter and fruit drifting in their wake like a second exhaust. She worked at the box's twine with her thumb.

"You pick Hawthorne on purpose?" Fiona asked.

"On purpose enough," Jan said. "Meeting a guy there. Marketing job. Pays a fortune if he likes me. Little black pills. I could sell the crap out of them."

She said it with ease, as if evil was a rational choice. Fiona felt the words like a fetid draft under a locked door.

Jan glanced at Fiona and continued.

"It's not multi-level marketing."

There were few things Fiona was sure about. One was this: if someone insists a job isn't multi-level marketing, then it certainly is. She'd seen the pattern too many times—someone crowing about *financial freedom*, waving charts and promising that all you had to do was sell a miracle lotion or vitamin powder and then recruit your friends to do the same. The product was always incidental. The real business was stacking a pyramid of hopefuls beneath you, each one paying for the privilege of climbing toward a nonexistent summit. Overhead, the crows shifted on wires, skeptical as ever.

Fiona had learned to smile politely, to let the pitch run its course, and to walk away before any hook was set. It wasn't cynicism; it was survival.

Fiona looked out the window. Fields stitched green and gold. A fenceline collapsed into its own shadow. Barbed wire. Cows. The radio made a static sound, then gave them a half-sentence of a preacher, then a mournful guitar. Delta blues on an old guitar.

> So—tomorrow, who knows?
> Tonight—who cares?
> And it feels like I'm next to nothin'
> So near to nowhere.

Jan turned the volume low.

"Ill-advised," Fiona said, thinking of Kimber.

"Advice is like pie," Jan said. "Best when you don't want it."

It was a weird turn of phrase. Fiona laughed, then quieted. The winding road surprised her—it was more present than she expected, like a person who listens. She let the day take her and let the name Hawthorne rearrange her mental furniture. She imagined bunkers under the scrub, deep cold storage for things that had to outlast other things. She imagined lake water holding its breath under wind. She imagined arriving and not arriving, both.

Then those pills. Black Death.

The idea of them tightened something deep inside her where fear lived.

They drove. Jan had a way with steering that made the car feel like it was thinking. Fiona glanced at her profile—steady, pretty in a way that made beauty obvious, road-written. Black hair, obviously dyed. She felt the absurd desire to ask about childhood, favorite breakfasts, worst mistake, although none of that was a right-now question. The right-now question was: did Kimber lock the bakery's back door? Of course she did. Kimber was a compulsive locker.

The sun settled into its late trick, appearing closer and farther in the rearview with each rise and dip of the road. Fiona opened the box and broke a cornbread end in half, handed Jan the bigger piece, kept the smaller and chewed. It tasted like kitchens do when the lights are off, good and simple and a bit melancholy.

"Kimber said you bake like you mean it," Jan said, not looking away from the road.

"I don't know how to mean it halfway," Fiona said.

"Hawthorne won't like you," Jan said.

"What do you mean?" Fiona asked.

Jan's mouth made a shape that could have been a grin or a grimace.

"First off, the ghosts. The dead of the abandoned mines—Lucky Boy, Fletcher Station, Nine Mile Ranch. They don't like city folk. Then the Army Depot. They built the bunkers on a sacred site. Indian spirits. But that's the least of it." She lowered her voice. "The bombs. Cold metal death." She glanced at Fiona, eyes steady. "Some find it creepy. I like it. If it was up to me, I'd light the fuse and let it all go."

By the time they passed through Lakeview—gas pumps glowing, the air cooling fast in the high desert dusk—and turned south, the road appeared ordinary and was, and appeared not, and was that too.

Drowsy, Fiona let the car carry her toward Hawthorne, a word that sounded like both a thorn and a thing with wings. Her mind drifted. Daylight slid west. Pies cooled in ranks. Somewhere, a map folded. Somewhere else, it opened. Fiona didn't put a frame around it. She didn't need one yet. The road would do.

Fiona: Hobbit Hills

THE HIGHWAY NARROWED as it slid into Hawthorne. Under moonlight, the town was ringed by low, dun-colored hills and endless rows of concrete bunkers that belonged to the Army Depot. Each bunker was a half-buried dome with doors painted olive drab with numbers in stenciled black. From a distance they looked like graves for giants.

At the edge of town, the neon of a shuttered casino buzzed faintly, though the building had been dark for years. A single bulb flickered above the door, as if it hadn't gotten the message.

Walker Lake lay to the north, flat as a sheet of hammered tin. Tonight the water was black and the wind carried the smell of iron and sage.

"The lake gets a life every year," Jan said. "Freely offered. There's no problem finding someone in Reno no one will miss."

Fiona could not believe her ears.

"That's horrible. Evil."

Jan glanced over. Her voice changed to steel.

"What's horrible is if we don't offer one, then the lake takes ten.

Ten of us. Ten we care about. You can't get anywhere in the world if you're bad at math."

As they passed, Fiona heard laughter—high, quick bursts that carried across the water. She told herself it was the wind, though she knew the Paiute stories of water babies—spirits of the drowned—pulling under the careless.

As they arrived in town, a depot siren wailed once, then cut off. No one seemed to notice. Fiona felt the sound in her chest like a warning meant only for her. She looked again at the bunkers on the horizon, their doors sealed tight and wondered what was really buried in that desert—bombs, munitions or something older. This was a gods-forsaken place, and it chilled her spine.

In town Jan pulled over, then turned to face Fiona.

"I've been thinking. You have a great work ethic and—except for a deficiency in math, you seem bright enough. If I get the job—and I know I will—you could work for me. To build a tight team, I'll need good people like you." From head to toe, she looked Fiona over. "Clearly, you can use the money."

That is exactly how a pyramid is built, Fiona thought. And there's nothing wrong with my math.

"No, thank you," Fiona said. "My destiny is to the south."

Jan clapped her hands.

"Shame. When opportunity knocks, you gotta answer the door. Next year, this wreck goes away and I'm driving a Mercedes. Not one of the cheap ones either, you see? My butt will settle in fine leather. Okay. This is it. Off you go." She pointed. "The Monarch is thataway. It sucks bad eggs, but it's cheap. Have a great night."

She laughed like she knew something Fiona didn't. And she did—plenty. Fiona intended to keep it that way.

The hotel was cheap, $29 including tax. Perhaps this was the cheapest hotel in America, but it was hardly worth it. The place was filled with bugs—buzzing flies, little black beetles and stealthy cockroaches. In the dingy bathroom, she crushed a scorpion and felt guilty. After all, they'd been here a million years before she—an angel of death—showed up. Too bad. If she saw one, she would kill it. Fair warning, arachnids. She hoped God would have a sense of humor about it. After all, he or she created platypuses and wombats.

There wasn't much to Hawthorne. The next morning as she walked on what passed for Main Street, she peeked in a coffeeshop window. Buster's Really Good Food. A hand-written sign said *Help Wanted*.

She walked in and the place was filled with soldiers. The cook was serving. A tween girl playing with her phone acted as hostess and cashier by pointing at empty tables and grunting.

Fiona addressed the cook.

"You Buster?" she said.

"You expect me to throw away a perfectly good sign?" he responded. "Name's Wally. The useless is Zymm, Z-Y-M-M—my granddaughter. About the name, I have no idea. Her mom was a hippie. Zymm is staying with me until her mom gets settled in Vegas with a blackjack dealer gig. Pay is a burger basket and nothing per hour, but you keep eighty percent of the tips. I keep twenty percent for Uncle Sam."

Like the taxman will ever see a dime.

What was she doing? She had money. But from deep inside, she felt that if someone offers a job, you should take it.

"I get all the tips, or I keep walking."

"City girl, eh?" he said. "Any experience slinging hash? What am I saying? Who cares? Place closes at two and we clean until three. Break a plate and you pay for it. There's a cot in the backroom if you need a place to sleep. What's yer name?"

"Fiona," she said.

In a loud voice, he addressed the room.

"You louts be nice to Fiona or I'll gut ya sideways."

She dove in and lost herself in the work. The tips were small—typically a buck or two, but they were busy all morning and she soon had an apron pocket full of cash.

Her last customer of the day was a tiny woman with dyed-black hair and over-plucked eyebrows who examined Fiona's figure carefully.

"Get tired of running around with these losers, you got everything you need to make real money at the ranch."

"What ranch is that?" Fiona said.

"The Chicken Ranch, honey. Learn to do the G-F-E and you'll

make a couple of grand a day."

Fiona laughed. She'd heard of the Chicken Ranch…one of the legal bordellos in Nevada. And, wracking her brain, she figured out what GFE was. GirlFriend Experience. She'd read about it in a People magazine. Sex was part of the bargain, but mainly these were lonely guys paying for companionship. With a vivid imagination, she pictured what that life would be like.

It would definitely be easier than running hot plates back and forth.

"No," she said after thinking things through. "Thanks, but that's not my vibe."

A few minutes before 2:00, Zymm turned the OPEN sign to CLOSED.

Two guys dressed in greasy overalls came in before she could lock the door.

"Closed!" she bellowed.

"Pay her laziness no attention," Wally said. "I'll make you a sandwich."

While Fiona watched, Zymm took bills from the cash register and stuffed them in her pocket. Then she sauntered out the door and up the sidewalk.

Wally shrugged.

"She gets fifty a day."

"What does she do with it?"

"There's a video arcade, if you want to call it that. A few games at the market. Kids hang out there. She drives the hormonal toads crazy. Keeps her busy, I guess. She's getting used to wielding the power of a woman's body. She'll figure it out or she won't—there's nothing I can do. If you can do something with her, I'd appreciate it."

He led Fiona to the backroom and pointed at a lawn chair with an inflatable mattress on it. Stacked on top, a pillow and blankets.

She checked—no bugs. It was already better than the roach motel.

"All yours," he said. "If you make yourself a sandwich, make me one, too. I'll be watching the baseball game. If it's too loud, too bad. My house, my rules."

Over the next week, she learned more than she ever wanted to know about munitions…their use and storage. Every other year, they would shoot samples at a range to prove the inventory was still viable. She didn't mind the soldiers, mostly they were young, earnest and serious about playing their part in protecting the homeland and doing their duty. Between shifts, the tribal cops would stop in and compare notes. As a notorious speed trap, they made a fortune in traffic tickets.

Fiona studied Zymm—who was not stupid but had to be the laziest person Fiona had ever met. Even when it was easier to do something than not, the girl would pointedly refuse to help. Her apparent plan was to have others serve her—particularly the boys who catered to her whims.

One afternoon, Fiona walked up to watch Zymm thumb around on her phone.

"What are you playing?" Fiona said.

"It looks to me like boys will do anything if there's the slightest chance they can cop a feel."

Fiona laughed.

"No, on your phone. What game are you playing?"

"Oh. Fallout."

Zymm said those words as if they explained everything that needed to be explained.

"It must be fun," Fiona said.

"It would be more fun if you weren't bothering me," the girl said. "Mosey."

Mosey was an interesting word and it made Fiona wonder if Zymm was smarter and wiser than she appeared. She was a puzzle and Fiona was determined to figure her out.

The next day, Fiona confronted Zymm.

"I swear, I've never met a lazier person."

Zymm looked up.

"I prefer to think of myself as highly efficient."

Fiona grabbed the phone and looked.

"This isn't any kind of video game I know. What is this?"

"Mind your own flippin' business."

Fiona studied the screen. It was something she'd never heard of.

Khan Academy. Introduction to Statistics.

Zymm grabbed the phone back. Wally rang the bell and Fiona walked to the IR heaters to pick up the order. She leaned over and raised her voice so Wally could hear over his sizzling grill.

"Don't worry about that girl," Fiona said. "She's going to be just fine."

"I was hoping you'd say that," Wally said. "Now, are you working or gabbing? Order up!"

To be annoying and redundant, he slammed his palm on the bell.

However, he was grinning and couldn't seem to stop.

Smelling the tang of chopped onions, Fiona pulled the chiliburger across, raised it and carried it to the table.

They were efficient in working together, so the restaurant—smelling of bleach and the vile industrial purple cleaning fluid Wally bought in 5-gallon buckets—was clean in 55 minutes.

Zymm was long gone, of course.

Fiona filled a plastic cup with ice and filled it with filtered water from the soda dispenser. She leaned back against the counter to catch her breath.

Wally approached, took the cup from her and drank deeply.

"Thanks," he said.

"Right, boss," she replied with sarcasm dialed up to 11 before turning to refill her cup.

"When do you figure on moving on?"

She had been feeling antsy and her mind had already taken the next step. Her pockets were full of cash. She was ready. However, she didn't know he knew.

"Soon, I guess," she said.

"I have a proposition. Wait until Sunday and take the Trailways bus to Las Vegas with her majesty."

"I don't want to be her babysitter."

"Let's call it an escort. And there's a hundred bucks in it for you. Your favorite. Easy money."

It sounded like about ten bucks an hour to Fiona, but she shrugged.

"Okay, I'm in," she said.

Soon, it was Sunday, and the three odd companions waited for the bus at the gas station that acted as depot. Zymm was chatting with a young man. When he leaned in to kiss her cheek, she gently pushed him away.

"Poor kid," Wally said as Zymm approached the bus.

Zymm shrugged.

"He was good practice."

Fiona and Wally exchanged a glance.

"She's something," Fiona said.

"Look," Wally said. "If you ever find your way back up here again…"

Fiona visualized the map, then laughed. Hawthorne was about as far away from anywhere as you could get.

"Unlikely," she said.

He grinned and held out his hand for a shake.

"Yeah, I know. I wish you gentle winds and easy seas."

"There's no need for all this extreme emotion," she replied. "Besides, we ain't going nowhere until I get the hundred bucks."

He laughed and fished the bill out of his pocket.

"Safe travels," he said.

The coach was surprisingly comfortable with seats much nicer than a modern commercial aircraft. Feeling vaguely superior, Fiona enjoyed being high above the road and looking down on everyone but the long-distance truckers…who she stared at eye-to-eye for brief but pithy instants of time.

Zymm had the aisle seat but spent all her time staring at the tiny screen on her phone—isolated from the world with earbuds stuffed in deep.

The landscape, though surrounded by distant ridges, was desolate.

The long trip would be boring without conversation and Fiona was determined to at least try. She wracked her brain for something to say.

She pulled out Zymm's nearest earbud.

"Those boys you are teasing?" Fiona said.

"What about them?"

"Like a gun, a car or a chainsaw, they're useless unless they're dangerous."

"So?"

"Most men are useful."

Zymm stuffed the earbud back in.

"Thanks for that pearl," she mumbled.

Fiona held on, tugged it free again.

"Give me a better response."

Zymm sighed, then smirked.

"Fine. Men are like chainsaws—hot, smelly and they'll take your leg off if you're careless. Not exactly a toy."

Fiona let the desert roll by a moment, then leaned in.

"True. But in the right hands, a chainsaw clears a path."

Zymm blinked, then gave a nod.

"Old people are strange," she said.

Impatiently, Zymm gestured. Satisfied, Fiona handed the earbud back, then leaned back in her seat. She couldn't hold back. A contented smile crawled slowly across her face. She did a head-to-toe inventory. From walking all day, she had toned her leg muscles, but they ached and her feet were very sore. Her shoulders and neck muscles were tight. Daydreaming, she weighed the cost of a Swedish tissue massage.

Maybe if I can get a deep, deep discount.

She wasn't fully asleep, but for hours, her mind drifted until the man behind her tapped on her shoulder.

"Next stop, Area 51," he said in a conspiratorial whisper. "Cost me a hundred in cash, but the driver is letting me off. I'm renting a Jeep and I know where to go. Got a map off the Internet. You want, you can come with if you split the gas with me. There will be plenty of money to throw around when we bring back undeniable pieces of aliens."

Turning, Fiona got up on her knees and turned to look down on the man. He was about 70 with a long, gray beard and hard belly bulge like half a watermelon under his Carhartt shirt. A serious professional drinker.

"The key," he said, "is to take a lot of water...at least a gallon a day. That's per-person."

He looked more like a gallon-a-day whiskey man.

Fiona tapped on Zymm's shoulder. It took a minute, but the girl finally looked up.

"Any interest in Area 51?" Fiona said.

Before replacing the earbud, Zymm grunted in derision.

"Tourist trap bullshit," she said.

Fiona grinned.

Good girl.

"Sorry, mister," she said. "You're on your own for this one."

At the Area 51 fleece factory, the driver did not pull completely off the road; he eased off to the side with hazard lights flashing while angry trucks whizzed by.

"Five seconds," the driver said. "Move."

The man was ready—standing by the front door with his knapsack, mirror glasses and floppy hat. With gears grinding, the bus moved again as the man's feet hit the gravel.

As they pulled away, Zymm lifted two fingers and waggled them.

"Have fun, prospector," she mumbled.

Fiona: Sin City

THE BUS TERMINAL at the south end of the Vegas Strip was mobbed with arriving travelers, panhandlers and dodgy men standing in the shadows with eyes that missed nothing. For an instant, Fiona felt a nervous pit in her stomach but realized she had survived the mean streets of Square City. In comparison, this was nothing to worry about.

They arrived right at dusk...the time when the city changed from hot, brown and dirty to color-bright and semi-magical. Almost immediately, a squat Native American man wearing a huge straw hat pressed a slip of paper into her hand.

"Discount massage," he said. "No funny business."

"Thank you," she said.

Surprised at the recognition—most people refused the paper and brushed by him—he looked her over.

"If you have strong hands, they can put you to work."

"No funny business?" she said.

He laughed and his gold teeth flashed in the waning light.

"Okay, everything in this town is funny business, but no one will make you do anything you don't want to. Want to be poor like me? Stay poor. Want to get rich? Tell them Juan sent you and Clarita will take care of you." He glanced at Zymm who was absorbed in her phone. "Both of you. Almost free."

Across the parking lot, an enthusiastic woman waved.

"Gotta run, *hermano*," Fiona said.

She tugged Zymm's arm and pulled her across the parking lot. Curious about the mother, Fiona studied the woman. She wore flat-heeled shoes and a black pantsuit uniform with gold braid. Nametag. Adina. *Roma*. Fiona glanced at Zymm. Odd, because ethnicity was something she was usually hyperaware of, but it was something she hadn't noticed before. Gypsy blood. Insight about Zymm's nature clicked into place.

A large floppy, black and gold bow was attached to the top of Adina's head. This didn't help her seem taller. She was small and slight. Mousy. There was a dusting of black and gold glitter on her cheeks.

The next thing Fiona noticed: Adina was not the mother. The sister—an aunt.

Fiona wasn't sure she wanted to know what happened to the mother. It was certainly a long, sad story.

After hugging the passive Zymm, Adina turned her eyes toward Fiona.

"Fiona, dear. It's nothing to brag about, but a pull-out couch is all yours for as long as you want it."

She was surprised, though she shouldn't have been.

"You know me?"

The woman smiled.

"Walzember and I talk, and the kid sends me a text message when she feels like it."

It took a few moments to sink in.

Walzember. Wally. Okay. I need to start paying closer attention.

Over her shoulder, she heard an announcement on the public address system.

Greyhound. Next stop: Flagstaff. Bay 7.

While still hugging, Fiona whispered to Adina.

"She's a decent kid."

"You were good for her."

Fiona pulled back.

"Say what? She hardly knew I existed. As far as she was concerned, I was wallpaper."

"No, you're wrong. She loves you. Thank you for everything."

"Are you okay?" Fiona said. "Need a few dollars?"

Adina laughed.

"We're poor, not broke. She make it sound worse? I deal blackjack clean, good tips, no trouble with my license. The lawyer's retainer set us back, that's all. We've got a pool at the complex, food on the table—we're fine."

Fiona pulled away and walked back toward the terminal. Halfway, she turned to look, but the two women were already gone. In their place, the Strip had come alive—flickering, gaudy and irresistible.

With a minute to spare, she bought her ticket and stepped onto the Flagstaff bus.

The noisy bus was nearly full of chattering Laotians, but she found a driver's side window seat toward the back. Not feeling social, she sat quietly and aligned her molecules to become as close to invisible as humanly possible.

Briefly, she wondered why there were so many of these women—where they were going and what were they doing. By listening in, she figured it out. It was a low-budget tour group, and their guide was completely incompetent. For example, he made a big deal out of their crossing of one of the eighteenth wonders of the world, the Hooper Dam. Listening, she figured out that these ladies worked at the fancy Phoenician resort in Scottsdale and their team had won an all-expenses paid trip. To save money, the big spenders at the Phoenician cut every possible corner, but the ladies seemed happy with their bus ride, gas station sandwiches and sleeping three-to-a-room in budget hotels. Maybe it was enough that they didn't have to work for three days.

She settled in and watched the scenery flow past—what could be seen of it via the cloudless night and three-quarter moon. To the north, the rugged Black Mountains (*Blank* Mountains described as haunted by the tour guide) were incredible—stark, desolate and scary. They *were* haunted. The tour guide had that part right. There were hulking cannibal creatures hiding in caves waiting for a wayward hiker. She shuddered to think of them eating the bone marrow of their victims. It was a miracle they had not been discovered in this modern age of satellites and cell phone cameras, but they ate almost everything and buried what little remained. This world still held many mysteries. In the creature's defense, they marked the forbidden trails but not with signs humans could understand.

They stopped for snacks and to pee in Kingman, then continued through Ash Fork and Williams. To the north, Fiona could feel the deep gash of the Grand Canyon. She could hear Zymm's voice.

It's a big hole. Who cares?

Zymm was right about that one. Sometimes a hole is just a hole.

Her seventy-pound seatmate—who looked like she was assembled from twigs—wandered off and was quickly replaced by something much larger. She didn't want to look. Like an ostrich, maybe if she didn't look, he wouldn't exist.

"That thing you did with the trolls—in the forest. Impressive."

"I did nothing."

"True. But you invoked. Who else could've done that? No one. Otherwise, you're ordinary. A flick of a talon and you're gone. The boss wants you alive for the ceremony. Did you think he was finished with your Minnie? He'll take her—body, soul, every way he pleases. She'll bear him half-breed sons until she's broken. When he's done, he'll blind her and hand her over to the orcs. If I'm lucky, I'll get a night first. Demon seed burns like acid, they say. The more she screams, the sweeter it is."

He leaned closer, jagged teeth gleaming.

"I'm in a mood. We could practice now. Climb on my lap—I'll give you a ride you won't live long enough to never forget."

For no obvious reason, she felt bold.

"Then do it, demon."

He laughed, a sound like gravel in a furnace.

"Let *me* show *you* something," Fiona said. She held out her hand. "Touch me."

He reached out with his claw and it passed through her hand like vapor.

"You don't exist. Neither do I. Physics says we're all empty space."

"You'll die screaming when Trevir tears your soul from your body."

The twig lady appeared in the aisle by the demon's seat. Reaching out, the bottle was offered to Fiona. Cackling, she said something like Loud Cow, but Fiona's mind translated.

Lao Khao.

This Laotian, rice-based liquor was strong and dangerous to the uninitiated. Her first impulse was to wave it away, then she thought, why not?

I'm not driving, Buddy is.

She took the bottle and studied it. It was crudely hand-blown with oblong bubbles left in the glass. The oily liquid sloshed.

She took a drink and it burned all the way down. Choking, she handed the bottle back and gasped.

"Very smooth. Thank you."

The seats on the bus reclined a lot…way more than an airplane seat. She pressed the button and the seat motor whined.

"You're tedious, and I'm sleepy," she said to the demon. "Go haunt someone who cares."

He leaned over, breathing rot, but she ignored him and drifted off. That insult stung, but he dared not act. His boss wanted her alive.

When the driver finally ushered everyone off, the apparition was gone—except for the stink he left behind.

Philip d'GreenApple: The Fine Art of Disappearing

AT THE CANTINA, the other drivers were looking at me oddly—like I didn't exist or like I carried a virus they didn't want to catch. It was subtle, but unmistakable. The place smelled of diesel and scorched tortillas. A boombox wheezed a *norteño* tune, the accordion sharp against the low murmur of voices.

With my plate of beans, I walked toward one of the card tables. They could use a fourth player, but they leaned in close over the cards, shoulders touching, cigarettes burning down to crooked stubs. No one looked up. It was clear they didn't want me there.

This was odd. As Vargas' golden boy, the others had always been open and friendly—we joked, insulted each other and passed a bottle of mescal. I didn't drink, but I'd fake a sip and they'd mock me mercilessly. Tonight was different. Their silence pressed harder than words. I took the hint and ate my dinner in a corner, the fiery beans cooling on the tin plate.

After a few minutes, the door banged open and José Luis stepped in. The hinges squealed, and the room seemed to pause. He scanned the room with a soldier's eyes, spotted me and marched over. Dust clung to his boots, and the smell of the night air—burnt rubber, mesquite smoke, and the faint chemical tang from the maquilas—followed him inside.

"My brother is looking for you."

"I know. I'm tired. I will go see him in the morning."

He shook his head once, sharp.

"He's getting irritated."

"Okay," I said. "After I finish my beans and pay a visit to *el trono*, I'll come to the big house. Okay?"

I put a nudge in my tone—enough to show I wasn't going to budge. I would appear, but on my terms.

He didn't like it, but he nodded, turned on his heel and left.

I lied to him; I wasn't even going to finish my dinner. I didn't like lying—it frayed the edges of my karma—but sometimes you must.

I'd said I don't believe in magic. That was a lie too, a small one. We slap a metaphysical label on things we don't understand. From childhood, we were trained by our fathers. We knew how to disappear.

I walked back to the Avalanche, pulled out my leather knapsack, and headed for the Avenida. The guards watched me, eyes flat, but didn't say a word and didn't try to stop me. The night smelled of exhaust and palo verde pollen. A dog barked somewhere down the block. I walked a mile, then climbed onto a rickety city bus. It didn't matter where it was going—as long as it was away.

After I slipped the required pesos in the slot, the bus groaned as it lurched from the curb with gears grinding like broken teeth. Inside, the cracked vinyl seats clung to passengers' backs, and the air was thick with sweat, diesel and the faint sweetness of pan dulce in a paper bag. A baby cried once, then went silent. The driver didn't stare at me, but I caught his eyes in the mirror—quick, assessing, then gone. The bus driver's world is a small one. Dusty roads. Litter. Old women slowly counting out coins from a meager pouch.

I slouched low, knapsack on my lap and let the rhythm of the engine cover me. Disappearing isn't magic. It's discipline. You don't run—you dissolve. You don't draw eyes—melt into the background. My father taught us to never move faster than the crowd and never look like you're searching for an exit. If you're invisible, it's because you've convinced yourself you belong exactly where you are. A trick is to leave pieces of yourself behind. A jacket draped on a chair, a half-finished plate of beans, a rumor whispered in the right ear. People chase ghosts while you slip out the side door.

The bus rattled past shuttered tiendas and warehouses with rusted roll-up doors. Sodium lights flickered on the Avenida, pinning us—all of us—like bugs in amber. The thought oppressed me, so I pushed it away. I didn't know where the bus was headed and I didn't care. The only thing that mattered was staying invisible.

I could've taken Vargas' pickup, gunned it across the border and put miles behind me fast—but then I'd owe him. And debts to Vargas never came cheap. So, what had I really stolen? The promise of a loyal soldier? A young gringo who slotted too neatly into his evil machine?

We travelers were slippery. We didn't believe in official bank accounts or government numbers of any kind. There were things we couldn't do—like board a commercial flight—but that was the price of freedom. We paid cash for everything. We saved in gold. In every big city, we had our own underground bank where gold could become paper and paper could become gold again.

You might wonder: how did we identify ourselves? That's where the coin came in. Lose it, and you were nobody until you got another. You could get a replacement, sure—but it took time, time and trouble.

I got off the bus by the bridge and walked across. The night air smelled of river mud and the honey mesquite growing along the riverbank. The chainlink fences hummed with the vibration of trucks idling in line. The Mexican guards waved me through without eye contact, as if I was transparent. Which I was: old boots, dusty jeans, sunburned cheeks, a broken-in San Antonio Missions cap with the red-and-blue flip-flop logo. Leather knapsack. Just an ordinary young working man.

On the Del Rio side, a U.S. border agent in a wrinkled uniform glanced at my cartel credentials, stifled a yawn and waved me on. No questions, no inspection. Ten minutes after stepping off the bus, I was back on American asphalt.

Rewarding my eternal optimism, there was a taxi waiting at the border crossing. I slipped in the backseat; the vinyl cracked and sticky from the day's heat.

"Amigo," I said. "Motel. Something cheap by the bus station."

With eyes unreadable in the rearview, the driver gave a nod and eased his old Toyota into gear. The engine coughed, then settled into a low growl. I felt sorry for his muffler. Like me, it was worn out and tired.

Outside the glass, Del Rio slid past in fragments—neon beer signs, shuttered tiendas and a stray dog nosing through trash. Inside, the cab smelled of gasoline, sweat, and the faint trace of a pine-scented air freshener that had long since given up the fight.

Deep in my gut, I felt a tug. West. After visiting the bank in San Antonio, I was going to head west.

Fiona: Flagstaff

SHE WAS THE last off the bus…she stood blinking in the morning light. The thin air was cool on her skin. Clearly, they were at altitude, but she didn't know how high. The jabbering, half-drunk Laotians streamed off to a Cracker Barrel restaurant. The driver, Buddy, a black man with a huge belly, sat on a bench under a tree and smoked a cigarette. For no reason, she sat beside him.

She pointed at the street sign.

East Lucky Lane.

"It makes me wonder if there is a West Lucky Lane," she said.

"I have no idea," he said. "Smoke?"

She shook her head.

"Nasty."

He grinned around yellow teeth.

"True that," he said.

His eyes were yellow, too,

Jaundice.

He patted his belly.

"More of me for me to love."

She considered.

"Suppose I could snap my fingers and you'd be free of all your bad habits..."

He laughed and his belly jiggled like he was made of gelatin.

"Without my bad habits, there would be nothing left," he said.

She thought about it and couldn't decide if she felt sorry for the man or not. He was who he was and seemed comfortable with it.

She was tempted to fix him anyway.

He seemed to sense that.

He pointed.

"See that cur sleeping under the juniper?"

It took a few seconds to find Waldo, but she found it.

"I see him," she said.

"That's old Sam. He's perfectly happy under that tree. Are you the kind of woman who would kick him in the ass just because you think he should be out doing something else?"

"No," she said.

"I didn't think so," he said. "Is the Flag your final destination?"

She thought about it. She'd simply been following her nose, but it did seem like she was going somewhere.

"That's the ticket I bought."

"That doesn't answer my question."

"Is there a Renaissance Faire around here someplace?"

He laughed and tears streamed down the side of his face. He mopped with a handkerchief.

"I ain't supposed to, but I can get you close. There's a rest stop where I can pull off for a minute and they won't fire me. I'll get a nastygram in my personnel file, but they'll forgive me if I tell them the ladies were going to pee their pants. No one likes cleaning pee off a seat. You follow?"

"You're starting to grow on me, Buddy. I like you."

He laughed and the mountain quivered under his smock.

"What's not to like?" he said.

It was almost ten in the morning when Buddy dropped her off. He left the diesel bus rumbling among the I-17 long-haul trucks while about half the jabbering ladies streamed off toward the restroom.

Standing at the door, she looked up at him.

"The RenFaire is south of Sedona," he said. "Fourth biggest in the U-S of A, I'm told. Big doins 'round these parts. Not my thing, but it sounds like fun."

"I can't thank you enough, Buddy."

"You can try," he said while rubbing his thumb and index finger together. I wouldn't look askance at a small gesture of appreciation."

The word *askance* stuck in her head.

She studied him more carefully.

Was his down-home, chitlin circuit image just an affectation?

"Buddy. Tsk," she said while palming him a twenty. "Greyhound don't allow drivers to take no tips."

"I'm just playin'," he said. "Take care of yourself, young lady and maybe I'll see you down the road someplace."

She turned and weaved though the grumbling trucks. In the center pavilion, there were concrete benches, but before she sat, she studied the highway map.

Sedona was off the track…it didn't look like there was an easy way to get there. There was a windy road to the north with a lot of switchbacks.

Maybe being hard to get to is part of the charm.

Waiting for inspiration, she sat on a hard bench and watched the cars come and go. A big, black, nearly silent electric SUV eased up and its batwing doors opened majestically. She'd never seen one up close before, it was cool. A young man emerged. He was beautiful…dressed in casual clothes that looked expensive. Something like six-foot-six. Tall, basketball tall. Lean. Huge, gleaming watch. Gleaming bracelets. Gleaming necklaces. Gleaming sunglasses. His longish brown hair flopping on his shoulders. He looked around the parking lot like a king admiring his kingdom.

He would make quite an impression on the ladies.

She realized he was making an impression on her.

Movie actor? Rock star? Crown prince of a middle eastern country she'd never heard of?

He was something. Deep inside her, there was a primal urge to bear his children. She pushed the instinct aside and decided to ignore him. Regardless of his handsomeness, he was irrelevant. He appeared to move randomly, but soon stood by her side, stretching and popping his back. She tried to make herself invisible, but the buzzing and humming deep in her belly would not allow it.

"Which car is yours?" he said. "Don't tell me. I'm good at this."

He had a subtle accent. East Coast something, she decided. Maybe New York, Manhattan, but mixed with Miami. Rich daddy. Raised on a full-floor condo a tall building with a doorman. In spite of all that, he was a good kid. Smart and unsullied. Protected from the raw and cruel world, but in a good way. He was on his way to being a good man.

He studied each car in turn.

She pointed at a Subaru Outback. It was one of the few that wasn't attended, so it had to be a candidate. With South Dakota plates, the little station wagon was covered with road grime and streaks from dead bugs.

"That one," she said.

He looked down on her—noting her handbag and battered suitcase—and considered.

"Bullsnot," he said. A thought struck him. "You know what? I'm going with you don't have a car here. What about that?"

"Did you stop for a piss?" She jerked her thumb over her shoulder. "Urinals are that way."

"My lord, no. This is not my kind of place. I just wanted to stretch my legs. I was getting a cramp. Are you stuck? Car breakdown?" He rubbed his chin and thought about it. "No, that's not it. You're going somewhere and this place is in between."

"Kindly, then, with no offense intended, please stretch those long pegs somewhere else."

He laughed.

"You have no idea who I am."

It wasn't a question. He seemed to enjoy the notion—like it was something weird that had never happened before.

"Barron," he said.

"The baron? The baron of what? Saudi Arabia?"

"No, just Barron with two r's. Guess what? I like you. But the problem is: everyone likes you."

Not everyone.

Besides, how could that be a problem?

She pondered.

He flicked a finger at his driver, who—with wary eyes flicking around—came out.

He was dressed casually, too, but not fancy like the King. Fiona could tell he was armed. Big-bore pistol in an expensive and inconspicuous waistband holster.

He handed Fiona a shiny, gold and black business card.

She didn't look at it, just dropped it on the bench beside her hip.

"You're my guest," he said. "Stay as long as you like, but don't go crazy with room service."

He tapped the driver on the shoulder, and they walked back to the car. Standing by the unfurled door, the young man turned and spoke.

"Sit tight and a car will come for you."

With dual-motors whining, the car backed up and hustled away.

It took fifteen minutes, but finally curiosity overtook her. She picked up the card and looked it over—front and back.

There was no writing, just a fancy picture of a gold palace against a glossy black background.

Barron of what? she thought. *Fancy cards?*

Externally, she was unimpressed. Deep inside was a different story.

She was beyond childbearing age, but that didn't matter. No matter how she might be sliced and diced, she was still a woman who responded to a good mating candidate.

Try as she might, she could not think of anything wrong with that.

After sitting another hour...doing absolutely nothing, a black Lincoln SUV cruised through the parking lot. Except for a gold "T" emblazoned on the front door, it was unmarked. While it idled at the curb, she spent a whole minute pretending it was not for her.

The driver, behind tinted glass, was invisible.

Finally, she gave up and approached. With a loud click, the side door unlocked and she pulled it open.

Twisting, the driver reached out for the black business card.

"I think I'll hold onto it," she said.

She slipped it in her blouse pocket.

Interesting that the driver did not get out to help with her bag. Maybe his instructions were to pick her up...but without added instructions to treat her special. If she ever saw the Barron again, she'd raise the topic.

I am, after all, the Queen.

This made her grin.

The Queen of cleaning toilets and refilling endless coffee cups. The Queen of Greyhound busses.

Once she was settled and her seatbelt was buckled, the driver eased out of the parking lot and onto the highway.

After a few boring miles, Fiona decided to engage the driver.

"How long have you worked for the Baron?" she said.

"It's just Barron," he replied.

This amused her. Referring to Barron as The Baron irritated them. So, she determined to keep doing it.

His mom should have picked a different name if it bothers everyone so much. What's wrong with Robert, William or David?

She made the rest of the trip with a smile on her face.

Fiona: Sedona

OTHER THAN AN elaborate gold T on the black gate, the private hotel was unmarked. Fiona figured it out. The locals didn't like chain hotels...particularly ones owned by an unpopular ex-President. She wasn't a big fan either, but looking around the place, decided it would be stupid not to take advantage of the situation.

She handed her handbag to the bellman. He couldn't have been impressed but hid it well. He reached in, pulled out her suitcase and placed it on a rolling cart. Rough-looking and lonely, it looked stupid all alone on the fancy cart. There was no checking in. She was hustled straight to her room. 107. She walked through the suite. Beyond the balcony, a creek gurgled.

"Oak Creek," the Bellman said. "Runs year around."

This struck her as an odd thing to say but remembered this was Arizona. A creek running year-around was noteworthy.

She didn't know why she teased him, but she did.

"Is there a room service menu?"

"Doordash works here," he said. "Domino's pizza will deliver. Or, the car will take you to town. If you give me your credit card, we will put it on file and take care of everything for you."

"Sorry," she said. "No credit card."

"Of course not," he replied. "Please go easy on us. I hope you understand...when the bosses have whims, it can be hard to get them to pay us back. Half the time, we eat extra expenses."

She thought things over, then decided.

"Can you give me two minutes to pee?"

He shrugged, then nodded.

After using the bathroom, she walked out on the balcony and looked into the foliage where, twenty feet below, the cheery creek gurgled and babbled. Reflecting fractured sunlight, it was peaceful and beautiful. Soothing. She held her palms out in the sunlight and soaked in rays—warmth from infrared and prickly needles of stinging ultraviolet.

She then turned to face the bellman.

"How far to the main part of town?"

"A little over a mile, but no sidewalks," he said.

She fished around in the front pocket of her jeans and found another twenty-dollar bill...which she handed to the man.

"What's this?" he said.

"I don't want to owe you anything."

He was confused.

"Are you checking out? I can drive you. Until you get to town, the road is not safe for pedestrians."

She plucked her suitcase from the cart.

Then. over her shoulder, she said, "No thank you. I will take my chances and walk."

A half-hour later, flushed and sweaty from lugging her suitcase in the hot sun, she regretted her decision. The bellman was right. The road was unsafe and the drivers were crazy. It seemed like a game to them to see how close they could pass by without hitting her. It was nerve-wracking.

But slowly, the commercial part of town came into view and her discomfort was forgotten. It was busy with cars honking and jockeying for parking spaces while pedestrians milled around with dripping ice cream cones. In the distance, the landscape was wonderful, but the crass commerce wasn't. She could see why locals might have an allergic reaction to an east coast billionaire building a chain hotel.

She marched by the gift shops and weaved through enthusiastic young tour company salesfolks dressed all in pink.

People-people-people, everywhere. There were too many of them.

She felt claustrophobic until remembering she could turn invisible. Instantly, things were better without hungry eyes weighing and measuring her net worth and trying to get her money. With no destination, she walked and walked until laying her eyes on a business off the main drag.

Meg's Bakehouse. Authentic European Bakery.

Until that instant, Fiona had not realized there was a hole in her stomach exactly the size of a crumpet.

No, two.

Lugging a suitcase that increasingly felt like it weighed a million pounds, she walked through the front door—enjoying the tuned tinkle of bells mounted above the door

Wiping her hands on a towel, a woman emerged from the back.

Like all good bakers, she was as wide as she was tall. Laying eyes on Fiona, her voice boomed.

"Where have you been! I've been waiting all year for you!"

Startled, Fiona dropped the suitcase.

WTF?

Sitting at a small table, a thin man looked up from his espresso.

"Meg, stop it. Look at this poor lady, you scared the wits out of her." He gestured to Fiona. "Pay no mind, she says that to everyone she's never met before. I'm Lemmy. That's Meg. Join me and take a load off those sore feet."

Staring at Meg, Fiona said, "I saw you in a dream."

"If so, sweetie, get yer money back. My life is so boring, my movie would be a still life. I'm going to guess your name—I'm good at this."

In a low voice, Lemmy said, "She's terrible—got one right in 1998 and has been insufferable ever since. Watch, you'll see."

Thinking, the Meg made a big show.

"Got it. Ester!"

"No one is named Ester, ever," Lemmy said. "Tell her."

Fiona pointed at herself. "Fiona."

"Even a blind squirrel never finds no nut half the time," Meg said. "You ruined my fun."

Lemmy wagged his finger at Fiona. "Don't bother trying to figure her out—you'll just tie yourself in knots."

Hovering, Meg said, "What are you having, dearie?"

"You have homebrew pollen tea. I can smell it."

"I'm impressed," Meg said. "Lavender, pekoe and cinnamon with local honey to take the edge off the bitter. You got it. Something to eat?"

"Yes," Fiona said. "Two crumpets, please."

Meg stared.

"Sorry, no crumpets. How about a croissant, scone or donut?"

Lemmy spoke up.

"You damned well make crumpets for yourself and have a stash of them in back."

"You wouldn't know a crumpet if it jumped up and bit you on the pecker...if your pecker could be found."

"Meg, settle down. For all you know, your customer is the sensitive type." Turning to Fiona, he said, "Are you delicate?"

For some reason, Fiona nodded her head.

"Yes. Very."

Meg exploded.

"Nonsense! In my own house! First, she eats all my crumpets and then wants to strangle me tongue. I'll not have it, not for a split atomizer. Next, she'll be asking for homemade marmalade."

Catching on, Fiona grinned at Lemmy.

"Yes, please," she said. "Apricot if you have it."

While eating their brunch, Meg calmed down. Now and then, she got up to serve a customer but always came back.

"When you dreamed about me, I hope you dreamed me fifty pounds lighter."

"And maybe fewer chin hairs," Lemmy quipped.

Fiona thought about it.

"I didn't dream of any pictures, just your name. I'm here to find my daughter."

Lemmy and Meg looked at each other.

"Daughter?" Lemmy said.

"Well, not my daughter exactly, but sort of. Her real mother died."

Meg pointed at the sky, then her head.

"The name is coming to me…"

"This is stupid," Lemmy said. "Your daughter's name is Minnie."

Disappointed, Meg said, "I was just going to say that. Why do you ruin everything? Don't you have errands or deliveries? We girls could do without your constant interrupting."

Lemmy glanced at his watch.

"Crap. You're right, I need to make a run for the Rennies."

"Good, now we ladies can get deep into life stories and gossip. I want to know everything."

"Rennies?" Fiona said. "Do you mean people at the Renaissance Faire? Could you run me out there?"

"Wait a minute," Meg complained.

"Sure," Lemmy said. "You want to go; I can haul you. I'll throw your bag in the back of the van."

Meg wanted to complain, but at that very instant, a group walked in the door.

"Where have you been!" Meg shouted. "I've been waiting all year for you!"

Lemmy and Fiona used the distraction to slip out.

After starting, the old van spit out clouds of blue smoke that eventually subsided as they merged into traffic.

"I have a favor to ask," Fiona said.

"Ask it," Lemmy said.

"I want to hide and call no attention to myself. I'm new to the world again and I want to take things slow."

"New to the world? What does that mean?" He glanced over and saw how serious she was. "That will be like trying to hide a spotlight under a wicker basket. But I will do my part. What are you hiding from?"

She thought about it.

"I guess I'm hiding from myself," she said.

Philip d'GreenApple: There's Always Free Cheese in a Mousetrap

IN THE MORNING, I put away three McDonald's breakfast burritos—it took that many before I felt satisfied. After dumping my trash, I walked down Veterans Boulevard toward the IBC Bank with a cup of decent coffee burning through the paper cup into my palm. The strip was already alive—semis rumbling past, the McDonald's golden arches glowing against the pale sky, the smell of tortillas drifting from Taco Bell across the way, and a car with an open window rolling by with talk radio hissing about complicated conspiracies.

By the time the bank opened, I was standing in front of a short line of impatient customers shifting from foot to foot and clutching their paychecks. Their day was wasting. They wanted to get on with it.

Promptly at nine, the glass doors sighed open and I stepped into the coolness of the IBC lobby. The place smelled faintly of floor wax and copier toner. Overhead, lazy ceiling fans circulated the air.

When it was my turn, I slid my fake ID and account slip across the counter. The clerk was young with streaky hair pulled tight and nails painted a glossy pink. Thick powder covered raw acne sores. They looked painful. She tapped at her keyboard, eyes flicking between the screen and me.

"I'd like to empty my account," I said. "Cash. Leave a balance of seventeen seventy-five."

Staring at her screen and pecking on the keyboard, her fingers froze for a moment, then resumed tapping. A crease formed between her eyebrows. She leaned closer to the monitor, then looked up at me.

Something was wrong.

"I'm sorry, Mister Dodd. It will take three days to gather that much cash. Can you come back?"

"I will be far away from here in three days. What are my options?"

"If you give me an hour, I could issue a cashier's check," she said carefully. "That's as good as cash."

Clearly, this was a trap. I considered just bailing and abandoning the money. She printed a receipt and slid it across the counter. I glanced at the balance. Low six figures. More than I expected. Enough to make me wonder why Alvarez goosed the account.

It was too much money to ditch.

I nodded, trying to look casual.

"Fine. Let's do that. I'll come back at ten."

I folded the slip into my pocket and walked out into the heat, the sun already baking Veterans Boulevard. An hour to kill. An hour to think about my life and the mistakes I made. The mistakes I would make. A line from a movie drifted in my head.

There's always free cheese in a mousetrap.

This made me smile.

The Way of the Gun. There were a lot of great lines in this movie. My favorite was a tangled mess delivered perfectly by James Caan.

I can promise you a day of reckoning you won't live long enough to never forget.

Grinning and mumbling, I'm sure the few people I passed on the street thought I was crazy. A plump Hispanic girl pushing a stroller crossed the road to get away from me. I knew I had to get away. Without breaking a sweat, Vargas' men could find me in Del Rio and haul me back across the river. That would not be good. Every minute spent lingering was dangerous. Oddly, I felt cheerful and light on my feet like my head was filled with Helium.

With nothing else to do, I walked. Past the Whitehead Museum, where the old cabins sat behind chainlink. Past Casa de la Cultura, its walls bright with murals and a poster for a *folklórico* class. A block over, the old firehouse had been turned into an arts council with banners flapping in the heat.

On Veterans, the Chamber of Commerce and Civic Center stood prim and official with flags snapping in the breeze, while across the street a stray dog nosed a greasy Whataburger sack. A billboard promised escape at Amistad Lake—blue water and jet skis—but the only water here shimmered in the mirages rising off the asphalt.

Through the window at Skillets, four airmen in rumpled green fatigues leaned over plates of Belgian waffles drowned in whipped cream and blueberries, laughing between mouthfuls. Their joy and comradery steamed up the glass. I stood outside, hungry for more than breakfast.

I killed the hour this way, circling the heart of Del Rio, watching the city breathe in the heat. Then I headed back toward the bank.

It was funny how an hour can—at the same time—be a blink of an eye and an eternity. But it passed, and I walked back toward the bank.

On the dusty street, sitting on a pale-green electrical box, a familiar figure.

Of course.

Alvarez.

Fiona: Ren Faire

AFTER TURNING OFF the paved road, Lemmy followed a dirt track outside the towering Faire walls, then checked in at the vendor entrance. The attendant with a clipboard, Paulie, made do with canvas overalls and a floppy hat.

Close enough for RenFaire work.

"How they hanging, Lem?"

"Same-same. Loose and lonely."

"I hear ya, brother. Who's your friend?"

Lemmy glanced over at Fiona, then turned back to Paulie.

"No one."

"Got it," Paulie said. "Half the folks here like to keep a low profile if you catch my drift."

"She could use a bed. Know anyone with a spare?"

Paulie thought it over.

"A couple options come to mind, but the safest? Have her try Spring."

"Roger that. How's business so far?"

Paulie grinned.

"You know as well as anyone—what with all the sold-out pastries you deliver. Gangbusters. Record year so far. We'll get a profit-sharing bonus this year, no problem. Hey, you wouldn't..."

Lemmy grinned while handing over an oil-drenched paper sack.

"You know it, brother."

To Fiona, he said, "Paulie likes cream puffs."

With his attention on the sack one hundred percent, Paulie waved the van in. On a rough passageway, Lemmy weaved around behind the array of wooden buildings. Behind the public areas, the facilities needed paint and repair—and always would.

Lemmy stopped and pointed through a gap.

"Spring runs the bookshop. If you're into mediaeval erotica, ask to see her private collection." He winked. "That stuff will put the damp in your knickers. Be careful, though—she'll put you to work."

Through the gap, Fiona could see a noisy crowd catcalling a juggler who tossed red rubber balls. His lips were moving, but she couldn't hear what he said. From the distant corner of her mind, she heard the wisps of a tune but quickly lost it.

"He has the best bawdy jokes—catch him when there are no kids around."

"Give me a minute," she said.

He looked at her. She wasn't having a panic attack but seemed to be headed that way.

"Take all the time you need," he said.

She settled herself, then worked on stillness for all of her cells, starting with the tips of her toes and ending with the frizzy hair on her head.

He was startled.

"How did you do that? I know you're here, but you're out of focus. It's weird. Did you go somewhere?"

To herself in a quiet, breathy voice, she recited a charm.

The breeze flows through me and we are one.

"Please," she said, "don't talk about me with anyone until I'm ready."

"Okay, but can I ask why?"

She thought about it.

"I'd tell you if I knew. I've been away and I'm not ready to engage the world yet, not fully. Can we leave it at that?"

"You got it. Need anything? Spread the word and I'll see what I can do."

She opened the van door and retrieved her suitcase.

"Thank you. I appreciate what you have done for me already."

"De nada," he said. "See you around. Give the door a good slam—it's sticky."

Firmly, she shut the van door and he rumbled away—leaving a miasma of harsh fumes for her to choke on.

Greyhound bus, fancy hotel shuttle, beater van.

She smiled at the vector of her day.

What's next? Rickety rickshaw?

Top it off, her feet hurt from all the walking with a 9,000-pound suitcase.

She took a deep breath and settled her cells one final time. Through the gap between buildings, she could see the sign.

Spring's Olde English Tomes—Books for Everyone.

Gathering her courage, she started walking.

Fiona-Face

HARRIET'S HUGE DRESSES looked like curtains from an old hotel; the colors were faded and the materials were thick and stiff. There was speculation that she made them herself with a sewing machine used for making canvas sails.

Patty was doctoring a cup of bitter breakroom coffee with Cremora and sugar when Harriet entered like a hurricane.

"The kids are up to something in the gym," Harriet said. "I saw Tara and a few other troublemakers sneak in."

"They're up early."

"She had a bucket of paint. We should check on them."

Patty looked at her steaming coffee with regret.

"That doesn't sound good," she said. "I suppose we should."

They bustled off and peeked through a slat of windows.

Inside, six girls argued over a sketch on the far wall. The loudest voice belonged to the meek Tara.

"We need to get the eyebrows right before we start painting. Less arch. We're making her look like she stepped on a spider."

"She has a point," Patty said. "She doesn't look like that." She laughed. "They got the wild hair right, though. Like a tumbleweed on LSD."

Harriet turned to look at Patty.

"Why are they painting a giant Fiona-face?"

"Beats me."

"This is clearly against school policy. Staff has to approve all art, then the school board gets involved. By the time a proposal is approved, the kids don't care anymore...which is half the point. Otherwise, we'd have Taylor Swift painted everywhere on everything. We need to report this."

Patty thought it over.

"Screw the rules...let's leave them be."

In concentration, Harriet's brows furrowed, then she made a zipper gesture on her lips.

"I didn't see nothin'," she said.

Fiona: Spring Time

LOVING THE SOLID clunk of antique tumblers, M slid the brass key into the lock, then walked through her bookshop's heavy mahogany door. Not just any bookshop. *Her* bookshop. After scrimping, saving and putting everything she had on the table, she had talked the retiring old man into lowering the price. He didn't need the money but wasn't giving away his life's work. However, it was time for it to be passed on and he wanted it to go to real lover of books, not someone who would make it into a fancy shop making money selling coffees with unpronounceable names and way-too-fancy pastries.

Thinking back, M vividly remembered their negotiation.

Through spirals of smoke, the old man's eyes held a piercing, steady gaze under bushy gray eyebrows. His tangled beard had embedded biscuit crumbs. He puffed on an ornate, amber-colored meerschaum and ivory pipe.

Though the bookshelves overflowed with interesting titles, the shop needed a serious airing out.

"M," he said. "That's an interesting name. Why do you call yourself that?"

"When I was younger, I was in love with the Magic Tree House series. I read them cover to cover, over and over. There was a character named Morgan Le Fay who signed her mysterious letters to Jack and Annie with ~M. I read those books far past when I should have, to be honest."

"Morgan Le Fay. Do you know where that came from? King Aurthur's mysterious stepsister, Morgana le Faye. *You cannot defeat me, for I am the shadow that lingers even in the light.*"

M shrugged.

"I was a teenager before I figured that out."

"Then what?"

"My fifth-grade teacher convinced me to branch out by easing me into the series about owls."

"Ahhh, I know that series. Wonderful books. *And in the still, deepest part of the night, four owls lifted into flight, their shadows printed on the hard desert sand below by the last spray of the moon's light.* Delicious, luscious writing. Go on."

"From there, I dived into Tolkien and the rest, as they say, is history. All my life: dragons, swords and sorcery. Through it all, the name stuck. I'm M."

The old man smiled; then and there deciding he'd found the shop's new owner. However, it was a small smile quickly hidden by fingers massaging his abundant, smoke-stained mustache as he prepared to negotiate.

Observant, M noted the man's brief smile and began thinking past the sale about what would stay and what would go as she made her mark on the place. She loved it as it was, but like everything else in the world, it could use vivid splashes of color. And, the military history section could be culled with discounts to make room for more children's books.

By crossing out his name and scribbling in hers, they reassigned the lease. In payment, he wanted gold coins. She pulled 10 shiny Krugerrands from her satchel and pushed them across the table. His accounts were kept in a large leatherbound ledger. She ran a slim finger down the numbers. The last one was large and unexpected.

"Is this right?" she said.

"To the *franc à cheval*, farthing and shekel," he said with fake offense.

"But…" she said. "…that means, basically I get the place for free."

"Listen, young lady. From an estate sale, I acquired a fine-condition, first-edition J.K. Rowling, *Harry Potter and the Philosopher's Stone*, with the spelling error on the back cover—along with a signed letter and book plate. I took payment in bitcoins at less than fifty dollars each—then held them. I have them now. How much do you think I care about your pennies? Besides, young lady, my surname? Harmsworth? The publishing Harmsworths? Does that mean nothing to you?"

It was embarrassing to recall, but back then, that name *didn't* hold meaning to her. Much later, she figured it out. Lord Northcliffe. The Daily Mail. Heaps and bushels of old publishing money.

She sighed.

Ah, to be young and clueless again.

Sipping her tea, her thoughts returned to history.

"Don't leave without advice. What will be the secrets to my success?"

He smiled.

"For an author's signing event, have them bring in inventory and take everything unsold away with them."

She thought about it.

"That's cold and cynical."

"True, but essential or you'll be swimming in hopeless books. Very well, how about this…don't let unsupervised children in the rare book room. Before allowing any entry, make the customers wash their hands thoroughly. And in there, no sweaty cotton gloves or Starbucks cups."

"That's like a basic intelligence test. Give me credit for having common sense. Give me something good."

"Don't buy books from customers—particularly Harlequin novels from spinsters. Instead, buy smart from estate sales where the spoiled heirs don't know what they have. Offer quick cash for everything and sort through it all later."

"I don't know anyone."

"I will pass along referrals until key people get to know you."

"Thank you. There must be more…"

Behind his bushy mustache, he smiled.

"In the locked case, there is a fine Jack Kerouac *On the Road* signed first edition with original dust jacket and authentication letter from Ken Sanders. Don't sell it cheap—the price is the price and the right buyer will be happy to pay it. If you get stuck, send me a letter. Handwritten, not typed or printed. If it's worth that much effort, I will help. Otherwise, no more freebies, young lady."

An old woman herself now, the shop was only open during the six weeks of the Ren Faire. To avoid being bothered, she hired girls to serve the public selling *Hunger Games* and *Twilight* books to preteens while she hid in the rare book room and read Liu Cixin, Haruki Murakami and William Gibson novels over and over until she felt like she understood them.

Of course, when entering the bookshop, Fiona knew nothing about any of this.

Fiona: Story Time for a Little Princess

M HEARD WHISPERINGS and murmurings from the East, that the Queen had finally awoke and was afoot in the world—hiding from the world and gathering her strength.

Somehow knowing Fiona would one day tread the worn wooden floorboards of the bookshop, M set to work, crafting a daily ritual with the simmer pot. Into the cauldron of scents, she tossed cinnamon sticks with bark curling like ancient magic scrolls and whole cloves, each a tiny orb of dark, potent spice.

She added orange rinds with peels like fragments of the sun's own skin and brown, sinuous twists of vanilla beans which whispered of distant jungles and secret rites. The room's air filled with steam carrying whispers of old spells and the promise of future gatherings, each welcoming scent a note in an aromatic symphony composed to welcome Fiona when she arrived.

In her soul, M knew Fiona could ground here and regain her wits. For everything to come, Fiona would need her strength.

As M went around and turned on the lights she hummed a little tune. The shop was an odd one. From the front door to the back door, the distance was less than three-hundred feet. However, inside, the passageways weaved through the shelves and stacks and the distance was much greater. It was hard to imagine how much. A mile, maybe. Or more.

How was this possible?

M smiled.

It wasn't.

She made her morning tea and sat on a cyan pillow covering the window seat to look out at the main street—watching the world slowly wake up as she planned her day. She got up and walked along with her feather duster and dusted book spines. She heard them giggle with delight. They loved to be tickled. She never had to worry about alphabetizing the books as she knew the hard-working book elves and faeries saw to that task during the night. M always left them little bowls of baked treats and mead to make their task more enjoyable.

As the village bells chimed, M muttered to herself.

"I suppose it's time to open for the day."

She hated it when the store opened late—the boss got really mad.

The fact that she was the boss was irrelevant; she didn't like being mad at herself.

She turned the wooden placard to *Open* and unlocked the front door. The neighborhood cat sleeping on the front stone stoop promptly stood up and walked inside as if he owned the place.

Which was true enough. A cat owns everything he or she sees.

"Well, hello there, Simon. Have you been waiting long? How was your evening? Are you ready for bowls of fresh water, cream and kibble?"

A chowhound, Simon purred excitedly and trotted behind M as she went in the back room to get the bowls. As she was back there warming up the cream, a customer came in.

"I'm back here—I'll be out in a minute. If you have any questions, I'm more than happy to help."

A small, faint "hmmmm" came in response, so M kept going about her task. Simon wouldn't wait for anyone, especially a customer who barely acknowledged his mistress M.

"There you go, Simon. Enjoy it all and don't make a mess like you always do."

She scritched his fuzzy marmalade head and went out front.

M did a quick scan of the shop. She never worried about people stealing from her; her prices were reasonable and if someone truly couldn't afford a book, M would work out a deal with them. She found the customer down the herb aisle. She had long curly hair and she turned to face M, she had the most stunning eyes. She was dressed in ragged jeans, Birks and a flannel vest with a t-shirt beneath. She had a well-worn backpack over one shoulder and smelled of jasmine.

"Fiona," M whispered to herself.

"Good morning," she said, playing it cool. "Is there something I can help you find?"

Fiona smiled.

The sun taking notice sent bright beams though the dusty windows. M continued.

"I just made fresh tea with herbs I grow in a windowbox. Nothing psychedelic, I promise, or not much, anyway. Would you like me to fix you a cup? Tea is always best when shared. The tea I brewed today is for strength of spirit. As crazy as the world is today, I figure we can all use some of that. It contains astragalus root, chamomile, lemon balm, linden leaf and flower, nettle, oatstraw, eleuthera root, red clover blossoms and schisandra berries. To sweeten the deal, I have wildflower honey from local bees or maple syrup from my cousin in Vermont."

Fiona's voice was quiet as she responded.

"That sounds heavenly. Thank you so much."

There was something odd about these faint words.

She felt stronger. For now, this is where she was meant to be. The bookstore cocooned her from the world; it felt cozy and sweet, magical and familiar.

"Great! I'll bring you out a cup and you can sweeten it as you will."

M turned on her bare feet to go out back.

As M was steeping the tea, a mother and her young daughter came in. As they looked around, the girl was clearly dismayed that the shoppe wasn't all flashy with colorful plastic toys.

"Just books," the disappointed girl said.

She walked through the maze toward the children's section. Brushing by Fiona, she smiled. Fiona instinctively followed to see what she would gravitate to. Along the way, she ran her fingers along the spines of the books and heard them giggling.

"What kind of books do you like, my young princess?"

"Books are boring. But what? You think I'm a princess?"

Fiona chuckled.

"Absolutely. There's no doubt."

"I like movies with faeries and dragons and gnomes and magic and animals and nothing extra scary. Those things have nothing to do with stupid old dusty books."

"You are exactly right. Besides, you don't know how to read anyway."

Looking up, the girl's face twisted into a red-faced scowl.

"I can read. I read better than anyone. I just don't care to."

Fiona held out her hand. After studying it for a few moments, the girl decided it would be okay.

Fiona knew there would be a place, but it was a longer walk than expected.

500 steps, give or take.

It couldn't possibly be.

But it was.

The passage opened into a small room with a wooden chair surrounded by an array of child-sized beanbag chairs.

Fiona studied the colorful spines on the bookshelves. One title jumped out at her.

Literally.

It vibrated like a jumping bean.

"Here's one," Fiona said. It's called *When the Root Children Wake Up*. You're a big girl. Please read it to me."

The girl puffed out her chest.

"*You* read it to *me*. I'm too tired and I like your voice."

Fiona smiled.

"I suppose I could…"

After arranging a stack of cushions on the hard wooden seat, she settled on the chair and watched while the little princess comfortably embedded herself in a beanbag.

"Are you ready?"

The girl nodded.

Fiona began reading. "Old Grandfather Winter slowly walks across the land. He knows that spring will soon be here. Climbing the mountain to his palace of ice, he turns to watch the snow melting behind him."

Fiona looked up.

"This is a boring story and too complicated for a young person."

"No, it's okay," the girl said. "Please carry forth."

Carry forth. Someone has already been reading to this little one.

After twenty minutes, the child's mother peeked in and listened. With every page that turned the young child's eyes grew wider. She felt like she was inside the story. Over the mom's shoulder, M peered around the corner and saw the princess clearly enjoying the read-aloud.

Ah, the Queen truly is magic.

Fiona read the last lines.

"Tucking them in for their long winter's nap, she kisses each one goodnight. As they drift off to sleep, Mother Earth picks up her lute and sings them a lullaby…"

Fiona closed the book.

"Wait a stinkin' minute," the girl complained. "Isn't there a song?"

"I don't have a lute," Fiona said.

"Sing it anyway."

Part of her wanted to swat the spoiled child and send her home crying, but a bigger part of her was willing to try. She opened the book again. She didn't know the melody and made it up as she went along.

Root Children sleep deep under the ground.
And while you dream the world will turn around
Then once again Young Robin will sing
Old Winter has passed. Wake up, it is Spring.

Fiona closed the book again.

"So, what did you think?"

The little girl said she loved it and that Fiona was the best reader ever—almost as good as her grandmother—then gave her a massive hug. Fiona had forgotten what physical human contact felt like, and it was wonderful.

"Buy the book, mommy, then you can read it to me a million times."

"Oh, Lordy," the mother muttered.

Giving in, she asked M…

"How much?"

"For this book, twenty dollars."

The woman looked over the cover.

"That's a lot for such a little book—and it's not in great shape."

With a grin, M continued.

"I have other copies. From the rare book archive, I have a 1941 first edition of the Helen Dean Fish version. It's two hundred. For an original Sibylle von Olfers' version in German, two thousand. *Etwas von den Wurzelkindern.* Don't scoff, kids pick up foreign languages quickly at this age."

"May I use a credit card for the twenty-dollar version?"

Mentally, M subtracted three percent from the profit on this sale.

"Of course," she said cheerfully.

After the sale was consummated and mother and daughter left, M approached Fiona.

"Ya know, I could use a hand here at the shoppe. It's not overly busy but you have beautiful energy and seem to love books."

"And tea," Fiona added.

"Yes, and tea. Truly, I'd love for you to stay for as long as you'd like. I live upstairs in a loft apartment. It's not much but it's home. You're more than welcome to stay up there or there's the old shopkeeper's space back here. There's a bed, a bathroom, and a small kitchen. Very cozy."

Fiona smiled.

Her eyes sparkled as she looked around.

"Yes, I might hover for a bit."

This was exactly what she needed.

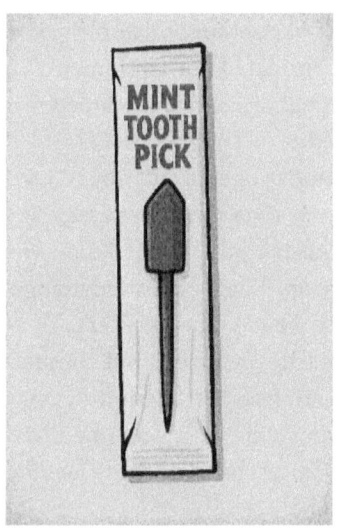

Philip d'GreenApple: Napalm in a Capsule

ALVAREZ WAS SCROLLING on his cellphone. I peeked. Apparently, he was in the market for a new boat. I blocked the sun and he looked up.

"Seventeen dollars and seventy-five cents," he said. "Cute."

I motioned for him to scoot over to make room for my skinny keister, then settled in beside him.

He continued.

"Unless you have Vargas in your back pocket, you don't have him. What's your plan?"

I had a toothpick in my shirt pocket...one of the minty ones in a paper sleeve. I focused all my attention on it—removing the toothpick, flattening the wastepaper, putting it back in my pocket and then examining the pick carefully before putting it in my mouth. I was able to stretch this out for over a minute while Alvarez shifted uncomfortably.

"At this point in our conversation, generally, I casually mention your family and friends back home and imply grievous harm might come to them if you don't complete your assignment."

I worked at a morsel of sausage stuck between molars.

Alvarez continued.

"But you're a slippery one, aren't you? You're not even a ghost in the machine. It's like you aren't in the machine at all. I don't know why it took me so long to catch on. I don't know your real name. I don't know where you grew up. I don't know anything about your family and friends. No paper trail. That's unusual. Very."

I dislodged the gristle and spit it out. Immediately an ant found it and after a quick inspection and an attempt to carry it off alone, scurried home to call in a scavenger crew. It was a small ant.

I'm more than willing to talk when I have something to say. In this case, I didn't.

"I could take your money. As easy as it appeared, poof, it's gone."

I had money in the real bank. I wasn't sure how much, but it was enough to buy a house if Minnie wasn't fussy about granite counters and a swimming pool. I didn't think she would be.

The idea of owning a tract house in a leafy suburb intrigued me. I didn't have a stable childhood and I could see the appeal. My kids might like it. My mind drifted to the concept of ownership. The idea that a small fraction of the Earth's surface could *belong* to a person was weird. We're on a rock flying through space for a billion years and we *possess* a fraction of its surface? Of course, we don't really own anything. If you want to know who really owns your property, stop paying property tax. Sooner or later, husky men with guns and badges will appear on your doorstep and usher you away.

Pay the man and keep paying or move along.

Impatient, Alvarez grunted.

"But I sense you don't care about money. Why not? You have a lot stuffed in your knapsack, I know you do. Is it enough? Help me, Amigo. I want Vargas on this side of the border with a couple of kilos of the little black pills. Then, we lock him up and take him off the street. He's a murderer. Fentanyl is a killer, but Black Death? That's Fentanyl on steroids. That's Fentanyl turbo charged. That's Fentanyl multiplied by the moon. You're in a key position to save thousands of innocent lives.

Just get me Vargas and we'll double your money. Triple it."

Alvarez was weird. His analogies were strained, like a man trying to play jazz on a broken trumpet.

I tried to think of better hyperbole.

Black Death is Fentanyl napalm in a capsule.

Black Death is a Fentanyl loaded gun in a child's hand.

Black Death is a Fentanyl plague rat in a velvet box.

Black Death is Fentanyl devil's breath, bottled and sold wholesale.

My mind kept spinning metaphors, each one worse.

Alvarez didn't care about imagery. He just wanted Vargas.

"Vargas says you invented Black Death."

"That's stupid. I'm just a cop."

"With the war on drugs, the penalties got harsher. Way harsher. That meant loads had to be more efficient. Each kilo had to be worth more to balance the risk. No more bales of coca leaves or bricks of weed—you needed powder, concentrated, weaponized. You created cocaine. And once you did, the merry-go-round spun around faster and faster until nobody could get off."

Alvarez leaned back and studied my face.

"Where did all this come from? Are you a Philonian now?"

I think he meant philosopher. Or maybe philanderer. It was hard to tell with Alvarez—his words were like loose wires sparking in the dark. I started to worry about his mental stability.

And what is a Philonian anyway?

I suspected he made it up or crossed his circuits. I was home-schooled. If there was such a thing, I would know about it. Probably. Unless it was one of those things they left out—like evolution, the alphabet people, or anything else that didn't fit neatly into a retro, classical education lesson plan.

"Did you do something about my check? If I go in, is the pretty lady going to say 'Sorry, sir' and press the alarm button?"

Alvarez deflated. None of his clever ploys were working. He surrendered.

As we know, that's when good things happen—when we give up and let the universe be what it is.

"Your check is in there. You're free to ramble."

"Great," I said. From the front pocket of my jeans, I fished out the paper Marisol gave me. "Vargas has a girl on this side. Disguised, he slips across and visits her every couple of weeks. That means, you and me? We're square."

He examined the crumpled paper. He was the kind of man whose lips moved when he read.

"Cienegas Terrace. Duck Pond Road."

"Correct," I said.

I got up and walked toward the bank.

He called out after me.

"When do you think he will visit next?"

I turned around and walked backwards so I could point my finger at him like a pistol.

"You're going to take all the credit," I said. "So, I need to leave you something to do. Don't hurt the girl."

Inside, there was no problem with collecting my check. There was even a little more added. The cashier had freshened her lipstick. I knew, if I asked her, she'd grab her water bottle and bag sandwich and we'd leave only dust behind as we hit the road. I reached across the counter to shake her hand. That was not allowed and the security camera videos would be studied carefully, but we didn't care.

I pulled her hand over and kissed it.

"You are going to have a great life," I said.

Instantly, tears dampened her powdery cheeks.

"I really needed to hear that," she whispered.

"I know, sweety. I know."

I didn't believe in magic, but I know people who do.

Back on the street, I walked to the bus stop. There was a Greyhound coach to El Paso at one o'clock. I would be on it.

Minnie: Rumors

AFTER THE FINAL child had scampered away like a sprite from an English folktale, leaving behind only the detritus of creativity—scissors like silver charms, art books as magical texts, pencils sharp as fairies' wands and fingerpaints as vivid as the hues of some enchanted forest—Minnie stood, her gaze sweeping over her quaint, makeshift classroom.

Here, amidst the chaos of mixed ages, she played the part of both disciplinarian and magician, endeavoring to keep the boys' minds engaged and their energies harnessed, a task as draining as if she'd been casting spells all day. She felt as if her spirit had been pulled through the eye of a needle threading a tapestry of exhaustion. Though it was still spring, and the classroom sat at an elevation of 4,000 feet where one might expect the air to carry the crispness of mountain magic, the day had turned unseasonably warm, as if the sun and landscape conspired to add to her woes.

The swamp cooler, dripping and sputtering like an ancient, overtaxed servant, rendered the tent's interior a shade less insufferable, yet Minnie felt dust and heat cling to her like a curse. In her mind's eye, she conjured the image of a cool shower—along with a spell to wash away the day's burdens.

The private, communal shower was half a mile away.

What were the chances she could slip through the crowd unnoticed?

She sighed.

Near zero, that's how much.

Of course, she was willing to lend a helping hand here and there, but only after rinsing off three pounds of sweat and dust. She looked at her hands and had to laugh. They were stained with streaks of paint that would forever be part of her. No amount of scrubbing would remove the rainbow tints.

She planned a route that started with the weedy path behind the old buildings. That way, she could grab her shampoo, a bar of Kirk's Original Coco Castile Hardwater Soap, fresh clothes, a fluffy towel and only be exposed to the staff and crowd for the last fifty feet. With twenty minutes of luck, focus and a tiny little cloaking spell, she would be standing under the acrid, deep well water—which after running for a minute, would be divinely cool.

The desert was blessed with water, but it was diamond-hard with minerals: Calcium, Magnesium and Barium. She didn't want to know that and didn't want to know how she knew. Unbidden, the vision of her mineral-frazzled hair came to mind. After she arrived at the Faire, this plagued her for a week until Meg gave her a tip.

Hard Water Wellness Shampoo. This vegan super shampoo has top-notch cleansing capabilities without harsh chemicals. And, it has a heavenly orange Creamsicle scent. You aren't clean until you're Wellness Shampoo and Kirk's Coco Castile clean.

It sounded like an annoying advertisement from an Internet influencer—one that pops up when you're trying to enjoy a delicious Lorde video for the ten-millionth time. She shuddered and felt double-dirty, but when a product worked, what could you do?

She realized she'd been standing for ten minutes while her mind was unmoored.

I'm losing my mind. Focus, girl.

She visualized the track—dodging cholla spines and stumbling over stones behind the dilapidated buildings, darting into the tent for her shower kit and invisibly slipping through the crowd to the shower stalls. It was a singular mission, and she knew it could be done.

Deep breath, girl. Get it done.

Everything worked per plan until it didn't. Tor and Gretchen were working the silver-coin mint. She could hear Gretchen working the crowd while sliding planchets under the mint.

"Gather 'round, ye lords and ladies! Witness the ancient art of the coin strike as done in days of yore. Here lie the dies, engraved with the Animal Interlace and the Egyptian Ankh—selected to represent the soul and essence of the proud purchaser. Punched with 40 tonnes of brutal force, each mark tells its tale now and forever. We weave history into metal and give you the gift of eternity."

Creaking, the 150-pound drop hammer was slowly raised to its full height of nine feet.

Gretchen continued her spiel.

"Hold steady the anvil and let the die's silver kiss be firm and fair. One-Two-Three, strike! By the hammer's might, let coin be born. Tally ho, the coin is struck."

She inspected the coin. After finding it acceptable, she handed it to the purchaser.

"Note the imperfections—they are marks of honor from the artistic hand of man and not the cold, perfect heart of automation. Each is as unique as the stars in the sky."

The shower building was in sight.

To sneak by undetected, Minnie walked on the opposite side of the throughfare with her head turned away while mumbling the cloaking incantation.

It didn't work.

"Minnie, girl," Gretchen called out. "You are a tonic—come quickly, we need you. String the medallions and bag them...we're running slow. Pip-pip, we need to pick up the pace."

Continuing to walk, Minnie pointed toward the showers.

Gretchen scoffed.

"It's so hot, you'll just need another shower right away. Our customers don't mind a little funk."

No, not fair, Minnie thought.

"Lads and lassies, we're saved! Let's have a vast welcome hurrah for our Savior, Minnie."

The milling crowd turned and applauded. The sound was deafening.

Giving up, Minnie turned and bowed.

Two hours later, as the remnants of the horde were herded through the exits, she was beyond fatigue and on the brink of collapse. She picked up her shower bundle and trudged toward the bathroom. The attendant stood outside.

"Sorry, Minnie, the pump went out. No showers today. Don't worry, we'll get it fixed for tomorrow. Come back in the morning."

Standing, Minnie looked up. The sunset was vivid and stunning.

Of course.

Spinning on her heels, she turned and caught sight of Al, the Vortex hunter.

She marched up.

"Let's go. You're taking me to the Arabella Hotel in your Jeep. Now."

"Oh, hi, Minnie. I'm in the middle of something, but in an hour or so, I can take you…"

He looked into her eyes.

"Oh," he said. "Yes. No problem. I can take you now."

At the hotel, in a tub full of cool water, she poured in the White Amber and Mirabella bubble bath bomb—including an extra bottle she talked the reservation desk clerk out of. She felt feverish and her skin goosed as she climbed in, but she ignored the discomfort and plunged. In a minute, her body adapted to the coolness, and she drifted. She could not remember ever feeling so good.

After a half-hour of bliss, there was an annoying buzzing like a wasp hive was in the bathroom with her. She ignored it as long as she could but finally opened her eyes. It was her little friends, the gentle Breena and fierce Nyx.

"I'm sure I hung out the *Do Not Disturb* sign. I love you both, but please go away. I will be ready to receive company tomorrow."

"Many apologies, dear Princess," Breena said. "In the wind, we heard rumors about something you need to know soonest."

"Our news is too important to wait for your convenience," Nyx said.

Minnie sighed.

"You're going to tell me my long-lost mother is at the Faire and works at the bookshop."

"You already know?" Breena said quietly.

"Who told you?" Nyx said. "I'll stab them in the heart and carve up their liver for a feast."

"No one told me. I know where she is. She knows where I am. We're linked. You should know that."

Breena and Nyx exchanged a look.

"I'm ashamed," Breena said. "I'm sorry."

"Why hasn't she announced herself?" Nyx said. "Why does she slink around and torture us? Doesn't she love you anymore? Are you feuding?" She unsheathed her spine-sword. "I love a family feud. To restore honor, I'll gore Fiona in the eye. Twice."

Minnie calmly waved her soapy hands.

"Relax, Nyx," she said. "Put your stabber away. There's no feud. There are good reasons for Fiona to stay away a little longer. Partly, she's still gathering strength, but there's something else. I'm not exactly sure, but when we're together again, it's like a countdown starts and the future begins again. Don't worry, this won't go on long. Now, if you don't mind, I want to get in the shower, wash my hair, and then sleep for 18 days."

Breena tugged at Nyx's arm.

"Come," she urged with a voice like the rustle of leaves. Turning towards Minnie with the grace of a courtier at a ball from another century, she continued, "We shall seek you at the morrow's Faire. In your tent of learning, the children are bringing forth a feast of potluck, dishes chosen with care from their kitchens. They will be all your heart's desires and to disappoint them would be to insult the joy woven into the day."

"Indeed," Minnie exhaled, the weight of her words carrying the weariness of one who has danced too long with the day.

"You shall see me then...though now, depart," she concluded, her voice a blend of command and fatigue.

With the flutter of dragonfly wings, they vanished from sight.

Minnie, embracing the hotel's comforts, indulged in an extended shower with water carrying away the soil and burdens of the day, before sinking into the depths of slumber as solid and unyielding as the stones of an ancient castle.

Fiona: Lost in a Book

AS EACH DAY passed, Fiona noticed she required less and less sleep. Night by night, her sleep cycle decreased by a handful of minutes, which slowly expanded to fewer and fewer hours. She began to listen to her body once again, honoring and marveling at its growing strength. When she awoke in the wee hours of the morning, she wandered through the bookstore and ran her fingertips along the spines of the books, delighting in their giggling as she left behind a trail of sparkling stardust.

Making herself useful, she often lent a hand to the bookstore elves and elementals, growing fond of their early morning conversations and songs.

On this particular morning, Fiona woke and made herself a cup of honey jasmine tea. She held the cup between her hands, cradling it like an offering to the universe. Her bare feet led her silently toward the rare book room. She rarely ventured there—not because it was off-limits, but simply because it didn't call to her.

This morning, however, the whispers beckoned. As she entered the room, the air smelled like vanilla and old parchment. Heavily bound books were carefully shelved or kept under glass. Delicately hand-drawn and painted pages and manuscripts were shielded from the light, protected behind special-made cases. The room felt sacred and hallowed, so Fiona left her teacup outside the entryway.

As she made her way around the room, she happened upon a first edition of *Illusions* by Richard Bach. Certainly not a rare book, but it was one of Fiona's favorites. The manuscript was handwritten by Richard himself, and she felt his magic on every page.

"I remember you. When I was younger and worked in a bookstore, you jumped off a bookshelf and fell at my feet. I thought I'd simply overcrowded the shelf, but you insisted I read you. You changed my life with your meaning of life, the power of belief and the nature of the soul. You with your barnstorming messiah Donald and skeptical Richard slowly coming around to the concept that the world that we inhabit is illusory, as well as the underlying reality behind it. I remember devouring you and then going back time and time again to glean more from your pages."

Fiona's voice drifted away as if lost in time. She sat on the floor holding the hardcover book with her eyes closed and remembering how it was when she first read the story.

When she opened her eyes, she found herself in a field with Donald Shimoda. He was frying pan bread and drinking coffee—black and thick as used motor oil.

"Ah, Fiona, I was wondering when you'd pop in. Nice to have you back. Richard flew off to the next county to get in a day's work digging a well, so it's just you and I, my dear. Come, sit and break bread. It's not the greatest thing in the world but you can always imagine it's a far cry better than it really is, and so it will be."

Fiona stood aghast.

Was she dreaming?

It didn't feel like a dream. She felt the warm morning breeze blowing through the tall grass, which tickled her legs. She smelled the bread and was lulled by Donald's voice.

"Taking it all in, I see. No, you're not dreaming, Fiona. You're inside the story. You have such reverence for this literature that I brought you inside. You say it changed your life all those years ago. Now it will give you strength. Come, sit and we'll talk."

Fiona willed her feet to move. The Earth felt cool under her bare feet and the sun felt warm on her shoulders.

"There we go, Fiona. Now tell me, did you ever find the Messiah's handbook? It will be especially important. I've seen what's coming to your world and I know what you're up against. You, my dear, need all the strength you can muster. Here, open it to any page and see what answers you find. Go on, it won't bite."

Fiona took the handbook in her hands. It felt warm and worn and buzzed with energy. Fiona closed her eyes and let her fingers be drawn to whatever page they so desired.

"Sometimes, the only way to win is to surrender."

Fiona, with the grace of a lady just discovering a worm in her apple, contorted her visage into one of mild displeasure.

"I was hoping for something more cheerful, Don," she remarked with a voice laced with the tone one might employ when discussing the weather with a particularly dreary companion.

"What you hope for and what you need are not always the same."

Fiona sighed.

Don't I know that all too well.

She quoted from the book.

"What do you mean? You know the past and the future of all things. You know exactly where we're going."

Don frowned.

"Yes, of course, as always. But I still try not to think about it."

He sipped, then continued.

"Yes, Fiona, there is much to ponder. But for now, for this moment, fill up with peace and wisdom. Focus your thoughts on what lay ahead, but don't dwell on it. You will know what to do when the time comes. And do you think you'll be alone? Think of the girl. She's the one with the most to lose and will determine who wins and who loses. When you leave, take the handbook. When you feel lost, when you have a question, turn to the book. Remember how you felt when you were young and first read the story. Think back to each time you read it. It gave you strength. Here, eat this pan bread while its hot."

Fiona took a bite. It tasted like sawdust.

"Now, think of it tasting like a warm honey roll. Savor the sweetness of the honey, the warmth of fresh bread. The creaminess of fresh-churned butter. Now, try another bite. Go on, try."

Fiona focused all her energy on how it would taste and when she took a bite, she smiled. It was fresh and warm as if it had just come out of her oven. Wildflower honey and sweet cream butter swirled around her mouth.

"How did you do that?"

"I didn't do anything, Fiona. You simply altered your reality to fit your expectations. There's no magic in that; there's simply believing."

He looked deep into her eyes.

"Fiona, dear, you know there are people looking for you—especially a little girl who isn't so little anymore. You're close. Why do you hesitate and hide?"

Fiona thought about it.

"I'm not hiding, exactly. She knows I'm here."

"Why hesitate? What's the point?"

"Good question. I don't know exactly."

"Never lie to me, Fiona. I know you too well."

She sighed.

"When we reunite, the cosmic clock starts ticking again and the black Prince will appear."

"King, dear," Don said gently. "He's King now."

"King, right. King of Rats, Roaches and Demons."

"As much as I enjoy your company, it's time for you to go. M is looking for you. She's approaching the teacup you left near the door, and it will break if you don't save it. Be well and stay strong...and always watch for a blue feather. You never know when I'll float one your way."

Looking down, she read the passage her finger was on.

Laughing on the way to your execution is not generally understood by less-advanced life-forms, and they'll call you crazy.

Fiona closed the book on her lap and slowly came back to the bookstore.

She heard M's voice.

"Fiona, are you alright?"

Fiona opened her eyes.

"Oh yes, I'm fine. I wandered back here and found this manuscript. It's one of my favorite books. I sat down to read it, and I must have dozed off."

"Ah, Richard Bach. Such a wonderful story. I'm so happy it found you. If you're okay, I'll leave you to your reading. We open in an hour or so but take your time. Don't worry about me dealing with all the customers and being in nine places at once with the schoolgirls who make more work than they get done. Enjoy the solitude and the musings of the reluctant messiah."

As M turned to go, she looked down and saw Fiona's teacup.

"Oh, what's this I almost stepped on? A vivid blue feather. In your cup. What's the color? Cerulean. That's it. Where did it come from? Did an elf leave a gift? Do we have parrots in the rafters? Did you come with a fancy feather boa hidden in your satchel? Grand mysteries of life."

M shrugged and walked away muttering.

"Perhaps so," a smiling Fiona whispered to herself.

She plucked the feather from the cup and flicked it away, then steeled her nerves for the store's opening.

Perhaps, indeed.

Fiona: A Visitor

IT WAS A dreary, rainy day. The skies opened early in the morning and the rain went back and forth between thunderstorm deluges and steady drizzles. Peering upward, Fiona looked out through the shop window at the sky.

A fragment of mournful music appeared in her mind.

It's a dull and dismal day…and the children in the dayroom want to play.

Fiona addressed the world.

"Why do you cry so today?"

M's answer came from behind.

"Because evil is afoot and the Mother is cleansing herself of the muck and mire that stains her skin."

Fiona looked down at the message swirling in her tea. The time approached when she should hide no longer. Feeling it in every fiber of her being, there was no need to speak of this truth. She just wanted a little more time to gather her strength and soak in the bookstore's magic.

Just a bit more time.

Fiona's trance was broken by an odd-looking fellow with a walking stick. He made an entrance through the door as if he expected everyone in the bookstore to bow down to his presence. Simon, with fuzzy tail raised high, looked him up and down and promptly rolled over on his stack of books, paying him no further notice. M looked at Fiona, who looked back. They played a mental game of rock, paper, scissors to see who would win the pleasure of dealing with the intruder. Fiona, losing, let out a sigh, plastered on a smile and approached the invader.

"Good morning. Is there anything I can help you find?"

He bowed with a flourish.

"Ah yes, good morning. My name is Gwydion-the-Wise, the wandering wizard. I come from Bakerfield in the grand state of California and am now featured at your desert Faire. Undoubtedly, my reputation precedes and you know of me."

"Hmmm, sorry, can't say as I do."

"Oh, I must say. Surely the roaming winds whispered my name to your delicate ears ahead of my arrival."

"No, sorry."

"Well, for communication, there must be a transmitter *and* a receiver. I can't take responsibility for all the deaf ears in the world— otherwise I'd have no time for other good deeds."

Fiona caught M's eye with a side-eye glance. M took a sip of tea before hiding a grin under her palm.

"Wandering wizard indeed," M muttered. "I daresay he's something more like what Simon dragged in, coughed up and left as a sad surprise for a bare foot."

"I shall leave you to your wanderings then," Fiona said. "If you're interested, there's a magic section along this way. It has all manners of texts with beginning spells and incantations—and history books about wizards and jesters. We even have something akin to *Wizarding for Dummies* if you're interested in getting started in the trade. Give a shout if you need assistance."

Turning away and barely holding her composure, she quickly slipped into an aisle. She was on the verge of erupting in laughter like a schoolgirl. Gwydion was displeased.

"*Wizarding for Dummies*. Such insolence. Who does she think she is? Clearly, she knows not of my great wizarding skills…"

His muttering trailed off as the stick spoke to him.

"Do not mess with the likes of Fiona. She sees more than she you know. She recognizes your ruse. Go find a book and be done with this shop. I'm wet and you need to wipe me down so I don't rot."

"Such impudence shall not be tolerated."

Gwydion tugged his long, scraggly beard. It was a soothing gesture—much like a child might rub a favorite blanket between their fingers and thumb. He had no idea what sort of book he was interested in; he truly only came in to get a glimpse of a rumored Queen and see what all the fuss was about. This lowly salesclerk could not be the one. There wasn't much to her—she fell far short of his expectations. Beyond that, she knew nothing of his reputation and adventures.

He perused the outer perimeter of the shop, haphazardly glancing at titles and running his fingers over the spines of the books. Fiona heard the books shutter and wince under his touch, and she promised to wipe them down once he had left the premises.

"In fact, I will do a smudge of the whole shop once he's gone," Fiona whispered.

He landed in the magic section and pulled up a chair. It creaked under his weight and hostility, and Gwydion decided he wouldn't sit for long. He looked over the lower shelves for something appropriate for his sorcererly standing. He never read books all the way through but loved being seen in public with them.

The more esoteric, the better.

"Ah, here we go. *The Secrets of Santa Muerte*. Cressida Stone."

He opened the book to a random page.

> *While she is caring, motherly, and generous with her devotees, Santa Muerte is also vindictive or wrathful to those who do not come through on her promises to her, who disrespect her, or who insult and disrespect her children.*

"Yes, that's the ticket. There must be good spells for raining wrath down on my enemies and the title will impress the rubes."

He was happy the stick was sleeping and didn't take notice of what he was about to purchase.

He got lost in the corridors and walked far more than he should have but eventually found the cash register where he dropped the book and rumpled currency on the counter.

"Ah, you found something cute," Fiona said. "*The Magic Mirror of the Mermaid Queen*. Good one. Let's go and ring you up so you can be on your way back to the Faire. I'm sure you have a whole host of things to attend to, being such an important wizard and all."

"What?" Gwydion sputtered. "That's not what I picked."

Quickly, Fiona reached out for the money. In the moment they touched fingertips, she felt energy Minnie had left behind. It was subtle, and most would not detect it, but she did. Minnie was not her birth child, but she was her daughter nonetheless and it was torture to be so close but unable to hug the waif.

She was overwhelmed with yearning. It tugged at her soul.

Across the country, Trevir slept and dreamed about his wedding.

She was there—on a plateau before a huge valley and pine forest as Minnie and Trevir exchanged wedding vows. She'd never been there and had never heard of it, but she knew the place. Mogollon Rim. Old Earth. It was destined—to save the world, Minnie would marry the Black King and bear his children. Only a miracle could save them.

She was jerked back to reality when Gwydion impatiently complained.

"I don't have time for games and I'm not paying for trash."

"Leave it, I will make sure it gets back where it belongs," Fiona said with forced cheer. "Safe travels and happy wizarding."

Gwydion huffed and turned on his heels to go. He gave one more over-the-shoulder glance to Fiona and walked out into the rain.

"Phew, I'm glad he's gone," M said as she emerged from behind a curtain. "He's a mix of creep and an annoying know-it-all. Fiona, are you okay? You look pale. Have a seat, love. You look as if you've seen a ghost. Tea. I will steep a cup for you right away."

"Perhaps I did see a ghost. An energy trail of someone I've not seen in a long time. I'll be fine; it just took me by surprise."

M stepped away and gave Fiona space to process.

Yes, the time would be soon. Fiona would soon continue her journey and set the wheels in motion once more...

Philip d'GreenApple: Learning to Crawl

THROUGH THE BUS window, the landscape blurred in a long wash of mesquite, caliche and sky so wide it felt like the bus was crawling. Every so often the monotony cracked open with a canyon cut or a creaking, wind-tilted windmill. Over a gaping canyon, the Pecos High Bridge flashed past like a rusty mirage, then it was back to scrub and road noise.

Mostly, the landscape was so tedious, it was hard to believe the bus was even moving. It was a perfect time to reflect on my life and what I had been through and try to make sense of it all.

Instead, I slept most of the way.

Cake for the Queen

IN THE QUIET, domestic confines of her kitchen, Meg moved with efficiency. This was experience; gentle slowness with no wasted energy. Bakers learned to conserve—everything was at hand and there was minimal lifting and reaching. The day had seen her hands busy with the alchemy of baking, creating endless cakes and cupcakes, not to mention chocolate croissants and muffins which multiplied according to a sly magic. The evidence of her labors adorned her; flour and frosting conspired to paint her in a mosaic of white and sugar-sweet hues. Her hair, once neatly pinned, now danced in unruly tendrils about her face, sweaty from the heat of the oven. As she passed beneath a bright, silver sauté pan suspended from the ceiling like a quicksilver moon, she glimpsed her reflection and could not help but let out a chuckle, a sound as light as the laughter of faeries in the quiet of the afternoon.

"Riddle me this. How do you show you're a baker without outright saying it."

As she bent down to pick up a stray scrap of parchment paper from the tile floor, a piece of paper blew past her. A telephone order form.

"Where did this come from? I don't remember seeing an order for a Tres Berry Tres Leche cake. I would have started soaking the layers this morning if I had known. What? It's for the afternoon pickup? Oh, good goddess. So much for knocking off early and soaking my sorry feet in brine."

Acting like she'd been bitten by a horsefly, Meg found the energy and gumption to start on the cake. She pulled berries from the walk-in cooler, hosed them clean and put them in a strainer to drain.

Blueberries, strawberries and blackberries make a nice topping.

She considered adding raspberries but remembered she'd eaten the last handful for lunch.

She pulled the mascarpone and pre-made cream cheese frosting from the fridge.

"Mystery customer, you're getting my version of the Sugarpine recipe. You'll eat it and like it or next time, you can buy a Land O'Lakes store-bought from the Whole Foods."

This was Meg's version of a pep talk. As the Valencia Mills flour flew, it seemed to be working.

From the walk-in cooler, she pulled out half-baked sponge cake layers. They'd been prepared for a wedding—a wedding called off when the groom was caught snogging the bride's former best friend.

Let not an infidelity go wasted.

She set to work splitting each layer in half and then soaking them in her top-secret tres leche mixture. Everyone knew the mixture was made of sweetened condensed milk, evaporated milk and whole milk but no one knew her proportions and that's what made Meg's cake so incredible. Making sure no one was watching, she dribbled in a few drops of Tahitian vanilla from her secret stash. As the layers soaked, she set to making up mascarpone cream cheese frosting. She was now settled in the rhythm of it all and forgot all about being irritated about the errant order form.

She hummed a jolly tune while spreading the frosting onto the layers and topping it with berries. She continued in this fashion for all four layers. Then she came to the top layer—smoothing out the top and laying on the final berries in a pattern that pleased her. She moved them around until the presentation was flawless.

"Ah, perfection. Sweet, sweet perfection." Meg mused. She

stepped back to admire the cake. "Not bad for an hour's last-minute work."

Lemmy walked in and admired her creation.

"A perfect masterpiece, Meg. You outdid yourself. I'll take it."

With a snap, she flicked a linen cloth at him.

"You'll draw back two bloody stumps if you touch it. It's for an order that blew in on the wind." She flattened the order form on the counter. Her reading glasses hung around her neck—she blew half the flour off the lenses and peered at the paper. "Deliver to the RenFaire. Bookshop. Some pastry hound named...Fiona."

Lemmy stroked his chin.

"I heard-tell of a Fiona. Mystery woman. There's plenty there to share a big piece, don't you think? In place of a tip? Does she sound like the generous type? How do I drop a hint?"

"I'll be generous with a flogging if you tip over my cake. The smallest jiggle will make it collapse into mush."

Carefully, she settled the cake into a box and taped it shut.

"Treat this as gently as a Fabergé egg and be gone with you," she said.

Trevir's Research Project

TREVIR STALKED THE conference room table like a predator with the soles of his shoes slapping against the polished floor. Each step was punctuated impatience.

"Find me one of the resistance cells," he said, voice low but sharp. "I want to see the enemy up close."

The team froze. Eyes darted between monitors and each other, unsure whether they'd misheard or misunderstood.

The wholesome were taboo—untouched by the Black Death opiate and immune to its seduction. They were mythic, dangerous and above all, unpredictable.

"Now if not sooner," Trevir barked, slamming a fist onto the table.

A coffee mug jumped and the team scattered like startled birds.

Twenty minutes passed in tense silence, broken only by the hum of data streams and the occasional curse. Then a young researcher raised his hand with trembling fingers.

"I got one," he said, voice cracking. "A cell. Small. Isolated. They're clean."

Trevir turned slowly, eyes gleaming.

"Prepare the transport," he said.

The dining room was warm with the scent of baked bread, roasted root vegetables and something sweet cooling on the windowsill. Trevir sat stiffly at the long wooden table, surrounded by faces flushed by candlelight and the woodstove's heat. The chairs were mismatched and worn smooth by generations of sitting. The children whispered among themselves and giggled, their eyes flicking toward him, then away.

They seated him at the far end, in a chair that rocked unevenly on the worn floorboards. Miriam, the mother, had paused before pointing him there—her hand hovering, her eyes flicking to the empty spot as if still expecting someone else to fill it.

"It's Eli's place," she murmured, almost to herself. "He's not with us tonight."

Trevir didn't ask. He didn't need to. The way her eyes lingered on the empty seat told him enough. He scanned the faces. Even here, in a tightknit family, he saw potential customers. The father, a broad-shouldered man with a long beard a beard thick and wild as bramble, stood and raised his hands. The room fell silent. Even the youngest child stilled.

"We give thanks," the father said.

He clasped his hands, and the room shifted. Chairs creaked. Sleeves rustled. One by one, the family joined hands in silence, forming a chain of flesh and faith.

Trevir blinked. Ritual. He hadn't anticipated that.

They waited.

After a beat, he extended his hands, completing the circle. Miriam's fingers were sticky—pie filling or honey, he couldn't tell. To his left, the young woman with flushed cheeks hesitated before taking his hand. Her palm was warm, damp, and trembling.

Trevir felt a flicker of something—future memory, maybe. Minnie's hand in his. The sensation twisted inside him, sharp and welcome. He didn't let go.

The girl's eyes dropped to the table. Her lips parted, but no sound came. A tremor passed through her arm, subtle but unmistakable.

Trevir didn't move. He watched her, watched the way discomfort bloomed across her face like a bruise. She felt it too. Not desire—something darker. Recognition. A primal force of nature.

He thought of Minnie's defiance. That would be corrected.

The father began the blessing, voice low and steady. The words were simple, reverent, but Trevir barely heard them. He was listening to the silence between breaths, the tension in the girl's shoulders, the way Miriam's grip tightened as if to anchor him.

"We give thanks," the father said, voice low and steady.

He closed his eyes, and the room followed.

"For the hands that tilled the soil," he began, "for the rain that softened the earth, for the sun that warmed the roots. For the beasts that gave their strength, and the grain that gave its body. For the labor of our children, the wisdom of our elders, and the mercy that binds us."

He paused, and the silence felt thick.

"We ask no favor," he said. "Only the strength to endure, the grace to forgive and the courage to remain whole."

"Amen," he said.

This was echoed around the table. With expectation written in their eyes, they stared at Trevir.

They were going to make him say it. He really didn't want to, but after a few uncomfortable moments, gave in.

"Amen," he croaked.

There was power here. Not the kind he wielded in the city. Something older. Something that didn't need wires or chemicals to bind people together.

And it made him feel exposed. He felt it like static against his skin.

The father nodded and seated himself. Plates were passed. Bowls of steaming food moved from hand to hand, each portion served with care. No one reached before another. No one spoke over another. It was...coordinated. Harmonious.

Trevir chewed slowly, watching.

"You're from the city," Miriam said, not unkindly.

"I am," he replied.

She nodded, eyes on her plate.

"Eli wants to go there. He says there's work. Opportunity."

Trevir said nothing.

"He's young," she continued. "Thinks the city will make him more. But it only takes."

The father cleared his throat, a gentle warning. Miriam quieted.

Trevir looked around. The children were listening. To his left, the eldest daughter, maybe sixteen, met his gaze with something like defiance. The youngest boy had jam on his cheek and was trying to sneak a second roll.

There was no signal here. No hum of the network. No flicker of the opiate's reach. It was quiet in a way Trevir hadn't felt in years. And it unsettled him.

He reached for his glass—water, not wine—and found his hand trembling.

"You miss him," Trevir said, surprising himself.

Miriam's eyes softened. "Of course."

Trevir looked at the empty chair. Eli's chair. The one he occupied.

He felt like an intruder. Not just in their home, but in something older. Something rooted. There was a force here, not technological, not chemical. Something he couldn't name.

And it filled him with dread.

Fiona: Feeble Creatures of Unconscious Habit

IN A FAR corner in the Philosophy section—which was isolated, quiet and peaceful, Fiona had hauled in a comfortable old, overstuffed chair and she was either reading or napping. It was hard to tell. What's the difference? A good book takes one on a mental journey—like a dream. Splayed on her lap was the big book by Susanna Clarke which she read with her eyes closed. It can be done. Try it sometime.

In a deserted corner of an impossible bookshop, one can only imagine what dreams might be influenced by passages such as this:

> There is a great deal of magic in books nowadays. Of course, most of it is nonsense. No one knows as well as I how much nonsense is printed in books. But there is a great deal of useful information too and it is surprizing how, after one has learnt a little, one begins to see...

With only dust motes for company, she dozed until a feeling of being watched overwhelmed her.

Who wants to be studied so carefully when sleeping?

It was creepy. Fiona didn't like it.

She snapped the big book closed with a mighty crack.

"You, sir, should know it's bad form to stare."

He took it in stride.

"Sorry, but I heard about you, and I wanted to see for myself."

She opened her eyes.

There was an expression.

Older than dirt.

That's the first thing that came to her mind.

"Please allow me to introduce myself. Seamus, that's me. Seamus-the-rude, some would say. I prefer Seamus-the-old-with-little-time-left-on-this-Earth-so-why-waste-an-instant. But that's long and clumsy, isn't it? Let's stand with Seamus and see how far we can get."

The fuzzy Simon purred and weaved through and around his legs.

Studying his craggy face, Fiona decided to give him a chance.

If Simon likes him, he can't be all bad.

From behind, a ray of sunshine illuminated the fluffy halo of his thin, gray hair.

"Until this very instant," she said, "I couldn't picture thistle-down hair."

He pointed at the heavy black book on her lap.

"You must be careful with a book like that. It can grab you and refuse to let go."

"Your stick is interesting. Can I see it?"

He pulled it back.

"It touches no hand but mine."

The stick, of course, had its own mind. It pulled itself out of his grip and fell across her lap.

"Can you comprehend the essence of rudeness?" he murmured, his voice a tapestry woven with the threads of old resentments. "To be disloyal and offer friendship only when the skies are clear and the sun shines—that, my dear, is the very model of treason. An old friend so quickly abandons a lifetime commitment just because a stranger thoughtlessly asks. It's impertinence and I've half a mind to find another useless old stick in the desert."

"Ironwood," she said. "You're old, but this rod is older." She fondled the ball carved on the end and studied its decorative ivory band. "If it could speak, the tales it could tell."

He reached out to take it back.

"It certainly does speak. When it's of a mind, you can hardly shut out its gabble to quietly ponder the endless mysteries of the universe."

She looked at him up and down.

"It's not just your hair that is thistle-down. Time hasn't left much of you. A strong wind could carry you away. And will. You woke me and I was startled and boorish. I apologize. Let's start again." She held out her hand. "I'm Fiona and I'm most pleased to meet you."

Simon turned tail and sauntered off—as if pleased with himself for doing a proper introduction and doing it well.

Seamus' hand was dry and bony like his flesh had melted.

"Apology accepted," he said. "You're the Queen."

"No, just a tired woman who has traveled too far and seen too much. Here I am, tucked away in a bookstore where no one knows me."

Seamus grunted.

"None, you say? Have you not discerned the gathering of souls who enter with a pretense of casual interest, only to linger like spirits bound to this Earth, before departing with nothing but a bookmark or a postcard in hand? More and more, they come, drawn not by mere curiosity but by the desire to behold you with their own mortal eyes."

"I hoped it was my hyperactive imagination."

At that instant, M entered the room with a tray. On a side table, she placed a steaming tea pot and mismatched mugs.

"Seamus," she said, "you old coot. I assume you still take agave nectar as sweetener."

"We are feeble creatures of unconscious habit," he said.

He reached for a ragged lump of cheese which he dropped in his cup to soften.

"Yak," he said. "Chhurpi from Nepal. Smoked. Hard as a rock, so don't break a tooth. Let it soften a while."

Fiona exchanged a glance with M.

"It's healthy and tastes better than it sounds," M said as she backed out of the room.

It took minutes of stirring and sipping before Seamus was satisfied. He slurped and clicked his teeth.

"Perfect," he said.

Her green tea was from a tea bag with the string wound around the handle of an old mug. Bigelow Classic sweetened with honey.

"Safe," she muttered.

He gave her a stern look.

"Boring," he said. "Now that we're friends, let's get to the point of my visit."

He reached into his robe, brought out two scrolls and placed them on the tea tray.

"What's this?" she said.

"I'll explain one. As for the other, let's leave it cloaked in mystery as a surprise to be unveiled in its own time. The first document is a free and clear deed for a 'Sconset house on Baxter Road."

She wracked her brain.

"Siasconset? On Far Away Island? Nantucket? Are you giving me a house?"

"Yup, more like a cottage, but don't worry, it's been upgraded and has modern conveniences."

"Like what? Solar panels? Radiant heat in the floors? Central vacuum cleaner system?"

He looked disappointed.

"It has everything you need. Running water, flush toilets and a pellet stove. Leave all the fancy, complicated things for the Cape Cod coofs."

"I didn't ask for this and I'm not signing anything."

Seamus shrugged and dislodged a morsel of cheese from a corner of his cheek with a skeletal finger.

"You think you have agency? I already forged your signatures and had the documents notarized. It's done. You'll need a place to go after the wedding."

She almost said *what wedding* but held her tongue.

There was no need to insult the old man.

"Stuff the scrolls away in your ruck," he continued. "Then, when you need them, you'll have them."

He drained his teacup and—with the help of his ironwood stick—got up.

He tapped twice and shuffled off—leaving her staring at the rolled documents. She opened the big, black book to a random page and looked at a passage hoping for an explanation.

> *The weapons that my enemies raised against me are venerated in Hell as holy relics;*
>
> *Plans that my enemies made against me are preserved as holy texts;*
>
> *Blood that I shed upon ancient battlefields is scraped from the stained earth by Hell's sacristans and placed in a vessel of silver and ivory.*
>
> *I gave magic to England, a valuable inheritance. But Englishmen have despised my gift, Magic shall be written upon the sky by the rain but they shall not be able to read it;*
>
> *Magic shall be written on the faces of the stony hills but their minds shall not be able to contain it;*
>
> *In winter the barren trees shall be a black writing but they shall not understand it...*

Out of context, these words meant nothing to her. Her mind was scattered and she could not concentrate.

At that instant a young man poked his head in the room. His hair was pulled back into a manbun and his chin had twin braids of beard with turquoise beads.

"I'm looking for collections of Calvin and Hobbes cartoons. Calvin is a subversive scoundrel. I'm researching for my Master's thesis. It's called The Psychology, Politics, Art, Love and Science of Stuffed Tigers.

She sighed and put the big book aside, then stood up.

"I'll show you," she said.

Philip d'GreenApple: The Bank

I STEPPED OFF the Greyhound in downtown El Paso. Payphones were long gone, leaving only faded rectangles on grimy walls. The art-history word *pentimento* surfaced—repentance in Italian—as if the glossy paint beneath each missing phone were an epitaph. I was too young to remember using them much, so why mourn? Everyone becomes a ghost eventually; there's no sense agonizing over it.

After I pleaded, the driver let me borrow his cellphone. I called my so-called bank in Maine, half-expecting there wasn't a branch within a thousand miles. But there was—just a few blocks away. I slipped the driver ten dollars, thanked him and moved on.

The air hit like an adobe wall; diesel from idling dually pickups, carne asada smoke curling from a food cart and the heat of concrete baked all day in the sun. After twenty-four hours on the bus—including the pointless 150-mile detour east to San Antonio before heading west—my senses were overwhelmed by the scents and sights of this sun-blasted border city.

The skyline was modest, but the WestStar tower glowed like a monolith, its glass catching the light at impossible angles. To the north, the Franklin Mountains rose against the sky, looming like castle walls.

As I walked, I tried to pin down my mood, but it was complicated. Looking on the bright side, I wasn't trying to sleep on a bus, so I decided to be happy. Soon, I was standing and looking up at the glass cube.

The WestStar lobby was wide, gleaming, modern. Behind a credenza, the belly of a tubby security guard strained his uniform buttons. I was scruffy and he gave me the once-over as I studied the directory, but he didn't challenge me.

I found the listing. Federalist Savings. Twelfth Floor.

The elevator whisked me up. After a short wander, I found the door. *Federalist Savings* was stenciled in crooked letters on a plain painted door, as if appearances didn't matter. The door was locked. I pressed a button that might have been a doorbell. While I waited, I scanned for cameras. I knew they were there, but I couldn't see them.

The lock clicked and I stepped inside. Whatever you imagine a bank to be, this wasn't. The place looked like a long-abandoned thrift shop with only a narrow path cut through the clutter.

I stopped at a webbed lawn chair—the kind that left a crosshatch on your thighs if you sat too long. Worth maybe two bucks. The tag read: *Contemporary Classic. On Sale. $499.95.* Any bargain hunter who made it this far would bolt.

The path through the clutter opened into a bare patch of concrete floor where a skinny old man sat behind a folding card table desk. He looked like he'd been poured into his chair decades ago and never got up. A banker's lamp glowed green on the table, its cord trailing across the floor.

On either side, half hidden by stacks of junk, sat two men who didn't belong in any thrift store. One was thick-necked, reading a battered *Reader's Digest* as if it was scripture. The other hunched over a tablet computer, thumb flicking, muttering in a low drone. They didn't look at me. They didn't care.

The old man did. His eyes were pale and sharp, like glass chips. He tapped the table with a yellow fingernail.

"Identification coin," he said, voice dry as paper.

The coin was wrapped in a sock, buried deep in my knapsack. I slipped the bag off my shoulder, unzipped it slowly and dug past clothes and notebooks until my fingers found the cool metal disk.

When I set it on the card table, the old man's hand darted out, quick and birdlike. He pinched the coin and held it up to the lamp. Gold light shimmered across its surface in a way that didn't belong to ordinary metal. He rolled it between his fingers, tilting it so the lamp caught the edges. That's when I noticed the markings. Not letters, not numbers— runes, etched in a ring around the Au. They weren't decorative. They had the look of something carved with intent, like a cipher or a curse.

I tried to follow them around the rim, but the symbols shifted if I stared too long, rearranging into patterns I halfway recognized. Memories stirred of half-forgotten textbooks and half-remembered dreams—but nothing I could name.

The old man's eyes flicked up, catching me staring. His faint smile deepened, as if he knew what I'd seen, or thought I'd seen. He set the coin flat on the table, and the runes pulsed once in the lamplight, like a heartbeat.

"Good," he said again, softer this time. "It remembers you."

I reminded myself…

I don't believe in magic.

He slid the coin into a slot on a small box. A green light blinked on. The coin clinked into a hidden hopper. The men in the corners didn't stir. The clerk smiled faintly, as if the coin had whispered something only he could hear.

"Good," he repeated, handing the coin back. "Now what?"

I pulled the cashier's check from my pocket and passed it across. Then I opened my knapsack and stacked the bundles of cash I'd been carrying. He flattened the check on the table and tallied the bills with a speed that suggested long practice.

The clerk flicked a finger and the *Reader's Digest* man set aside his magazine and walked over, gathered the check and the cash, and hauled it into the back. I heard gears grinding—there was a vault hidden back there.

"Debit card?" he said.

"What?" I said.

His eyes skimmed me and I knew what he decided.

I was a moron.

"It's like a credit card, but it draws against your account. There are millions of ATMs around the world—machines waiting to spit out your money in places you never heard of. I can issue you a titanium card in two minutes. With it, you could buy a house or a Maserati for your girlfriend. In most markets, a decent house is the obvious choice."

"Why do I want a house?"

He nodded, satisfied.

To him, I confirmed being a moron.

"With the money you have, that would be your most common purchase. You might not care, but your girlfriend will."

He pressed a button and a printer hummed. A slip of paper slid across the desk. I picked it up. Somewhere in the world, in my name, 190 ounces of gold were stored. It made sense to me and my family, but anyone else might think this was an odd bank.

"One advantage of the card is you don't need as much walking-around money. Flashing your cash can make you a target." He giggled again. "Flashing your cash. I like that. You don't want to flash your cash."

He was truly an odd man.

I decided.

"Yes, please," I said. "I would like a titanium debit card."

He lied. It took five minutes, not two. When the card was ready, he pushed over a keypad.

"Don't let me see it," he said. "Punch in a four-digit PIN. That's a Personal Identification Number. Anyone with the card and the PIN can get to all of your money, so protect it. Don't tell me. Don't tell your girlfriend. Don't tell anyone."

I shielded my hand, pressed in my code and slid the keypad back.

He giggled.

"I was kidding. Like God, I know everything about your account. PIN 9931." He leaned closer. "But seriously—don't tell anyone else."

I studied the card. It was metallic, heavy. I tapped it on the desk.

"Yes, it's literally titanium," he said. "Nearly indestructible. Don't lose it. We appreciate your business. Take care. Be good. Have fun. Come back and see us anytime."

I was dismissed. I shouldered my knapsack and weaved my way out.

Elevator.

Lobby.

Then I was back outside, blinking in the bright sunlight.

Other than a subtle magnetic pull toward the West, I had no plan. But I was hungry. I tried to decide what my gut wanted.

The Denny's Juan and I liked was a few miles west, so that fit. I set out walking. If I was lucky, I could hitch a ride.

I was lucky.

Minnie: Jalapeño

MIDAFTERNOON, MINNIE TRIED to resist the odor and allure of a Sonoran dog, but the resistance was futile. Maria, the cart vendor that day, made her two.

"No, *gracias*, I can only eat one," Minnie protested.

Maria, with a gappy smile from missing teeth, pointed at her ears and pretended she did not understand English.

"No *habla*," she said. "*Dos.*"

This was irritating because Maria was born in California and spoke better English than half the rennies. Minnie spotted an empty picnic table under a palo verde tree and marched to it. As soon as she was settled, Maria's boy, Pedro, dropped two ice-cold Fanta Orange bottles at her elbow. Grinning, he ran away before she could complain.

I don't need these empty calories.

The bottles spoke to her.

"We're made with cane sugar, not high fructose corn syrup *meado*."

"Shut up," Minnie said. "That's a distinction without a difference."

The bottles laughed at her.

Someone approached from behind.

Grumpy and salivating, Minnie reached for a dog. She was determined to ignore anyone who might bother her.

Seamus settled in beside her.

"Perfect," he said. "I've been craving one of these all week."

"They're both for me," Minnie said.

Seamus leaned his stick against the warped wood of the table.

"No, they aren't."

With complete concentration, they ate and in a matter of minutes, both dogs were memories. For dessert, Minnie nibbled her grilled jalapeño and spit out the seeds.

"The seeds are the best part," Seamus said.

"Shut up," Minnie replied.

"That was perfect." He turned toward her. "Guess what. Some absurd nonsense ends today."

She felt like fighting.

"Oh, yeah? Forget it. What nonsense is that?"

"Today," he said, "right now and without delay, we're going to the bookstore."

Trevir: The Harvest Begins

THE SUITE WAS glass and chrome, perched like a predator above the city. Trevir stood shirtless at the window, the skyline bleeding into the city beyond. His skin caught blue light from the wall-sized display behind him—data streams, surveillance feeds, heat maps of unrest. The suite smelled of ozone, sweat and the faint metallic tang of fresh blood.

Troll Srenzo lay sprawled across the leather couch with one arm draped over her face and the other clutching a tumbler of something expensive and amber. Her leather jerkin was unbuttoned, her boots still on. She looked like a fallen angel who'd traded wings for algorithms.

Trevir didn't turn around.

"They're gathering," he said.

Srenzo grunted. "Who?"

"Just outside Sedona. RenFaire. Minnie's there. Fiona too."

Srenzo sat up, blinking.

"That's not what I expected to hear today."

Trevir's jaw flexed.

"It's not cosplay. It's resistance. They're using the Faire as cover—rituals, encryption, old-world symbology. I've seen drone footage.

They're building something."

Srenzo swirled his drink.

"You think the patchouli crowd is a threat?"

Trevir turned, eyes cold.

"They're not just stoners and artisans anymore. They're nodes. And Minnie's the keystone."

He walked to the table, tapped the surface. A hologram bloomed—Sedona, Arizona. The RenFaire grounds pulsed with heat signatures. Tents, bonfires and clusters of bodies moving like blood cells through a vein.

"Look at this," Trevir said. "They're off-grid. No Soma penetration. No Trevir Protocol uptake. They're immune."

Srenzo leaned in. "That's not possible."

"It is," Trevir snapped. "And it's spreading. Pockets of resistance in Tennessee, Utah, the Dakotas. Places where family values still mean something. Places where people still look each other in the eye."

He zoomed in on a cluster near Sedona's edge. A woman in a pirate hat with a fake eyepatch. Another in a long dress and Doc Martins boots. The drone's thermal lens caught their faces in profile.

"Minnie," Trevir whispered. "And Fiona."

Srenzo exhaled.

"You think Fiona returned?"

"It was inevitable. Too much empathy. Too much poetry."

Trevir walked to the bar, poured himself something dark. He didn't drink it.

"I gave them what they wanted," he said. "Euphoria. Status. Identity. And they spit it out like spoiled wine."

Srenzo shrugged.

"Maybe they want something real."

Trevir's eyes narrowed.

"Realty is obsolete."

He downed the drink, slammed the glass on the counter.

"It's time I made this partnership official and married Minnie," he said. "Take her off the board. Make her mine."

Srenzo raised an eyebrow.

"Why do you think she'd agree."

"Easy. Kill everyone she loves if she doesn't."

The suite's lights dimmed as the system detected a mood shift. Trevir's vitals spiked—heart rate, cortisol and aggression index. The AI adjusted the ambient temperature and morphed the music into a minor key.

Trevir paced.

"They're using old tech. Analog signals. Carrier pigeons, for all I know. Fiona's an unconscious cryptographer. She's building a firewall against me."

Srenzo stood, stretched and casually exposed a breast.

"So burn it down."

Trevir stopped.

"Not yet. I want to see it. I want to feel it. I want to walk through their little renaissance and watch their faces when they realize the future hates their small-minded fairy tales."

He tapped the screen again. A new feed appeared—interior footage from a farmhouse in Nebraska. A family gathered around a table. No devices. No Soma. Just conversation, laughter, prayer.

Trevir's lip curled.

"This is the virus," he said. "This is the rot."

Srenzo walked to the window and looked out at the city below— neon veins, digital arteries; the hum of engineered desire.

"We built a machine," she said. "But people aren't machines."

Trevir smiled, but it didn't reach his eyes.

"They will be."

He turned back to the map, zoomed in on Sedona. The Faire was growing. More tents. More bodies. More heat.

"I want a team on the ground," he said. "No uniforms. No drones. Just eyes and ears. I want Minnie's scent. I want to crack Fiona's spells. I want the Faire infiltrated."

Srenzo nodded. "And if they resist?"

Trevir's voice was ice.

"Then we harvest early."

He walked to the bedroom, stripped off his pants, pulled on a suit—black, tailored, lethal. He adjusted the cuffs, checked the mirror. The face that stared back was handsome, symmetrical, and utterly devoid of mercy.

Srenzo watched him from the doorway.

"You ever wonder what you'd be if you hadn't been born into power?"

Trevir smiled. "Dead, or worse. Ordinary."

He picked up his tablet, scanned the latest reports. The resistance was growing. Not fast. Not loud. But deep. Like roots.

He hated roots.

They implied permanence. History. Things that couldn't be bought or branded.

He walked back to the window, stared out at the desert.

"Minnie thinks she's safe," he said. "She thinks Fiona can protect her."

Srenzo lit a black cigar, blew smoke toward the ceiling.

"No. The opposite, I think."

Trevir turned slowly.

"Then I'll kill them both."

The room went silent. The AI dimmed the lights further, sensing escalation.

Trevir smiled again.

"But first," he said, "I'll offer her everything. Love. Power. A throne beside mine."

He tapped the screen. The slogan appeared.

"Soma: Because Empathy Is for Losers."

He stared at it.

"Not good enough," he said. "We need something primal. Something that bypasses reason."

Srenzo flicked ash into a crystal tray.

"Like a grotesque clown face?"

Trevir didn't laugh.

"That was the appetizer. Now we serve the main course."

He turned to the wall, tapped a final command.

"Activate the Trevir Protocol," he said. "Full saturation. Coast to coast."

The map lit up like a Christmas tree in hell.

Trevir watched it burn.

Philip d'GreenApple: Breakfast at Denny's

THE DENNY'S SAT low and wide beside the frontage road with its yellow sign buzzing against the desert sky. With a friendly wave, I thanked the driver and hopped from the cab of the stake bed truck that picked me up on an I-10 onramp.

Inside, the air smelled of coffee, fryer oil and faux-maple syrup. A young woman at the counter laughed, and for a second the sound was close enough to Minnie's that I turned my head. Not her, of course. Never her. But the echo stayed with me as I slid into the booth.

After scanning the seated diners, I should have been surprised, but I wasn't. Juan was already there, tucked into a corner booth with a cold plate of half-finished eggs and hash browns. He looked up, grinned, and waved at me.

"Boy, you look like hell," he said.

"I've been banking," I told him, sliding into the booth.

He laughed.

"Whatever you been doing, think about slowing it down."

I ordered coffee. When Lupita left, I leaned across the table and told him about Jim Alvarez, José Luis and Vargas. Juan listened, chewing slowly, eyes steady. Half-lidded, he seemed to be awake and paying attention, but it was hard to tell.

I topped off my story by telling him about the bank. When I finished, he wiped his mouth with a napkin.

"You sure you didn't dream all that on the bus?"

"I wish."

He chuckled.

"Figures. You always find weird corners of the world."

Lupita brought my coffee. I dumped in sugar, stirred, and tried to decide if Juan believed me. He had trucker's patience, the kind that comes from long miles and stranger stories than mine.

"You got the bank card?" he asked.

I slid it across the table. He picked it up, turned it over in his thick fingers, tapped it against the Formica.

"Damn. Titanium. Never seen one of these."

"Nearly indestructible," I said.

He handed it back.

"So, what now?"

I shrugged.

"I don't know. West, though. I feel a pull."

Juan smirked.

"West, huh? What's there?" He grinned. "Don't tell me. The girl. Minnie. Am I right or am I right?"

I hated being so transparent. The truth was, she's always in my head—threaded through every mile of my journey.

Time to change the subject.

"What's news with your son?"

His resigned grunt told a story. Mateo had done something and wouldn't be getting out anytime soon.

With the change of mood, we ate in silence for a while. The clatter of dishes, the hiss of the grill and the low murmur of other diners filled the space. It was ordinary, blessedly ordinary, and for a moment I almost forgot about Alvarez and Vargas.

When the plates were cleared and the coffee refilled, Juan leaned back and stretched.

"Well, lucky you. My next load's west. I'm deadheading to Sedona. You can ride along if you want."

I froze with my coffee cup halfway to my mouth. Sedona. Minnie. The name hit like a coin dropped on glass—small sound, big crack. I'd been pretending I didn't know my destination, but the truth was I knew.

Juan didn't notice my pause. He was already talking about the route, the weigh stations and the long climb out of El Paso. To him, it was just another haul. To me, it was the road to the one person I couldn't stop thinking about.

I set the spoon down and nodded slowly.

"Yeah. Sedona sounds good."

Juan grinned.

"Then it's settled. The two amigos, reunited. Finish your coffee, pay the tab and we'll roll."

Had he known I was coming? I had the sense he'd wait a year for me to show up and cover the breakfast bill.

I leaned back in the booth with the taste of burnt coffee on my tongue.

The magnetic pull to the west sharpened.

I knew exactly where I was going.

Minnie: Cuttlefish

SEAMUS WASN'T EXACTLY manhandling Minnie, but she sensed that if she dragged her feet or resisted, he would do so.

Their journey across the faire began with just the two of them, but as they traveled, people started to follow. At first, it was only dusty children—looking up from their game of marbles—who joined the procession. Then, actors from the Fairhaven Feast Hall joined in. Soon, jugglers, orators, jousters and jesters formed a colorful, lively mob. Then came musicians with lutes, recorders, drums, and bagpipes, adding melody and rhythm to the march. Hearing the music, dancers joined in with their bosoms heaving and skirts flying.

Then came the nobility and courtiers; people dressed as lords, ladies, knights and squires, emitting authenticity and grandeur. The wandering crowd of Renfaire customers joined in. Most were casually dressed in shorts, jeans, floppy hats and t-shirts, but some had appropriate garb assembled with varying degrees of enthusiasm. Some just wore an ornate hat or a vest, but some were decked out from head to toe in medieval garb.

Looking back, Minnie rolled her eyes. She didn't want any of this— she wanted to slip away, find her tent and enjoy an afternoon siesta. With

Keela, she could hide in her blankets and disappear from the world.

Where was Seamus taking her?

Deep inside, she knew, but her guts were in a swirl.

They headed directly toward the bookshop and in a minute, there was no doubt about their destination.

Was this a good or bad thing? Was it really time? And what would Fiona feel about being ambushed?

After ten minutes of racket and mayhem, they stood before the front door of the bookshop. After a half-minute, M came out and studied the crowd.

"What's all this then?" she said.

Semus refused to answer. He tapped his stick on the ground like a circus ringmaster and grinned.

She pointed at Minnie.

"You only," she said. "The rest of you lunatics can wait outside."

Inside, it was quieter.

Idly, Minnie fingered bookmarks by the cash register.

"Go," M said.

"Go where?" Minnie replied.

"You'll find her."

Minnie sighed and decided to stop being obtuse. She wanted to see Fiona. With every cell of her body, she did.

But, did Fiona want to see her? If she did, why was she so close, but at the same time, so far away?

Resigned, Minnie nodded.

But she *didn't* know where to go. The shop was small, so it probably didn't matter. No matter which way she went, she'd be where she was supposed to be.

She didn't know, but her feet did. They led her to the right—along a passage with books stacked to the ceiling.

This place would be a big mess if there was an earthquake.

She had been on both sides of this store, so she knew the distance from front to back was only 300 feet, give or take. So, how was it possible that she could walk and walk? Looking back, it was ten feet before the corridor turned and she could see no further. Ahead it was the same.

Impossible.

She stopped to look at leather bound books.

Apparently, she was in the Zoology section.

Why does a Renfaire bookshop have a Zoology section?

She couldn't get her mind around it.

Titles included *The Expression of the Emotions in Man and Animals* by Charles Darwin and *Tempo and Mode of Evolution* by George Gaylord Simpson. On impulse, she pulled down a book and turned to a random page. *Animal Behaviour* by Niko Tinbergen.

> *When a cuttlefish happens to expose a shrimp by whirling away its protective blanket of sand, the shrimp quickly covers itself again. This is its undoing. The cuttlefish, which might have overlooked the shrimp if it had remained still, detects the movement. Instead, the cuttlefish immediately shoots out its tentacles and seizes the shrimp.*

Life is cruel, Minnie thought. She didn't want irrelevant and useless information about cuttlefish in her brain, but knew she'd remember this factoid for the rest of her life.

One must be very careful about what one reads.

The price sticker showed the book had been discounted to $1.95. She put the book back and tapped the spine.

"You stay right there," she whispered. "Eventually, someone will love you."

It was completely impossible, of course, but it seemed like she'd walked for an hour deeper and deeper into the bowels of the shop. The corridor grew narrower, and the light faded until she was stumbling around in the dark. Ahead was a doorway with dim, dusty light showing around its edges. Standing before it, she considered knocking, then considered slipping away quietly and forgetting this whole thing.

This is not the right time. Maybe it will never be the right time.

The Arctic Circle is nice this time of year.

She shivered from an imaginary chill.

No, too cold. I'm young. I could learn zoology and specialize in studying tropical cuttlefish. I could be an international expert and get on the Discovery Channel.

Minnie took a deep breath, then pushed the door open.

Almost three thousand miles away, Trevir held court in the Presidential Suite of Washington, DC's Four Seasons hotel. The dining room furniture had been removed and replaced with a conference table. Perched on an ergonomic chair that cost more than a car, Trevir stood at the head of the table with a stunning view of the Chesapeake and Ohio Canal. The guests all sat their pampered butts on folding chairs…with wooden seats that were as uncomfortable as could be found.

All day in 30-minute slots, heads of flailing NGOs had come and gone. With their funding slashed, they were desperate for financial support. Each made it clear they would do anything to keep the money flowing and maintain their staffing. Roma Thomas from Children First International was stunning and perfect. CFI had over a thousand employees. Trevir enjoyed teasing her.

"I like helping little girls."

"Of course," Roma said. "We do great work with underprivileged girls. Medical care, education and opportunities."

"I'd love to get a hundred of them for a special program. Let's say 12-years-old. Orphans. Clean ones. Pretty. Untraceable ones no one will miss. No questions asked."

Roma licked her lips.

"With adequate funding…"

"I could start with two-hundred million to support your good works…"

Roma calculated.

"I could deliver in three weeks."

Trevir stood up.

Something was happening to the west. His spine tingled.

He loosened his necktie and waved at Troll Srenzo to clear the room.

"I will get you our wire transfer information," Roma said.

"Leave your brochure and we'll get back with you," Troll Srenzo said while ushering the woman from the room.

Once they were alone, Troll Srenzo said, "What's up boss?"
He grinned.

"It's happening," he said. "Fiona and Minnie. Out in the desert. Get my plane ready."

Fiona and Minnie

IN THE DIM confines of the room, an elderly lady in a wingback chair lay in slumber. Her neck was cocked at an uncomfortable angle and her slack face bore indelible marks of weariness, as though the essence of fatigue was baked in—infusing her features with the solemn grace of one long-challenged by the world.

I will tiptoe past and find Fiona.

On a crystal cakestand with a dome, there was a white cake with creamy frosting around seven inches in diameter. It was topped with a creamy frosting and a scatter of mixed berries.

Unbidden, the name for the cakestand popped into her mind.

Cloche.

Hot water burbled in an electric teapot. Cups, saucers and utensils were ready. The air was filled with exotic aromas of loose tea, ginger and cinnamon.

Slipping to the side, the woman had a folded quilt on her lap. Minnie reached out to pull it back over the woman's bony knees and tuck it in.

That's when it hit her.

Fiona.

An elderly Fiona from twenty years in the future.

Minnie didn't know what to feel.

What had this poor soul been through that aged her before her time?

At the same time, she was thrilled to be reunited.

Whatever Fiona gave, it was not for herself.

Fiona stirred, then her eyes opened.

Many of the years fell away. Her eyes sparkled. She rotated her head and neck to dispel the kinks.

"Sit, Minnie, please. I want to feast my eyes on you. It's been a lifetime and a half."

She busied herself with preparing oversized mugs of fragrant tea.

"Before you tell me everything about everything, cut the cake, dear. The Meg made it for us."

Minnie grinned.

The Meg.

"Oh, Fiona," Minnie said. "Prepare yourself for a real treat."

On the world's stage, this quiet reunion reverberated. Like the radiating flux of atomic fusion, a wave of energy rippled outward.

Across the country, Trevir slept in his suite under satin sheets. In an instant, he woke.

There you are, he thought. I see you.

Fiona and Minnie: Cake for Breakfast

THEY TALKED DEEP into the night, but at some point, while holding hands, they fell asleep in their chairs. At a mysterious hour deep in the night, Minnie opened one eye, then another to find Fiona watching her. The only light came from flickering candles.

Minnie wondered.

Had the candles been here all along without my noticing them?

Her throat was dry. She took a sip of cold tea.

"I've missed you something fierce," she said. "I don't want to leave you again, not even for a minute."

"Me too," Fiona said.

"But if I don't find the bathroom soon, things will get messy."

Fiona laughed and tilted her head toward the door.

"I don't know how it works, but there's always one close by."

Minnie took her turn in the washroom, followed by Fiona. Once they had returned to their makeshift sanctuary and settled in, Minnie broke the comfortable silence.

"There are still diehards camped outside, waiting for you to appear."

"I know," Fiona murmured, her gaze lost to the shadows. "What wisdom do they seek? Words that might echo from the Temple Mount itself? I am fresh out of inspiration."

"It's closing day for the Faire. If we sit here until the gates open... then everyone will be too busy to pay any attention to us."

"We need to discuss Trevir. He's coming."

Minnie spoke and her words weaved through the air like threads of fate.

"I've been visited by vivid dreams," Minnie whispered, her eyes distant. "I see us standing on a ridge with the wind whispering destinies with our silhouettes stark against the bruised sky of an impending storm."

"Doing what? Pushing him over the edge?"

Minnie exhaled a breath heavy with the weight of inevitable fate.

"No, we're standing before Trevir's orcs and harlot. Getting married with you and Philip as witnesses."

Fiona's complexion drained to the hue of moonlight on snow, her eyes wide with the terror of prophecy.

"That can never happen. Please. No."

"I don't understand it," Minnie whispered, her voice a mere thread in the silence. "There's a path through shadow and doubt—the only way peace might grace our troubled Earth."

"What follows? You live in a castle and bear his children? I'd sooner die."

Minnie clasped Fiona's hand, their fingers entwined like the roots of ancient trees, drawing strength from the Earth below.

"Don't speak so. I don't know what lies ahead. If I must bind myself to the black prince for the sake of our world...I see no other choice."

"King. He's the undisputed King now."

"Right," Minnie said in a faint voice. She changed the subject. "How did you defeat the trolls?"

"I don't know. It wasn't me. It was the Earth."

"See, that's it. I sense that if Trevir and I stand at one particular place, then mighty forces will rally to our aid."

"This must be a special place. Where is it?"

"To the East. In my mind's eye, the scene is clear as day, but it's nowhere I've trod before. Jagged boulders. A ridge made of Toroweap and Hermit Shale at the edge of vast, deep valley. Scrubby Pinyon and Ponderosa Pines. When the time comes, I will know the way."

"Your vortex hunter?"

"Yes, my own personal vortex hunter. He's cool. You'll like him when you meet him. And Tor and Gretchen."

"And Gwydion the amazing?"

Minnie let forth a laugh, the sound bubbling with unexpected delight.

"Gwydion the Pompous. A blowhard, liar and pickpocket, but otherwise, harmless enough. Grandiose some? In Welsh tradition, the Milky Way is called *Caer Gwydion*. Gwydion's Castle. Imagine taking a name like that. And my kids. Closing day or not, they will be in school. I can't wait for you to meet them all. If only there were a way to slip out here and avoid the menagerie waiting for us out front..."

Fiona winked with a sparkle of mischief in her eyes.

"I know a back way."

"Of course you do," Minnie said.

There were two slices of cake left over, solitary survivors of last night's feast like islands of sugar amidst the sea of their brewing storm. Minnie eyed them, her gaze softening.

"How do you feel about cake for breakfast?" she said.

"I can't think of anything I'd like better," Fiona replied, the promise of sweetness a momentary respite from their foreboding journey.

Philip d'GreenApple: The Long Road

THE SEMI GROANED west on I-10, dragging its shadow across the desert. I rode shotgun with the seat too high and the seatbelt cutting into my shoulder. The cabin smelled of diesel, cold coffee and Juan's tobacco pouches.

Outside, the desert rolled by in shades of beige and rust. Mesquite, scrub and the occasional billboard promising fireworks or pecan pralines. Hours of nothing.

Juan drove with one hand on the wheel, the other drumming the dash. He looked amused, like he was waiting for me to say something.

"You're quiet," he said.

"Not much to say."

He chuckled.

"Long trips lower the threshold."

I looked over at him.

Threshold didn't seem like one of his words. I wondered if he was more educated than he appeared.

I took a chance.

"Where'd you go to college?"

He turned his head to grin, but I could see his reflection.

"Didn't graduate."

"That wasn't my question."

We travelled ten miles before he answered.

"Couple years at Texas Tech."

I studied his profile. With lumpy, leathery skin, he was not an attractive man. Husky. Stumpy. Road worn. He was a great actor because it had never occurred to me that he might be educated.

He glanced over.

"Soon as I said *threshold*, I knowed it was a mistake."

"Just stop," I said. "Stop."

This new realization gave me a lot to think about as I stared out the window. The horizon shimmered with heat bending the sky. I tried to think about anything but Sedona, but her name circled like a horsefly.

Minnie.

Juan shifted gears, the engine growling.

"You think you're all complex and mysterious, but you're not. I read you like a road sign."

"You read me like a speed limit sign. That means you pay no attention whatsoever."

Complex.

That was another word that wouldn't be used by the Juan I knew.

He continued.

"Yeah. You're chasing someone but taking the long way around."

I didn't answer.

He grinned.

"See? That silence right there—that's confirmation."

Somewhere in New Mexico, we stopped at a rest stop. A family huddled under a shade ramada with their station wagon hood up and steam rising. Juan wandered over and glanced. After a few minutes he returned.

"Head gasket. They're screwed. Already called for roadside. Nothing we can do."

I saw him hand over cash for the vending machine and watched the family hustle for cold drinks and snacks.

"Nothing," I said. "Right."

When we were a few miles along, Juan sipped from his thermos.

"You remind me of Mateo, before he screwed up. Always running around something, never right at it."

I glanced at him.

"That supposed to be advice?"

"Call it perspective."

Perspective. That did it. I mentally scolded myself for letting my lazy mind accept his character-acting stereotype. I should have been onto him right away.

The miles unspooled. Billboards for gas stations, casinos and Jesus. The desert didn't change, but the light did—it was harder and flatter as the sun climbed.

Juan hummed along with the radio, some old Eagles tune. He looked content, like the road was his natural habitat. I envied that.

I can't tell you why . . .

"Know what I think?" he said finally.

"You'll tell me whether I want to hear it or not."

"I think you already know where you're going. You just don't want to admit it and make it real."

I shifted in my seat. The belt dug deeper.

He laughed.

"See? You don't have to say a word. Your posture does the talking."

We rolled through Lordsburg, a town that looked half-abandoned and half-waiting for Judgement Day. Old railroad yards stretched along the highway with boxcars graffiti-tagged and rusting—parked like they'd been forgotten for decades.

Juan nodded toward them.

"Storage. Cheaper to let 'em rot than scrap 'em. Whole country's like that—junk piling up, waiting for someone to remember it."

I watched the cars blur past.

"Like people."

He grinned.

"You're catching on."

A dust devil spun across the frontage road and for a moment the

Sonora Desert felt like it was dissolving back into sand.

Farther west, Deming spread out low and flat, the air sharp with chilé fields drying in the sun. On the frontage road, peppers hung in *ristras* outside roadside stands, bright against the beige. Juan pointed with his chin.

"Best chilés in New Mexico. Burn your tongue, clear your head."

I nodded but kept my eyes on the horizon. The fields blurred past, green and red patches stitched into the desert, gone as quickly as they came.

At one point I dozed, head against the glass. I dreamed of a gold coin pulsing with light and a woman's laugh that wasn't quite *hers* but close enough to hurt.

When I woke, Juan was still driving, still amused.

"Sleep well, banker?"

"Not really."

The road stretched on, straight as a ruler, pointing west.

Later, past the mad tangle of Tucson, the horizon sprouted wings. Hundreds of airplanes, row after row, parked nose-to-tail in the desert. Some still gleamed, others sagged, stripped for parts.

"The boneyard," Juan said. "Every bird gets grounded eventually. Even the big ones."

I didn't answer. The sight of them—machines meant for flight, reduced to silence—sat heavy in my chest.

We rolled on. The desert didn't change, but the light did—it got harder and flatter as the sun ratcheted across the sky.

By midafternoon, Juan swung the rig off the highway at Picacho. A Dairy Queen squatted by the exit with its sign faded and its parking lot half empty.

"Best soft serve between El Paso and Phoenix," he said.

"Bullsnot," I said. "All the fake ice cream is the same. Same factories. Same sugary slop from plastic bags."

"Location, location, location," he said.

Earlier, I would have let a comment like that slip by—assuming it was random nonsense. Now that I was onto Juan's schtick, I thought about it. He was right. A cold treat after a long haul through the desert was notable and welcome—even if it was really the same crap you could get anywhere.

We sat in a booth with cones dripping faster than we could eat them. The place smelled of fryer oil and sugar. At the counter, a family of tourists argued—Dad pushing kiddie sizes, the kids demanding mediums. I watched idly to see who'd win, but we left before the verdict. Dad was on the verge of folding. My money was on the kids.

Back on the road, the miles unspooled. After a couple of hours of dodging drivers who thought the freeway was a video game, Phoenix rose out of the haze with low buildings and casinos smeared against the horizon. I shifted in my seat, the belt digging deeper and slipped a hand into my pocket. The titanium card was still there, cool and heavy, as if it was waiting. For a moment the dream came back—the pulse of light and the laugh that wasn't quite hers. I shoved it deeper, but the weight stayed with me as the freeway funneled us through the city.

After the tunnel, we turned north on I-17 and battled for over an hour before the traffic thinned as we climbed out of the valley.

The desert opened up beyond Anthem. I let out a breath I didn't know I'd been holding and thought of her. Juan glanced over, grinning like he was reading my mind. He didn't say a word. He didn't have to.

The landscape turned jagged and the air thinner. The horizon pulled me forward. The road stretched north, and every mile was hers.

Fiona and Minnie: School's Out

IT FELT LIKE an eternity. The women walked a mile down a corridor until they stood before a door painted in deep black.

"This is going to be fun," Fiona whispered with a grin. "We're backstage at the Blackfriars Theatre. For the final show, they're putting on a risqué twist on *A Midsummer Night's Dream.*"

Fiona nudged the door open just a sliver, peeked inside, then slipped through. The room was a whirlwind of activity, filled with women in various states of undress, pulling on costumes or shedding them. In front of the vanity mirrors, wigs were being styled, and bold makeup was applied with theatrical flair. Fiona grabbed Minnie's hand, pulling her into the vibrant chaos.

Suddenly, a tall man, flamboyantly dressed as a woman, scooped up little Minnie, spinning her around with delight. His breath, sweet with the scent of mead, carried his lines with gusto.

"If we shadows have offended, think but this and all is mended, that you have but slumbered here while these visions did appear!"

With a flourish, he left a smear of red lipstick across her cheek with a messy kiss.

Despite the disguise, Minnie knew him at once.

"Put me down, Leonard," she hissed, trying to maintain a semblance of anonymity. "We're trying to keep a low profile."

His response, however, was anything but discreet.

"We will make amends ere long; else the Puck a liar call!" he boomed, his voice echoing through the room, drawing laughter and curious glances from all around.

They slipped out through a side door into the bustling Faire grounds, where closing day was notorious for wild, unrestrained festivities. Crowds had journeyed from far and wide, some from hundreds of miles away, to soak in the spectacle.

In the bustling heart of the central square, Seamus sat ensconced at a rickety card table with his fingers tracing a life story etched in the lines of a pimply teenager's palm. From fifty feet away, he spotted the women, his face lighting up with a mischievous grin. His walking stick, leaning against his chair, quivered as he refocused on the eager customer in front of him.

Fiona leaned in close to Minnie, whispering.

"He's telling that lad he'll soon meet the love of his life."

Minnie gave a small shrug.

"Hope springs eternal," she replied with a wry smile.

Above them, the blazing sun promised a sweltering day ahead. Minnie caught sight of one of her students and swiftly took hold of the boy's arm.

"Come with me, we'll have a lesson," she proposed with enthusiasm. "I want you to meet Fiona—she'll read to you."

The boy recoiled, shaking his head.

"Everyone knows there's no schooling on closing day. Today we set aside the books and play. We can school tomorrow."

As they watched him dash away, Fiona gave a nonchalant shrug.

"I guess school's out," she remarked with a playful tone.

While they were standing still, Gwydion spotted them and marched up.

"Come with me," he commanded.

"Crap," Minnie muttered.

Undaunted, he tugged on their sleeves.

"Let's go," he said.

Looking around at the colorful craziness, Minnie surrendered to the day. Gwydion herded them like errant goats and soon they found themselves skirting a long line of customers at the Pirate's Pub.

"Not the turkey-leg pirate," Minnie said. "He's annoying."

They watched the transaction as Captain Blacke slipped twenty dollars into Gwydion's greedy hand.

"Arrr, wenches," Captain Blacke bellowed, pointing his finger. "The big'un can swill mead like a true pirate. The wee lass can mind the coffers. Good with numbers, ye be, Minnie, or so I'm told by a man who lies less than yer average scallywag."

While Fiona looked on with amusement, Minnie stomped her feet.

"I'm not working for you," she said.

Captain Blacke spoke like his words settled the matter.

"A hundred doubloons extra for every mate when we sell out our wares—and we shall, quicker than ye can say 'shiver me timbers'!"

Minnie turned to Fiona.

"I told you he's annoying. Every heard of a pirate from Nouth Dakota?" Making a decision, she said, "Two-hundred."

"Ah, ye be holdin' a defenseless merchant hostage, do ye? With a heart as cold as the depths of Davy Jones' locker, robbin' him of his hard-earned booty? Plunging an evil blade into his innocent belly, ye scurvy cur?"

Minnie tugged at Fiona's hand.

"We're out of here," she said.

"Hold fast, ye scurvy barnacle! Double curse ye, but I be needin' yer aid. Done fer. Two hundred doubloons snatched from the gobs o' me starvin' wee ones."

"Each," Minnie said.

Captain threw them aprons, then lifted his fake eyepatch to scold them properly.

"Aye, two hundred doubloons for each o' yer thievin' purses!"

While the crowd enjoyed their closing-day afternoon in the sun, Minnie and Fiona spent the dregs of their energy ferrying plastic cups of mead and running the overflowing cash register. Two hours before the Faire closed, they sold their last smoked turkey leg and the final keg of mead was tapped out.

Captain Blacke rolled down the screen and they were closed for the season. From a plastic garbage bag, he counted out bills for the staff's bonus, then poured shots of Coroni Heavy Trinidad rum into rustic wooden cups.

"Hold," he said.

With his oversized hairy fist, he squeezed lime drops into the cups.

"Lime to scare off the scurvy," he said. "Did you know that's why they called Brit sailors limeys?"

They raised their cups.

"Just like that," Fiona muttered, "the pirate-talk is done for the season."

"Yes," Minnie replied. "Just like that."

"Aren't you too young to drink?" Fiona said.

Minnie stuck out her little tongue.

"I'm marrying the evil King, birthing his demons and you're worried about my drinking?"

"Valid point," Fiona said.

She clicked her wooden cup against Minnie's.

"May we colors ne'er be lowered and our tankards ne're run dry."

"Shut up and drink, Anne Bonny," Minnie replied.

Minnie and Fiona: Embers

AT MIDNIGHT, THE RenFaire grounds shimmered under a faint quarter-moon—a tapestry of tents, firelight and music. The air was thick with incense and roasted meat, laughter echoing off the red rocks looming over Arabella and Sedona like a spell. At the end-of-season celebration, the Faire bloomed into something ancient—half festival, half rite of passage.

Minnie stood near the central bonfire, her red pirate cloak pulled tight against the desert wind. Someone had grabbed her and braided her hair with copper wire and dried lavender. All around, dancers spun in ritual circles with their feet kicking up dust and memory. Drums throbbed like heartbeats. Wooden flutes sang like meadowlarks.

Fiona approached. She carried a half-eaten pomegranate. Her eyes were sharp, scanning the crowd.

"They're here," she said softly.

Minnie didn't flinch.

"Trevir's spies?"

Fiona nodded.

"Three, maybe four. Dressed like us, but wrong."

Minnie turned, her gaze sweeping the revelers. Jugglers, smiths, herbalists and poets. Children with painted faces. Elders with stories etched into their skin. It was a living archive of resistance—analog, embodied and defiant.

Tipsy, Minnie mind free-associated.

"They don't understand us," she said. "This isn't nostalgia—it's armor."

The like-minded Fiona responded in kind.

"Our friends use beeswax and bone for communication."

Minnie grinned.

"I have no idea what that means, but I love having you around. Let the future choke on technological silence."

"Dueling non sequiturs," Fiona said.

A burst of laughter erupted from the ale tent. A bard sang a bawdy song about a knight who fell in love with a sentient mushroom. Somewhere, a petting zoo goat bleated.

But beneath the revelry, tension coiled like a snake.

Trevir's eyes were everywhere.

In the shadows near the archery range, a man watched with too much focus. His tunic was perfect. His boots were new. He didn't drink. He didn't dance.

In the candlelit apothecary, a woman asked too many questions. Her smile was rehearsed. Her hands were uncalloused.

In the stargazing circle, a pair of twins whispered into crystal devices disguised as pendants.

Fiona marked them all.

"They're mapping us," she said. "Trying to decode our rituals. Our songs."

Minnie's voice was calm.

"Let them. They'll find nothing here but myth and metaphor."

Fiona frowned.

"Trevir believes in focus groups and manipulation. He doesn't believe in metaphor."

Minnie turned to her, eyes fierce.

"We'll teach him fear."

The bonfire roared higher. Sparks danced into the night like fireflies on a mission. A circle formed—elders, children, warriors and weavers. The Ember Circle. The final rite of the season.

Minnie stepped into the center. She raised her arms. Silence fell.

"We gather," she said, "not to escape the world, but to remember it. To remember what it means to touch, to speak and to bleed."

The crowd murmured in agreement.

"We are not algorithms. We are not avatars. We are not products."

She looked directly at the spy near the archery range.

"We are the virus in the evil machine."

The spy flinched.

Fiona stepped forward, unrolling a scroll. Symbols glowed faintly—old runes, mathematical spirals and fragments of song.

"This is the firewall," she said. "Built from memory and myth. It cannot be hacked. It cannot be bought."

The Ember Circle began to chant. Low, rhythmic, primal. The kind of sound that bypasses reason.

Trevir's spies recorded everything, but the data was useless. The chants scrambled their devices. The symbols triggered hallucinations. One spy vomited behind the blacksmith's tent. Another wept uncontrollably.

Fiona smiled.

"We're not just resisting. We're rewiring."

Minnie closed her eyes. She saw Trevir in his glass tower, watching, calculating and burning with rage. She saw the map lighting up. She saw the harvest coming.

But she also saw the roots.

In Tennessee, a grandmother taught her grandson how to carve a flute from cedar.

In Utah, a father built a loom from scrap metal and taught his daughter to weave.

In the Dakotas, a boy buried his phone and planted corn over it.

Minnie sipped home-brewed root beer from a plastic pirate mug. She tapped Fiona on the arm and gestured.

"I want to show you something," she said.

Leading the way, they stumbled along a rocky path to the top of a hill.

"Cinders," Minnie said softly. "Left behind after the volcano herds stampeded through."

At the top was a stone used as a bench. Seats were carved in it, but it was still hard and uncomfortable. They faced the east.

"What do you see?" Minnie asked, her voice soft in the quiet night.

"Stars," Fiona whispered, eyes fixed on the heavens.

A gleaming dot streaked silently across the sky—the satellite's cold trail brushing past scattered pinpricks of starlight.

"No, really look," Minnie urged.

Fiona blew out her cheeks.

"I'm wore out. Don't make me work."

"This matters," Minnie insisted, her finger stabbing along the horizon. "Tell me what you see."

Across the dark line of the Mogollon Ridge, splashes of color burst like fountains—violet, emerald and molten gold sliding into one another.

"What are those?" Fiona squinted.

"Energy vortexes," Minnie said. "The Earth reaching up to space. Maybe it's not scientific, but that's how I see it. Go deeper."

Fiona's gaze caught the largest, swirling above the cliffs.

"Oh," she breathed. "That's wild."

Minnie nodded, her eyes never leaving the horizon.

"The Mogollon Rim breathes, you know? In and out. Whole lot of secrets get sucked in, more than most folks ever guess. Around here, they say those secrets stack up higher than the pines. Me, I think it's untamed—not scary. Like Mother Nature threw a fit and spewed magic everywhere."

She took a slow sip, voice dropping conspiratorial.

"Ever heard of the Mogollon Monster? Folks say he's bigger than the biggest bear and hairier than a herd of sheep with shiny eyes watching from the trees."

Her hand swept across the view, painting it with words.

"But there's more than monsters. Some nights, there's strange lights—shooting straight up from the cliffs, like the ground is reaching for the stars. And if you're real quiet, you might hear the trolls whisper or spot a sprite flicking her tail in a creek. Old-timers say there's places out here where the world feels thin. Like you could take one step and land somewhere magic."

She grinned, eyes sparkling.

"Truth is, the Rim's bursting with stories—true ones, half-true, and pure nonsense. Out here, you never really know where real ends and stories begin. That's my favorite part. Makes everything feel possible."

Fiona glanced sidelong at Minnie.

When did she become so certain, so grown? What happened to my little girl?

"And that's where I will marry Trevir," Minnie said, voice steady.

Fiona recoiled, old fears rising hot in her throat.

"No, child. Never. Don't even think such a thing."

Undaunted, Minnie turned and clasped Fiona's hands. Her eyes met Fiona's, shining with something wild and resolute.

"Tell me you see it. Out there on the Rim. The Earth will accept what it wants and turn away what's not meant to be. It's the only power I know that is strong enough to stop Trevir."

"But...the risk—" Fiona began.

"If the Earth accepts the union, then I'll be Trevir's and I'll bear his children." Minnie's words pulsed like prophecy. "If it doesn't, we walk away. There's no other way."

Fiona shook her head.

"No. Not as long as I live and breathe."

"What else can stop him?" Minnie pressed, voice low but relentless.

Fiona searched desperately for another answer—but nothing came to mind.

Dammit.

Below, the Ember Circle's chants rose in a spiral. Shadows darted and disappeared as Trevir's spies scattered to the dark. The bonfire surged with heat and light lapping at the night—and, somewhere far off in the desert, the future cracked open.

Fiona Greets the Black King

THE ARIZONA SUN bullied late sleepers. In their borrowed tent, Fiona groaned, throwing an arm over her eyes. It was barely past eight and sweat already dampened her skin.

Minnie, sprawled in shorts and a t-shirt, had cast off her covers and commandeered the fan, its rattling voice the only relief in the stuffy morning. Her scarlet pirate cloak, dangling from a nail, shielded her eyes from slivers of sun poking through the tent's nylon seams.

This child's grown up desert tough, Fiona thought, admiring Minnie's anticipation of the light.

Sitting up, Fiona rubbed her eyes, taking in the girl's tranquil face. Years together, years apart—a wild ride she cherished more than life itself.

Reaching for the fan, she tilted it toward her own face.

"I love you, honey. But you can't have all the air."

Outside, the whomp-whomp of a low-flying helicopter churned the air, rattling the canvas overhead. It swept past with its engine whining as it settled nearby. The turbine wound down and quiet unfurled over the camp.

Fiona, still unused to the RenFaire's rhythm, couldn't tell if arrivals like this were routine or something more. The hush made her curious.

She gathered her toiletries and slipped outside, squinting as sunlight slapped her cheeks. The camp's makeshift bathroom—a flatbed trailer lined with portable toilets—offered a hint of cool relief. With her fingers, she worked at her unruly curls with quick, practiced strokes, catching glimpses of herself in a scratched metal mirror. A halo of hair and lines around her eyes ran deeper in this harsh light, documenting years.

Back in the open, workers wove through the camp—vendors folding canvas booths, food trucks disgorging yesterday's trash, roadies calling as they hefted crates and banners. Hungover crew dragged hoses and cables across gravel with eyes half-shut against the day.

U-Haul trucks idled at the edge with doors yawning for stacks of costumes, props and excess inventory destined for the next RenFaire stop. The party's truly over now, Fiona thought while weaving between laughter and the leftover confetti of last night's revelry.

Her attention snagged on the helicopter's resting place—a patch of dusty field beyond the fire circle. People clustered with backs turned and voices low and tense. Beyond the usual rhythm, something was happening.

Drawn by curiosity and unease, Fiona wandered closer, brushing flyaways from her forehead and scanning faces for clues. The sun pressed heavier. The future felt poised, as if today might begin another wild ride.

One by one, with unhurried precision, the entourage dropped from the black helicopter and gathered in the dust, surveying the camp with predatory calm. In the hard sunlight, they looked like hired muscle—private security if you didn't know better. But Fiona saw past the sunglasses and tailored jackets. Their disguises were only skin-deep. Ohrkks.

A hulking brute stepped forward, extending a hand to help a tall, sleek woman down with her wary, cuckolded husband following.

She knew these faces.

Troll Srenzo. Kelpht, the ohrkk.

Their presence meant only one thing.

Trevir. The Black Faerie Prince.

No—she corrected herself—King now.

Once, she'd have been terrified. Not so long ago, even thinking his name sent a chill through her veins. She ought to be afraid—any rational person would be.

But as the heat shimmered and the helicopter's engine ticked in its wake, Fiona glanced inward with strange detachment.

What had changed in her?

She searched for familiar fear and found nothing. Only dry, electric curiosity—and a thread of amusement that cracked a laugh from her lips. She pressed a fist to her mouth, stifling it.

So much had happened. Years—lifetimes—of surviving, losing and finding and losing again. Each chapter of her life burned something away and left her steelier deep within. Unafraid. Whatever would happen, would happen. She felt light, almost weightless.

She couldn't explain how she'd crossed that last threshold, but she had. It was the end of fear.

Minnie's promise came back, vague and echoing. If the Earth accepts the union, I'll be Trevir's. I'll bear his children. If. Not certainty, not surrender—something ancient, conditional and bound to forces even Trevir couldn't command.

Fiona drew a slow breath and approached the helicopter. Reluctantly, the ohrkks—hulking, predatory—parted for her with eyes flat and watchful. She barely noticed. All her focus sharpened on the figure ahead.

He emerged: slender and elegant with his suit as sharp as cut glass. But beneath the gloss, Fiona glimpsed gnawing, coiled hunger—the twisting monster inside. The Black Faerie King.

They stood face to face as the clicking of cooling metal and distant camp noise folded into hush.

"Where is she?" he said, voice cold as a blade.

Fiona and Minnie: Breakfast at the Mead Hall

A PARADE OF booted steps cut through the rising dust as Fiona led Trevir's entourage past sleeping tents and crates loaded with gear. The camp stirred in slow waves. Vendors hosed down tables while children darted about with paper crowns breathing the sharp tang of firewood mingling with spilled ale beneath the new sun.

At their tent, Minnie's blankets lay neatly folded with the complaining fan still thrumming against the heat. Fiona's heart switched between hope and dread. She stopped a nearby woman balancing a tray of mugs.

"She's not here," Fiona murmured, her voice tight.

The woman tilted her chin toward the main path.

"Mead Hall for breakfast, looked like. With her adopted folks."

Relief and apprehension tangled inside Fiona as she hurried on. The entourage shadowed her: ohrkks hulking in silence and Trevir gliding close, never quite out of sight.

Inside, the Mead Hall glowed with warmth and life. Steam curled from mugs, and laughter ricocheted off rough-hewn beams. Breakfast plates towered high. At the long table, Minnie beamed—cheeks flushed, hair tangled, grinning between Gretchen's broad smile and Tor's steady, weathered gaze. Blueberry pancakes vanished in bites—Minnie savored each mouthful as if sweetness alone could shield her from whatever waited.

Gretchen's arm rested protectively around Minnie's shoulders, pride and love radiating, as though to reclaim lost years. Across the table, Tor lifted his eyes—gray and kind—offering Fiona a quiet nod filled with unspoken joy.

Fiona paused at the threshold with time stretching and collapsing. It had been so long—years torn apart, journeys divided, wounds and stories unspoken. Now, in simple everyday comfort, their reunion wrapped Minnie in belonging so deep it made Fiona ache. She drew a breath and stepped closer, laying her hands on Gretchen and Tor's shoulders. Their heads turned, faces alight with welcome and disbelief.

"Thank you," Fiona whispered, her voice trembling with gratitude and regret. "Thank you so much for looking after our girl. I should...I wish..."

Gretchen squeezed her hand, eyes shining.

"Of course we did, love. She's family. She always was."

Tor rumbled through his beard, feigning gruffness, though Fiona caught the warmth beneath.

"Weren't much bother. Mostly tolerable."

For a moment, Fiona let herself forget Trevir, the ohrkks, and the shadows trailing in his wake. The world narrowed to this small circle, mending connections—a shelter against whatever storm pressed in.

Then the bubble burst. Warmth was disturbed as Trevir approached with his presence chilling the air. Minnie glanced over her shoulder at the king, at Troll Srenzo and Kelpht.

Trevir's voice broke the spell—polished and poisonous.

"We have business," he announced.

Minnie's reply rang out, clear as a bell in the hush that followed.

"Join us for breakfast."

Trevir's expression barely shifted.

"We have no time for trivialities."

Minnie met his gaze, unwavering.

"Mind your manners," she said. "I wasn't asking."

Fiona, Gretchen, and Tor stared—astonished by the authority in Minnie's voice, the bravery of a girl hardened by heartbreak, desert and experience.

The tension between the two sides stretched, thin as wire. Then, in a flash of false charm, Trevir let a smile flicker—acid and veneer mingled on his lips.

"As it happens," he said, motioning to his entourage and settling at the table, "I could do with a bite."

As the hour wore on, there was a natural outflow of people with things to do—replaced with Minnie's friends. First was the Vortex Hunter, Al Bailey—accompanied by the baker, Meg. Both carried toppling boxes of warm-from-the-oven scones. As people left, most helped themselves.

"If anyone doesn't like scones with currants, cranberry, goat cheese, cracked black pepper with a lemon glaze, then remove yourselves and be happy with Hostess Donettes from the Circle-K gas station. On closing day, I make what I like. Eat them and be happy."

Minnie laughed as she plucked one from a box and placed it on a napkin in front of Trevir.

He looked down his nose at it.

"No, thank you," he said.

"You heard the Meg. Eat it and be happy."

Fiona marveled. A strange authority resonated in Minnie's small voice. With a sour look, Trevir broke off a chunk of pastry and nibbled. Surprised, he shrugged.

"Not half bad," he said.

Clapping her hands, Meg threw her head back and laughed.

"Every year, the same thing," she said. "Skepticism, then fans for life."

The fake wizard, Gwydion, poked his head in and immediately pulled back when he saw Meg. He still had a crease in his head from Meg's rolling pin after he'd said something ill-advised. She'd promised if she saw him again, she'd hit him again—and there was no doubt she meant it. As he left, he passed the real wizard, Seamus.

"Bro," Gwydion said. "Snag me one of those scones, will ya?"

With his ironwood staff, Seamus pressed him aside.

"Bug off, cretin," Seamus replied.

Inside, Seamus grabbed a pastry and took a big bite. With crumbs in his beard, he spoke to Minnie.

"I told you. You'll agree to marry…that thing."

Minnie pressed a delicate finger to her lips.

"Don't spoil my surprise," she said.

The last person to enter was M from the bookstore. She dropped a ragged booklet in front of Minnie.

"I brought you something, dear."

With a hand that wasn't holding a scone, Minnie picked it up.

Duties of Woman in the Marriage Relation.

M leaned over and whispered.

"Second printing," she said. "1848. I quote: It is not degrading to submit to rightful authority. The wife who cheerfully yields to her husband in all things lawful, not only secures his affection, but promotes her own happiness. Rebellion in the household is the fruitful source of misery."

She picked up a pastry and made the rounds, hugging Gretchen, Meg, and Fiona in turn, then the men—Tor, Al, and Seamus. Giving wide berth, she avoided Trevir, Troll Srenzo, and Kelpht. After minutes of camaraderie, Minnie tapped her spoon on the table. The room fell silent and all eyes were on her.

"The King will ask a question and I will answer," she said.

"I'm not asking," Trevir replied.

"Fair enough. The question is whether I will accede to your demands."

"You will," Trevir said.

Minnie turned to look at him.

"You need to learn how to win," she said wryly before continuing. "As I was saying, with Mom's permission, I can legally marry next year and I am ready to agree to Trevir's terms. He can keep his," she glanced at Troll Srenzo, "…dalliances. I will bear his children. In fact…" She raised M's gift. "I will use this as a wonderful handbook and accept its wise guidance."

Sarcasm oozed from the word 'wonderful.'

She turned to a random page and read aloud.

"'Let her prepare his food with care, serve it with cheerfulness, and receive him with a smile. Let her not greet him with complaints or coldness, nor burden him with the troubles of the day before he has laid aside the cares of the world.'" She laughed. "All that and more," she said.

Gretchen could not hold back.

"No," she said.

Fiona put a gentle hand on the woman's shoulder.

"Faith," Fiona whispered.

"I can't listen to this," Gretchen said.

In tears, she got up and scurried out.

Catching Minnie's eye, Tor spoke softly.

"Sorry."

He rose and followed. A moment of silence followed before Minnie raised a finger and spoke.

"With only one little condition…"

"You will submit without condition," Trevir said.

"All you have to do is ask my Father for my hand. If he says *yes* then it will be so."

"He will agree or I will have his head," Trevir retorted.

Troll Srenzo whispered in Trevir's ear.

"Wait," he said. "You don't have a father…never even knew him. What is this trick?"

"No trick," Minnie said. "We all have Fathers. Our Father Earth. You will politely and respectfully ask and we will abide by his decision. Even more, I will sincerely beg our Father to grant your request. I will promise on my soul that this holy marriage is what I want. At noon today, Father willing, at the rim on Schnebly Hill Road, we will have our engagement ceremony and then, on my sixteenth birthday, I will be yours."

"I tell you," Trevir complained. "You don't tell me."

Again, Troll Srenzo whispered in his ear. Trevir's face twisted in anger. He slapped his hands on the table.

"Okay, so be it. I command it to be so."

"Bring a ring," Minnie said.

Fiona and Minnie: Way

AL LOUNGED IN his camp chair, arms folded and boots kicked out, the morning sun burning away what was left of the morning's cool.

He watched Fiona circle Minnie with hands practiced and gentle as she wove slender twigs of ponderosa pine through the girl's dark hair—an ancient ritual, maybe, but beautiful all the same.

Al cleared his throat—not to interrupt, more to reset the mood. Stories in his head wanted out, and this felt like the kind of morning for them.

"Schnebly Hill. What do you know about it? Why there of all places?" He nodded toward the distant Rim, voice turning thoughtful. "Folks go up chasing views and vortexes and all that, but what gets them is how the place takes you. You leave Sedona's gods behind—sandstone spires, golden desert light, all pretty enough for postcards. But then the road throws you up and it's all pine and limestone. It's different up there. Different air, different rules."

He paused, his gaze tracing the line of the crest beyond camp, where rays of light struck ancient stone and disappeared in shadows.

"Once you're up here, it's the Rim proper. Sheer drops—

thousands of feet straight down. Makes grown men feel small. And all that canyon—Oak Creek, Wilson Mountain, the cathedrals of red rock—spread under your boots."

As Minnie leaned into Fiona's touch, Al stooped to snag a pine twig from the ground, rolling it between his fingers. He smiled at the memory.

"They say the Ridge is older than anything we could hope to build. Pines outlive memory and legend clings like burrs to your boots. Stories spread about Earth energy up here, how the wind doesn't flow straight and the light hides things. If you feel something tingle, that's not just cold air—it's the place shifting you sideways."

The wind played through camp, and Al squinted toward Fiona, his voice dropping with the tone of old secrets.

"Hawks, too. They ride the Rim like it's a runway. At sunset, the cliffs go purple and orange—stained glass better than any saint ever imagined. Not just beautiful. It's deep. It's the kind of magic you don't get for free."

He grinned, earthy and knowing, as the sharp scent of pine resin mingled with a faint chorus of laughter further up the slope.

"When the vortex crowd asks me, I say: sure, there's energy here. But it's wild and old—it doesn't pick favorites. Some folks come out changed, some just get a sunburn. Magic here? You gotta earn it."

He tipped his battered hat, watching Fiona tuck the last twig—her hands lingering for a moment, as if sealing something invisible. Magic in the making, and the Rim watching on.

"Leastways, that's what the stories say," Al added, finishing with a shrug.

Minnie glanced up at him, her eyes lively.

"I've never heard you speechifying so much," she teased.

Al's humor softened his face.

"Sorry. Must be something in the air this morning."

Fiona straightened, focusing on the practical.

"What do you have for a pretty dress?" she asked softly.

Minnie looked herself over—dusty blue jeans and a ragged t-shirt screen-printed with faded red rocks and the words 'Sedona Dirt Squad: Wandering Since Forever' grinning back at her.

"What's wrong with what I'm wearing?" Minnie protested, tugging self-consciously at the shirt's hem.

Fiona sputtered, but before she could reply, the tent flap lifted and Gretchen appeared—triumphant, a hanger in her hand.

It was a mid-calf dress, calico patched with squares of old patterns and long strips of lace, sun-dried and irrefutably fancy.

Gretchen beamed, lifting it like a prize.

"Look what I found."

Minnie groaned, backing away.

"No way."

"Way," Fiona replied, already advancing with a spark of mischief in her eyes.

Ken Coffman and Kristen Lolatte

Philip d'GreenApple: The Long Road North

THE SEMI RUMBLED off I-17 at Sedona's exit, groaning as Juan eased it down the ramp. Pine-dusted air streamed through the window—cooler and sweeter than the arid urban valley. The hard angles of Phoenix had given way to red stone. In the distance, the land rose in mythic folds.

Juan jerked a thumb at the road.

"I ain't up for navigating the round-abouts and tourist traffic, so you're on your own, Amigo. Thumb a ride and find your gold coin."

I climbed down from the cab, the steps big and mean, boots hitting cracked asphalt. I studied Juan's profile.

Was this it?

After all the miles we traveled together, all the secrets they shared...

"It's been..."

With his eyes on the horizon, Juan interrupted.

"Well, *chamaco*...all this distance, all this dust—every long road's only worth a damn if someone's waiting at the end."

He reached for the brim of his battered hat, adjusting it against the sun.

"There's more roadwork ahead. For you and me both."

He nodded—final, absolute—and slammed the truck into gear. I closed the door and watched as the semi grumbled and rolled away. With dust in my eyes, I stood for minutes—long after he was out of sight—before walking toward the west. I didn't know where I was going, but I felt a pull in that direction.

There was steady traffic, but no one took sympathy on a dusty young man with a knapsack until I'd walked at least three miles. Then, a Subaru Outback pulled over.

"Dona downtown?" she said.

I wasn't exactly sure where I was going, but anyplace I might enjoy air-conditioning for a while sounded good.

I studied her.

"I know it's a cliché," she said. "A dyke driving a Subaru. Get in or shut the door—cold air's escaping."

I slipped in, pulled out and latched the seatbelt and settled my knapsack at my feet.

"Philip," I said.

"Call me Hank," she replied.

She worked the clutch and forced her way back onto the road.

"Was it easy to find a car with a manual tranny?"

She laughed.

"Buster, you don't know the half of it. Plus side? Keeps my friends from borrowing the car. How do you like that?"

I flashed on the trucks I'd been driving—muscling though the gears mile after mile."

Wouldn't stop me.

She was a talker.

"What drags you out this way? Seeing the sights? Job?" She glanced at me, up and down. "No, it's a girl, isn't it? Don't say it, I know I'm right. How do I know? I know about girls. I once drove three-thousand miles in three days for a girl. Then she broke my heart—or maybe I broke hers, I don't remember. Maybe I know your girl. I know everyone around here. What's her name?"

I waited a few seconds to make sure there was a gap and she really wanted an answer.

"Minnie," I said.

This surprised her.

"Minnie," she muttered. "I know one. Tiny little thing, sharp tongue. Big spirit. Smart. Tough. Could that be your Minnie? Rennie?"

"What's a *rennie*?

"RenFaire crowd. I'm not sure you're in the right place. Most of them are packing up and leaving. Denver is next, I think. Or maybe North Carolina. Is that your Minnie? Any chance?"

"Sounds likely," I said.

"Been a while since you've seen her? Long road from there to here? Man, this is something. I can hook you up with her. Wait, that didn't sound right. You're too young for hooking up. I meant reunite you two. But the point remains. If she's still here, I can probably take you to her. Wouldn't that make my day? Wait. She going to be happy to see you?"

"Yes," I said.

Probably.

As we approached, the city felt like a waking dream—Sedona, with its iconic rocks looming to the south and the red cliffs cut sharp against a sky too blue to trust.

"I need water."

She looked me over.

"Right, you look dryer than a Gila lizard. We'll stop at Safeway. You got money?"

I nodded.

Yes, I had money.

It was an odd feeling. I never thought about money—now I had a ton. It had to be my imagination, but my titanium debit card seemed to vibrate in my back pocket.

At the Safeway, the sliding doors whooshed open, air-conditioning hitting harder than expected. Inside, Sedona's unique blend of spiritual gear and hiking boots mingled with designer sunglasses and tie-dye. I threaded past a rack of "Sedona Rocks!" shirts and made for the coolers.

Behind foggy glass, the colorful display of water overwhelmed me.

Why do we need 100 brands?

At random, I grabbed a liter.

Fiji water.

I wasn't sure where Fiji was. I hoped they had good water there.

For six bucks, it had better be good.

As I headed to the self-checkout, a flash of red and green caught my eye—mountains of apples. Gala, Fuji, Pink Lady, Honeycrisp, Jonagold, Red and Golden Delicious.

And my favorite.

Granny Smith.

Like gleaming emeralds, they fit in my mind like a final puzzle piece. I filled a doubled-up plastic bag with as many as I could carry. I had no idea what I would do with them, but I had to have them.

Outside in the bright light, Sedona moved in vigorous swirls. Pink Jeeps hauled tourists along the main drag while hikers sat at a coffee shop and fussed with their pristine Timberland boots and iPad maps. Feeling the ground pulse with possibility, I stood in the shade with water in hand and apples slung over my shoulder in their plastic.

I drank a quarter of the bottle in one go while a massive raven swooped low and snatched a crumb off the overheated sidewalk. Across the parking lot, Hank waved vigorously.

She cupped her hands like a megaphone and yelled.

"Move your ass, slack-toad. There ain't no flippin' time to waste."

I could hear her better as I got closer.

"Your Minnie is getting married. No, not married, engaged to be married to some rich city dude with a helicopter. Move your rusty keister, bub."

At that moment, a black helicopter—headed east—swooped by.

"That chopper," she said. "Hurry and we'll follow it."

There wasn't even a moment of panic. I knew whatever the day held, it wasn't going to end with Minnie engaged to anyone.

That said, I still wanted to bear witness.

"What's with all the apples?" she said.

"Stop jawboning and drive, woman," I said.

Bethrothed

THOUGH IT WAS late summer, at this altitude, it got cold in the winter. The wind emanating from the valley bore cool traces of the upcoming season. It was refreshing and ruffled Minnie's hair and dress.

She stood on the edge of the sheer cliff and looked down on rocky talus and scree a thousand feet below. She restrained an impulse to jump—to launch herself into space and fly. She looked for any signs of the sheet vortex that lived here, but there was nothing—not even a whisper in the breeze.

But the power was there. She could feel it coiled and waiting. The immenseness of it was terrifying. It could pick her up and fling her to the moon without any effort.

Behind her, the helicopter, beating the air like a bad dog, circled to find a landing spot…finally deciding on a gravel turnout a hundred yards away.

Wary of the edge of the cliff, Fiona slowly approached to speak with Minnie.

"This is not a good idea," Fiona said. "Truly. Let's get in Al's Jeep and run. Please. The world is big. We can find a safe place to hide…in

Timbuktu, Senegal or Wyoming."

There was quiet confidence in Minnie's voice.

"Wherever we go, if we're together, the mad King can find us. You know that." She took Fiona's hands. "Trust me. This is the way."

They turned to watch Trevir and his entourage jump out of the helicopter. Troll Srenzo pulled at Trevir's arm and argued with him.

"She knows," Minnie said. "She wants him to leave."

While they watched, Trevir slapped the troll with all his strength. With her hand on her cheek, she stepped back. Her husband, Kelpht, the ohrkk, stood watching silently with his shoulders slumped.

"See that," Fiona said. "Marry him and that's your future."

"Maybe so," Minnie said.

With the entourage trailing, Trevir marched to join the women.

"Is that how you intend to treat your bride? With violence?"

Trevir smiled.

"I promise you, no one will touch my Queen. Not me, not anyone. Treated like royalty, she will be the mother of us all and will be lavished with loving respect and adoration." He thought for a moment. "If she behaves, of course. Sometime a husband must raise a hand to his wife, but only under the most severe provocation. Never, unless I have to, then rarely. I promise."

With tears streaming, Fiona spat at his feet and turned away.

"This is an abomination," she muttered.

"Let's see the ring," Minnie said.

Trevir gestured to Troll Srenzo who opened the lace on her leather pouch and brought out the ring. Heavy, it was hammered white gold with a throbbing ruby.

"It beats with my heart," Trevir said proudly. "Money means nothing, but you should know, I paid over three million dollars for this bauble. And, of course, you are worth it, every penny. Three point three million if you want a precise number. But never mind that. How shall we do this?"

After taking the ring and weighing it in her palm, Minnie turned to look over the crowd. There was a baker's dozen of people gathered. All of her desert friends.

Including the Meg, baker.

M, the bookshop owner.

Tobias, the bard.

Her guardians, Gretchen and Tor.

Seamus, the wizened wizard.

Miss Epona, the schoolteacher with her students Steph, Chloë and shy Penny.

They all looked scared, but also hopeful.

They thought Minnie's betrothment was something they should be happy about.

But the thin man?

He was not right for her.

They did not understand.

Further along the cliff's edge, Fiona, with her back turned, kicked stones under the guardrail and into the void.

Penny approached.

"Miss Minnie," she said. "We made a *blomsterkrans*...a flower wreath...for you to wear. Miss Epona made it, but I helped. We all helped. It has Mexican Poppy, Owl's Clover, Fiddleneck, Globemallow, Bluedicks and Fairy Duster." She glanced sideways at Trevir and whispered. "And spiderwort, too."

Minnie leaned over and Penny carefully arranged the flowers on her head.

After stepping back, Penny looked up in awe.

"You look like an angel," she said before running back to her group.

"Okay," Minnie said.

She reached out for Trevir's hand and pulled him to the edge of the cliff.

Troll Srenzo tried one last time.

"This is a trick, Trevir. She's..."

Trevir pushed her away.

"Don't forget who I am," he said. He turned back to Minnie. "What now? Let's get this done."

"Now you ask," Minnie said.

"Ask what? Ask who? There's no one here."

Right, Minnie thought. There's no one here.

"Just say, 'Father, grant me the hand of Minerva to be my wife,

Queen and mother of my children'."

"You're making me feel stupid," Trevir said.

"Just do it."

Annoyed, he stared into the distance, then took a deep breath and spoke. His words tumbled past the wind and the cracked stones at his feet.

"Father, grant me the hand of Minerva to be my wife, Queen and mother of my children."

For a moment, nothing moved. The cliffs fell away in silence. From a thousand feet below they heard only the murmur of scree. Cloud shadows drifted over the crowd; faces that were hopeful or pale as ghosts. Far away, a distant raven cawed.

Minnie met the wind with her crown trembling—flowers bright against the coming dusk. Something vast uncoiled, invisible but near, as if the world itself was waiting to see what would happen next.

She smiled—a barely-there crescent at the corner of her lips— fleeting as a sigh and enigmatic as moonlight. Perhaps it was resignation, a flicker of sorrow, or something ancient, unnamable and beyond the grasp of any human tongue.

"Now we wait," she said lightly, as if greeting a guest for tea rather than awaiting a response from stone and sky.

And so they did. For a long time, no one spoke. Far below, the land groaned. The breeze gathered wishes and the Mogollon Rim held its breath with judgment suspended, until someone, somewhere—perhaps the very Earth itself—was ready to reply.

Then came a rumble of stones and a faint rainbow of energy from below.

Fiona, Minnie and The Black Faerie King: Judgement Day

A SOUND ROSE—an unearthly rumbling, deep and resonant, as if the very marrow of the Rim was awakening. The crowd shrank back. Gravel shivered. Some among Minnie's friends fell to their knees, impelled by ancient instinct to worship the old ways from before the volcano world sprouted into green foliage and blue water.

Light threaded through cracks in the talus and scree, weaving blue-green, gold and a shade beyond red, as if the sun itself twisted and bled. Hair on every arm stood up; even Trevir appeared smaller, his jewels modest and his grandeur threadbare.

In that unsteady hush, the Rim spoke. It was not sound, not exactly. It was the pressure of ancient water behind stone, the weight of a mountain's intention, the memory of bones ground to dust, deep as dreams beneath their feet.

Minnie's flower crown flared—not with flame but with impossible colors, poppy and spiderwort and fairy duster blazing strange new hues beyond nature. The wind spun around her, petals lifting until she seemed

370

to hover—neither wholly of Earth or sky.

Trevir, still gripping Minnie's wrist, tried to shout an invocation, a threat or a plea. But the words collapsed. One by one, his entourage staggered to the ground with their faces wet with tears they didn't remember shedding.

Fiona called Minnie's name, but the air was thick. The syllables drowned before they reached the Rim's edge. The Meg muttered a half blessing. Gretchen's arthritic hands twisted hemp dress until threads snapped.

From the air—from a presence older than storms—came the pulse of an answer.

Minnie did not look at Trevir. For the first time, she was utterly herself: vast and impossible. Both a girl and the symbolic wisdom of old rivers and burned forests. She clutched the ring. The white gold bent in her grasp as if it were wax.

Her voice thrummed like the Earth after rain.

"No one owns me," she said.

The sky cracked open—not lightning, but shivers of light, rainbows layered on shadow as if every possibility was visible and reachable for a single, breathless instant. The flower crown lifted from her hair and spun upward, scattering seeds finer than dust, each carrying memory, wish and promise to distant grounds—fertile and hungry.

For the witnesses—baker, wizard, children, guardians—the moment would live longer than any of them. Some would call it magic, some a miracle and some would lie and say it never happened. But none would doubt the gravity of old places, or what a girl might do at the edge of the world when the Earth itself decided to speak.

A hush descended, vast and endless.

Then, deep below, a bell of stone rang—once, twice, three times.

All the wildflowers on the rim shivered.

Judgement was passed.

Minnie looked at Trevir. Somehow, he had shrunk—his power suspended, grandeur gone. For now, he was merely human: small, limp, haunted.

The final word from the Earth resonated in every mind.

This mortal man can marry this woman.

It took her breath away.

Man or magic King, she did not wish to be united with him. But her hope that this bonding would be denied was dashed.

She had gambled and lost.

Trevir looked around in wonder.

"So," he said, "this is what normal feels like. Can't say as I like it. But if temporarily being a man is what it takes to claim my bride, I suppose I can handle it. You want the words? Fine. Minerva, will you be my wife and bond with me as my Queen?"

It was on her lips; she had no choice.

The inevitable word was *Yes*.

But a hairy arm came between them.

Kelpht, the ohrkk.

With steady, firm pressure, he pressed Trevir back—back—until Trevir's legs hit the guardrail. There they stood, eye to eye.

"I command you," Trevir said.

"You command me no more," Kelpht replied, quiet as dusk, pressing further until Trevir was hanging in space, desperately scrabbling at Kelpht's knobby arm.

As he fell, Trevir screamed—his voice echoing, turning from rage to something smaller, lost in the stones below.

Everyone gathered round and looked down.

Kelpht took Minnie's hand and studied her shocked eyes.

"It had to be done while he was human," he said. "Now we go."

"Do good," Minnie begged. "Please. Do good."

Kelpht nodded.

"I'll do my best," he said. He reached out and took his wife's hand. "We'll do our best."

Hand in hand with the wind whipping around them, they walked back toward the helicopter.

Philip and Minnie

BEFORE HANK'S CAR was fully stopped, Philip jumped out. With his dark hair flying in the downwash, he looked up as the helicopter ascended.

After gathering his knapsack and apples, he nodded thanks at Hank, then walked toward the cliff's edge. Like Moses and the Red Sea, the crowd parted and he was face to face with Minnie.

"What did I miss?" he said.

Philip d'Green-Apple

MINNIE JUMPED INTO his arms. After kissing his grimy neck, she pulled back.

"You missed my marriage proposal."

She was still holding the ring, but it had melted into a lump. The ruby still glowed blood-red but no longer pulsed with life.

She held it out to him.

"It cost three-point-three million."

"Do tell. I have one for you. My dad made it. It cost about three bucks."

"Let me see it," she demanded.

He put her down and dug around in his knapsack.

"I know it's here somewhere."

While he pulled out dirty clothes, she pointed at his plastic bag.

"What's with the apples?"

"Here it is," he said while unwrapping it from a dodgy handkerchief.

After slipping it on her finger, she said, "Perfect. How did he know my size?"

"He has an eye for that sort of thing."

"What's it made of?"

"Knowing him, it's probably made of old nails and electric box slugs he melted down."

"Perfect."

"You already said that. Is that what I'm getting? A girl who repeats herself all day?"

"Is that what I'm getting? A boy who is never around and is always five minutes late?"

"We're perfect together," he said. "So, that's it? We're engaged?"

She counted in her head.

"That's been a store-bought fact for almost eight years."

Penny tugged at Philip's shirt.

"What's with the apples?" she said.

Philip picked up the bag and walked to the cliff's edge.

"The Black King went over?"

Minnie nodded.

"The Earth made him human and Kelpht made him dead," she said.

"Good," Philip said. He gestured to Minnie. "Toss it."

She studied the molten ring, then flipped it out into space.

One-by-one, Philip passed out apples.

"Hold," he said.

Once everyone had an apple—and for some reason there was one for everyone, even Hank who had joined the group—he made a tossing gesture.

"Why are we wasting perfectly good apples?" Minnie said.

"You, of all people, will complain when we do something irrational?" Philip said. "Think of them like flowers on a grave." He turned to the entourage. "On the count of three…"

In defiance of gravity, the apples soared outward before falling.

All but one apple. Penny was eating.

"I was hungry," she said.

Philip crouched before her and, with a dirty thumb, cleaned a dribble of juice from her chin.

"Toss it and I'll buy you lunch."

"Deal!" she said.

Epilogue

IT WAS A September evening on the Island, a time when the rocky speck sighed with relief. The tourist season's gaiety—echoing with painted throngs and summer laughter—faded with the receding tide.

Tethered boats were covered in canvas and no longer prowled the coves. Children, sunburnt and wild, retreated to the hallowed brick reverie of their schoolhouses; and those who truly belonged—those with saltwater in their veins—began the subtle rituals of belonging.

Fiona rested upon her porch with a quilted shawl laying across her stooping shoulders—a garment of sea-worn wool, embroidered with silver thread that winked when the light caught it just so. The porch faced west, toward the burnt coin of the sun as it kissed the lips of the brackish cove with an audible hiss, as if reluctant to leave behind such beauty.

Colors bled across the sky with the glorious carelessness of the world's first painter—riotous oranges smudging edges into blushing roses and opaline blues. Each hue held the memory of a hundred other sunsets, all distilled into this lingering moment.

Sean was inside with his clattering pots creating a rhythm like an orchestral timpanis. He hummed as he prepared their supper: chard and crisp greens from Bartlett's Farm and a loaf of something yeasty and fresh-baked. He brought out a chilled glass of rosé—Fiona's favorite, a pale vintage from the vineyard at the far side of the Island, where grapes huddled against the wind in bent rows, remembering the hands that tended them.

"I picked up fresh greens and parsley, and a dessert-of-mystery Matt swore you'd love," Sean said, setting the glass in her palm, his other hand tracing the wrinkled map of her knuckles. "You will have to tell me what it is, I don't know it."

"I asked for Malachite ice cream."

"No more until next summer, dear. He says you'll like this better."

There's nothing better, she thought.

"I'm sure it will be fine," Fiona murmured softly in the thickening air.

Sean drew up his rocker next to hers, their chairs creaking together in ancient counterpoint. He took her hand into his; it was veiny, rough, warm and alive, a testament to all the kindness she had worked in this world. They watched the sun slip lower, thinning, then pooling, then vanishing, leaving only a flash of green, then a shimmering seam of gold at the world's edge.

"How did we ever get so lucky, to be together in this small heaven? Thirty miles out to sea—our own little cottage in Madaket ringed with the salt's memory and a blanket of mist?"

Fiona's white curls fell down her back, curling like the scrolls of forgotten maps. The crow's feet at her eyes fanned more deeply now with every line feathered with humor, sorrow, delight and loss. Her eyes, so blue they recalled the deep sea at noon, flickered with wisdom—the ancient kind that comes only to those who have witnessed the world's silent transformations. Tattoos from wilder years meandered down her arms and legs, gleaming faintly with the memory of full moons and midnight dips in coves and the wild coupling of bare limbs beneath the elms. On her back, the crow fluttered its ebony wings.

She smiled and squeezed his hand.

"Luck is what's left behind when all the striving falls away. It is the tune that lingers after the dance is done, the tide that comes and goes of its own accord. We worked and we wandered but look—here we are at last…at peace, mostly upright and awash in the hush that only comes at the end of a very long song."

Seagulls gathered along the porch railing, jostling with practiced indignation. With a murmur and a scattering, Fiona tossed the required breadcrumbs into the dooryard, securing an ancient pact: so long as she fed them, peace would reign above and she would not be visited by raucous chaos or streaky droppings. Her envious neighbors had not figured it out; their roofs were all elaborately decorated.

"When will Minnie and Philip arrive, do you suppose? I miss the commotion they bring—the crosstalk of voices and mischief."

"Oh, darling," Sean replied, lips brushing her knuckle. "Remember? They missed the ferry. Phoned from Hyannis—they'll be on the first boat tomorrow. You know how those two are, always in league with delays, accidents and the secret clockwork of adventure. We'll meet them at dawn."

"Ah, yes, I did know that," Fiona sighed. "I lose things. Pieces slip away through cracks."

Sean looked upon her with gentle sorrow. Old she was—her strength less now, her years gathered about her, but her spirit undimmed. Time inked its story on her face, but the fire still glimmered beneath. In their next book, when the moon hangs high and the air is thick with jasmine, they will run down to the water—naked as their first summer—and let the waves baptize them anew.

"For tomorrow's tea, I will fetch elephant ears."

She nodded, wriggling her toes in anticipation.

"Yes, yes. And don't forget raspberry bars or Minnie will curse your soul."

As the last glimmer of sun melted into the sea, Fiona and Sean rocked gently on their porch, fingers knitted together, their silhouettes a single knot on the tapestry of twilight. Around them, faeries of light—some human, some less so—flitted. Inside, the hearth was kindled. Flix and company set out candles, laughter echoing off the fine old beams, calling forth the spirits of child and memory, kin and companion, hope and peace.

In their cottage by the foxglove border, Queen and King sat in mild majesty, islanded by ocean on all sides and by enchantment on all others. There was no need any longer for battles or crowns, for futures hurried or pasts regretted. Here, on a September evening's porch, twilight was just twilight—neither a beginning nor an end, merely a passage from one tender moment into another. This story surrenders to peace.

Music drifted on the breeze. Always, music.

Let the years unspool their colorful threads
Down island roads where golden sunlight weaves,
Let laughter echo where the whales bled
Old secrets in the salt-crusted sand.
The hearth remembers—faithful, glowing and kind—
A shawl of sea-mist formed of dusk and dew.
On moonlit porches, hearts swell and meld:
Love dwells in magic's hush, and love renews.

And so, dear reader, this is where we bid farewell to Fiona's journey.

A Queen with her King in their magic-washed haven where the tide, sun and years come and go and love does not diminish but grows ever stronger, wilder and stranger, washed in the vivid colors of eternal dawns and sunsets.